" 'TIS ALL RIGHT," SHIVAHN WHISPERED URGENTLY. " 'TIS GOING TO BE ALL RIGHT. PLEASE, BRAVE ONE, *PLEASE*—"

His groan exploded into an outcry. He arched against her, even the arm she'd splinted with two molding boards and the few remaining clean cloth strips from her bag.

"Nay!" she ordered him in a vehement rasp, and instantly felt contrite for it. . . .

Shivahn darted desperate glances around the cell. Dear God, how was she going to protect this man from himself?

Only one effective tactic came to mind.

She swiftly slid her lips to his and sealed them there. She expected the fever-induced heat of him. She expected the sweat-drenched slickness of his lips, even the instinctual warrior's resistance his body raised against her. . . . She did *not* expect him to return her kiss.

She first thought his mouth's responding pressure as the beginnings of another groan. But when his good arm wrapped up and around her like an erotic tendril of candle smoke, taking slow possession of her from the base of her spine on up . . . *oh, blessed saints*, her mind shrieked; what had she gotten herself into?

Heaven, came her heart's ringing cry of reply. . . .

The Promise of Your Touch

Annee Carter

A Dell Book

Published by
Dell Publishing
a division of
Bantam Doubleday Dell Publishing Group, Inc.
1540 Broadway
New York, New York 10036

ISBN: 0-440-22294-X

Printed in the United States of America

Published simultaneously in Canada

April 1997

10 9 8 7 6 5 4 3 2 1

OPM

For Adrianne Ross . . .
Thank you for ducky power and dolphin dreams,
for pixie dust and fairy dew,
for wisteria adventures and sunflower fun,
for laughter and tears, sharing and caring . . .
Thank you for being such a special Irish treasure.
Thank you for being my precious friend.

Extra thanks to
Julie Greenspan
Danielle Myers
and
Teresa Ozoa
I couldn't have done this one without you!

And very special thanks to
Eric Kunze
"Why does Saigon never sleep at night?"
Because *you're* singing to it!
Thank you for giving me Kris
through the magic of your talent.

Chapter 1

"Bloody Jesus, Johnnie . . . who's *she?*"

The words themselves, Shivahn Armagh had heard, yet learned *not* to hear, a thousand times before. It was the stares she would never get used to. Those stares that matched the filthy English soldier's tone shade for shade. Bold. Bald. Morbidly interested but cruelly indifferent, as if gawking at some artifact pilfered from one of the local chapels, not a woman who'd been ordered from her bed after a night of delivering one baby, stitching two heads, and sleeping three hours.

Nay, she would never get used to the stares.

Nevertheless, she surrendered not a fraction of her pride as the soldier called Johnnie pulled her through the ankle-deep mud and oatmeal-thick fog surrounding the gates of Dublin's Prevot Prison. She forced her shoulders to support her tattered shawl as if she wore Queen Medb's own robe; her patched sack of herbs and ointments might have been a velvet pouch of emeralds and perfumes bouncing against her left hip.

But most of all, she did not lower her gaze. Shivahn returned the soldiers' stares with determined serenity, silently telling the swine this Irish bauble was not as crushable as their conquests on the Wexford battlefield last year. *This* foreign oddity had edges sharpened on the whetstones of injustice long before the screams of that night were buried beneath the winter of 1798.

As she half expected and fully hoped, her mettle worked—for half a minute. First, both men nervously darted their stares from her regard. But the venture only funneled all Johnnie's fervor to his arms. Like a human grappling hook, he clamped his hand tighter around her upper arm.

"She's the healer the captain ordered us to find last night," he told his comrade in an equally agitated tone. "So let me through, Thor."

But Thor—whose mum clearly had the Sight when christening him—shifted only his hairy brows, causing a deep scowl across his leathered forehead. "The healer? You mean the one with them strange powers? The harpy who fixed that rebel's leg back to him like it were no more than a doll's joint?"

"How the bloody hell should I know?" Shivahn felt Johnnie's discomfitted squirm before he jerked her forward by another two steps. "Look, I'm tired and I'm—"

"She don't look like a harpy to me."

"Thor!"

The soldier cracked a grin, his teeth looking a jumble of dirty pebbles crammed against fleshy gums. "C'mon, Johnnie. No foul meant." The smirk slid higher. "I was just wonderin' if harpies has the same parts as other birds."

At that, Johnnie's attitude transformed, as well. As slick as the sweat he reeked of, he sidled closer to Shivahn. She stiffened, but his other arm caught her waist, locking her against him. She barely held back the rush of bile surging from her belly . . . or the dreading pound of her blood in parts lower than that.

"Ahhh." The soldier growled into her nape. "*Now* I ken your meanin'. I must admit that very question ails my own head."

Thor chuckled at his comrade's stress on the last word. "Well, when *my* head aches, I rub it."

"Me, too." The swine's mouth moved to her neck. His hand slithered around her bottom. "C'mon, healer harpy, what d'you have in your magic bag for my poor throbbin' head?"

She yearned to scream with every ounce of air in her lungs. But she emitted not a sound. Doing so would only make her the breakfast "treat" for the entire regiment. Instead, Shivahn answered him with the hardest, wildest struggle her depleted muscles would yield. But when Thor added his brute's strength to Johnnie's wiry tenacity, she found herself dragged, dumped, and flattened to her back in the mud behind the guard house, watching the younger soldier kneel and flip open his breeches with practiced speed.

"Not yet!" Thor growled urgently at his mate. "We gotta blindfold her first!"

"*Blindfold* her?"

"They say she can make your staff fall off just by lookin' at it."

"Bloody blinkin' Mary," Johnnie muttered, grabbing at his groin. "Use your neckerchief, then. Tie it on her good."

Shivahn fought Thor's hands, tossing her head back and forth, but with a gritted oath, he grabbed her hair, holding her in place while he secured the kerchief around her eyes. She grimaced at the feel of the grimy cloth against her face, but some other part of her actually thanked Providence that she would not have to witness the taking of her innocence, only listen to the deed. Another part of her mind told her she also should be grateful for having seen her eighteenth summer without being defiled yet by these bastards. *That* thought was not so easy to honor.

She tried to turn the sting of her tears into spring raindrops, in a world she envisioned beyond her squeezed eyes. A world where folk smiled at each other again on the streets of Dublin, where children *played* in this mud . . . where English rapist bastards had been sent to Hell, where they all belonged.

But the picture was not strong enough to obscure Johnnie's pleasureful grunt as he leaned forward, thrusting aside the last of her underskirts.

Which doubled her surprise at his shocked oath, as he leapt away from her.

Nay, Shivahn discovered as she pulled off the blindfold a moment later, not leapt—the soldier had been yanked clear of her with seemingly no effort on the part of the medal-encrusted officer now towering over her. As she and Thor looked on, Johnnie dangled in the man's grip like a mutt caught with his muzzle in the stew pot.

"Mr. Treakle," the officer intoned with little movement of his thin, grim lips, "and Mr. Rankin. Good morning, gentlemen."

"M-Major Sandys," Johnnie squeaked. "W-we didn't hear you comin', sir."

"Then it's your fortune I wasn't a brigade of United Irish Insurgents." Again with naught but a tremor of strain, he flung Johnnie back to the ground, before delivering a hard kick to the V where the soldier's breeches still gaped open.

"Bloody Jesus!" Johnnie doubled over, tears in his eyes.

Thor stared at his comrade in silent sympathy but dared not a gesture otherwise. The big soldier's features reflected legitimate panic about the severity of *his* fate at Sandys's hands. He fumbled into a trembling salute as the senior officer turned back to him. Mud sucked at the soles of Sandys's costly patent boots, the only sound in the morn's dense air.

Sandys stopped before the soldier before flicking a brief glance at Shivahn. His nostrils flared in disdain, as if regarding no more than a mound of donkey droppings.

"Mr. Rankin," he said with equally efficient frigidity, "did Mr. Treakle inform you of the urgent need for this woman in Cell Block Three?"

"A-a-aye, sir."

"Ahhh. And the last time we discussed the meaning of 'urgent,' Mr. Rankin, I believe we also discussed the meaning of delays."

"A-a-aye, sir."

"And their unacceptability to the proficiency of this facility."

"A-a-aye, sir."

During Thor's tremor-ridden grovelings, Sandys pivoted slowly back toward her. Shivahn winced before prudence could overcome impulse, for in one fleeting twitch across the man's hard-etched features she saw the vague temptation to finish Johnnie's violation between her legs.

Relief came in a dizzy flood when he regarded her as donkey leavings again. "Get up," he ordered.

As Shivahn stiffly obeyed, he motioned Thor over with a flick of his hand. "Deliver her to Cell Block Three with *no* further delays," he directed.

"Aye, sir!" Thor betrayed his own relief with the transparency of a three-year-old.

On the other hand, Shivahn's reprieve was cut ruthlessly short by a second shiver, permeating her whole body. The dread thickened to the consistency of the gray slime coating the stone hallways Thor led her down, farther and farther. Dear God. Cell Block Three. She was journeying to the section of Prevot where they held the most notorious members of the most radical insurgent brigades. When such valiant souls were finally brought here, the rumors claimed, they should treasure the memory of their last sunrise, for they would surely never see the sun again. They should also store the memory for the days, perhaps weeks, of agony and suffering to come before execution brought the mercy of death.

That thought spurred her third and most violent shiver. It was followed by one slice of inner question: If the rumors of this abyss were halfway toward truth, what did Sandys want *her* for?

The answer was too petrifying to contemplate. And, by now, too final to battle. The number of insurgents she had healed was hardly a secret, but, she had assumed by now, hardly worth Sandys's time, either. If he wanted to make an example out of any one link in the United Irishmen's chain of aid, there were many more renowned than she.

That thought gave her little comfort, especially when a thick iron door banged to a close behind them. She looked to Thor, who directed her toward a row of twelve more portals, smaller but equally ominous, stretching into the oily murk ahead. Sandys entered the area from a door to their right. "Number six," he commanded her, and snapped his fingers again in bidding. He dismissed Thor with a jerk of his head.

He didn't say another word as they paced to the

appointed cell, making Shivahn certain that the whole prison heard her heart thundering for release from her chest. She twisted tight fists into her shawl as Sandys rifled through a ring of keys, praying he had somehow lost the fit for number six.

But her heavenly hosts were clearly off hunting celestial stag. With an economy of motion, Sandys produced the proper key and scraped it into the rusted lock. As metal scratched metal and finally clicked into place, she ordered herself to face the fate beyond the portal with the dignity the world had come to know of the Armaghs.

She *was* thankful for the life she'd had. She could not have asked for a finer heritage, nor a more beautiful place to call home. Her memory would be honored in Trabith Village for a fortnight, and the cottage she shared with Gorag, who had become both mother and father to her, would be well tended by the village matrons until Saint Peter found the courage to come fetch that old man, as well. *Oh, Gorag, I love you . . .*

Sandys jerked the door open. The door screeched on the stone floor like a dragon having its claws torn out—much like the sound made by every one of Shivahn's nerves. She struggled to remember her last sunrise. She saw only the weeping, cold opening before her, the ooze-covered walls spitting onto a floor covered by a mat of unrecognizable refuse.

And upon that mat, she saw the man.

She held back her horrified outcry but could not repress her healer's impulse to rush to him. She was glad Sandys did not try to stop her, either, for the man would find his arm broken in the doing.

She dropped to her knees beside the unconscious rebel, hardly aware of the sharp pebbles cutting through her thin skirts. Since he was rolled over on his side, tangled dark brown hair shielding his face and mingling with the blood on his upper back and shoulders, she could not tell if the *Sídhe* had brought her to one of the missing brigade members from Trabith—but she dreaded the moment when she *did* find out.

With a determined breath, she gave his shoulder a gentle push. When he sprawled over onto his back, the air left her with a mixture of relief and pain. She knew him not, yet she had known him a thousand times over since requesting permission to forsake her shepherding duties to fulfill her healer's calling on the battlefields. She had known him in a thousand agonizing moments like this, when another broken rebel took over another part of her soul.

And yet there was something different about *this* man . . .

As she searched his features for the accounting to that intuition, a moan vibrated from his full and uncommonly curved lips. The revelation came then, inundating her senses. *He does not belong here,* she silently raged. *He does not belong here. Lips like that should be flirting in Heaven, not dying in Hell.*

He shifted then, and a cut in the corner of that mouth released a crimson trickle down a jaw pummeled to resemble a quart of pickled octopus. And that wound comprised the *best* of the devastation. Shivahn did not know why they chose to blacken only one of his eyes, unless they agreed their handiwork on the first was impressive enough. Most of his left eye and jaw had been transformed into a giant black splotch, and a bloody ooze dripped from that side of his strong, remarkably unbroken nose. His right arm twisted out at an unnatural angle—broken in at least two places, she surmised with seething certainty—with an older scar dividing the breadth of his upturned palm. Smaller scrapes, nicks, and gashes peppered the rest of his face, as well as patches of skin that showed through his tattered shirt, threadbare waistcoat, and mud-encrusted breeches. The man's body was the battlefield of Boyne all over again.

Yet he was the most beautiful sight she had ever seen.

"My God." Tears rasped her voice, but Shivahn did not care. She reached for him again, not flinching back this time. Her movement sent creatures scuffling into the shadows at her invasion of their moldy home, but she barely noticed the vermin. She only saw the unconscious face that she leaned over and began to wipe with a clean portion of her faded apron.

"My God, Brave One," she whispered to him, "what have they done to you?"

Two impatient boot scuffs sounded from the doorway. "Save your mollycoddling for your gutter brats, Mistress Armagh," Sandys's snarl followed. "This bastard is slated to die next week as a criminal, not this week as a martyr. Can you keep him alive until then or not?"

Shivahn secretly admitted her insecurity about the reply to that, but she directed a steady nod at the officer nonetheless. She had no doubt this rebel had been through the ordeal of Sandys's dreaded triangles, run the gauntlet of the battalion's knives, and endured God-only-knew-what other atrocities of the English and their "necessary" measures to ensure a "peaceful" transition toward their Legislative Union with Ireland—yet he lived. More than that, he *fought* to live.

And if he could put up such a battle for his life, so could she.

"I need some water and some time," she said to Sandys, managing to summon a haughty command to her tone.

Sandys jerked a quick nod. "You have thirty minutes."

"I need sixty."

The officer's nostrils pinched. "Very well." But as he

turned to go, he snapped back once more, pinning her beneath the talon of a raised eyebrow. "It would behoove you to remember the door *will* be watched."

She only nodded again, not trusting her mouth to any more civilized words at the monster who stalked away into the gloom. After the water arrived—if the pan of filmy muck brought by a drunken lackey qualified as "water"— she wiped away all she could of the crimson stains and clinging hair along the rebel's face and neck, then prepared to direct her ministrations lower. With shaking fingers, she peeled his shirt away from his chest—

And suddenly realized she did not shake wholly out of fear. A hot, unfamiliar sensation made itself blatantly known in Shivahn's thrumming pulse . . . surging to a flush across her face . . .

"By Saint Catherine!" she berated herself. Her healer's hands had touched more shirtless males than an average doxy!

But this time, 'twas different. This *man* was different. Like the felled prince from one of Gorag's more romantic fairy yarns, the rebel's courage and honor were evident even in his wounded slumber, even in the food-deprived and battle-hardened muscles surrounding the broken bones of his arm. Aye, she saw his defiant strength in the bold jut to his swollen jaw, she felt it in the dogged heartbeat beneath the strokes of her suddenly shy fingers.

So much strength, yet so dependent on her alone.

That awareness blasted through her like a gleam of sun on the morning waves at Skiddy's Beach, driving her into a tempest of motion. She tore open her sack and dumped out the contents, then began a swift, silent system of activity, moving according to soul-deep instinct and heart-consuming determination.

And finally, painstakingly, the heat began to come. It

arrived as it always did, starting at the center of her mind, then stealing behind her eyes and into her nostrils, finally down through her mouth and filling her throat. Her senses ignited with the strange fire, alive with burning dread and joy, of frightened awe and reverent acceptance.

And after what seemed a minute and an eon in one, the heat spiraled down her arms and swirled into the tips of her fingers. One by one, they tingled to life, like a swirl of fire-flies in each tip.

At that, she knew the time had come to set aside the bottles and ointments. After doing so, she turned back to the rebel, hovering her hands but inches from his battered torso. Her breath came in increasingly sharp spurts as she slowly, steadily lowered her arms.

Then she started to administer him the medicine of her soul.

But minutes into the Giving, something went wrong. No, Shivahn amended herself, not wrong, *different*. Dear God, incredibly different. The heat did not drain from her, as it always did. She grew warmer, instead, suffused with a shining sensation she had never known before and never wanted to be bereft of again. Her heart froze yet raced. Her mind exploded yet sang. Most of all, her soul reeled with its first taste of true completeness, of whole acceptance, of utter oneness . . .

Oneness with this man she had never met.

But this spirit she had known forever.

She had no awareness of the tears streaming down her face until a shower of them splashed through her fingers and into his open cuts. The rebel flinched at the resulting stings, his eyes squeezed, his lips exploding on a groan.

"Oh, no," Shivahn blurted, hastily dabbing at him. "Oh, Brave One, I am sorry. I am so sorry."

He sighed as if in response to that, and her own breath

clutched in her throat. When he rolled his head toward her, stretching in a way she could only describe as innately sensual, her heart and lungs shut down, as well.

But she still had the ability to move. Responding to a force beyond her will, Shivahn slid one arm beneath his head, the other into a careful embrace around his chest, and pulled him into the shelter of her lap. He sighed again, a more contented sound, and she smiled into his slumbering face, unable to remember the last time she had smiled with such undiluted joy.

Until he suddenly spasmed, and a moan vibrated his body. "Nay!" she rasped, pulling him closer and slanting herself atop him, as if the pain was cannon fire from whatever battle they had captured him from. "You will not die on me, you bastard," she commanded him in a fierce murmur. "You will not dare. If you die, they have won. Do you hear me? Those British whoresons have won—do you want that? Do you?"

She pressed herself around him, willing herself into him, praying for the Giving to work far beyond what it ever had before. But he continued to lay limp in her arms, fevered sweat now breaking out on his upper lip and down his temples. He groaned with deeper resonance.

" 'Tis all right," Shivahn whispered urgently. " 'Tis going to be all right. Please, Brave One, *please*."

His groan exploded into an outcry. He arched against her, even flailing with the arm she'd splinted using two molding boards and the few remaining clean cloth strips from her bag.

"Nay!" she ordered him in a vehement rasp, and instantly felt contrite for it. In apology, she cupped his stubble-roughened jaw. "Brave One, you must be still. You are going to rip yourself asunder! Can you understand me? You must be—"

He only moaned and writhed against her once more.

Shivahn darted desperate glances around the cell. Dear God, how was she to keep this man from killing himself beneath her own fingers? She dared not call to the guards to aid her; the rebel's existing wounds provided enough testament of how the beasts would interpret the purpose of "calming" him.

Only one effective tactic came to mind. She had no time to ponder the rightness or recklessness of the notion.

Shivahn swiftly slid her lips to his and sealed them there.

She expected the fever-induced heat of him. She expected the sweat-drenched slickness of his lips, even the instinctual warrior's resistance his body raised against her. She did *not* expect the hard, hurting intensity of the moan when it finally came up through him and echoed down through her, joining her to him with a shattering intimacy.

But most of all, dear saints, she did not expect him to *return* her kiss.

She first thought his mouth's responding pressure as the beginnings of another groan. But when his good arm wrapped up and around her like an erotic tendril of candle smoke, taking slow possession of her from the base of her spine on up . . . *oh, blessed saints*, her mind shrieked; what had she gotten herself into?

Heaven, came her heart's cry of reply. Oh, aye, the oily cell and its stinking garbage and its despairing walls fell away to a world of soaring clouds and eternal stars, of blinding light and the strength of joined souls. In this beautiful rebel's embrace, Shivahn fled this life and place; in the joining of their mouths as he urgently parted her lips, she flew to a world where she no longer needed dreams, because they had all come true.

Finally, both breathing short, shallow breaths, they pulled apart. In the following moment, Shivahn looked into his eyes for the first time. And she trembled then, for she beheld a depth of green found only in the heavenmost boughs of the tallest pines or in the deepest dominions of the seas.

The realms of an enchanted prince.

The power of his stare shamed her but held her; she yearned to hide her own gaze's deformity from him, but he wouldn't let her. He looked on her as if the differing tones of her eyes were not witch's orbs but two priceless amethyst stones. Not only that, but he seemed to draw those stones directly into the lockbox of his soul, meaning to cherish them there forever.

Shivahn swallowed back tears in favor of an awed smile. Her Brave One reciprocated with a weary upturn of those distracting lips. At the same time, he slid his good hand forward, around the curve of her shoulder, then up to her face. His thumb found the embarrassing line of light peach freckles along the bridge of her nose. But beneath his soft, savoring touch, embarrassment became a feeling of her past. Beneath *his* touch, her skin felt perfect and precious . . . and sensuous.

When Shivahn smiled wider and leaned her face into the cup of his hand, her prince actually chuckled. "My God," he wondered on a dry, strained throat, "what kind of incredible leprechaun have the *Sídhe* sent to me?"

As answer, she gave him halted time and stunned silence. Half a moment passed. Another. Only then did Shivahn's mind claw past the shock in her chest long enough to order her body into a leap of retreat, as if recoiling from a six-foot-long lizard. The rub was, as far as she was concerned, the figure on the floor had transformed into exactly that.

The man's brogue was thin as Sandys's face. No, she amended that thought, the man's "brogue" was more mush than sound, more a strange, wearied attempt at effect than a natural whisper on his lips.

Dear merciful God. Her "Brave One" was *not* brave. He was *not* an adventure tale prince. And he certainly *was not* Irish.

The bastard sprawled before her was a bloody Englishman.

ristian fell back against the floor as the leprechaun stumbled back and hit the wall, shock exploding from her lips in a sharp, high cry.

He knew this scene had been too good for truth. At first, he'd even supposed himself dreaming it all, when consciousness returned with not the agony he'd dreaded but the kiss of a golden-haired fairy with healing warmth in her touch and healing magic in her eyes. Ah, God, he ruminated, her *eyes* . . . not only a double blessing of color, but a color he hadn't seen since those long-ago summer days so mistermed his boyhood, when escape from Grandfather meant an afternoon in Castle Clay's arbor, and freedom meant running beneath the wild wisteria. The path had glowed in sun-dappled lavender and lilac, the shadows shifting with deep violet and royal velvet . . .

A boy could get lost for days in the splendor of wild wisteria.

A man could get lost for days in the splendor of that woman's eyes.

Who the bloody hell was she?

Then again, came his mind's backlash, he didn't need to know. His few words had accomplished the necessary explosion to destroy the dangerous bridge they'd connected to each other, and they were both better that way. She now regarded him as she should, with mouth clenching away the last flush from his kiss in favor of an abhorring glower. In other words, she looked like a woman beholding a country-man of the monsters who'd slaughtered *her* countrymen.

And dear God, Kris knew he'd still never seen a sight more beautiful. Hell, maybe she *was* an enchanted leprechaun.

He'd never have the chance to find out. Clearly roused by her outburst, Sandys marched into the cell with four mutated baboons in tow. With a wince, Kris rose to one elbow as the primates managed the feat of training bayonets on him, fanning their weapons in a neat semicircle around his heart.

Kris returned the greeting with a relaxed, excruciating smile. "You shouldn't have, mates," he drawled. "But I'm touched. Next time, the soiree's on my shilling, I promise."

The biggest baboon curled a lip in warning and jabbed his weapon closer. A restraining hand from Sandys sent the soldier into retreat. But Kris didn't rush to compose a humanitarian tribute to the man. Sandys would allow him to breathe through the next five days for a single purpose: to make him an example on the gallows come next Sunday. A *big* example.

"Well," Sandys stated then, rocking on his heels, "I see we've all had the chance to get acquainted."

As the bastard spoke, Kris switched his gaze back to the leprechaun, effectively tumbling his hair back into his face. He didn't know if the move was a fatal mistake or a stroke of genius. Something strange yet weirdly pleasant squeezed his chest as he saw a flicker of remembrance twitch her features, and he knew she recalled the same moment as he, when she'd summoned him from unconsciousness by stroking these dirty strands from his face . . .

"Acquainted," he murmured, deliberately reweighing Sandys's term on the scale of their intimate secret. "Aye, I suppose that's what you'd call it."

That same flare of unnameable heat ignited between his ribs as her hands flew to her flushing cheeks. "Th-this man is *B-British*," she blurted at Sandys.

Sandys slanted her a brow with droll deliberation. "You *are* observant, Mistress Armagh."

Kris couldn't help it. His mind eagerly seized the man's last word. *Armagh.* Damn his earlier prattle about the advantage of anonymity; even the knowledge of her last name seemed to fit somewhere inside him like a customized key to a lost castle dungeon. In this case, that didn't veer very far to the fictional. In the castle of his life, his soul was definitely the dungeon.

And she was definitely an Armagh. From the graceful pride of her upheld chin to the firm stance on her thin-soled ankle boots, she heartily earned the nobility of her family's name. Goddess Armagh, Kris wanted to call her, come to save the dungeon of his soul before death really occupied it.

But before he could proffer his first worshipping gaze, Sandys's boot blasted a mound of dirt into his face. The baboons guffawed, just before Sandys's sneer came: "Oh, aye, Mistress Armagh, he's British . . . on the *outside*."

Kris heard her move. She pushed away from the wall and took one tentative step toward him. He couldn't escape her gaze upon him, quiet but intense. "What do you mean?" she asked softly, suspiciously.

Sandys only responded with a guttural chuckle. The baboons followed suit.

Her footsteps exploded then, small in accordance with her size but thudding across the chamber with demanding force. She scuffed to a stop next to Sandys. "What do you mean!" she actually demanded of the bastard then.

Sandys seemed to hesitate. Kris should have been glad. The next moment, the man's hand dug into his hair and jerked, pulling him to his knees and nearly ripping his head off his neck. His face, now encrusted with more dirt than an alley mutt, came inches from the amazing porcelain beauty of her own, and he wished Sandys really would yank a little harder and finish the goddamn job.

"Mistress Armagh," the bastard crooned, "I'm afraid I owe you an apology. How neglectful of me to ignore the basic formalities. Pray allow me to introduce you to Mr. Kristian Rayne Bastion Montague, lord of absolutely nothing, and the biggest traitor recorded in his country's history."

The baboons added obscene enhancements to the introduction, poking Kris's back as if tenderizing a roasting boar. Bloody hell, they must have spent the night sharpening the blades. Still, the new wounds were almost worth it, for the pain sharpened his senses to every shading of the confused consideration now shading his goddess's face, wondering whether to believe in the bond they'd shared before he'd opened his mouth, or the horror she'd known after. Damn it, he didn't know why he so desperately wanted her to believe in the "before." He just did.

"Enough," Sandys finally growled at his men, and everything from Kris's shoulder blades to waistline began a posttorture throb. He yearned to drop onto the floor and pass out. Sandys kept him mercilessly hoisted, worsening the ordeal by lowering his ugly rodent features into Kris's limited sights.

"Come, come, Mr. Montague," the rat finally goaded. "Don't tell me you have no more curses to fling at your hosts now?" He glanced at the goddess with a mocking pout. "Pity, really. He had such an entertaining vocabulary earlier, with the triangles as his muse. But perhaps that's what gets a traitor . . . excited. They say pain can be a powerful aphrodisiac." He curled a greasy smile at Kris's face—then lower. "Perhaps we should have a look at *this* traitor's excitement . . ."

"Go to hell!" Kris lurched forward, coming back around so forcefully that his good elbow connected with Sandys's gut between the lungs.

"Christ!" The bastard released his hold in order to breathe. But before Kris hit the floor, the baboons were upon him, the smell of their bloodlust filling his senses.

Yet even through the din, Sandys's commanding bellow cut as strongly as—well, a rat's fang through molded cheese. "Don't touch him!" he shrieked. "Don't—touch—him!"

When the baboons shoved away with disappointed grunts, their faces were replaced by Sandys's raging glare. Below that, the tip of a finger at the end of an outstretched arm spasmed in the center of Kris's vision.

"You are *mine*," Sandys rasped with low, evil satisfaction. "You are mine, and I will destroy you. Mark my words, *Griffin*, I will destroy you."

Shivahn gasped. Loud. Even through his fury, she saw the responding upturn of Sandys's lips. She had given the bastard the exact reaction he intended, but containing her shock was like asking her to tie down the wind.

Griffin. Her ears heard the emphasized word, but comprehension would not come to her spinning mind. *Griffin.* Sandys had called the man *Griffin.*

She stumbled back several steps, as if standing at the entrance to the magnificent cathedral in Clonfert, and only moving back would bring the entire spectacle within her comprehension. Within the last six months, the Griffin had already become a legend to not only the United Irishmen but all the Irish people. Dublin's children awoke to impromptu holiday mornings when toys appeared overnight on front stoops. The burned-out villages around Newry and Ballinamuck received sudden cartloads of blankets, candles, lumber, and even herds of goats. And most important of all, the rebel troops counted a few less casualties due to incredibly timely arrivals of weapons, ammunition, boots, and, every once in a while, intercepted messages detailing British troop movements.

Yet this mysterious savior of their land never loitered for thanks nor, it seemed, for rest. The only evidence of his presence always lay inside one white envelope marked with a boldly stroked "G." The package's content: a single dark green feather.

Dark green . . . like the tops of oak trees and the depths of the ocean. Dark green . . . the color of the Griffin's feather. Always "flying in" where the English slammed their fist down the hardest.

Because the Griffin himself was English?

Could it be so blatantly simple as that?

"Blessed Mary," Shivahn whispered. She stared at Kristian Montague with a shaking swallow. She took in the body she'd so boldly touched, the eyes she'd so audaciously glared at, the lips she'd so deeply kissed—

Stars and saints. She had kissed the Griffin.

"Blessed Mary," she blurted to him again. "Blessed

Mary, I cannot believe I am here. I cannot believe *you* are here. My God, you—you're—"

"Nobody!" Montague spat back, sending her a look of wild animal's pain, and Shivahn nay blamed him. Sandys had well near broken her Brave One, her gentle rebel, her discovered Griffin. She longed to have her own turn on the bastard's gut—with her dagger in hand.

"Oh, tsk." Sandys did not make her effort at restraint any easier with his flagrant play-act of courtesy. "Now you're getting testy, Griffin. This isn't fun anymore."

Montague attempted what he could of another enraged lunge. "How many times do I have to tell you, you misbegotten whore's spawn, that I'm *not* the Griffin?"

Sandys smiled slowly. "Then tell me who is, and we'll forget this ugly little incident."

A replying silence fell so thickly, it bordered on utter stillness. At the end of that pause, Montague wearily folded back to the floor. Gloating triumph nearly radiated from Sandys on light beams, like a medieval painting of Satan conquering Christ in the wilderness. Shivahn's hand drifted toward her pouch, where she had tucked her dagger. How she yearned to kill the monster, burn the fact that her blade would double as the pen to her death certificate. But if she died, so did Montague.

With the calm only a demon possessed, Sandys produced a small brush from inside his coat and dabbed it at lint on his lapels as he turned to his lackeys. "We have duties to attend, gentlemen; unlike *some* Englishmen, we've sworn allegiance to our king and country." To the largest soldier, he stated, "Tucker, you shall replace Deergood on cell door watch." He ignored Tucker's grimacing reaction. "Brandewyne, Yarborough, you are dismissed to quarters. And you—" Shivahn started at realizing he'd run out of minions to dictate and now pivoted toward her. "You have twelve more minutes."

She shot an accusing glare up the officer's skinny leg. "You promised me an *hour*."

"I did," Sandys concurred. "And you have had that hour. It is over in twelve minutes."

Shivahn sucked in breath for her enraged reprisal but instead, released a hard sigh. She dreamed of collecting every lint mote in the cell and shoving the resulting wad up the bastard's nose. She ground her fists against the floor instead. Even a sneeze of contention would cost her the precious remaining minutes with Montague, perhaps even send the man back to the torture rooms above. Sandys's imperious show of an exit relayed *that* much as piercingly as the glint off his medals.

Yet with that same soul-deep certainty, she knew that if they indeed came back for him, they would have to make their way past her dagger first. She would fight them without hesitation.

She would fight for this *Englishman* without hesitation.

Why? her mind and soul raged.

"Why?" her lips whispered, beseeching the word into the face she now cradled into her lap again . . . the bruised yet captivating angles her fingers gingerly touched again.

Montague attempted what he could of a bewildered scowl. "Wh-what?" he rasped back, confirming the instinctive apprehension that had crept up her spine in the last few minutes, as his skin had paled and his eyes gotten more glassy.

Still, beyond her volition, angry words hissed past her clenched teeth. "Why have you let them do this to you?" she demanded.

Surprisingly, the right side of his mouth jerked up at her. "You think I had a choice, Leprechaun?"

"You could have given them the bloody name they want!"

"No," he interjected, suddenly appearing the first cousin to a carved tomb top. "No, I couldn't have."

"Then you could have done more than just protest your innocence. You could have given them proof—"

"They have *more* proof." He stopped to emit a strained cough, his whole frame shuddering with the effort. "All . . . documented," he continued shakily.

"Such as what?"

"The usual," he supplied with a shrug, as if being accused and tortured as a traitor was more typical for him than a hair trim. As she again stroked his thick tangles from his face, Shivahn wagered that assumption not too far afield from the truth. "I was caught too many times stealing away on 'cigar breaks' in the wrong offices," he explained. "I wandered manor house gardens at odd hours of the night, instead of heeding invitations to my hostess's bed. Then last week, I checked my ship and crew into Dublin Bay stating passengers as my cargo."

A small moment passed before Shivahn replied. Shamefully she blinked herself from the reverie of stroking his right eyebrow, arched in its recklessly male way. "And I take it you had no passengers?"

"I had plenty of passengers," came the disgruntled reply. " 'Tis only they were chickens, not humans." Before Shivahn could decide whether to gasp or laugh at that, he burrowed his face closer to the hand she had moved upward, to now caress his forehead. "That feels good," he murmured, as his eyes slid shut.

A faint smile curved Shivahn's lips as she continued to touch him like that for a minute longer, exploring him, she shamefully admitted, with more than just a purpose to heal. Still, just for this moment, she indulged the longing to simply hold him, to touch him, to desperately wonder of him.

Who are you?

Who are *you, Kristian Montague? Nemesis or hero? Witless man or mythical savior? A cruel trick of fate or an incredible gift from Heaven?*

Then again, did the answers matter? Loyal Englishman or Irish legend, he was going to be Sandys's "example" on the gallows next week, and she already knew a part of *her* would die that morning, too.

That meant she had an astounding challenge to face between now and then. She could not let Montague take any more of her soul with him.

God only help her with the ordeal, because even now as he stirred against her, pressing his head closer beneath her breasts, she could not ignore her body's exquisite awakening to him . . . nor her soul's strange aching to be with him.

Chapter 3

ristian didn't know how much time had passed—and, through a sleep-fogged brain, berated himself for not caring. Condemned men were supposed to treasure each passing moment like gold dust in an hourglass, or some tripe like that, but he had no idea how much of the stuff he had left to sift.

He pried open his eyes, finding himself stomach down on a bed of cleaner, if not spring-fresh, hay and saw *her* there.

God's glory. Whatever moments comprised the rest of his life, they'd surely be a prelude to Heaven if he spent them like this, sights filled with her golden beauty as she sat next to him, mashing a mortar against something in a bowl and humming a meandering melody. At a skewed angle atop her head was the same handmade cap he'd craved to peel off her head when she'd first "awakened" him, yet now long spirals of her hair fell loose from the thing, like the copper-touched beams of a sunrise escaping morning clouds. And as she leaned harder into her task, tumbling one of those beams across her cheek, Kris found himself suddenly wanting to know what a sunrise felt like.

Thanking the *Sídhe* she'd picked his good side upon which to set up her apothecary, he slid his hand across the floor and two fingers up to that errant golden strand.

The moment he caught her hair, her song came to a startled halt. Her head snapped up at him.

Kris's hand froze, following the stunned lead of the rest of his body. The shock compounded when he almost found himself giving thanks Sandys's noose awaited, for he wondered how long he'd live anyway if her gaze impacted him like this every time they looked upon each other anew. Even more revealing, he confessed the jolt had less to do with the rareness of her two-toned stare than the purity of the violet and lavender depths themselves, like the core of a candle flame, penetrating to the core of *him*.

"Do not move," she suddenly dictated to him, her voice permeating him with warm intensity . . . just as she sounded in the dozen dreams he'd had of her. "Do not move," she repeated, scooting to his side in a pair of swift movements. "This will take but a moment."

Yet in direct contrast to her soft words came her first excruciating dab at his back. Whatever weird salve she'd prepared stank worse than the floor slime and stung worse than his original injuries.

For the first time in his life, Kris decided to succumb to torture. In one motion, he flipped over onto his good arm, then flung the other, now encased in a fortified splint, at her in a gesture of stiff entreaty. "Please," he growled, "stop. Enough. *Stop*."

She did, thank God. But she also fell back onto her heels with an expression of such alarm and wariness, Kris wondered if his words doubled as some evil spellcasting in the Gaelic tongue.

"I-I'm sorry," he hurried to stammer, though a part of him pondered why. *He* wasn't the one setting *her* spine on fire with what felt like a mixture of illegal whiskey and smoldering coals! Still, as he gently lowered the fingers that dangled from the end of the splint down over her coiled knuckles, he repeated, "I'm *sorry*. I didn't mean to . . ."

The sentence had an ending. He was certain of that. But the phrase was damned to the nether regions of his conscious as she dropped her gaze to the place where his fingers met hers so lightly, fused to each other with a force as powerful as their locked gazes. Thicker than the damp air around them, the awareness of her swirled around his senses, until he concluded a man really could live without breathing.

"It—it is I who should be asking forgiveness," his sprite said then. She averted her gaze, darkening both eyes like facets of a prism turned in a different light. Would he *ever* tire of looking at her eyes? "I thought you still burned with the fever," she hurried on, "and would not notice my touch so strongly."

At that, Kris couldn't contain a soft chuckle. "My little leprechaun, I could be tossing in the throes of the pneum and still, most assuredly, notice your touch."

"I beg your pardon?" She began the reply correctly enough, spouting the words taught by all good mothers to all good daughters as "safe" ground in times of confusion. But then she glanced up again and beheld the meaning Kris made no effort to cloak from his gaze. Her final word ended in a trembling rasp.

The sound made Kris feel the rabid wolf with his paw up a maiden's dress. He pulled back his arm as he buckled a more neutral expression to his features and fumbled to find an equally bland subject toward which to guide their words.

"So, Mistress Healer, how did you come to so swiftly determine the state of my fever?" Now that was winningly bland. If only Grandfather were here to see those hours of etiquette lessons weren't entirely for naught.

"Oh, one look can be the telling," she answered with an easy sweep of her hand, assuring Kris he had met success in his effort to assuage her trepidation. "And you looked very much fevered, I assure you."

"I did?" He couldn't help a bemused grin. "And what is such a 'look,' that I embodied it so completely?"

She cast him a sideways glance of her own. "You would like me to be honest?"

The smirk gave way to a frown. The wonder of her eyes aside, Mistress Armagh surprised him more frequently than any woman he'd ever met. "Of course."

She shrugged. "All right, then. You looked fairly much like a dolt."

"A—"

"Dolt. 'Tis true; you were nay the one looking at you, so stop gawking. Your mouth was all screwed up like a lover getting ready to pleasure his colleen, and your eyes did not shine much clearer, mooning at me like I was the Forest Queen herself, the most desirable thing you had ever seen."

Kris couldn't help himself. As she dedicated herself to her description, he felt that "mooning" look taking over his features all over again, so that the moment she finished, he defied the pain in his arm to tug her down next to him—just

so she got a better look this time, he justified sardonically.
And ah, God, how *he* looked at *her*. He doubted Sandys
had left him with the strength for full arousal, but that most
life-affirming part of him definitely stirred with the first
throbbings of need, and he wanted to yell out with the elation of it.

Instead, with huskiness derived straight from the bittersweet tension in his blood, he asked her, "And it surprises
you that a man would look at you so?"

This time, she didn't beg his pardon. This time, Kris
knew, she comprehended every syllable of what he said. As
he watched that realization transform her face into tremulous elation, Kris thought of nothing less than the sea awakening beneath the sun, lifting its crests toward the heavens.
The revelation filled him with a humbled awe, as if he'd just
lent a hand in a miracle.

It made him long to kiss her. Hard. And long. Then
longer, and harder. He told her so by pressing his splint
across the small of her back, then drawing her to him with
the wanting length of him. "Leprechaun," he whispered as
she slid nearer, "Leprechaun . . ."

She sighed. Or so he thought she did. But the next
instant, he discovered the high-pitched sound for its real
purpose. It was a protest cry, seconds preceding her vehement escape from him. She pulled herself far back away
from him, hands pressed to cheeks flushed brilliant as the
sky over the morning sea he'd just conjured.

She remained like that for eternal moments, until her
throat found her voice again. "Who *are* you?" she rasped
fiercely at him. "And blast you, why are you beleaguering
me so?"

Kris didn't answer until he struggled onto his good
elbow. "Come now, Mistress," he replied with a courtly

casualness that nearly gagged him, "we *have* been introduced . . . though I gather you have a first name other than 'Mistress'?"

"Introduced! And Sandys's little tea party makes us cozy as bunnies in the winter, does it?"

To emphasize, she gesticulated furiously with her arms, then slammed them into a tight coil against her chest. "Kristian Rayne Bastion Montague," she declared, giving each of the syllables an assessing distinctness of their own, "for the bard's own epic length of your name, I don't think I've been 'introduced' to the half of who you are."

Kris gave a shrug of finely feigned confusion. "I have no idea of what you speak. I *am* sorry to disappoint you, but you get what you see. I am Kristian Montague, London gentleman and international shipping merchant. I was only going about my normal business in Dublin, when caught in a series of bizarre circumstances beyond my control."

She renewed her derisive chuckling from the moment he uttered *gentleman.* "Oh, aye, and *I'm* just Shivahn Armagh, innocent Irish village healer who fancied to take to the streets of Dublin for the adventure of it."

Kris bore a twinge of genuine guilt when her shoulders suddenly slumped, and she muttered a curse involving a dozen saints. She'd discerned her lips' blatant slip just as his own mouth spread upward in triumph.

"Shivahn," he repeated softly. There was no need to compound her chagrin by making the word a Handel overture, but the syllables did feel so damn nice on his lips. "So that's the Mistress Armagh's elusive identity. 'Tis very befitting, I think. A strong name, but hinting of a woman with a secret chink in all her armor, after all."

She arrowed him a scowl. "I have *no* idea of what you speak."

"Oh, aye, you do," Kris interrupted on a subtly sensual drawl. "*Shivahn*. Your name itself speaks of a woman filled with many dreams . . . and many desires."

He let out that finishing sibilance with slow deliberation, so the sound curled between them like smoke from a scented candle. As he did, he watched her expression change, the light in her eyes hovering hesitantly, expectantly, above the flame of her awakening womanhood . . .

A flame that could easily become a forest fire—a fact he'd be wise to repeat like a High Mass for the next week.

Because if he began *this* conflagration, he wouldn't be around to put it out.

"This has nothing to do with answering my question, Kristian Montague," she broke into his thoughts. She punctuated the demand by blinking her way to a guarded frown again. Hell. He needn't have worried about snuffing the taper, after all. She did it for him.

Nevertheless, his comeback came easily. "Only after you answer *mine*, Shivahn Armagh," he murmured with deliberate challenge. "I'll tell you who I am, if you tell me who you are. Then we'll prick our fingers, become blood brothers, and take all that lethal knowledge to the grave with us."

At that, against every obvious objection in her body, Shivahn Armagh smiled.

He didn't misinterpret the look this time. Oh, aye, she *smiled*, and with that sight came the awareness that he didn't hurt anymore. In place of his wounds and bruises came a sensation he imagined the sun would feel like if melted and poured through his being.

No, Kris revised, not the sun. The sea. 'Twas Neptune's own power he held responsible for forming this creature, with her mermaid queen's eyes, spray of coral-light dots across her nose, and that *smile*, straight from the treasure troves of Atlantis itself . . .

"You are . . . so strange," she finally said, her smile at last slackening to a perplexed moue. "And I am naught but an Irish village lass, of no consequence. Why am I so important to you?"

Why, indeed. Kris could have, should have, presented the words to *his* soul. But he didn't want to. And damn it, he didn't have to. He supposed a condemned man had a few liberties left, after all.

"I offer the same query to you, Shivahn," he returned once again. "I am naught but an arrogant, empty Englishman—your enemy. Why am *I* so important to *you*?"

She could have been one of the wall stones for all her reaction. But abruptly, a furrow of such deep confusion crinkled her brow, Kris bit his inner cheek to hold back his grin. He scribbled a reminder note in his mind's journal: Befuddlement did adorable things to leprechauns.

"It would seem," she finally said on a sigh, "we have reached a stalemate."

Kris shook his head. "Not necessarily a stalemate. I would prefer to call it . . . a friendship."

He didn't think she could render a more motionless response than her previous stillness. But the paralyzed gaze he endured now revised that conclusion. A full minute passed of her unmoving two-toned scrutiny. A minute more.

"Well," he finally said, struggling for a blasé smile. "At least you didn't say no."

"I did not say *aye*!"

If the woman's intent was to appear a spark exploding off a fire, she achieved the job with honors. Yet somehow, Kris lunged across the floor with equal alacrity, managing to catch her by one knee. As he did, he gritted to her, "But you did not say nay!"

The words were filled with the pain he paid for the action. The moment he caught her, he had to let her go, anyhow, dropping to the hay as his body screamed its disapproval of his exertion. That was when he found out blessings sometimes came in peculiar disguises. Immediately a wash of healer's concern brought Shivahn down next to him.

"By the sky and stars," she muttered furiously, running fingers over his wounds and bruises. "You obstinate man, do you even know of what danger you speak? Do you? What on God's green earth am I supposed to say? *You* supplied the words to seal your own coffin in this matter! You're an arrogant, empty *Englishman*, and why would I want aught to do with you? Why?"

Kris stopped her hand with the firm but gentle grip of his. Half a dozen flippant replies raced to his lips, but they vanished as he found himself only longing to speak one thing to this woman: the truth.

"Why, Leprechaun," he said, completely confronting the amethyst glory of her gaze, "is because I *will* be in a coffin next week . . . and you'd make the journey there a bloody hell of a lot easier."

At that, he lay down and closed his eyes, and let himself breathe once more. There. He'd endured the worst of the blasted ordeal.

Hadn't he?

Damn it, his soul raged as he reopened his gaze. *Ah, goddammit.* He'd only tasted a drop of what this torment could be. He realized that the hard way, as he watched Shivahn's stare fill and glimmer at him, like rainpools beneath a hurricane-tossed sky. Only rainpools didn't reflect a spirit vacillating between striking him and saying Mass for him.

In the end, she did neither. Instead, she slumped forward

and bathed his hand with her tears as she whispered, "May the demons torment your next hours, Kristian Montague. I dreaded you would say that."

Dread, Shivahn concluded as she trudged along the River Liffey an hour later, only began to describe the tangled sense of foreboding Kristian Montague had wound around her soul. But commanding herself to forget the bounder yielded a protesting uproar from her mind, as it proved in the images that appeared every time she even blinked her eyes.

She remembered him with that cocky lad's smile creeping at the corners of his mouth . . . then with that man's pain twisting the length of his body. But most clearly of all, she recalled him swallowing every drop of his formidable pride and confessing *she* was his sole dying wish.

The thought brought the pain again, sharp and yet sweetly intense, between her breasts. The strange sensation had driven her to her knees in his cell, affecting her as no other force, not even the inundation of The Giving. Now the attack forced her to stumble to a tree, bracing herself against the rough bark as her breath came hard between her locked teeth.

"Oh, Kristian," she finally whispered, "why can't you order up two pints of poteen and a fine cigar, like any other condemned bastard?"

But she already knew the answer to that. She'd supplied it herself when looking upon him in the cell, and knew she saw only the outer covering to the inner labyrinth of this man. His maze delved to levels no poteen could intoxicate or cigar could cloud. It mattered not that he hid his soul's depths behind a heathen prince's smile—she knew of Kristian Montague's labyrinth as surely as she knew of the same bottomless maze twisting through *her* soul.

And for that reason alone, she would return to him again. For the precious hour Sandys permitted them together each day, she would be Kristian Montague's friend for the rest of his life.

Five more days.

Five more days.

A soft sob echoed across the river. Only a moment later did she realize the sound had emanated from her own throat.

"By Matthew, Mark, and Luke." Shivahn furiously back-handed the salty wetness now making an appearance on her cheeks, as well. "Put your ducks back in a row, Shivahn," she chastised herself. "He's just a lonely, luckless English-man, and you're—"

Her heart doubled its frantic beat. *What, indeed,* are *you to him?*

Her soul echoed the words as her gaze scanned the Liffey for the answer she could not fathom. A liquid tapestry of reflections flowed before her in the coming morning's haze, the waters first a flat flannel blue, then a ribbon of hazy gray, then a thread of amber sun.

Yet one thread was all she needed. In that sole flash of sunlight on the water, Shivahn received her answer. She smiled as she pronounced the safe finality of it aloud.

"Convenient," she said. "Aye, you are *convenient* to him, and no more. You can surely accept that, Shivahn. And you can surely grant what the poor wretch asks of you. 'Tis five days of your life, and no more."

Feeling lighter, she took up a more spirited step back to the waterfront "warehouse" she and a handful of the other Trabith Insurgents called a Dublin home. "Nay, 'tis not as if your world is going to upright itself in that time," she assured herself on a laugh into the wind. "And if it were, 'tis not as if an *Englishman* were capable of the uprighting!"

No matter how green and penetrating his gaze, or blissfully magical his touch, or strangely, sweetly close his soul.

Chapter 4

Two nights later, Kris jumped to his feet when he recognized her presence on the stairway. Her soft-soled shoes presented no contest in volume to the boots of the two guards flanking her, but he knew she approached as surely as sensing the rise of a tide or the coming of a dawn.

He cursed himself then for never completely appreciating tides and dawns.

The footsteps halted, and the key grated into the lock. For every moment it took the guard to battle the door open, Kris's heart pounded in his throat fifty times. *Dear God, Montague,* a voice pronounced from that safe, logical part of his brain that wouldn't remain conveniently behind in England, *can you be any more pathetic? Has your existence come down to this, then?*

He answered that with a surprisingly shameless laugh. "I

suppose it has." Then, with one brow quirking in perplexion, "I think I even *hope* it has."

But no time remained for bewildered brooding now. With
a screech of metal against stone floor, the door swung in.

She entered with her eyes downcast, which Kris gave
instant thanks for, since the simple sight of her made him
wonder if a fever had struck him anew, with sweating heat
and weakened limbs. The added onslaught of her gaze
might truly have reduced him into something to label
"pathetic."

Not that he didn't come bloody close to filling the order
as it was. For the better part of a minute, he stood there mute
and motionless, taking her in as if she'd entered dressed in
nothing but the attire God gave her at birth. Even if she had,
he didn't think his eyes could widen any further to fulfill his
need for the sight of her.

And God's troth, the sight of her . . .

Not a thread of dingy work clothing hung from her proud
shoulders tonight. Instead, the torch flickered fingers of
amber light over the pale lavender frock encasing her curves
with simple lines and sweet perfection. A prized length of
faded lace acted as fichu to the dress's neckline, directing
his sights where he ordered them not to trail—yet where he
trailed, anyway, loitering much too long where the lace disappeared into lightly freckled mystery.

"Good evening, Mr. Montague," she greeted him as soon
as the guard departed. She reached a hand up to check the
angle on her lace-trimmed cap, trying her hardest, Kris
knew, to camouflage a waver of feminine uncertainty
beneath a show of careful nonchalance. Kris barely checked
his pleased grin. No guessing game was required this time;
he liked being the cause of her nervousness. He liked it a
great deal.

He should have continued along with the game, spouted

a string of enough ballroom flattery to fill her dreams for the next three years. But those words were playthings, as satisfying as the champagne and canapés he'd learned them by. This woman deserved more than words spoken between bubble-filled wine and air-filled bread.

"Shivahn Armagh," he murmured, drawing out each word so that he almost sang them to her, "you are . . ." *the most incredible thing I've ever seen.* "You look . . ." *you look like my dreams. You look like the fantasies I have when I dare to think beyond tomorrow.*

"Nice," his numb lips blurted, instead.

"Nice?" Shivahn flung him a ruthlessly sardonic arch of brows. "Mr. Montague, surely you are not telling me a glance at a hand-me-down wedding frock has stripped all the silver off that sterling tongue of yours?"

She finished the invective by breaking into a small smile, clearly awaiting a comeback of matching wit. Nothing obliged Kris save a look reflecting the storm front gathering in his chest. "*Wedding* frock?"

To his puzzled but strangely pleasant shock, she let out a chiming laugh. "Not *mine*, you simpling. This is a maid's dress, not a bride's."

"A *maid's*—"

"Aye." She laughed again, but the gleam in her eyes softened beneath the same mist sneaking into her voice. "Today 'twas a happy day for my friend Adrianna. She was joined at last to her David, which has been no small miracle in the making, mind you."

"Oh?" Kris tilted his head, hoping the act encouraged her on, as he grew more enraptured with this girlish side of the healer who healed too much and smiled too little.

"Aye. You see, the whole village had given Davey up for dead in the Battle of the Diamond. When he returned to us a full year after the atrocity, Adrianna was actually stitching up the last of her mourning weeds." Her eyes twinkled brighter. "We raised a fine fracas, thanking the *Sídhe* for their magical hand in the matter. But 'twasn't half a celebration compared to the doings of *this* day!"

In emphasis of that, she went up on tiptoes, pirouetting like an orchid twirling on a spring wind—only more beautiful, Kris concluded. He battled not to scoop her up out of that whirl and crush his mouth against the nectar-sweet softness of her.

A dream, he reprimanded himself. *Just a dream. A vision to cling to as they tighten the noose around your neck, and no more. You've made your last request, and she's granting it, and your condemned body better be satisfied with it.*

With a determined sigh, he looked back to her again. Sweet God, she was lovely. Even her freckles were flushed with joy, and her lips twitched with hidden mirth, a creature happy to be alive in this moment alone.

But that was the trouble with moments. All too swiftly, they disappeared into time. And time, Kris conceded, was no longer a luxury he could claim—therefore, he had every right to cheat it by extending this moment as long as he could.

He softly requested, "Tell me more about it."

At that, she dropped back to her feet and stepped away. The maiden Shivahn had been out playing too long. The rebel Shivahn returned, swiftly dropping her shoulders and averting her eyes.

"Not much to tell," she muttered. "Certainly 'twas not the fancy paradings you're used to in Londontown."

The barely hidden bitterness beneath her words conveyed her meaning blatantly enough—but Kris had encountered worse disdain from Glengesh farm children. With one step, he closed the gap she'd created. She'd carried flowers during her friend's ceremony, he guessed. He smelled the lingering traces of heather and roses in the excruciating nearness of her.

"I'll wager you had just as much fun," he asserted with painstaking gentleness.

His reward came when her lips quirked upward again. "We probably did. The fairies indeed kissed our dancing meadow with magic dew this eve."

Kris raised both brows. "*Magic* dew?"

"Of course," she replied as if he'd merely confirmed there was still snow on the summit of Mount Carrantuohill. "You do not think a new bride would dance on *everyday* meadow dew?"

"God forbid," he muttered.

"Beg your pardon?" she returned over her shoulder, as she turned, knelt, and began unpacking the contents of her sack. Kris was saved, as it were, by female nature; he watched her "feathering" his prison "nest" with the ale, bread, wedding sweets, and herbal healing concoctions she'd smuggled in for him. In that moment, he knew he could let her fairy fantasies fly safely away by not uttering another word of them.

He could do that. He *should* do that. He'd never become more of a "bloody bastard Englishman" by hacking apart her dreams with the blade of his disbelief.

But the sight of her drove all the *coulds* and *shoulds* from his mind. He watched the changing angles on her lips as she hummed some lively Celtic tune. Her shoulders, curved more beautifully than swan's wings, dipped and swayed in time to her music. Finally, his stare moved to her hands . . . those hands that had glided over him and infused him with a sensation he'd never known before. Such innocent hands, yet so knowing what he needed. Such tapered and small fingers, capable of such amazing power. And magic.

Aye, he could forget her fairy drivel right this instant.

But he didn't want to.

Because he desperately wanted to believe, too.

Kris moved to where she'd almost finished setting their "picnic" array. He slid to the floor next to her, propping his good elbow on one bent knee. Without a word, he loosened her fingers from the chunk of dark bread she was slicing and lowered both food and dagger to the napkin at her knees.

"Fairies," he said then, gazing into the sparkling violet depths of her eyes. "Magic . . . fay spirits . . . miracles . . . they're all real to you, aren't they?"

She looked as if she wanted to scowl. But she didn't. "Well," she at last replied, "aye."

The words were barely more than soft utterances, which was why, Kris surmised, he heard the screams of his body so clearly as she leaned closer to him, closer. "By the spirits and saints, Kristian," she murmured, lifting her fingers to the side of his face. "Don't *you* have magic and miracles in your life?"

He didn't know whether to kiss her or curse at her. To his surprise, Kris battled the urge to do both. *Damn her*, his mind raged, instead. Damn *him*, for purposely placing himself close enough to her touch, for now adding the heated torment of his body to the clamoring confusion of his senses.

He turned away from her, shaking visibly until he regained control by curling a hard fist. "The *Sídhe* don't save miracles for people like me, Leprechaun," he finally growled.

Her outraged snort erupted behind him. "Bull fodder. Of course they do. But they *only* do for anyone who helps them along in the effort." A sharp sigh came next. " 'Tis bloody hard, Mr. Montague, even for the *Sídhe*, to spin miracles for those who do not want them spun. And it seems to me that you have plenty of flax, but the only thing you're spinning is a ball of blazing knots."

Now he didn't know whether to kiss her or laugh at her. Kris decided on the latter, indulging a sardonic snort as he turned a stare back to her full of similar meaning. "What are you talking about?"

"Well, *that* should be plain as day." She harrumphed. "If, as you keep claiming, you are not the Griffin, then why are you letting Sandys punish *you* for his crimes? *Now* do you see?" Her hands flew back up to second the motion. "A ball of knots!"

As those arms descended, Kris reached forward and caught them by the wrists. He slid his grip down until his fingers entwined with hers. He felt her stiffen and prepared himself for her attempt at escape, but Shivahn didn't move save to look down where their hands locked, then back up into his eyes with a gaze as curious as it was startled.

He allowed the magic of that stare to wash over him, wash through him, for one inexpressibly perfect moment. Then the moment was gone, Time continuing its merciless pace, slapping him with the recognition of what he must do next. Of what he must say next.

"A ball of knots, eh?" he heard himself reply to her. The man who spoke was a monster filled with bitterness and frustration and fear—a man he'd left behind in another life, another place. "So you really think that if I proved I were Admiral Pitt himself, that bastard upstairs would believe a thing I said? Do you? *Do you?*"

Shivahn didn't move an eyelash. Nor did she whimper or cry out at his tightening hold. She gazed at him with nothing less than her convicting anger and her desperate confusion. And *that* spoke her response louder than any shriek or curse.

Kris's hands slackened, finally dropped to his sides. His gaze followed the same course, tracing a trail of black goo on the floor as he rose and retreated from her into the equally lightless depths of the cell.

"Please," he finally grated, sinking against the wall. "Please leave me now."

Shivahn had wanted to disobey him, of course. The moment the hoarse appeal left his lips, every muscle in her body had lurched with the desire to hurl herself at him, then force him into grabbing her again and squeezing until her fingers snapped off. At least then, she'd know he was still angry. At least then, she'd know his blood still burned with the fires to fight.

At least then, she'd know he still wanted to live.

Oddly, that was the dilemma which had given her the will to leave. She could stand there all night, or even squeeze *him* into a mass of darker black and blue, but she could not replenish Kristian's thirst to live. She did not have the power, or the right. No one did.

The conclusion did not provide the makings for peaceful dreams, and Shivahn had paid for her loss of such through the hours of the following day. Yet now, making her way through Dublin's darkening streets, she barely blinked for fear of wasting even that time on her way to Prevot's gates. Without faltering a step, she struggled past a flock of sheep, down the middle of a children's tag game, and through countless mud holes. Her breaths came through stinging lungs, but she rushed on toward her ironically vital goal.

Ironic? her mind reiterated. *Do you not mean* insane? *Is not* that *the word, Shivahn? You surely cannot be anything else, returning to the man who cast you away like used pot grease.*

"No," she whispered vehemently, jerking her shawl tighter around her shoulders, increasing her pace still more. *"No."*

Finally, she turned the last corner and sloshed through the mud pit before the prison's entrance. She approached the guard and managed to weave enough "healer's talk" between multiple mentions of Sandys's name that the lazy-eyed lad didn't raise one word of question about her unscheduled arrival.

Getting from the guard shack to Kristian's cell was another matter. For all the time they took in sending an escort for her, Shivahn surmised she could have taught the entrance guard the "Hail Mary" in two languages.

She didn't know if that was a good sign or a bad sign. As she marched the last length of the corridor in Cell Block Three, she tried not to let the trepidation churn her insides into gruel, either. Of course, Fate could have asked her not to breathe and gotten more successful results.

The guard jerked the door open. For a long moment, Shivahn could not bear to look inside. She scrutinized her escort's face, instead. His expression showed only weary disgruntlement at having to interrupt a good dice game to deliver her here.

The soldier grunted impatiently. Holding her breath, Shivahn stepped through the portal.

And let that breath out in a stunned gasp.

He was alive. As a matter of fact, if she hadn't borne witness to the contrary, she might disbelieve the man had just spent four days and nights in a prison dungeon—a dungeon that now seemed shrunken against Kristian's overwhelming presence. He stood with weight evenly dealt to both long legs, his good hand flat against one defined thigh, the splinted arm held at a proud angle across his high torso, topped by shoulders thrown back in what she almost termed defiance.

He was strength and courage. Pride and respect. He was larger than life, a hero straight from one of Gorag's adventure tales, complete with battle scars to impress the little boys and a gaze to melt the little girls. In short, he was missing absolutely nothing.

Except half his hair.

Ridiculous, Shivahn's senses railed. *Surely your weary body plays at false sights with you.* But even after she shook her head to free it from the image, she looked up at the same man as before, only discernibly lighter by at least a pound. Where Kristian's dark mane once fell well past his shoulders, now the thick waves teased the top of his nape at best, played around the edges of his ears, then teased in shorter strands against his face and forehead.

Only the *Sídhe* knew how long she'd have remained gaping like that, if not for the awkward half grin Kristian finally flashed at her. "What do you think, Leprechaun?" he quipped with equal clumsiness. "I'd . . . just been thinking I needed a trim, anyway." He ran a slightly shaking hand from temple to nape. "What the bloody hell. Perhaps this will start the newest fad in London."

Shivahn swallowed deeply. The realization struck her that his "new fad" of a look did not frighten her at all. 'Twas his Sunday-in-the-meadow pretense of an attitude that made her stomach clench in anticipating dread. "H-how?" she finally forced herself to blurt. "And why?"

She knew not whether to adore him or strangle him for the chuckle he had at the ready to that. But when the expression fell just as swiftly, succeeded by a heavy gulp then a rapid turn to the wall, all temptations vanished to do anything but rush forward and hold him.

Hold him very, very close.

"I'm . . . glad you came tonight," he said at last. But the floor heard the words more than she, as he braced both hands to the wall and dropped his head between his shoulders.

Her belly twisted tighter. "By the saints, Kristian," she demanded, "what is happening?"

He cleared his throat twice before replying. "It's just that I owe you this apology—"

"What? You are making less sense than a swill-pot on New Year's eve!"

Shivahn hastened an instinctive step back as all the tension in his tone exploded through his body, and he whirled back at her with a stare of commanding fierceness. "I *am* making sense," he snapped, "and you will hear it out, damn it."

He stopped then, sucking in a harsh breath while closing his eyes, clearly searching for a calmer mien from which to continue his explanation. "Shivahn," he began again, in a measured murmur, "last night, my behavior—" He let the breath out in another rough rasp. "I had no right to snap at you like some rotten-toothed old man, no matter how much I felt like one. And . . . I'm sorry."

Shockingly, Shivahn found it her turn to give him a bemused smile. "You are not a surly old man."

A strange expression came over his face in response to that. Nay, Shivahn amended the next moment, the look was more an *absence* of expression . . . a lineless blank of neither anger or sadness, hope nor despair.

An expression very similar to the toneless deliverance of his next words.

"As of tomorrow, I won't have to worry about being *anything* of an old man."

He paced to the opposite wall again. Against her will—

against the horrid new thunder of her heartbeat—Shivahn
followed him. Yet she stopped short of touching him. She
stopped short of touching the shoulders clenched so taut,
they pressed at the tatters of his shirt with their spasmings.
She stopped short of pulling his hand back into hers and
pressing its strength to the relentless pounding between her
breasts.

"Wh-what do you mean?" she softly blurted. But no
matter what the answer was, she dreaded it with every drop
of bile now searing her belly. She had told herself this
would happen if she cared. A thousand times, she had told
herself *not* to care—

That was when they still had time to pretend life
was real.

That was when they could count that life in minutes, not
moments.

"What do you mean?" she heard her trembling lips
repeat. "Tomorrow—tomorrow is only Saturday."

"I know. But it seems . . . um . . . Sandys wishes to
change his plans a bit."

As he said that, Kristian began to pace a small but swift
circle before her. He awaited her to prompt him on, Shivahn
knew, but her jaw worked on empty air, her lungs labored
on shallow breaths.

"Go . . . on," she finally forced out.

He threw her a relieved glance. "It . . . seems that my
execution will make a better 'example' tomorrow, on
market day . . . that even though I'm English, the Insurgents
would find a way to make me a martyr with an execution on
the Sabbath."

Now Shivahn could only nod. Nearly word for word,
he'd recounted what she'd expected—yet couldn't bear to
accept. *But why?* her mind railed. *Why do you grieve for one
inch of this bastard? Is he not the token of vengeance*

*everyone has prayed for? The Londontown flirt who has
hunted fox and shared gallons of claret with the monsters
out there trampling the heather and burning the villages of
your country? He is one of them. He nay wears their colors
outside, but he bleeds their blood inside. He is one of them,
and you do not care about him . . . you do not!*

Why did the words not resound in one beat of her heart?

Why did her soul consider this man's death and know not
a drop of vengeful satisfaction?

Why did *none* of this violence suddenly make no right
nor sense?

"The hanging—" She finally choked out. "It—I suppose—" Beyond her volition or caring, the tears came,
silent and searing, and she tasted their bitter salt with her
rasped finish. "They'll do it at sunrise, then?"

In the ensuing silence, Shivahn battled to compose herself. The effort exacted two completely clenched fists and
such a good portion of her concentration that she never
noticed the increasing intensity in Kristian's pace. Nor did
she catch the transparent uneasiness in the one glance he
gave her. Nay, she noticed not a thing in his transformed
mien, until it was too late.

Too late to contain her dread when she realized his
announcement wasn't over.

"Er . . . that's the other interesting thing," he stammered,
as if they merely stood in some fancy drawing room, and he
forgot a point to a postdinner joke. "It also seems that
Sandys feels a . . . um . . . beheading will make more of an
impact. He feels that—"

"A *what*?"

Shivahn stumbled back, pleading him with her eyes to
pull the spear of his statement out from her writhing heart.
But with a silent, almost imperceptible tightening of his
jaw, Kristian only drove the spear in deeper.

"N-nay." Her lips formed the sound with foundering disorientation. "Nay, damn you." Her voice resounded in her senses as if she heard herself playing a part in a nightmare, only she could not wake up. Why could she not wake up? "Damn *them*! He—they cannot—oh, God, they cannot!"

"Leprechaun." Kristian was as heinous as Sandys himself with his infuriating, controlled gentleness. "They *can*. That's why they cut my hair—so the blade won't be hindered—"

"Stop it. Stop saying that! Do you think I *want* to hear that?"

Through the blur of her tears, his form stepped toward her. "Shivahn—"

"They're barbarians, and so are you! *Look* at you! A body would think you're looking forward to being dishonored like that—to having your head—oh, God!"

"Shivahn."

Before she could think to protest, his hands encompassed her wrists as his command echoed through her being. He pulled her closer with his good arm, his touch commanding, but calm. "Shivahn, please . . . it'll be all right."

"The bloody *hell* it will!" She wrested one hand free enough to drive a fist into his shoulder, both pleased and ashamed at the soft *oof* of pain she induced. "It shall *never* be all right. I didn't *want* to be your friend. I didn't *want* to care! Damn you, Kristian, it shall never be right again!"

She cried the words out as punishment, as his trial and conviction in one, but when the syllables ceased echoing off the walls, the silence cast forth a verdict against nobody but her. And dear God, Shivahn realized, the judgment was fitting. She was guilty, so guilty, ready for sentencing at the hands of her own denied pride, her own compromised soul . . . her own surrendered heart.

That heart meted that sentence now without delay. It guided her hands up his chest, along his neck, and around the back of his head . . . then pulled his mouth to hers in a kiss they'd shared before only in the realms of her most secret dreams.

Chapter 5

t's true, Kris conceded from the deepest realms of his being, from the roaring eruption of his senses. *Ah, God, she's speaking the truth. Nothing will ever be right again.* Not after the ultimate rightness of this; not after the completeness of her body pressed to his, the consummation of having her against his lips, in his arms, in his soul.

In his soul.

The realization blasted him as he shifted from not only acceding to her assault, but joining in her passion. Oh, aye, somewhere in that soaring moment, as he brought her closer with a fierce jerk and made her whimper with a hungry downsweep of his mouth, he recognized the motions for what they were: primeval play-actings at strength to camouflage how thoroughly she'd annihilated his defenses, how completely she'd come to live in his thoughts and dreams of what would never be.

Thoughts and dreams of holding her just like this.

No, not exactly like this. For a flicker of an instant, he pulled away to fix the single element amiss about her. With one feverish motion, he shoved away her cap and hurled it to the shadows. Like a waterfall of melted sunset, her curls flooded into his hands. Like a waterfall's din, his blood thundered in his ears.

"Jesus," he breathed, spreading his fingers into the thick, warm strands, "Oh, Jesus, Leprechaun . . . you're more beautiful than I—"

She cut him off with another upslant of her mouth. But this time, Kris was ready.

This time, he met her lips, then parted them.

The world ignited into pure sensation: softness, wetness and heat; pliant, melding lips and eager, trusting tongue; surrendering woman's moan and sweet woman's body. One filled his pounding heart, the other swelled the length between his thighs until he groaned in return and rocked against her, needing her to heal him with her touch, begging her to save him with her embrace.

I don't want to die. Ah, God, Leprechaun, I'm afraid. Make me forget. Let me forget. I don't want to die. I don't want to die!

Harder he pressed, in time to that desperate litany, suckling his mouth to hers as he slid more urgently against her. And even that felt right; aye, so right; and he moved to guide her down to the hay, driven by pure feeling and raw need—

But he suddenly stood holding nothing but the remaining scent of her on the air. He heard nothing but her rapid, panicked breaths.

He snapped his head up and beheld nothing but the terrified shame in her eyes.

Those amethyst facets glittered brighter with moist pain as she raised shaking fingers to her swollen lips. "I am . . . sorry," she rasped, and tears trickled over her slender knuckles. "I should not have come back. I should not have agreed to all this to begin with. I am so sorry."

"Shivahn—" He hadn't pleaded with anyone so fervently in years, but his pride could incinerate in hell, where his heart already plummeted. "Shivahn—it's all right—"

"Nay!" She spread a hand out to stay his approach. "It is *not*! I cannot feel these things, Kristian! I cannot!"

"Shivahn!"

But he lunged at the emptiness filled only with the echoes of her fleeing footsteps.

The night descended and progressed in an ironic plod of minutes that felt like days, hours that felt like years. Many classics of poetry were created in moments like these, Kris reminded himself; sometimes men wrote epics of immortal wisdom, or, at the least, a pithy proverb to last throughout perpetuity.

He didn't give a thumbnail's damn about perpetuity.

He circled the cell a hundred times and saw only Shivahn. He searched in the corner where he'd tossed her cap and saw only Shivahn. He scooped up the garment he'd resented and now clutched it like a monk with a rosary, shutting his eyes as he inhaled the fabric's capturings of sunshine and meadow clover.

With the scents, he felt her, too. His arms remembered the exquisite fit of her. His thighs remembered the submitting softness of her. And every beat of his heart remembered the powerful passion of her. Dear sweet God, the passion of her . . .

Until she'd fled from him like a nun caught at an Orange Order meeting. *I cannot feel these things, Kristian.*

"These things?" he muttered sardonically as he finally slumped to the floor, bone weary and yet hours away from real sleep. "Ah, Leprechaun, if you feel half the things *I* feel, then you can indeed feel them."

Hades' fire, can you feel them.

"Stop," he ordered to himself, slamming his head back against the wall. And he tried. Hell, how he tried. He attempted to divert his thoughts by pondering the sludge and slime surrounding him. His arousal didn't diminish an inch. He counted cracks in the wall, told himself to sleep. His mind only overflowed with more images of her. Beautiful, carnal images of her. He saw that flood of gilded hair spilling against the arch of her bare back . . . then his hand, trailing the sleek indenture in that back. At last he guided his fingers lower, cupping the curve of her body there, lifting her willing body against his as he guided himself inside her . . .

And then, he even pictured her ripe with his child. And he saw her with that babe in her arms, taking nourishment from her full, beautiful breast. After that, he envisioned her standing next to him in a dew-kissed meadow, smiling features captivatingly redefined by the paintbrush of age, in an Ireland where soldiers had become farmers and prisons were converted to schools and theaters.

An Ireland that would someday be.

Filled with children he'd never see.

Something moaned then, an animal's sound reverberating with the kind of pain that embraced death as much as battled it. Strange, Kris thought as a black abyss finally rose from his conscious to consume him, the sound followed him into a chilled slumber, because it came from *inside* him . . .

He fought to ignore the echoes of his misery, and almost succeeded, until the sounds took on the form of words. Shivahn's fairy demons had finally come to get him, came his first surreal conclusion, as the voices called, ever more earnestly, *Kristian . . . Kristian . . . come on, Kristian; please, Kristian . . .*

"Kristian!"

A lad's face suddenly wobbled before his blinking eyes. Kris batted at the image, groaning in protest, but when he tried to slump back over, two arms gave him a hard shake.

"Kristian, blast you, wake up!"

Then the lad kissed him.

This time, he woke up.

Sputtering a mouthful of expletives, Kris lunged at the boy. He didn't know why, but he wasn't surprised when the lad retaliated with an equally vehement shove and a vibrant oath.

"Are you ready to behave yet?" a furious rasp followed. "Because if not, I shall leave you in here to lose your batty head, after all!"

For one stunned and wordless moment, Kris fell back against the wall. The next, he let out a low yet delirious chuckle.

The next, he hauled the lad back to him and considered never letting go.

"Shivahn," he said into the dirty stocking cap hiding the wad of her curls. Into that utterance, he poured all the things he'd spent the last hours dismissing from his world: tenderness, hope, exhilaration, anticipation, strength, weakness, and joy . . . *joy*. "Shivahn," he repeated. *"Shivahn."*

A soft but distinctly baritone cough cut into his reverie. Kris looked up. The source of the cough—a chap who matched him in height, but doubled him in grith—grinned back through whiskers so dense and white, he appeared foamed up and ready for a good shave. A second man stood to the right, holding a torch as gaunt as his stark frame and whiskerless face.

"Kristian," Shivahn interceded, "this is Billy, and Duncan." She motioned to the men accordingly. "They're going to help."

Still absorbed in the elation of simply having her in his arms again, he scowled, not comprehending. "Help?"

"Aye. They have both been through the escape passage before, and I convinced them to come——"

The men released derisive snorts in unison. "Convinced?" Billy said with a wry twist of lips. "Ohhh, nay, missie, ye ain't switching yer words so easily on us this time. No *convincing* went on more than *bribing*." He turned to Kris with a commiserative raise of white caterpillar brows. "No offense to ye, o' course, but we don't normally be in the habit of casting ourselves into Prevot's bowels to *save* an Englishman."

"The thing is," Duncan picked up from there in a voice as pointed as his features, "we would nay even be standing here gawking at ye, if not for this brave lass. Last year, she not only pulled me off the middle of a battlefield, then a lead ball out of my leg, but she closed up the hole without a stitch!"

"Duncan . . ." Shivahn interceded with none-too-subtle warning. Her spine tensed beneath Kris's hands.

But as Duncan backed down, Billy thumped a meaty hand against his chest. "That story is a bedtime tale, and he knows it. *I*, on the other hand, had three bayonet stabs directly between my ribs. And what Shivahn did——"

"What I did nay matters *now*!" she broke in with an urgency Kris felt down her entire frame. She disengaged herself from everything but his hand, yet that she gripped with tight intensity as she looked into his eyes. "You must answer me with the truth," she demanded softly. "Are you all right? Can you walk? Can you run?"

Kris smiled and lifted his other hand in a brief caress to her cheek. "Up the Cliffs of Moher, if I have to."

"Well," she returned, "you may have to. Billy, Duncan, let us away."

They stepped over two bound and unconscious guards, snuck past four more with their foreheads locked over a card game, then down a maze of tunnels and countless flights of narrow stone steps. Every twenty-five to thirty feet, Billy halted the group and cocked his ear to the ceiling. Watching the man's brows and beard twitch as he assessed "sounds" from the passages above, Kris began to wonder if the man was part sheepdog. His own ears heard nothing but the fizzes and crackles from the torch—and Shivahn's increased breathing as they descended farther beneath Prevot's dungeons.

When they paused for a fifth time, he felt her trepidation as plainly as the sweat droplets in her palm and the pulse galloping to win the Grand National in her wrist. The truth be known, *he* seriously questioned their course.

Three stops later, Kris prepared himself to voice a protest. But as he stepped forward, Billy turned back on them. The sheepdog didn't cock his ear this time. He motioned Duncan and the torch closer. The light threw shadows upon a thick fissure in the wall, seemingly created by a stray stream of water flowing from God knew where and *to* God knew where.

Billy stuck both hands into the fissure. After a soft grunt, he threw his mighty weight against the crack. Slowly yet distinctly, stone rasped against stone. In a cloud of dust and age, another recess in the wall absorbed the sliding panel into its invisible depths.

"Thanks be to all the spirits of luck and life," Shivahn

murmured. She released Kris's hand to signal her gratitude with a fervent clasp of her fingers, which she fitted into the crook of her chin.

Those hands whitened to the shade of a Milan statue as Billy stepped away from the opening.

"Knew I could still do it," he declared with a casual shrug and a ponderous wheeze. Then he bowed to them with a proud grin. "M'lords and lady, freedom awaits!"

But Shivahn might as well have become that marble artwork for all her unmoving tenacity to the spot she stood. When Kris urged her forward, her spine answered with equally stone-hard resistance. He threw her a quizzical glance, only to behold features as pale and immobile as her hands.

"B-Billy," she stammered, "th-that's *not* the escape passage."

"Sure as spring rain it is. Gotta thank Duncan here and his mates for discovering it, too."

"Bloody right," Duncan added. "Didn't know where the blazin' thing led the first time we tried it, or if it led anywhere at all." He jabbed Kris with a commiserating elbow. "Kinda like my first trip to the hay loft with my Essie."

Billy chuckled. "Guess if ye let Mother Nature run her course long enough, she'll help you out in the—"

"*Billy.*" She *did* move then—to coil fingers into the man's sleeve with fierce force. "You told me not that the tunnel was only three feet wide."

Billy laughed again. "Aye, but don't ye worry a whit about me, darlin'. I made the trip before with nary a hassle, and I can do so again."

But Kris felt and observed the depth of Shivahn's fear. He nearly smelled it in every shiver of her body, in every gleam of the terror glazing every inch of her eyes. This paralysis went beyond a passing fret about Billy and his paunch. This reaction screamed of deeper—much deeper—terror.

She confirmed that impression by jerking away from them and scrambling backward along the walls. Her hands scraped and cut against the stones, but she barely noticed beyond a few fast winces.

"F-fine," she blurted. "*You* all get out with nary a hassle. I shall take the hassles, thank you,"

"What?" Billy and Duncan blasted their disapproval in gaping unison.

"You heard me," she snapped. "I am not going in there. Take Kristian and go, Billy. *But I am not going in that tunnel.*"

Chapter 6

"**L**ass," Billy growled, coiling his shoulders so tight, Kris wouldn't be surprised if the man's shirt hid raised hackles, too. "Lass, don't be a dunderpate! The alarm will sound any moment now!"

Shivahn bit the inside of her cheek. "I know."

"And you are the first thing they'll search for!"

"I know that, too. I shall be careful."

"You shall be *dead*!"

"Shivahn." Duncan approached on a less vehement step than his mate, yet Kris didn't doubt the man disciplined his children using the same patronizing mien. "Shivahn, *now* is not the time to decide to become a woman."

"For God's sake," Kris finally snapped. He shoved his way between both the men to endure another wrench of his gut at the sight of her, pale and wide-eyed, forcing herself to remain standing.

Yet though she wobbled like a fawn, one glance showed a man he encountered *no* uncertain newborn. Beneath the grim line of her lips, she raised her jaw with as much resistance as she'd given Sandys. The line of her shoulders rivaled any duchess for determined fortitude. Oh, aye, he knew the strength she possessed—all too well. All too heatedly, he recalled her ability to not only wrap her arms around his body but twine her spirit around his senses, as she'd plundered his mouth and threatened to detonate his desire . . .

"Duncan," he at last said, "look again. She already *is* a woman."

He didn't take a breath for a moment to follow. The words—and the caress of a tone he murmured them on—were an enormous risk, blurted before these men who might tear his cods out in recompense for the intent he'd clearly stated toward their ward.

But the only movement between the four of them came with the beginnings of a smile, faint yet glimmering, at the corners of Shivahn's lips. That look stirred bold new words on his tongue.

"Oh, aye, she's a woman," he continued, still watching her. "A strong woman." That was when he made his deciding action. During one smooth step forward, he reached and twined his hands with hers. "She's also a woman who can easily travel this tunnel, if she puts her will to it."

The smile vanished. Her hands twisted inside his. "Nay," she told him, struggling harder. "Nay, she cannot."

"She *can*."

"She cannot!" Her head darted in correspondence to her gaze, now glancing at the walls as if they'd grown poisoned talons. "You do not understand, Kristian. You *cannot* understand. You do not fathom what you ask of me, so do not ask it!"

"Shivahn—"

The rest of his assurance would never be heard. It was annihilated by a series of panicked bellows from above, then an explosion of action: clamoring feet, slamming gates, urgent curses, clattering bayonets.

The alarm had been sounded.

"Balls and blast," Billy growled. "This is it, mates. We have to move!"

"Kristian," Shivahn immediately followed that, "let me go!"

Amazing, came Kris's reacting thought. She fired the words at him with the authority of a royal mandate, while her gaze expanded wider in her battle to escape him. He might even have laughed at the ironic sight she made, if the ceiling didn't start to rain dust from the impact of Sandys's regiment searching out the halls and cells above them.

"No," he told her in lieu of the laugh, the command allowing no quarter for obedience. "I'm not leaving without you."

The line of her lips twisted into a pained grimace. New moisture shimmered in her eyes. "I *cannot* do this! There are reasons, Kristian—from the past—too many reasons for you to understand!"

"Try me."

"Nay!"

"Montague," Billy broke in. " 'Tis a prison we're breakin' ye from here, not a confessional. Can we be off? Now?"

"Aye, Billy. We're *both* coming. *Now.*"

As his lips assured the man, he shifted behind Shivahn, adding his bodily presence to his verbal campaign. He effectively left her with only one direction to proceed: forward, into the passage.

Or so he thought.

He should have known better, he reprimanded himself. Aye, the woman had only burst into his world five nights ago, but he imagined a baboon could have fathomed by now that when Shivahn Armagh didn't like her options, she planted her heels where she was, no matter how solid-packed the dirt floor beneath her feet, and refused to move.

Which was precisely what she did.

Even as Sandys's men began to shout their agreement about their next course of action. "To the caverns!" came some soldier-ape's bellow. "They've gone beneath ground, I'm sure of it! To the caverns!"

More shouting voices agreed with him. "Go," Shivahn ordered him amid the ensuing echoes. "Damn you, Kristian, *go*!"

She, on the other hand, should have known better of *him*. Setting his own feet in line with hers, he jerked her within elbow's length of him, struggling to give her only one vehement shake, instead of the thorough brain-jostling she clearly needed.

"Shivahn," he gritted, willing that same coiled control to his low tone. "I know you're fright—"

She cut him short with her hurting burst of a laugh. "You know nothing!" she spat, eyes gleaming the sheen of a sword blade embedded with amethyst shards.

Kris didn't break away from that gaze, yet his arms didn't stop spasming with their effort at control. *Don't let a snip of an Irish chit break your war record now, Montague,* came that survivor's voice from deep in his gut. *Whatever little else Grandfather believed you capable of, the "Mountain of Montague" never doubted your ability to padlock*

*your emotions until they'd do you the most good. Don't let
the old bastard down now.*

"You may not think so, Leprechaun, but I *do* understand." He braced an arm to the wall on either side of her
head. "I understand how terrified you are, because that's
how frightened I am that those bastards will capture you."

At that, they swallowed deeply together. Kris had deliberately omitted a phrase to his confession, and they both
knew it. He'd deliberately not mentioned that after capture,
she'd eventually be executed—yet death would be her
mercy after Sandys and his men had settled their due with
her. Torture took on new meaning when a *female* prisoner
was brought and spread-eagled in chains . . .

Kris shoved away from her and made his way toward the
tunnel, lest she see how hideously close he came to emp-
tying his stomach at the thoughts *now* introduced to his
mind's eye.

Despite that excruciating awareness, he commanded
himself not to react when he heard Shivahn's tentative step
in his wake. But when her hand slid up into his, so cold and
trembling and *trusting,* he couldn't abate the bruising intensity of the grip he returned to her poor fingers.

"Just don't let go," she said from a hoarse throat, her fingers squeezing him back just as fervently. "Please, Kristian,
don't let go."

Kris was again glad she couldn't see his face, nor the half
smile he couldn't help at this new version of the goddess
Armagh, issuing her orders with a shaking scepter at best.

The man, Shivahn conceded a minute beyond an hour
later, was amazingly true to his promises.

Kristian had not let her go for an instant—not even when
Billy had slid the secret wall shut behind them, sealing them

into darkness relieved only by the torch's meager glow. She had spun back toward the door, thirteen years of half memories and nightmares suddenly squeezing in on her, just like the black air around them. Just like that black night on the eve of her fifth birthday . . .

But he had not let her go.

He held fast a dozen steps later, when they had rounded the tunnel's first curve to discover the ceiling plunged in on them by another three feet. Into his arms she had fallen as her knees buckled, turning the consistency of the sludge around their ankles. He still did not let go a half minute after that, when an unexpected subterranean wind snuffed the torch out, and she'd emitted a scream to wake the dead in every sepulchre of the city.

A mortified flush rushed up her face at the remembrance of the moment now. As even the back of her scalp burned with embarrassment, she sent up a thankful prayer for this eve's concealing sliver of a moon, because in that same moment, her gaze was again inexorably drawn to the man who had gotten her out of that moment alive.

Extraordinary, she ruminated, that even gazing upon Kristian now, immersed in his exhausted slumber in the hay mound across the ox cart's bed, she could remember him at the height of his strength with one effortless thought. Without trying, her memory yanked forth every second of her terror in that thick-as-pitch darkness. Once more she heard the shriek that had ripped loose in her throat, shrill with mindless fear. She remembered the years falling away from her mind, until only a five-year-old Shivahn remained, lost in another blackness that demanded even her breath . . .

But suddenly the darkness had been conquered. A lean, powerful arm had pulled her up and held her close. A strong, sheltering chest absorbed her scream while steady fingers cradled the back of her head, rocking her without ceasing.

Yet most wonderful of all, she remembered the warmth of a voice in her ear then along her neck, *oh, his voice*, murmuring things that only made half sense to her head yet found completion and comprehension in her heart. The voice became all-important, a soothing waterfall of sound over her senses, that she stopped screaming just to hear it better.

After that, she knew they would make it. All she'd had to do was hold one powerful hand and follow one powerful voice.

On that reflection, she fought yet another yearning to crawl across the hay and take refuge in those amazing arms again. "Dear saints," she beseeched beneath her breath, "forgive me and help me for my sinful longings."

The prayer had as much affect as Admiral Pitt's petitions to Parliament. By furtive inches, her gaze continued its path along Kristian's reclining body. Her blush deepened as her imagination wondered what that hard chest and those long, carved thighs would feel like if pressed against her own tingling limbs, her own aching breasts . . .

The torment was worsened by remembering their stolen moments of passion in his cell. But those were desperate instances, she clarified. Those were frantic gropings at meaning in a world where nothing was real anymore. Yet now . . . oh, now, she wondered what it would feel like to lie with this man on pillows and on sheets, to feel the magic of his long, sweet kisses as well as his heated embraces; kisses that meant he really *wanted* to be with her . . .

"So what the hell are ye goin' to do with him now?"

In spite of Billy's constant growlings that the Insurgents placed their faith in too much magic and not enough might, moments like this made Shivahn wonder if the man was truly a high druid in disguise. He slid down next to her and asked the question just as her mind's answer to it hovered between a vision of Kristian's thigh wrapped around her waist and his hand sliding down her leg.

Sinful thoughts. Dangerous thoughts.

'Twas why she fervently abolished those fantasies now, and answered Billy, "I do not know, exactly." She dropped her cheek atop her bent knees. "I do not know." A sigh made a gentle escape from her lips. "Mayhap the answer does not lie with me at all."

Billy's prolonged pause didn't put her qualms at ease. Then he cleared his throat. She had never heard him clear his throat, save for the day he had come to the meadow where she and Adrianna were making daisy crowns and told Adrianna they had not been able to account for Davey in their battle . . .

"Tell me a little somethin', lass . . . how much *do* ye know about this nobby?"

Aye, Shivahn decided then, the man was quickly working himself to high druidness. How else could Billy know all the questions for which she had not a dandelion wisp's worth of an answer?

Unfortunately, the conclusion gave her *no* inclination to throw herself before him with reverent awe. Instead, she averted her eyes, reshuffled her cramped legs, and retorted, "Sandys was not inclined to give me a life's history on the patient, Billy."

"And ye never thought of askin' the patient himself?"

"The patient himself?" She made the rebuttal with a healthy borrowing of Kristian's sarcasm. "You mean the man so far gone to a fever he did naught but babble the first two days I saw him?"

"The lad was speakin' just fine when *I* met him."

"Well, healing is ofttimes a complicated matter. We had *other* things to do when he finally came around."

The words barely left her lips than Shivahn desperately wished them back to the depths of her throat. Billy's lusty chuckle sealed her mortification.

"Other things." He snickered. "So that *is* the way of it."

She knew her swift punch to his shoulder would only deepen his conclusion, but the wallop was so gratifying, she added a second. "That's not the way of it and you know it, Billy Brayshaugh."

He raised his hands in tolerant surrender. "All right, missie, all right." He chuckled. "O' course I know it. But even if ye nay tumbled him, I think me 'n' Duncan have the right to know what kind of Englishman we put our balls on the choppin' block for."

Now here was a query to which she could rally with confidence. "You found him in Cell Block Three, didn't you?"

Billy didn't flick so much as an eyelash. Shivahn retaliated with a peeved glower. "Oh, Billy, think about it. Not even Sandys would hold one of his own countrymen in that hell if he did not have serious support for his charges."

At that, the man at least began to stroke his thick whiskers. "And what *were* the charges?"

Shivahn swallowed. Spirits help her, she could not simply make up charges against Kristian off the top of her head. Not for allegations significant enough to land him in Prevot's most notorious cell block—offenses against English "laws" Billy knew more thoroughly than the hairs his fingers scratched now.

On the other hand, an easy "I don't know" or "I don't remember" would not suffice, either. Billy knew her too well. He had trained her himself, painstakingly teaching her the methods for writing down every detail of her prison visits on the most convenient "quill and paper" to be found: her brain.

This time especially, the man would be glad to know he accomplished his task well. She remembered so much about Kristian Montague, down to every gold fleck in those deep green eyes and every dark hair sprinkling the backs of those strong fingers, that no room remained in her chaos of a brain to concoct a quick and easy lie about him.

'Twas a quandary that quickly became a problem.

"By Saint Peter and his pearly gates, Shivahn," Billy finally growled at her reticence. " 'Tis not as if the man is the bloody Griffin."

She gulped again and arrowed her gaze down to her shifting feet. Oh, blazes. Now she would have to come up with a really, *really* good lie.

"Shivahn?" the man prompted again—only this time, with an altogether different undertone. The summer day ease of his voice resonated with a gathering thunderstorm of intent. "Shivahn, look at me."

She did not move.

"Shivahn, *look at me*."

"Nay."

"Shivahn Nicoleen Armagh . . ." he rumbled more ominously. "Who helped hold your stubborn little head at your first baptism? Who changed more of your dirty nappies than your own father? Who could not *look* at his sweetlin' for two weeks, after the bruise you put in his privates whilst pretendin' he was your enchanted horse? And who—"

"Stop." She squeezed shut her eyes on a pained grimace. The enchanted horse story. She crumbled when he used the enchanted horse story, and he knew it. "Damn you, Billy," she muttered, knowing she owed him no apology for the profanity.

"I love you, too," he replied with no remorse. "Now look at me."

Shivahn had no choice but to comply.

"Lass," he began with the soothing gentleness she hated as much as the enchanted horse story, "do ye realize this has gone beyond whatever feelings you have for the lad?"

"For the twentieth time," she interjected, "I have *no* feelings for the man."

"Fine. Then you shall find it no effort to look at me now, and tell me true: Who is he?"

With every drop of will in her body, she forced her gaze to remain steadily aloft. This time, anything to the contrary would serve only as a full confession in the court of Billy Brayshaugh.

"He says he is a merchant," she stated. "He says it was all a mistake."

"A mistake?" came the caustic comeback. "That landed him in Cell Block Three? Why did he not tell Sandys that?"

"He did. And Sandys said he could go free . . ." She took a measured breath, forcing a steady, fact-giving tone to her voice. "If he gave the name of the real Griffin."

Billy whistled softly. "But why does Sandys think *Montague* knows that?"

"I do not know."

"For that matter, why did Montague not simply give over a false name?"

Shivahn shook her head, continuing to look at Kristian. "I do not know," she repeated, though somehow, with his features reposed in the simplicity of sleep, she almost felt as if she could reach over, touch him, and at last know all Kristian Montague's secrets. *Almost . . .*

"By Jesus and all the saints," Billy uttered. "Under those circumstances, if I were Sandys, I might even call the man Griffin myself."

Shivahn tensed every muscle to maintain her pose, to give up not a hint of overt reaction to that—but then she swallowed, deep and hard. And Billy watched. Close and intently.

"Bloody damn! Sandys *did* call him that, didn't he?"

Shivahn clamped a restraining hand to her friend's upper arm. "Billy, Kristian denied the stories, even after Sandys tried to beat them out of him! He denied them even when he was alone with *me*!"

"I've no doubt he did," he replied breezily. "If the Griffin wanted himself known, he would be leavin' somethin' more to mark himself than a paltry green feather, aye?"

The man, Shivahn admitted, made unnerving sense. But as she looked back across at Kristian, a renewed surge of longing overcame her—an ache different from her need of before, when she had so easily imagined herself wrapped safely in her Brave One's arms. With this stare came the vision of holding *him* in *her* embrace, of folding herself around him so completely, nobody could ever gawk at or accuse him again; nobody could ever call him Griffin and beat him to a half-dead pulp because of it.

The feeling gripped her with more force than that first sensation, too. Her throat clutched on a throbbing ache, as if she had raced Duncan too many times across the village on a chilly autumn day. And still the pain went deeper, engraved on the very essence of what made her woman, a surge of primeval awakening.

The pain, she realized, must be what a wolf felt when she fought hunters to the death to protect her lair.

And aye, Shivahn also conceded, she would fight, as well, if necessary.

"Billy," she stated, intensity surging in her voice, "Billy, you must promise me something." She clutched both her friend's hands. "Promise you will say naught of this for now. You *must* promise me!"

Her ribs threatened to collapse against her heart when the man jerked back as if she handed him two smoldering coals. "The *hell* I shall." Billy looked close to licking his fingers as proxies for his wounded pride.

"Just *for now*," Shivahn pleaded, and emphasized by grabbing his shirt front this time. "If not for me, you prideful ass, then think of Trabith. Think of what might happen to the village the English have seen to leave alone so far, if they discover 'tis now a haven for the Griffin. A man who only *might* be the Griffin, at that."

Billy's face screwed tight in mulling disappointment, before he finally growled, "All right, damn it. For the time being, Mistress Weasel, your secret is secure by me."

He raised hands against Shivahn's forward rush to hug him. "Oh, no; do not count this a favor, lassie. 'Twill come the day when you shall really need one, for I do not know how long this matter shall remain *my* choice."

At that, he lowered his gaze into hers with a purpose that Shivahn had only seen on his face a select number of times before. The occasions had all been funerals.

"You may have done something much bigger than rescue your man from prison, Shivahn. Something bigger than us all."

She tried to heed the very serious meaning of her friend's words. She tried to consider the very real concern, the very real threat they brought to all of Trabith with every mile of terrain churned beneath the cart's wheels—but she could not regain, much less recognize, her fear through the unexpected sparks of joy now exploding in her heart. The sparks kindled by but two of Billy's words: *your man*.

She was certain he no more meant them than his constant teasings about her big feet and church steeple neck. More than that, the mere implications of them were as dangerous as they were impossible. A hopeless dream. A dance without steps. Two worlds crossed in the very wrong time, in the very wrong place.

Her man.

Never to be.

Chapter 7

She was there again, like a mystery in his dreams, but if solving that secret meant waking up, then Kris pleaded for eternal unconsciousness. He begged Providence for the unending stroke of her cool fingers on his brow, for a forever of lying like this, cradled in her lap, blanketed in her arms, senses filled with the misted sea fragrance of her, imagination nourished by the unending sea dreams of her.

Dreams . . . aye, he wanted an eternity filled with these kind of dreams . . .

So why did she insist on waking him up?

"Kristian," came her entreaty. Somewhere at the edge of his senses, he tried to push against her but only seemed to bring her closer, instead. Her lips brushed the crest of his cheek as she whispered, "Kristian, come, you must wake for but a few minutes. We are here."

At that, despite the lead his eyelids seemed formed of and the armies of needle-footed ants laying siege to his limbs, he pried open his eyes and lifted his good hand to rake back his hair. Next, he slid that hand into the junction of her neck and jaw.

She smiled. He smiled back.

Perhaps, he mused, consciousness wasn't so bad, after all.

"All right, Your Majesty," he teased in a gravelly murmur. "I'm awake. Now how are you going to make the feat worth my while?"

At that, her head lowered. Her hooded gaze met his. And the incredible, inexplicable explosion of awareness ignited between them again. With his thundering heart now assuring him he had truly awakened, Kris slid his hand around to her nape, parting his lips as he pulled her warm body closer, closer . . .

"Kristian." Both syllables came stressed by adamant pushes of her hands on his chest. "Kristian, we—you—not *now*."

But every syllable only thickened the brandy-sweet throb in his blood—very fine brandy at that, he qualified. Oh, yes, she could murmur those protests for another five minutes, but she no more wanted him to stop than Juliet wanted Romeo to disappear off her balcony, a conclusion affirmed by every lilt in her voice, now echoing the urgent need in his body.

Kris laughed softly as he cupped her squirming fingers and began kissing them one by one.

He thrust her away as if she'd turned into a banshee when his laughter gained a distinctly older, distinctly *male* echo.

The motion slingshotted Kris back into the cart's slats, igniting fifty bonfires of pain up his still-healing back.

Before he regained enough thought to control or regret it, the crudest of expletives flew off his lips.

That crotchety old voice snickered at him again.

"For bloody sake, Gorag!" came Shivahn's heated whisper. "Sandys has nearly turned him into the walking dead, and you stand there and chortle like a fishwife?"

A surly snort cut through the damp air prior to the rebuttal. "Save your preachings for someone who cares a piss about 'em, girl. *I* like the lad already." The voice added in a disgruntled mutter, "Just a shame that the first bloke we get here who knows the right direction to point his rudder is also a god-be-damned blueblood from the big isle."

Kristian decided he might give this Gorag person another chance. If exhaustion didn't permeate every bone and muscle in his body, he might have seconded the old bounder's next chuckle, in response to the tangible force of Shivahn's rising agitation.

But instead of blistering both the old man's ears with a tongueful of scathing fury, she narrowed her attention on *him*. After scrambling across the cart in two eye blinks, she pulled him back into her lap and ran her fingers over his scalp with probing but sensitive swiftness.

"I am sorry, Brave One," she murmured—*not* helping his body's discomfited state by brandishing the magic of her touch with such exquisite care. "Have you been hurt again? Be still and let me inspect you."

"Leprechaun," Kris responded with a husky chuckle, "if you do much more 'inspecting,' I shall order you to examine the strain I have in *lower* muscles, as well."

He received the response he intended: the instant drop of her hands in tandem with yet another bark from the old man. It hurt nevertheless, especially when coupled with Shivahn's steady glower, which had him feeling the imprudent bridegroom returned three hours late from the tavern.

Dear God, came the secret plea from deep inside his wrenching chest, *if only my life could be so simple. If only my world could be so real.*

But he allowed himself to believe the fantasy just a little while longer, as Shivahn hopped down from the cart with haughty alacrity. "I think you are strong enough to get along from here, Mr. Montague," she said. With a barely suppressed smile, Kris hastened to obey her.

A moment later, he didn't find the grin difficult to repress at all. His mouth gave way to a gape of astoundment, instead.

For all intents and purposes, he sat on a normal little cart in a normal little road winding through a normal little Irish hamlet—*if* he were a character in a storybook.

The phenomenon began with the road itself, weaving a perfect ribbon of oval stones to the far end of "town," denoted with a fountain ruled by a green stone mermaid and her carved contingent of fish and dolphins. From the pool at the sea goddess's feet, white-fingered mists ascended off the water with as much grace as any ballet Kris had seen, then spun their way around the darkened houses and buildings along the lane.

And as for those structures . . . he stared at the thatch-roofed, simply built homes with quiet awe. He took in the gardens with their overflowing flower boxes and hand-hewn bird baths; he smiled at the forlorn gaze of a jowled hound dog confined to the front stoop for the night. Then he took in a breath, inhaling air redolent with fresh-cut wood and chimney smoke, spiced with hot honeyed cider and stew prepared with hours of care and pride.

All in all, the scene was dipped in a giant vat of . . . peace.

Kris's throat tightened. Maybe Shivahn *had* magically taken him on a journey into a fairy tale. Or had he existed without peace for so long that now, he considered it a piece of fiction?

"So you're the blueblood."

Again, he recognized the croak of the coot Shivahn had called Gorag—and again, he inwardly thanked the man for rescuing his thoughts from paths he did *not* wish to travel. Because of that, he coerced his aching muscles to turn and acknowledge his host with a respectful stance.

"Aye, sir. I'm the—"

For the second time in as many minutes, his jaw went slack in surprise.

He'd expected an old man, of course. Perhaps someone like Grandfather in country clothes, only with laugh wrinkles instead of scowl lines. But his first thought upon beholding Gorag was a memory of a visit to the Harbingers' country estate when he was twelve, where the mantel displayed an ancient stuffed raccoon. The problem was that the cat had chosen the piece as its playmate, giving the raccoon a ratted coiffure, one hollowed eye socket, and two heartily gnawed paws.

With the exception of the paws, Gorag could pass as the animal's twin.

Kris quickly corrected himself on that point. The raccoon couldn't deliver that distinct cackle of a laugh, which *this* coot wielded with glee.

"I do be an eyeful, eh?" he cracked, then let out a heartier snicker at his joke. He gave Kris's chest a good-natured backhand. "Beggin' yer pardon, lad. Yer most likely ready to declare yourself ready for the graveyard with weariness. Come, I'm of a certain Shivahn's taken herself off to your room to fret over the last speck of dirt on the floor and wrinkle in the bed."

Kris couldn't argue the old man wrong on either of those assertions. Indeed, as the mountain wind shushed through the treetops overhead, the breeze also carried the last of the stamina from his limbs. And when they entered the nearest cottage, a modest structure with tiny roses growing around the door frame, they found Shivahn in the low-ceilinged loft, fussing at a cot made up with several thin blankets and one hand-woven quilt. As she bent over the bed, her jerkin rode up on her torso and revealed her breeches-clad bottom in all its exquisitely rounded beauty.

That was when Kris *knew* the old man was right. He *had* died of exhaustion and ascended to Heaven.

"Lass," Gorag growled, "the man is going to sleep in the bed not paint a picture of it. Go on, *go on;* out of the way—"

"She's not in the way." Kris stated the objection with as much respect for the man as possible, but he couldn't conceal the trembling urgency in his fingers as he reached for her in emphasis. Fate again smiled their way. The nuance escaped Gorag's notice, but not Shivahn's. She lifted her head, and her gaze met his with the warming assurance of a lavender-skied dawn.

She returned his grasp with that same crushing but strangely comforting pressure she'd used in Prevot's dungeon, before murmuring to the old man, "I shall stay to make certain Mr. Montague is settled, Gorag. Then we shall share that cup of cider I promised. Will you go down and rekindle the fire?"

The man prefaced his reply with a cynical grunt. "Yer to settle him between the blankets, lass, and naught else. 'Tis half my sight those Orange Order bastards stole four years ago, not my hearing, and—"

"I shall be wise to remember that," she finished for him with the fluency of one who'd done so a few hundred times before. Still, as Gorag muttered his way back down the loft's narrow ladder, a tender smile lingered on her lips for the man who clearly adored her with every heavy breath he took.

"He means well," she explained to Kris as they sat together on the cot.

As he leaned to pull off his boots, he cocked a grin at her. "He also loves you."

"I suppose . . . he does."

"You sound amazed at that," he stated with the honesty that came more boldly with each hour in her presence.

Her answering silence provided the sole moment needed for a thick intimacy to permeate the air between them . . . again. Kris's body reeled in the flood of feeling as his mind struggled to comprehend this spell they cast over each other. But he could no more resist this bittersweet sensation than he could understand its consuming magnetism.

"Shivahn," he whispered then, shamelessly using the courage of the feeling to cup her downcast chin in his fingers. "Don't you believe it would be easy to love you?"

She made a halfhearted effort to shake her head. Then, in a quivering rasp, "I do not know what I believe anymore."

At that, every muscle tightened across the breadth of his chest. His every nerve ending grew unbearably aware of her trembling softness. Before he thought of the motion, Kris lifted his fingers on her chin.

"Believe in *this*," he commanded silkily, in the moment before he closed his mouth over hers in a possessing kiss.

With Gorag less than ten feet beneath them, they both shuddered with the repressed force of their ignited desires. To Kris's mutual dread and delight, that imbued the moment with a fiercer, naughtier excitement. Ah, God, how he wanted to press her back against the straw mattress, exploring her until she gasped mindlessly with her passion's release. But he could only express his need to her through urgent strokings and silent, seeking kisses.

She felt wonderful against him; so wonderful, his senses teetered beyond caring if the Pope himself shuffled around the room below. "Shivahn," he said on a hot breath into her ear. "Shivahn . . . *Shivahn* . . ."

"Shivahn!"

With a barely tamped growl, Kris jerked away from her. Once more, Gorag and his bark had rescued him from himself with excruciatingly accurate timing.

"Shivahn!" the old man called again, now attacking the ladder rungs with what sounded like a pewter mug. Kris almost emitted a wry laugh. The din comprised an uncanny echo of the turmoil in his body. "Lassie, this cider o' yours is fast going cold!"

Shivahn turned and raised her chin as if to issue a reply but, at the last moment, looked back to Kris. Her gaze was a wide plea . . . a petition that said she didn't want to go drink cider. She wanted to stay and kiss him again.

It took every drop of what little fortitude he had left to return her stare with steady control. It took one more moment to summon the strength for a soft smile, as he told her, "Go. Your cider awaits, m'lady."

He released a relieved sigh as she nodded in agreement. But his following breath clutched in his throat as she halted her exit to turn and give him one more stare . . . and a soft, but sparkling smile. And with that smile, Kris identified another thread in the tangle of emotions this woman kept stitching into the lining of his soul:

Happiness.

At least 'twas what he *thought* the sensation felt like. He wasn't sure if he remembered happiness, really . . .

But ah, God, how he longed to.

"Your pillow awaits, m'lord," Shivahn teased him back then, leaning for one more stolen kiss. But her whisper took on a solemn tone as she lingered a moment longer, gently pressing her fingers to the side of his face. "Sleep well, Kristian. You have naught to fear in this place save a fairy's spell or two."

Kris joined his own smile to hers. Yet after she blew out the candle and disappeared down the ladder, his lips descended back into a frown.

"A few fairy spells," he repeated as he lay back and stared hard at the cottage's ceiling timbers. "Ah, Shivahn, if only Sandys and Castlereagh and a few thousand bounders across the sea would see things through your eyes."

Only then I would have naught to be afraid of, Shivahn. I wouldn't have to worry that every horse or cart or carriage on that lane below might be the soldiers you've invited by sheltering me.

I wouldn't have to think about what they'd do to you after killing me.

She'd said to sleep well. But the better part of two hours passed before Kris's exhaustion overwhelmed his terror, delivering his dread-filled visions into dreamless slumber.

When he awoke, a dark gold glow suffused the sky outside, and the air smelled of fresh-tilled earth and well-worked plowhorses. But Kris's nostrils welcomed the pungent smells, for they told of a day spent nurturing the land, instead of gaining a battle position upon it. He guessed even Billy and Duncan had replaced their rifles and daggers with hoes and horse reins, and now shared bawdy jokes with their countrymen as they trudged in from the fields.

He liked the scenario so much, he let his mind indulge several more moments of it, before a melody of bells chimed from the direction of the mermaid fountain. The sound repeated several times at rising octaves, lending the twilight an ethereal beauty.

The signal not only stirred his senses but expanded them to the awareness of another collection of aromas. He detected beef fat on an open fire . . . simmering soup with healthy portions of sweet onion . . . a rich cake with fresh fruit filling . . .

Stirred senses, he concluded then, were a precious thing to enjoy. A stirred stomach was not. And he couldn't remember the last decent food he'd eaten besides Shivahn's smuggled prison tidbits.

Shivahn. He smiled as his mind reverberated with her name. From even his casual thoughts, he realized, his leprechaun didn't stray far lately. As he descended the ladder and let his nose lead him the correct direction outside the cottage, he kept his gaze open for any sight of her.

At last, after circling to the opposite side of the mermaid fountain, Kris slipped inside what was obviously the community dining hall. The modest but high-beamed structure was filled to the rafters with—well, the *community.* And maybe, he half jokingly speculated, the population of the next two towns around the bend, as well.

Everywhere he looked, benches, chairs, and walls were occupied with what looked like the village chorus crowd from one of the Paris Opera's more lavish spectacles. Babies squirmed on their mums' knees while bare-handedly turning their food into artwork. Husbands traded fishing tales while wives traded tart recipes. Fresh-faced maids batted eyelashes at puff-chested youths. Beneath everyone's feet, mutts alternated between hunting down the cats and the food scraps. In a word, the scene was chaos.

In a heartbeat, Kris fell in love with every detail of it.

For a moment, even concern for his barren stomach

retreated to the back of his senses. He closed his eyes and inhaled the happy din as he would a lungful of bracing sea air.

There was only one problem with the moment. He heard himself take that breath.

A tidal wave of silence had suddenly crashed over the room.

In the pause he took before opening his eyes, Kris's instinct told him what he'd encounter when he did. Assuredly enough, a horizon of unblinking stares met his gaze. Even the babes found him fascinating, their soiled fingers flying into mouths as mute and serious as their parents'.

Only one unusual sound rasped into the silence: Kris glanced to his right at two maids huddled together, their wide gazes fixed upon him and their giggles barely contained behind cupped hands. Did that mean he should smile, or start checking the road for the quickest way out of here?

Fate didn't take long to render its reply to that. In tandem with a lockhold around his knee came an insistent tug at his breeches pocket, followed by an angel's face that filled his downcasted vision. Indeed, he wondered if Heaven had truly tossed down a special helper just for him, a seraph with the sunshine of childhood in her cheeks yet the wisdom of the ages in her sky-blue eyes.

"Hal-lo." The charmer followed the singsong greeting with a bow-shaped grin—thus securing the reaction she so blatantly sought from him. Without pause, Kris knelt to the lass's level and gallantly kissed the back of her tiny hand.

"Hal-lo," he returned in the harmony to her offered melody.

His audition garnered audible approval from the giggling maids. A younger version of the same erupted from the angel with her fist still wrapped around his finger.

"Well, sir," she declared then, "ye *are* rather comely, fer a lad and all. If only yer clothes were nay such an awful mess."

The maids gasped in unison. Kris, on the other hand, secretly thanked his miniature guardian for disengaging her hold in order to point at the splotched front of what had once been his brocade waistcoat. As he dipped his head in order to follow her direction, he was able to release his enchanted smile without ruining his appropriately solemn reply. "Mmmm hmmm."

"Ye baffle me with all this dirt," she blurted on. "Unless, of course, ye be an enchanted prince in disguise. I would greatly like *that* sort of an excuse."

Me, too, angel, Kris heard from the deepest regions of his heart. *Me, too.* By all ten of God's toes, how achingly easy the visions came of an overstuffed throne and days of boring diplomacy compared to the merciless tension that lurked at the back of his mind even now . . . the cold realization that even in this fairy-book world, he lived on borrowed time.

He lived solely to turn around tomorrow and walk back into Sandys's path again.

Otherwise, he resolved more steadily, there was no other reason to live.

"Ye got a name?" the angel's voice sliced into his thoughts. "*My* name is Rhianna," she rambled on with a proud lift of her chin. "It means I am a goddess."

Kris could no longer hold his smile in check. "I do not doubt *that* for a moment," he replied. He gave her a regal bow. "I am Prince Kristian, and I am honored to be at your humble service."

But the giggle he expected never came.

Instead, as he lifted his head, his guardian angel released a scream worthy of Hell's deepest chamber.

Somewhere in the midst of the paroxysm, the girl ripped

her hand from Kris's hold and raced to wrap herself in the skirts of a woman who looked like a Rhianna fully grown. "English!" she shrieked as she did. "English bastard! Mummy, 'tis a horrid English bastard!"

Kris wasn't surprised when the woman didn't lift a finger of reprimand toward her daughter. As a matter of fact, Rhianna's hate might as well have been a mask the woman reproduced for her own face, as she clearly prepared to hurl her own epithets at him. She'd have to wait in line. A dozen of her peers beat her to the privilege the next moment.

"Monster!"

"Murderer!"

"Whoreson swine!"

"Lying, chiseling bastard!"

He drew no breath to combat the mob. Nor, Kris admitted, did he want to. But rather than tear through his senses in search of the sanity he'd obviously lost, he stood and let the crowd use him as a pin cushion for the barbs of their grief and frustration—many of those barbs stained with the blood of their husbands and brothers. Blood *he'd* seen on far too many occasions to shove under the rug of his compassion.

Still, as news of Rhianna's discovery reverberated through the crowd, the assault of hatred swelled to a pummeling force—literally. First, the shouts came punctuated by vegetable chunks, beef bits, and half-eaten tarts. But Kris found himself reconsidering the distance out the door when a hard-crusted roll slammed into the bandage topping his left eye. In the immediate wake of the bread came an eating dagger, its perfect arc concluded when it took a gouge out of his right ear.

He spun around, only to find his path obscured by the well-fleshed curves and fury-taught stance of a very formidable woman. "How dare ye!" the wench spat, tossing her head of unruly red curls. "Filthy English vermin. Thinkin' just because ye lost yer friends and happened to get lost in *our* woods that we'd just take ye in like a wee orphan? We got enough orphans here, thanks to *yer* murderin' king! Occchh! I spit on ye, British bastard! I *spit* on ye!"

The woman screwed up her mouth in preparation of doing just that. But suddenly the wench—and everyone else in the mob—jumped and jerked startled stares toward the source of the loudest scream in the fray yet.

Kris didn't jump. But he did stare, gripped by amazement once again, as the source of the sound made her presence indisputably known. Through the throng she shoved like an enraged goddess in her own right, her hair a wild gold conflagration around her face, her glare radiating the violet core of surely every Samhain bonfire that ever blazed.

He'd never seen a woman more infuriated.

Or breathtaking.

Surprisingly, when Shivahn spoke, her voice came low and modulated—though wrath rippled through the words like the heat waves off the fire in her eyes.

"Maeve O'Gleary," she addressed to the wench first, "you shall recant that slur as well as the rest of the unfounded swill you've slung at this man." She spun and decreed at the rest of the mob, "As will you *all*!"

She forced down several hard breaths after that, but her voice still shook as violently as the fists she stretched out, almost beseechingly, at the rafters. "My God," she uttered. "I have called you people *kin* since the day I no longer had any. And I was proud of that! But now—"

"Now you have brought an *Englishman* into our midst, and you expect us to accept him with open arms," Maeve O'Gleary snarled.

"Aye," Shivahn retorted, meeting the woman's glare with a smoldering but steady regard, "as a matter of fact, I do. You especially, Maeve. We paced some long nights together through the births of both your bairns. We know many stories and secrets of each other. And you should know that if I brought King bloody George of England himself here, it would be because I believed in the good of my action and that I would believe the same of you."

Maeve appeared to test those words in her mouth, shifting lips and tongue as if merely rendering judgment on the balance of spices in a stew. " 'Tis not so simple as that, Shivahn," she mumbled.

"And why not?"

"You know why not! An Englishman took my brother's life!"

"*This* Englishman saved mine."

At that, even Maeve joined in the crowd's newly considering stares and newly contemplating murmurs. Kris looked for a glint of satisfaction to at last enter Shivahn's eyes or, at least, a pose of vindicated confidence. But therein lay his mistake: expecting this woman to act like every other person in the world. Aye, she rocked back on her heels with a happier mien, but the gaze with which she beheld her people sparkled only with a proud devotion, as if she said to herself, *There, 'tis more like it.*

" 'Tis true," she reconfirmed when the buzzing murmurs abated. "Despite that a good deal of you think otherwise, I would not have survived *this* particular ordeal without this man. If you are wanting sanction on that, ask Billy Brayshaugh and Duncan Thornberry. They were there, and they shall tell you I was steps away from becoming last night's prize fruit on Prevot Prison's hanging tree. This man refused to let that happen."

The mob's regard of him took on a soft-gasping intensity. And the woman before him savored every dramatic second of it. "His name is Kristian Rayne Bastion Montague," Shivahn declared with a shamelessly insolent grin, "and he is my friend."

The crowd shifted uneasily. Unbelievably, Maeve herself was the first to snap their reticence, stepping before Kris with an attempt at a smile. "Well, Master Montague," she stated, "I cannot fathom why yer mum cursed ye with a name longer than the day, but I know I owe ye an apology thrice as big. I suppose I also owe ye a bowl o' stew. Ye must be famished, aye?"

Kris grinned an eager agreement to *that*. As soon as he did, the crowd went back to their former chaos, leaving him to a much-needed moment of solitude. He used that opportunity to fill his stare with the leprechaun who'd saved his hide . . . again. Lucky happenstance, he ruminated as he watched her cross the room to retrieve his stew, that this was Ireland and not some Oriental outback where a man gave over his life in servitude to the bloke responsible for preserving it.

Then again . . . he caught her tilting her own surreptitious glance back at him, as well as the blush that assaulted her cheeks at her awareness of his attention. 'Twas the same dark rose shade, Kris noticed, that rushed to her face after she'd been soundly kissed.

And at that, he wondered how far away the Orient *really* was.

By the time Shivahn escorted him back out of the dining hall with an amply filled belly, the moon had risen high enough to throw the tops of the pine and birch trees into silhouetted relief against a sky silvered with stars. The air smelled of rising night winds and diminishing hearth smoke; the mating song of a night bird orchestrated with a ballad played on a tin whistle in a nearby cottage. Kris didn't miss the irony of the scene—that but hours ago, this community had generated such noise, only to turn around and hold a collective breath in homage to the wonder of the night.

The observation transformed his small smile into a soft chuckle. From the corner of his eye, he noticed the responding uptilt of Shivahn's head.

"What was *that* for?" she asked.

"Nothing," Kris returned amiably. "And everything." He made a gesturing arc with his good hand. "This place . . . that's what it seems to be. Everything, and nothing."

"What do you mean?"

What do *you mean, Montague?* Kris tipped his head back as his brain seconded her request. And once more, simple honesty had never presented itself as the more perfect answer. So he took a measured breath and plunged in.

"When we first arrived here, I thought you and your fairy friends had taken me inside one of the storybooks I loved as a tyke. Everything about this place was so perfect, so unreal . . . so I thought it *wasn't*. It had to be an illusion . . . a nothing." He paused as they came upon a shadow-dappled footbridge over a sparkling creek. "But then . . ."

For once, common sense caught both his thoughts and words at the same time. He trailed the last of the statement away in desperate hope Shivahn would fill in her own conclusion.

Hope didn't favor him tonight. "But then what?" she persisted, following him onto the bridge.

Kris turned and forced himself to look at her. Once he did, he wondered if he'd ever tear his sights away again. He drank in the halo of the moonlight on her curls, the kiss of starlight on her cheeks, the intoxicating intensity of her gaze . . .

And for one moment, he again considered the truth—all

of it—as his answer. For one moment, her presence ignited his discretion like one of those thatch roofs beneath a flaming torch, making it all too easy to release the words trapped in the dwelling of his soul beneath . . .

Instead, he presented her with an all-too-acted shrug. "But then what? Then I woke up."

"To one of Trabith's notoriously warm welcomes," came her wry return. Kris chuckled again but pivoted back around to find her profile etched in enchanting moonglow—and taut anger.

For a long moment, that expression rendered him motionless. Yet the more he beheld her ire, the more he fought the need to yank her close, cocooning her like a precious gem on a bed of protecting velvet. He couldn't remember the last time someone had gotten enraged on his behalf. He couldn't remember the last time he'd cared.

"Leprechaun," he finally said, taking a soft step toward her. "You're really upset, aren't you?"

"And you imagined I wasn't?" Kris felt the rush of air off her swirling skirts, so rapidly did she spin and march to the bridge's opposite side. Once there, she grabbed the rail with what looked like the intent of ripping it off its moorings. "Since the days before my great-great-grandda was village speaker, Trabith has stood for compassion, tolerance, and acceptance," she said. "We welcomed the Scottish gallowglass soldiers with open arms. We sheltered unregistered priests in the hardest days of the penal laws and even nursed victims of the Black Death when their own families would not.

"What Maeve and the others did this eve . . ." She spun again, making the bridge's boards endure the brunt of her fury. " 'Twas contemptible."

"What they did this eve was *understandable*." His comeback was adamant enough to sway the bias of Robert

Emmet himself, but Kris couldn't help his good-natured grin while leaning his good elbow against the rail again. "Shivahn," he continued gently, "for all the tolerance your people have shown the world, it hasn't given much back, at least not wrapped in British red. And I actually didn't mind everyone's unconventional little greeting . . . er, until that wedge of bread decided to become best mates with my head . . ."

"Heavenly saints." She gasped. She whirled and rushed to his side. "I am as horrid as they! I forgot all about checking your head! And your *ear*—Kristian, your ear; why did you not say anything? Both wounds could be infected even now, and here we are, strolling about as if you were not beaten within an inch of your life a week past . . ."

But with each passing sentence of her diatribe, Kris's smile only grew wider. He even thanked the bounder who hurled that roll in the first place, for Shivahn's concern now brought her sweetly, wonderfully close . . . close enough that the curls atop her head tickled his chin; close enough that he breathed deeply of the unique way she smelled tonight, like apple tarts and forest berries . . . spicy, tangy, delicious.

He forced himself out of the sensory reverie as certain parts of her one-sided dialogue no longer impacted his brain like words but warrior spears. Kris reentered the "conversation" just as she deliberated her treatment of his wound between a dragonwort poultice or a witch hazel rinse.

His memory quickly summoning the stench and sting of the "rinse" she'd used on him in Prevot, he grabbed her probing fingers with one hand and silenced her babbling lips with the other. "I am *fine*," he issued. "I'll have no poultices. No rinses." But he counteracted his rebuke by lifting her fingers to his lips and softly stating, "Leprechaun, you have done a fine job of putting me back together."

"Of course I have." She tossed her head as if insulted, but

not before Kris caught the betraying quaver of her chin. Still, she gave an impressively adamant jerk against his hold—to which Kris didn't submit an inch.

"Kristian . . . you may release me now."

"No," he countermanded. "No, I don't think so. Not yet."

She pulled at him again. "Kristian, cease this nonsense."

"There's no 'nonsense' to cease. My terms for your release are simple: I shall let you go . . . the moment you tell me what you're so afraid of."

If he'd blinked, Kris would have missed the first reacting expression on her face—as if he'd landed a bull's-eye dead center in her soul. All too rapidly, she covered the look with a forced laugh. "You must be in jest."

"I think you know I'm not." He dropped his tone yet another octave. "I think you know exactly what I'm about, Leprechaun, judging by that look on your face."

"The look on my—I know *naught* of what you speak."

"The bloody hell you don't. You're as pale as a wraith, and your hands feel like they just left the grave, as well. Shivahn—" He slid his grip from her hands to her elbows. "You look exactly like you did in the tunnel at Prevot."

"Kristian." She attempted a dismissive laugh—and failed miserably at the endeavor. "This is ridiculous."

"Your fear of failing me—that I may have contracted even a tiny new infection because of your negligence—it has something to do with why you froze up in the tunnel, too, doesn't it?"

"Stop it." She began to jerk against him again—this time, with panicked force. "Stop it and let me go."

He only entwined his fingers tighter around her. "And what did you mean in the dining hall, about 'surviving this particular ordeal' because of me? Were there *other* ordeals? What are the *other* pieces to this, Shivahn? How many other times in your life have you been so terrified, so cold enough to pass for a corpse?"

To his shock, she reacted to that with another laugh—if only for the fact he couldn't describe the sound any other way. In truth, enough pain etched her face that he ached to look at her.

Softly, brokenly, she finally uttered, "You do not want to know the answer to that."

Kris responded by raising his hands all the way to her face, cupping them on either side of her tear-shimmered eyes. "Oh, aye," he whispered, his lips barely an inch above hers, "I *do*."

A hard swallow vibrated down her throat. "Why?"

Kris slowly shook his head as he traced her nose's soft freckles with his thumbs. "You saved my life, Leprechaun. Hell, you saved it more than once. And yet . . ." He stilled his hands. And he plunged his stare, deeply and intently, into the unfathomable lavender mists of her own. "And yet, I don't know who you are."

If the bridge rail didn't still anchor his stance, he imagined her response would have hurled him over it in shock. "Well, then," Shivahn issued back in a tone too suddenly bright to be genuine, "that makes two of us." She stepped out of his slackened hold with a brisk snap of her skirts. "Because until you are ready to tell *me* who *you* are, Kristian Montague, I am not ready to answer your questions, either. And now," she concluded in a honeyed soprano worthy of any pretentious London virgin, "I shall bid you a good night."

And she did. Kris no more than blinked before she presented him with her stiff spine, her rigid shoulder blades, and the maddening sway of her beautiful little bottom as she marched into the shadows.

Kris spun back on the rail with a clenched, low moan. As

if answering his call for primal companionship, the creek's shores began to rustle with the comings and goings of various night creatures. A perfect ending to the evening, he surmised wryly. All the beasts of the earth, snarling together in flawless harmony.

"Ah, Shivahn," he muttered hoarsely into the mists now adding their own eerie ambiance to this demented gathering, "you go ahead and say your good nights. I, on the other hand, shall stand here and say my thanks to God."

He inhaled deeply, attempting—in vain—to introduce some semblance of order to his senses with the creek's bouquet of water ferns, pimpernel, and night moss. "I'm going to thank Him I'm leaving you for good tomorrow, Leprechaun," he softly finished then. "For only He knows how long I'd survive if I didn't."

Chapter 8

The next morning, Kris awoke with a violent start. He threw back the cot's blanket and lurched to his feet, part of his mind still trapped in the nightmare he thought he'd finally escaped but had now reassaulted his sleep with a horridly bizarre variation.

The last six months had disappeared, and he trudged the battlefield at Wexford again. His feet slipped and slid on the blood of his dead comrades. He blinked against the constant sting behind his eyes; bile was an incessant flame in his throat. But he didn't stop. Not until he found the body he searched for . . . praying to God he wouldn't.

But after three more steps, he saw it: sprawled facedown against an embankment, where shelter was obviously sought before death came. The corpse was clad in distinctly simple country clothes—now blood-soaked country clothes. *Rayne,* he heard his dry lips rasp. *Ah, God, no, not Rayne!*

Still, he forced himself forward, until he knelt by the body, now cold but not yet stiff. Whispering another prayer for strength in his frozen muscles, he shoved against the corpse's shoulder and held his breath to behold the face, now pale with death.

And when he did, he screamed.

The body didn't have Rayne's face.

Shivahn's lifeless eyes gaped back at him.

Kris raked a hand over his head, now covered in the same cold sweat breaking from every pore in his body. When he lowered his hand against his thigh, his fingers trembled.

"Just a dream," he told himself in a hoarse mutter. "It was just a dream."

Wasn't it?

Or could nightmares become reality as easily as the stuff of dreams . . . as easily as storybook villages with mermaid fountains, as fairy children named Rhianna, with the sky in their eyes?

As absurd as his next actions seemed, Kris didn't hesitate about commencing them. He only knew he had to see Shivahn again *now*. 'Twas why he nearly flew down the ladder that had seemed tantamount to the summit of Ben Nevis two nights ago. 'Twas why he crossed to the cottage's front window in three strides, throwing open the shutters to reveal the sun-drenched lane.

'Twas why he released a breath of relief upon hearing a familiar leprechaun's laugh.

Taking caution to conceal himself behind one of the shutters, Kris felt guilty for but a second before granting himself spying privileges over the scene on the grassy knoll outside.

"Whose turn is it now?" a fiery-haired hoyden cried, almost toppling Shivahn to the ground as she embraced the woman's knees. Not that Kris would have minded such an occurrence—not in the scene he beheld her in now.

Last night's simple muslin dress was still the essence of her wardrobe, only now she'd shed her kitchen apron in favor of a daisy chain belt and matching bracelets. An impressive, multi-flowered crown encircled her unbound hair. At this moment more than any other, he decided, she was a fairy goddess become visible to the mortal world, with her breasts high and full with laughter, her laughter ringing with life and passion . . . and that passion promising an indescribable Heaven to the man who at last tapped it . . .

" 'Tis *my* turn, I think," piped a mirror image of the first girl. She ran up the knoll and reached for Shivahn's crown.

"You had your turn yesterday, Sarah!" the first twin objected. " 'Tis Rhianna's turn now."

" 'Tis *mine*!"

"Sarah," Shivahn broke in, joining her rebuke with a peace offering of her left arm's daisy bracelet, "I believe your sister is right. 'Tis Rhianna's day to be Queen of the May. But"—a smile tilted her lips as she extended the second bracelet to Sarah's sister—"she shall need two ladies-in-waiting."

The twins let out identical gasps of delight. "Ladies-in-waiting!" Sarah giggled, grabbing her sister's hand. " 'Tis a lovely thing to be!"

After that, Kris could hear only their laughter, as Shivahn escorted them farther up the knoll, patiently giving "lady-in-waiting" lessons along the way. He felt his own lips play with the possibility of echoing their happiness with a soft chuckle of his own—

When someone else's laugh filled the cottage, instead.

Kris pivoted to Gorag, less unnerved about the man's

arrival than his absolute unawareness of Gorag's approach. Good God, he inwardly condemned himself. Only two days out of prison, and he'd already let his instincts soften.

It was this place, he determined without a doubt. This magical place—and its dangerous effect on him.

The conclusion caused a fresh sheen of sweat to trickle across his brow.

His new companion, on the other hand, bared a grin crooked as the stones of Giant's Causeway and serene as a cat who'd just drained the sweet cream. "What're those little lassies up to now?" he asked on a mischievous cackle.

Kris followed Gorag's gaze back out toward the knoll, where Rhianna had arrived for her "Queen of the May" coronation. Shivahn and the twins sang a simple but sweetly melodic tune as they draped her in daisy-chained finery.

A heavy swallow thudded down his throat as the tune drifted across the grass to the cottage. The thick Gaelic words spun together with the wind's whispers in the tree-tops, with the distant calls of sheep and cows, again causing Kris to look around in wonder. By the moment, all of this felt more surreal.

Worse than that, all of this felt more right.

At that moment, he blinked. And for that moment, his heart froze in midbeat. Was he about to wake up back in his cell in Prevot, remembering this as nothing more than a dream from the imaginings of his childhood?

Fate granted him a reprieve. The dream continued, completely intact. Rhianna twirled and laughed. Shivahn and the girls began a second verse of their song.

"It's pretty," he murmured then to Gorag, "but what does it mean?"

" 'Tis a tune from the ancient days," the old man murmured. "Before Saint Pat and his like came 'round. Back then, great pagan fairs were held to celebrate the spring.

'Twas a time for great feasting and dancing—and, o' course, a Queen of the May." He curved a shrewd grin. "But knowing my forefathers' forefathers, this little ditty translates into some queenly attribute those tykes should *nay* be singing of."

They shared deep chuckles at that. "Hell," Gorag said, punctuating with a grunt. "S'pose we must preserve the old language any which way we can, eh?"

Kris didn't answer. In motionless silence, he savored the last note of the tune, sung by Shivahn alone, like a lingering sip of the honeyed brandy he was allowed to taste during those boyhood story hours. He finally said, as another upsweep of wind carried her voice away to the heights of the distant mountains, "It's the most beautiful thing that I've ever heard."

Another moment passed before he realized Gorag hadn't issued a single sardonic grunt or snort to that. When Kris turned the old man's way, he found Gorag regarding him with such unstinting potency, he forgot he received such scrutiny from one eye alone.

"Hmmmph," the man finally muttered. " 'The most beautiful thing.' Is that why ye say it as if yer bangers are bein' chopped off at the same time?"

Despite the boulder still lodged in his throat, Kris rocked his head back on a laugh. "You have a unique way of phrasing it, my friend."

"But 'tis the truth."

Kris lowered his gaze with a markedly different mien. Slowly. Intently. "What do you mean?"

Not a hair of Gorag's brows—what remained of them—quivered from the scrutiny. "Exactly what I said," he returned. "Shivahn . . . she enchants you, lad."

"She *what*?"

"She enchants you."

This time, Kris snatched his own turn to level a hard snort. "The hell she does."

Gorag only slanted him a small sideways glance—though his features were drenched in maddening self-assurance. "No shame in confessin' it, lad."

"Bugger off." Violent frustration exploded off each syllable, practically as visible as the fists Kris now added to his pose. But damn it, he couldn't very well strangle an ancient raccoon for stating the very thought that hovered at his every waking moment.

No.

No, his senses echoed in resounding determination. He would not let one starry-eyed village chit destroy the good of the freedom she'd help him win. He owed her the commitment, for God sake. What else *could* he give her? Certainly not a few hours of mindless, desperate passion, no matter how clearly they both envisioned such whenever even their gazes joined . . . no matter how openly those magical eyes of hers begged him to take just that from her . . .

But it would never be just that with Shivahn. She deserved more, a man who would give her children and laughter and a rose-festooned cottage of her own. An existence where those incredible hands of hers would mend skinned knees and village squabbles, not legless soldiers and tortured prisoners.

That was what he owed her most of all. What he owed her *people* most of all. And he would not fail them in the task.

Not this time.

"So," Gorag interjected then, again with irksomely perfect timing, "we be agreein' she enchants you."

"She—does—not—enchant—me." Kris punctuated it with his fist against the window ledge. "She—" His teeth ground together as they forced out his inevitable conclusion. "She terrifies me."

He didn't know what to make of the responding chortle he received from Gorag. "Well, well, well," the man crooned cryptically.

"What the bloody hell does *that* mean?"

Gorag only gave a one-shouldered shrug as he shuffled himself into a well-worn chair by the banked hearth. "Why don't ye unhand that poor window ledge and help me rekindle this blaze for dinner?"

Wordlessly Kris heeded the request, settling himself onto a low stool opposite Gorag. He added a new log to the brazier even as he studied the faraway sheen that had seemed to glaze over Gorag's good eye between one blink and the next.

"Shivahn ... is a very special lass," the man finally murmured.

Kris attempted to soften the edges of his replying sarcasm. Then he decided he didn't care. "I'll run out and carve that in stone," he growled, snatching up the poker and jabbing the log.

Good thing the blow ignited a sufficient shower of sparks in the hearth. He never administered a second stab to the thing. His arm went motionless when he looked to Gorag's face again and beheld the old man's expression of unguarded surprise.

"You already know, then?" Gorag asked in a tone more suited to a moonlit spying mission. He leaned forward with almost leonine concentration.

This time, Kris managed to contain his frustration to an exasperated sigh. Barely. "That she's special?" he returned. He waved a hand toward the open window. "Doesn't it take just a few moments to fathom that, old man?"

"Oh, lad," Gorag replied, shaking his head in a manner

reminding Kris of his boyhood French tutor, grappling with his tenth failure to properly conjugate *partir*. "I be afraid, in Shivahn's instance, it does not."

But unlike those exasperating French lessons, Kris knew he was not going to *learn* something. He only wondered why that thought made him raise his gaze to Gorag with what felt like a thunder storm gathering in his brain.

"Ye be a keen bounder, Kristian," the man began with quiet surety, "despite all that English blood stainin' yer innards. So there's a fair chance ye've figured Shivahn's ma and da have been gone a while. 'Tis I who have been both to her the most o' her life."

Kris nodded, wordlessly urging the man to continue. As Gorag did, he turned his gaze to the fire, the flames illuminating the faraway expression again claiming his wizened features.

"Daniel and Megan died five summers after the fairies brought Shivahn to 'em. They never had any other children—somehow, Daniel became . . . er, incapable . . . after being attacked by street thugs in Dublin—but in truth, they never yearned too much to question Fate's turn. In their minds, Heaven had dropped them an angel, and they wanted for naught else."

"How did they die?" Kris asked in a guttural murmur.

The burgeoning smile the man indulged during his memory now fell prey to the shadows of a grimace. "For a while, a very *short* while," Gorag continued roughly, "the stench of the country's political strifes at last slunk over the mountains into Trabith. At the heart of our village's version of the broil were Daniel and another young man, Blake Kincaid. Blake's da had been a captain in the Defenders terrorist group in the sixties, and Blake's blood simmered with that same unpredictable heat. As the boys grew older, and it became clear Grattan's parliament was doin' no better for *them* than it had for their fathers, battle lines were drawn against the government"—Gorag dipped a meaningful glance in emphasis of his finishing point—"at least by Blake."

Kris raised both brows in understanding. "And Daniel?" he prodded.

Gorag held up both hands, as if his answer was the only explanation possible. "Daniel was a smitten da of a five-year-old. He wanted his daughter to grow up in a world o' peace . . . *and* he truly believed the reforms in Dublin, though small, were to be followed by more."

Kris released a quick grunt. "Made him the toast of the crowd on Blake's end of town, I'll wager."

"We'll never know for certain," Gorag returned. "One night, after the lads were sent home by Maeve for letting their fists take over their debating in the dining hall, both of their cottages were burned to the ground."

Kris pursed his lips on a slow, low whistle.

"Their wives and children were with them."

The whistle died—slashed to its death by a sudden throatful of shock. For long moments, Kris could only sit and rotate Gorag's words around in his mind, striving to reach any conclusion other than the absurd imaginings he had *now*. "Th-their—" he stammered, "their wives and—"

"Children," Gorag supplied softly.

"But Shivahn—"

"I dragged her from the cottage just before it collapsed completely." The man shook his head once, as his lips twisted into a sad half grimace. "Barely found the little wretch, too. She was so covered in soot, she looked a very part o' all that smoke, but I tripped o'er her, thank God, and—"

"And she was alive," Kris interjected with an urgency gathering unnervingly and uncontrollably in his blood. He leaned forward just as Gorag had minutes past, hands gripping his knees. "Right?" he continued. "She was *alive*. Her parents perished . . . but she survived, right?"

And yet, some part of his instinct knew the answer to that already. He knew it in the long moment Gorag took before even sucking in breath for a reply . . . the moment his own lungs struggled to find sustenance, as his mind fought to find logic in the words to come. His allegations to Shivahn, growled recklessly on the footbridge last night, now haunted him with reverberating echoes: *How many other times in your life were you cold enough to pass for a corpse?*

"I held her as I watched the last of my best mate's cottage burn to cinders," Gorag finally went on. Remembrance ground his voice to a hoarser murmur. "I don't know how much time passed . . . the others said 'twas about seven minutes; it felt more like seventy years . . . but before I knew it, they were tryin' to take her from me. 'She's gone, too,' they said. 'Shivahn is dead.' "

As the image increased its stronghold in Kris's mind, a numbing chill spread in his gut, as well. "What did you do?" he asked lowly.

"Told 'em to go rut with the cows," came the harrumphing retort. "And . . . I kept holdin' her." The last of that came more softly, as the man swiped a thumb beneath a telling glimmer in his eye. "I held her even when somebody brought her favorite lace shawl, sayin' how odd it was she'd left it behind at dinner that night, sayin' how right it would be to bury her in it . . .

"Bloody idiots," Gorag again growled. "Even when then blatherskitin' priest came with his holy water and his last rites, I held her . . . aye, lad, I held her."

As he said the last of that, Kris didn't miss the smile starting to thread its way back across the man's lips. And he'd wager a thousand gold guineas he already knew the explanation for that smile. He knew it . . . while he endured his logic's screaming denial against it.

"O' course," Gorag continued in a low but decidedly more humored voice, "the priest stopped when Shivahn blinked up at him, grabbed his rosary, and asked which poor soul he was sayin' the rites for." Reliving the moment, despite the miraculous implications of it, induced a hearty laugh in the gnarled face. "The little mite was breathin' again, as certain as ye and me now."

For a long moment after that, Kris could only sit with his elbows resting on his knees, blinking slowly at Gorag. His logic screamed strident protests at the story, yet in his gut, in that deep part of him he'd come to trust more than any other instinctual message in his body, he recognized his instant and even easy belief of it.

A slight smile curled his own lips as he asked the man, "What did you do then?"

"Started countin' stars," came the sarcastic sneer of reply. "What the hell would *ye* have done? I let the mite get up, then followed her to the dining hall." Gorag leaned back while indulging a grunting laugh. "Maeve pranced along behind us, declarin' to one and all 'twas a miracle by all accounts *she'd* ever known, and surely the saints and the *Sídhe* had conspired to work great deeds through the life of this precious girl."

At that, however, that strange solemnity crept its way into the man's wrinkles again. "But balls and bones, lad . . . do ye know . . . the shrew was right."

Outwardly Kris only gave the man more of his silent, intense attention. But inwardly he shouted giddily: *Yes. Oh, yes, old man,* this *I* do *know.*

"Ye see," Gorag hastened on, "that very night, that very moment, she proved it. There she was, a lass of barely five summers, joltin' outta my lap like the very firefly she looked akin to, and—well, ye know *why* she raced to the dining hall first? 'Cause she knew that's where they took the men who had tried to put out the fires. And what she did when she got there . . ."

The man shook his head like a man trying to explain he'd just seen the Loch Ness serpent. "W-well," Gorag stammered, "I would nay tell ye so if I did not see it so myself, but . . . she—well, she worked magic on those men. With naught but a smile and a gentle touch o' her tiny hands, she . . ."

He dropped back in his seat with a snort and a nervous glance, as if suspecting Kris would have him carted off to an outer island for spouting such insanity. Still, Gorag continued. "The next morn, the men said their burns only itched and their bruises had all but vanished. Christ's feet, I know this all sounds bloody damn odd—"

"No," Kris interjected. "No, my friend, it doesn't sound one whit odd."

He said it as he rose and paced back across the cottage—back to the door this time, which he opened to achieve a full view of the knoll. And he said it as he, too, remembered. As the stench of Prevot invaded his senses again, as the distant screams of tortured Insurgents filled his ears, as he lay in a dark cell of his own, knowing he'd never see light or feel warmth again—

Until an angel brought them back to him with the music in her voice and the miracle in her touch.

The story didn't sound odd at all.

As a matter of fact, it sounded wonderful.

That conclusion became the kindling for the renewed bonfire in Kris's gut . . . for the searing terror in every breath he took. For now, he realized, he had begun to believe. He had heard, from perhaps the most skeptical codger on this entire island, that his fevered hallucinations in Prevot weren't impossible illusions at all. He had witnessed, both last night in the dining hall and now out on the knoll, that he wasn't the only one who thought Heaven was missing an angel named Shivahn.

And once more, for the first time in ten years, Kris began to believe in a ridiculous thing called magic.

He even began to believe there was some of the stuff reserved for *his* miserable existence.

And *that*, he conceded with a pounding heart, was the most dangerous thing of all to believe in. Magic didn't save a man when he stared down a pistol barrel. Magic didn't spare his neck on the gallows or the guillotine block.

Magic sure as hell wasn't going to change the English blood in his veins, nor the Irish blood in Shivahn's.

He had to leave this place. Before it really did let him forget who he was. He had to leave this place. *Now*.

He wanted to leave. *Now*. Shivahn sensed the urgency in Kristian the moment she turned and beheld him in the doorway of the cottage. A shiver claimed her as she drank in the sight of him, a figure tall and magnificent with his usual erect pride, but now, with a spine held even more rigid by a strange, extra something. A restless something . . . an apprehensive something.

As if, in the utterly immobile way he stared across the grass, he were looking at her for the last time.

With that thought, none of Shivahn's muscles would work, as well. She could not even blink away the appalling sting entrenching itself behind her eyes.

"Oh, fiddle!" she heard Rhianna pout somewhere near her knees—though only the back reaches of her mind registered the words. "There is Maeve with the midday bells. We have to go help serve the stupid stew!"

"Stew will make you strong and pretty, pet," she rebuked—or at least attempted to, past the iron chains constricting around her throat. "Now off to your chores."

"While *you* are off to your enchanted prince?" came the countering giggle. *That* caused a momentary slip of Shivahn's sights—down to where the ringlet-headed nymph and her mates showed their clear awareness of the wordless but potent forces swirling from here to the cottage and back. Shivahn silently thanked God when the midday meal bells sounded again, sending the trio skipping off and saving her from having to answer Rhianna with the blush now suffusing her face.

The blush that grew in direct proportion to the heaviness in her chest, as she walked down the knoll toward the entrance of her home.

"Good day, Mr. Montague," she said softly when she arrived, battling to ignore the increasing size of that weight as she took in the alluring jut of his unshaven jaw, the innate regality in his doorway-filling stance. Somehow, her feet stepped their way up onto a tree stump Gorag often favored as an afternoon sunning bench. The new positioning placed her a head and a half taller than Kristian. For this conversation, she suspected, she would need that advantage.

"A good day to you, Mistress Armagh." He offered the words quietly, politely . . . *too* politely; though a smile twinged his lips as he added, "Your ceremonies were beautiful enough to rival the shows of our own courtiers. *Bravissimi.*"

As for what his last string of syllables meant, she had no fathoming, but his tone, silken as morning rain falling through the pines of Trabith Wood, imparted his meaning with more prismic clarity than a rainbow after that rainfall.

Shivahn listened to her heart beat out an erratic tattoo as she watched her toe trace the stump's age rings with equal agitation.

"Aye, our May Queen was beautiful," she concurred in a murmur to match his, "but she needed a king." She dared to tilt a glance up. "Mayhap tomorrow, Kristian, you will afford our court the honor of . . ."

"Shivahn." He said it past the discernible tautening of his jaw. Shivahn's own body braced itself for the words she had expected—and dreaded.

The words she now knew she would fight with every wit and instinct at her disposal.

"Shivahn," he prompted again, "we need to talk."

She dug her toe against the wood with painful intensity now. "Talk about what?"

Kristian averted his gaze. As she watched him search for anything to look at beside her, the weight on her chest might as well have solidified into a lead anchor.

"I think you know, Leprechaun," he stated at last. "I think you know I've stayed here too long already. And every moment I *do* stay only jeopardizes you and everyone in this place—"

"And *I* think we must get you into a bath and some clean clothes," Shivahn sliced back before he could utter another syllable—before he could jerk that anchor's chain even another inch further. "You are beginning to stink beyond the realms of decency, Mr. Montague, and I refuse to converse with you in such a state."

She did not entirely lie, she justified. The man *did* smell, though Shivahn found his male musk, joined with the smoky, foresty scent he had absorbed since arriving here, an enticing mixture. As a matter of fact, on the footbridge last night, she had a fine view of his bruises from an arm's distance, but his scent had drawn her closer, until she got close enough to breathe the full essence of him . . .

"Then there is the matter of your arm," she went on rapidly, the remembrance of their midnight moments fanning higher those forbidden flames only Kristian seemed to kindle within her. "Well, *look* at it," she charged. "The splinting is falling asunder, and I wager you have utterly soaked the dressing, as well. How can you expect the break to keep healing, set in a tangle such as that? Aye, we shall have to do something about that before talking, as well."

But her chatterings released naught a line of tautness in his face. Not even the shadow of a chuckle teased the corners of his mouth, as it always did when she ranted at him, just before he shook his head as if to say *what am I going to do with you* now, Leprechaun?

But all Kristian did was take a step closer to her, softly, evenly. He was the noble bloody Englishman in every last composed muscle, while inside, *she* felt like a dying rose, about to crumble and blow away on winter's merciless wind.

"My arm," he finally said, "is fine." Then with low, pointed meaning: "At least fine enough to travel."

"Nay." As she issued it from locked teeth, Shivahn gulped back the horrifying sting behind her eyes again. "Nay. I—I shall set it correctly after you bathe. I shall gather the materials I need whilst you visit the lake. 'Tis beautiful at the lake this time of the day; you shall like it very much. And when you are done, you can put on the clothes I left on the table next to your cot. Gorag found an old tunic he never wears, and Maeve brought over some breeches she has stitched up. The woman is as fast with a needle as she is with her tongue. And I think your boots will be fine after a good—"

He caught her off guard by breaking from his serene

shell with sudden ferocity, clearing the distance to her in one movement.

"My *boots*," he finished, while yanking her down from her perch, "are going nowhere but down that road. And damn it, Shivahn, I wish you'd stop making this harder for me."

She should have swallowed down her next words along with the weight now growing in her throat, as well. But her desperation sprinted wildly toward the point of ignoring logic and acknowledging only pain. "Harder for *you*?" she spat from the pith of that pain.

"Aye." He emitted a harsh breath, past teeth she could almost hear as they ground together. "For Christ's sake, Shivahn, you've got to know how difficult it is to do this. How difficult it is . . ." His voice waned to a discomfitted mutter. "To leave you."

At that, she let her head fall forward as her eyes squeezed shut . . . as the tears finally, silently seeped past her heart and onto her lashes.

Why? that heart clamored at her with every searing drop. *Why do you care what is hard or difficult for this pompous Englishman who lures Sandys closer with every moment he remains here? You have done your Christian and your human duty for this man, Shivahn! Let him go, and good riddance to him!*

And yet she knew, as she lifted her chin once more and retightened her fists against the folds of her skirt, that she would fight the stubborn ass to the death before watching him march out of sight down that road and into Sandys's waiting guillotine. For if his head, in all its hard obstinance, meant that much to the English at the top of a stake, then surely it meant much more to the Insurgents still secured to his spine.

And for that reason alone, she reconfirmed, she *had* to

save the man from his own folly. Aye, as far as she was concerned, he could sail himself off to the midst of the Asian seas, but she owed Kristian Montague's safety to the good of her people now.

With that conviction, she bounded off the stump and advanced upon Kristian with singular intent. "I only know *one* thing, Mr. Montague," she accused as she did. "The only one making this harder on you is *you*."

When but a step's distance separated them once more, she jabbed an emphasizing finger into his chest. "If you are so bloody anxious to return to your ships and your merchants and your trading—*if* that is what you truly do—then go. I shall not hold you back another step. Though 'twill serve you well to remember that Sandys and the Dublin port authorities may nay be so understanding as I!"

She could scarce believe it, but one of her tirades seemed to finally penetrate the man's maddening armor. A tiny timbre of hope echoed in Shivahn's heartbeat as at last, the taut composure of Kristian's features surrendered to the deep V between his lowering eyebrows. "What the hell are you getting at?" he demanded, inhaling sharply again as he finished, as if he fiercely fought the urge to grab her by both arms and shake her.

"Not a thing," Shivahn countered with utterly feigned blitheness. Inside, she rattled off a swift penance for the charade, now vitally necessary to the success of her purpose. "After all," she continued lightly, "I am just a country lass, and Irish at that, barely learned of these sorts of things. What do *I* know? I suppose, if you are so confident about the task, that you *could* ask Sandys to let you pass his port blockades, and he would be agreeable about the whole affair. I suppose *you* know that he shall be utterly tolerant of your back, still festering with wounds from his sword, and your arm, still too weak to hold a serving ladle, let alone a musket or saber with which to fight him off."

She paused to emit a strategically timed sigh. "Oh, aye, Kristian, you *do* know these things much better than I. You must know Sandys shall see your ship and your crew, and know 'twould be utterly—how do you toffs say it?—oh, aye, 'twould be utterly *beyond the pale* to satisfy his vendetta for *you* by taking *their* lives. That, of all things, makes not a pittance of sense to me, but I *am* ignorant of these things, after all. You English are indeed a different lot than—"

"All right, damn it." He cut her off with a snarl bettering any lion she saw on those fancy Dublin mansions. "All right, you've made your bloody point."

He pivoted from her and paced a fresh groove into the cottage's front walk during a tense, silent minute. Shivahn's heart pounded in time to every one of his hard strides—but those beats never neared the thunder in her chest when he swung back upon her, his gaze the darkness of pure jade again, his features the severity of pure granite.

"You have your way for today, wench," he muttered. "But tomorrow, Sandys himself may look like a portrait of mercy next to you."

Shivahn merely reacted by remounting her stump, battling not to appear the vanquishing warrioress smugly taking her throne. She failed, of course. She also failed at thinning the elation from her voice as she cocked a brow back at him and quipped, "We shall address that tomorrow then, shan't we?"

But they did not, of course. How could they, when tomorrow's morning brought the first smell of spring berries on the air—and thus, a glen of them to be picked for fresh tarts at dinner? And how could they discuss the matter the next day, either, when Kristian spent the morning helping

Billy find a lost sheep on the south meadow and the afternoon fulfilling his duties as King of the May to three girls who *all* wanted a turn at being his queen?

Still, as the sun set on that day, Shivahn entered the cottage to find Billy and him hunched over a satchel packed full with supplies and foodstuffs—all the necessary comforts for a cold night's hike through the mountain pass back to Dublin. She glared from one to the other of them. Kristian only spared her a glance in return, but his message was clear: *Don't you dare try to stop me.*

Billy, on the other hand, gave her more than a glance, and *his* message was even clearer: *Don't worry; we shall stop him.*

She had no idea where the man eventually carted Kristian off to but readily kissed Billy the next morn when he reappeared with a Kristian who had obviously been given too many whiskey salutes during the "farewell festivities" the men had arranged. And once Kristian arose from his half-drunken slumber—around noon the next day—Maeve paid an unannounced visit, huffing her disbelief in the rumor he had never milked a goat before. To Shivahn's profound but delighted surprise, when Kristian confirmed the report as true, the woman hauled him off to the dairy, rendering her rectification of the problem by giving him two hours of lessons at the task—then putting him to work at it.

Shivahn watched these goings-on with soft giggles from a knothole in the dairy's south wall. Yet her laughs comprised mere bubbles on the surface of a wellspring of joy newly formed within her . . . a wellspring flowing with the magic of one beautiful realization:

The whole village was falling as deeply as she under Kristian Montague's spell.

Not that she wondered why for one moment. With each passing hour, it became harder to remember this man had entered Trabith five days, not five years, ago. At his easy grins, the young maids sighed. At his appreciative appetite for their berry tarts, the matrons cooed. At his mastery with a sword, the youths grunted approval. And at his fearlessness of hard work, the men welcomed him into their ranks with, of course, a "farewell party."

But most of all, Shivahn saw, they had all begun to look at their world through a very different set of eyes. Eyes through which they all saw Trabith as if *they* had just entered it for the first time and felt their senses stop in awe at the beauty around them.

Shivahn felt that awe, as well, and reveled in the sensation—but for her, Kristian's eyes possessed even more meaning . . . a significance she shared only with The Almighty these last glorious days, for fear her new awareness was only a desperate concoction from the depths of her heart.

'Twas the same awareness she ached with as she sat opposite him before the fire at nights, staring at the reflection of the hearth flames in his fathoms of green eyes, which in turn stared at her with such focused intent that her blood heated to honeyed poteen with the effect. With that look, he swirled her head with sinful images of what it would be like to drop her mending and go to him . . . aye, just go to him and press herself to him, and whisper to him of these feelings he stirred in secret, precious parts of her . . .

If only she knew what to *call* these feelings.

If only she was not so terrified to discover that answer—or its deeply dangerous implications.

So instead, Shivahn told herself she was happy with moments like the one the *Sídhe* gave her now, laughing another stitch into her side at the sight of Kristian maneuvering his long frame from beneath a short azalea bush, with a triumphant grin on his face—and a squirming rat in his hand. As he handed the animal back to a wide-eyed Rhianna, who expressed her thanks for the rescue of her pet with a sloppy kiss, he nonetheless looked at Shivahn with a smirk not unlike a knight who had gutted a dragon for his princess.

Taking in the whole view of him, she surrendered her grin to a heavy sigh. She reached up to pluck tiny twigs from his hair, which had grown into deliciously thick waves again, and muttered a rather *un*princesslike oath as she fingered the rip in his left shirt sleeve.

"You nay need to worry so much about Sandys getting you again, Mr. Montague," she muttered affectionately. "You are doing a fine job of destroying your clothes on your own."

Yet at that moment, she regretted getting that close to him once more. From beneath his lowered eyelids, he began to burn that *gaze* at her . . . the intense stare he usually reserved for the fireside.

"But Rhianna was going to lose her pet," he told her in an equally intimate undertone.

"And Rhianna could nay have 'saved' the thing herself?" she admonished, folding arms over her chest—while commanding every muscle in her face to control her laughter.

"Of course not," came the instant answer—in a voice as different from Kristian's as fairy song from warrior chants. "Do not be silly, Shivahn," Rhianna continued from the bench where she'd plopped to tidy the rat with a comb fashioned of pine needles. "Prince Kristian *had* to come to my rescue."

"Oh?" Shivahn tilted one brow. "And why is that, Mistress May Queen?"

" 'Cause."

"Because why, Rhianna?" Kristian's lips twitched in anticipation of the chuckle he'd have at the girl's answer.

" 'Cause 'tis what ye do," came the slightly exasperated answer. "All the good things . . . ye do them 'cause ye are the Griffin, Kristian. And good things are what the Griffin does."

In the crashing, stunning moment of silence before Kristian looked back up at her, Shivahn already knew what emotion to expect across every inch of his features. Her lurching stomach and clenching heart ached as horridly accurate messengers.

Surely enough, as his head snapped up, his glare stabbed into her, gleaming with accusation and sharp with a thousand shards of betrayed fury. Helplessly immobilized by that look, Shivahn managed only glances at his locked teeth beneath the embittered snarl of his lips. But glances were enough of that—more than enough. If only she could experience her heart's terrified shock in such temporary measure.

"Kristian," she finally managed to rasp. "Kristian, *I* did not tell her such—" She spun upon the girl. "Rhianna, where did you hear this? From who?"

The girl shrugged, thankfully too intent with her rat's tresses to notice the intensifying turmoil between the grown-ups. " 'Twas at Sarah and Rachel's house, the other night, when I ate dinner with them. We had peach tarts for dessert, too! Their da said it to their ma, and he said he heard it from—"

"That's enough, princess," Kristian bit out. "I can wager a good guess at who he heard it from." He drove another glare into Shivahn. "As well as who knows about it now. And why it suddenly makes sense I've been welcomed here like a member of the bloody family."

A laugh did escape him then—a brusque, bitter distortion of the sound he'd first contemplated. "Silly me." He sneered at the end of it. "I actually thought they'd stopped throwing bread at my face because they *liked* my face."

With that, he spun on his heel without a backward glance. Shivahn followed with matching resolve. She caught up to him at a full run and stopped him only by yanking on his elbow with both hands.

"Kristian!" she lashed out as she did, driving the words into him along with her own frustrated glare now. "Damn it, you must believe me. I had no part in this!"

The tension slackened in the muscles beneath her grip. But as Kristian pulled away from her, she sensed he'd jerk from Medusa's clutches with less impatience. "I don't know what to believe anymore," he muttered. "Not in this place. Perhaps not anywhere anymore."

At that, he turned and left her once more. But this time, he trudged heavily along the path, his stompings replaced by the distinctive gait of a man alone and well used to being that way. And as she stood watching him, hands balled at her sides and pain wedged in her belly, all words fled Shivahn except the question searing from her soul and screaming down the path behind him.

Dear God, Kristian Montague . . . what kind of life have you known?

No answer came except the drumming of distant thunder clouds in background to Rhianna's contented humming. But that void only induced Shivahn's heart closer to its next determined resolution:

She would bloody well discover the answer for herself.

And her quest would begin right now.

Chapter 9

She followed him to the lakeshore, ten steps beyond where the south meadow yielded to a short but steep bank of rocks, a small but ageless forest, then a stretch of gravelly sand. The result was an alcove that looked gleaned of medieval legends, shrouded in cool shadows even on the sunniest days, cloaked in misty solitude during thunder-clouded twilights such as this.

Shivahn peered down the ledge at his figure, now crouched at the water's edge. If not for the tension coiled around her middle, she would have smiled. Her own soul sought this hideaway in which to escape to her thoughts, so it came as no surprise—but a cherished discovery—to find Kristian poised as she had so many times, staring unblinkingly, seeking solace in the depths that stretched like liquid pewter before him.

She made her way down the slope, but stopped upon a

large boulder when she reached the bottom. She curled her legs beneath her as she watched him stab long fingers into the dark gray water. Then, with barely tamped violence, he hurled the water across his face.

Shivahn jumped a little in surprise—but the jolt gave her the fortitude to lift her chin from her folded arms, and call to him. " 'Tis not holy water, Kristian," she stated gently. "It only washes the stains off your skin."

His hands paused on either side of his face, but his response revealed no surprise at her presence. "Go away, Leprechaun," he commanded softly.

As she rose, she tried to tell herself he only used the words to vent his anger—and fear. But as she issued her rebuttal, her lips obeyed the churn of her heart. "Mayhap I should have done so when I came to get you out of Prevot."

He gave a wry grunt. "Mayhap you should have."

Her stomach joined the turmoil of her heart. "You do not mean that."

Kristian rose himself then, the vehemence of the action scattering pebbles into the water like a miniature hailstorm. "Just like you didn't mean to tell the whole village about my 'secret identity,' right?"

With the accusation, his bitterness molded into a double-edged blade, driving into the center of her. Shivahn retaliated with a seething advance of her own. She halted when she arrived at the water's edge, close enough to see every taut edge in his face.

"I know not what sort of 'honor' your British belles invoke when they promise to hold confidences," she charged, "but in Ireland, our secrets follow us to the grave if need be. *I* have not attached your name to the Griffin's in a single sentence, Kristian. Billy deduced your 'secret identity' the night you arrived here. I denied his claims, of course, but Billy has never listened to his own mum with a full ear. The truth is, I am surprised he held his tongue about it *this* long."

She paused then, expelling a tired breath. The next moment, Kristian emulated the action, which looked to drain at least his shoulders of their tension.

"Billy," he muttered, his lips twisting sardonically. "Well, that makes sense, doesn't it?"

Shivahn knew her answer did not have to be spoken. She also knew his consensus was all she should expect of an apology right now. One look to the gold and green shards still piercing his stare provided enough evidence of the battle even those words had waged to be expressed.

"I am more surprised at the children's tranquillity about it," she said instead. "But in another way, I am not. In their eyes, you are a hero already."

That was *not* the right thing to say. Kristian's snarl, brandished with more sharpness than the original blade of his fury, told her that with no doubt to be had. "Stop," he ordered, presenting his taut spine to her once more. "Damn it, stop it!"

"Why?" she fired back. She took a step closer and pressed her hand to his shoulder. *"Why*, Kristian?"

He flinched away from her touch. "I am not a hero, Shivahn." Every word rasped hard through the misted silk of the air. "I am the farthest thing from it."

For a long moment, Shivahn did not speak. Because in that moment, in a voice soft as the wind rushing through the trees overhead, this man had, despite his pain and fear, commenced a precious symphony in her heart . . . the symphony of his life's song.

A tear joined the mist upon her cheeks. She needed to hear more of the symphony.

"What is it, Kristian?" she beseeched in a whisper. "Tell me . . . please. Tell me what this demon of yours is."

The fairies could have transformed him into a lakeside statue, so stony and unmoving was the outward response he gave her. "I don't know what you're talking about," he finally returned from taut lips.

"The bloody hell you do not," she rebutted. "Kristian . . ." She yearned to run to him, to wrap her arms around the turmoiled heart of him . . . she dared not. "You are not just running from Sandys, are you?" The retightening of his shoulders gave her all the confirmation she needed. "From what else are you escaping?" she pressed. "Or whom?"

"Please," he gritted, "*don't*. 'Twas a long time ago, and—" He jerked a gruff shrug. "It doesn't matter any more."

"And I am the great Brigid of the Judgments," she snapped. "Or mayhap I am only a fool, for thinking you a 'Brave One' at all."

She shook her head as the symphony began to fade, leaving only the sound of the lake waters slapping uselessly at the shore stones.

"I cannot dictate what the rest of my people will think or say," she finally said to him. "And now I think you know that I never have. But do know this, Kristian Montague: I shall never confuse you with the Griffin again."

Damn this woman. Ah, damn this woman back to the bold, beautiful fire from which she'd surely been formed.

Kris's mind raged with the contention, yet his protest amounted to the heat of a wax taper next to the bonfire of Shivahn, her heart a violet fire in her eyes, the trail of a lone tear blazing at him from her cheek. Convicting him. Burning into him as none other could—perhaps as none other ever would.

That confession comprised the beginning of his end. If

only she demanded a simple white flag as her compensation. Instead, his lips moved to fulfill the excruciating terms of Shivahn Armagh's peace pact: the words of a story he had spoken to no other in his entire life.

He began quietly, awkwardly, jabbing his toe into the shore as he struggled to push the words to his lips. "The ghosts of my past are many, Shivahn. They begin . . . with my parents."

He heard her intake of breath at that. "I am sorry," she murmured. "My mum and da were both taken from me, too. I was five. That was when Gorag took me in."

"I was six," he returned. "But I had no Gorag. There was only Malcolm."

"Your brother?"

"My cousin." It surprised him, how flat and composed his voice sounded, even as all the old unsurety and insecurity ignited back to life inside, as if the last time he'd fought this need to drive a hole through an oak with his fist wasn't eight years but eight days ago. As if he were fourteen again, turning his back on Castle Clay for the last time, and feeling no anguish at all about leaving the mausoleum he'd been forced to call home.

"Your cousin?"

Shivahn's prompt reminded him an ocean now lay between him and that life. Safe; he was safe here, he reminded himself, and it was all right to speak without fear of being "corrected."

"Our fathers were brothers," he continued, "determined to relive the glory of their boyhood by taking the families out on an ocean fishing expedition for the day. But my mother wanted to cancel it and wait until another time. There were dark clouds on the horizon, and she feared a storm was approaching."

He stopped then and peered across the lake. Dense clouds

had sneaked in over the hills, an enveloping blanket of gray joining the mists off the water. "I remember the look in her eyes as she looked to those clouds . . . as if she somehow knew what tragedy they were bringing with them . . ."

He didn't notice Shivahn moving to stand beside him, until her fingers curled into his. Kris didn't have the strength nor inclination to resist her. Her fingers were warm and gentle; her presence soothed the wound he tore open farther with every new word he uttered.

"What happened?" she softly asked.

"Everybody laughed at her." His brow furrowed on the memory. "I remember Aunt Ilona calling her a 'silly, sour fish' out to ruin the 'lovely party.' "

"So you sailed?"

"So we sailed."

"And the storm came."

"And the storm came." He punctuated it this time with a hard swallow. "It came upon us like a phantom. One moment we were alone with the blue sky, and the next, rain and sleet and wind were plummeting at us." He finished in a rough mutter, "It was terrifying."

Shivahn clutched him tighter, making him realize he was shaking. "I don't remember many things about it so clearly," he stammered on, "except . . ."

"Except," she repeated quietly, "what?"

"Except . . . the sight of my mum as she wrapped herself around the rail and looked at me for the last time."

"Oh, Kristian." She gasped. "Kristian—"

"Her teeth were chattering," he continued rapidly, now commanded somehow by a force beyond his own will. "She was soaked to the bone, and her skin was so pale. But when she looked at me, her eyes were so peaceful."

He scanned the horizon as he concluded, seeing not the shifting mists of Trabith anymore, but that unforgettable stare which still haunted his dreams. "I suppose she'd already accepted her death," he murmured in realization. "I know *I* thought she was already dead. 'Tis why I looked away from her, frightened by the sight of her."

He pulled his hand from Shivahn then, needing to be alone, mentally and physically, as he finished the account. "When I turned back to her again, she was gone."

From behind him came a small utterance mixed of sympathy and pain, but beyond that, Shivahn remained silent. She let the lapping waters speak between them, telling him she understood all the words he couldn't clarify of that night a lifetime ago, a yesterday ago.

Finally, she told him, "I am so sorry, Kristian."

"I know. I . . . know," he repeated, hoping his tone conveyed the thanks his compressing throat wouldn't allow.

"Tell me what happened after that."

Kris didn't thank her for *that*. He issued a protesting sigh. He didn't want to go on. Perhaps 'twas why he'd locked all this behind a wall of numbness in his mind. Reliving it exhausted him as much as enduring the storm the first time.

And yet, with every bulwark of memory he tore down, it seemed a flock of ugly, dark birds took flight out of his soul. Birds that had been crammed inside him for so many years, they'd blocked out all the light from his days.

So he swallowed again and swung a determined ax at the next wall inside him. "The next two or three days passed in a blur. I was cold and wet, then fevered and frightened, and then, just alone. Nobody ever really *told* me they'd both died . . . I just knew, when I woke up in a strange bed in a strange house, and they weren't there—" He jabbed a hand along the side of his head. "Well, I just knew."

"Where were you?" Her voice was the guiding keel he

needed in traversing this ocean of memory. She spoke with empathy but not pity. Softness but not sorrow.

Borrowing from that wondrous fortitude, Kris went on. "I came to find out Malcolm and I had drifted pretty far into Saint George's Channel. And ironically, we were spotted by a fisherman and his crew."

"That sounds less like irony and more like fate."

He looked up to catch the serene smile she attached to that. "You're probably right," he agreed, giving a half smile of his own.

"Who was this fisherman?"

As he answered her, Kris's smile grew. "His name was Gregory Kirkpatrick," he began, "and if fate brought him to us, then I wager he was an angel on loan from Heaven.

"Without a second thought, Greg took us home that day, to his wife, Faye, and his son, Rayne. And in their house on the Howth Peninsula, I knew six of the happiest months of my life. The nightly rough-and-tumble games before we went to bed . . . the backbreaking chores that made up our days . . . even Greg's badly acted tales of sea serpents and enchanted mermaids . . . it was the medicine I craved. They gave me a fair place to put all my grief and anger."

She nodded, though her brow creased as a prelude to her next question. "Six months . . . what happened after that? Did somebody finally come for you?"

A bitter grimace swept Kris's smile away like a wave wiped footprints from a shore. He inhaled deeply again, fighting back the acrid distaste invading his mouth.

"Somebody came, all right," he stated. " 'Twas none other than the *great* and *honorable* and *righteous* Emery Dominick Montague."

"Who was that?"

"My *beloved* grandfather." He stripped the words of all their syntaxed meaning with the brutal slice of his tone.

"My grandfather who came sailing into Howth Harbor with half the Royal Navy, then stormed into our house with an entire battalion at his heels."

He heard Shivahn trying to dilute the shock from her quick gasp yet failing. He didn't fault her.

"B-but," she stammered, "why?"

Kris turned from her then. He turned because in this moment, he admitted to being the coward that she had branded him. He couldn't bear to watch the revulsion take over her face as he relayed the next part of his story.

"When the 'authorities' in London tracked Malcolm and me down, it was their opinion that Greg and Faye had kidnapped us, intending to eventually kill or ransom us."

She gasped again. "Why would they assume such poppycock?"

"Why has any of this madness continued?" he returned. "Somebody leapt to one wrong conclusion, which led to another, then another, until my grandfather was forging the Irish Sea with half of George's fleet in tow."

That was when she uttered the words he prayed she wouldn't. "What did they do then, Kristian? Your grandfather, and the soldiers?"

He swallowed before continuing. "They barged in on our supper prayer. Grandfather immediately commanded Malcolm and me to his side. Malcolm happily obeyed. He fairly well abhorred our life in Howth. He called our chores 'Greg's tortures' and wasted no time in spouting that to Grandfather."

"What did *you* do?"

"I told Malcolm to shut the bloody hell up. And he didn't, so I jumped on him." Hearing the tale on his lips now, Kris marveled at how innocent the moment now seemed; at how easy the shrug came to his shoulder, like a youth simply relating the latest tavern brawl he'd instigated.

Good Christ, how he wished it had been just a tavern brawl.

"We got into the row rather well," he forced himself to continue, "and Greg ended up stepping between us. He had to violate a soldier's order to do that, and that soldier did not find Greg's disobedience so tolerable. He came down on Greg with the butt of his rifle, which brought Faye into the mess, and—"

His churning gut forced him to stop. But then Shivahn's hand curled back into his from behind. And immediately, magically, her touch began its healing power on his senses, on his soul. When she urged, "And what, Kristian?" he was somehow able to summon the words again.

"Everything happened so bloody fast," he grated. "Shots rang out, and I remember watching Faye fall to the floor, next to Greg."

"Oh," came her tearful rasp. "Oh, Kristian!"

"They were lying there together, so still . . . and I wanted to go to them. I struggled against the guards; I kicked and scratched, but they yanked me out, along with Malcolm and Rayne, as they set the house on fire."

"Dear *God*."

"They set Rayne free, yet he didn't run. He stayed and watched from the shore, standing there as his home burned, as they wrestled me aboard the ship. He stayed there until he and I could see each other no longer. I watched him, too, as I was forced back to a country I knew I'd never call 'home' again."

He concluded that by digging his toe at a stone with ruthless force, then watching it skip out onto the water and disappear into the mist . . . much like the years that vanished from his life, leaving an angry, insecure six-year-old boy standing at a ship's rail, watching the last thing he'd known as a family vanish in a smoke-filled Irish twilight.

"Life with Grandfather was everything I could have desired," he proceeded in a tone controlled in every aspect except one: the raw contempt punctuating the end of each word. "That is, if fine lawn on my back and pheasant in my stomach were what I desired."

"They were not?" came her sincerely curious query.

"They were *not*. And I exploited every chance I had to tell Grandfather so, in whatever manner I had at my disposal. My resentment and pain only grew through the years, fed by rules I never obeyed and punishments I soon learned to endure." He booted another rock into the lake. "Beatings can only hurt the body, you know."

"Nay," Shivahn asserted with clenched intensity. Yet then her voice softened, wrapping around him like the mist itself. "Nay. They hurt much more than that, Kristian."

Still, Kris retreated from her again. He fled to hide the wash of emotion bathing his face. He turned so she wouldn't see how desperately his spirit had waited to hear somebody say just those words. But he still felt her; he felt the tendrils of her soul, as full of healing warmth as her hands, reaching to him over the ramparts of his composure . . .

"Don't," he spun back at her and commanded. "Don't do that!"

"Do you think I can *control* it?" she lashed back, spreading her hands in pleading desperation. "Do you think I can douse my feelings as easily as a candle wick?"

"And don't *you* yet understand what I'm trying to tell you? I am not the conquering hero at the end of your little fairy tale, Shivahn. I let those years with Grandfather embitter me, not strengthen me. I was at war with him by the age of ten, and if not for one Castle Clay fencing instructor who knew where to place my aggressions, I'd have probably followed that with a declaration on all of England, as well."

"Attila the Hun, waiting to be anointed?" she quipped, now crossing those arms while cocking both eyebrows.

Kris held back from snatching her bait. Instead, he maintained his level stare upon her and told her with equal concision, "The day I turned fourteen, that fencing teacher helped me pack a bag of traveling gear, steal my favorite horse from the Castle Clay stables, and leave for good. I didn't look back, nor have I returned since."

At that, she lowered her arms. And her brows. Kris read her emotions in her eyes: the sharpening amethyst glints there, as she began to really see the dauntless youth who turned away from a world of footmen, maids, and fencing instructors just to find the completion for a cavern of despair inside him.

"Where did you go then?" she at last asked.

"Straight to the docks of London. I suppose it was instinctual . . . mayhap some need to avenge the ghosts of Mum and Greg. No matter what the reason, it didn't take long for me to drop Grandfather's name in all the right places and find one of his own ships, the *Hades Plunder*, bound for Ireland."

Despite a marked effort to repress the expression, her features quirked in bemusement. "The *Hades Plunder*?"

" 'Twas a vessel aptly named," Kris returned grimly. "If Hell could float, it certainly did so with my grandfather's blessing, beneath the helm of one Captain Righteous Prathing."

He began to pace the shore again, rolling his shoulders, trying to free them of their renewed yoke of tension. "I shall spare you the details of the treatment we all endured at that man's discretion. Suffice it to say that I almost didn't survive the voyage at all, so the shores of Tramore were a very welcome sight to my eyes.

"But instead of putting in ashore immediately, Prathing commanded that we dock in a hidden cove over that night. I was puzzled and damnably disappointed, but at dawn's first light, I discovered the reason for Prathing's cryptic behavior."

He stopped as he came to the end of a small, flat jetty, bracing his feet on the largest of the big gray stones as he slammed his arms across his chest.

"Prathing ordered the pillaging to begin with less concern than he gave the *Plunder*'s watch rotations," he stated in a tone as flat as the rock beneath him. "I, bloody fool that I was, thought none of my fellow crewmates would agree to tossing their honor so far overboard like that."

He shut his eyes and shook his head. But his fight to shut out the memories was waged in vain. "God," he gritted, finally unable to restrain the break of his voice, "was I wrong. They razed that village like children at play in a sandbox. They didn't look back as they stuffed their sacks and their mouths, then pulled screaming women from their beds, while murdering their husbands. I tried to help . . . *God*, I tried to help, but I was fourteen, damn it, and they threw me aside like I was just another buntline to be tossed across the poop deck."

"What . . . happened then?" he heard Shivahn ask, a broken and faraway voice from that place he no longer lived: the present day.

"I'm not sure," he replied. "One moment, Prathing was backhanding me with his pistol as he prepared to rape a maid no older than I. The next, I was blinking up at a young warrior shoveling stew into my mouth and ordering me to swallow."

He finished that, unbelievably, with a chuckle—

prompting his mind back to the present and a small huff of perplexion from Shivahn. "Who was it?" she asked, and he smiled, for once relishing her tenacious attention to his story.

He turned with an equally savoring grin. "It was Rayne."

Her huff dropped into a gape. "What?"

" 'Twas he," he affirmed. "You see, as boys, we'd gotten the notion one day of becoming blood brothers—only we weren't satisfied pricking just our fingers to seal the pact. We decided to gash open our whole hands."

Her gaze lowered as he turned his left hand over. "Your scar . . . " she murmured with unfolding realization—and a growing smile.

Kris nodded. "So even after nine years and much growing up betwixt the two of us, Rayne knew fate had at last conspired to bring his brother home."

The edges of her smile softened in awe of the tale's incredible turn. "So what kind of trouble did you two heathens get into then?"

"Plenty," Kris stated. "After living hand to mouth for many years, Rayne had been recruited by a small, secret band of traveling rebels. These men were the elite of the Insurgent force, endeavoring raids so dangerous that even many of the Insurgent leaders were not aware of their presence. 'Twas in their camp that I awakened that night, and 'twas there that I knew I'd found my new home, as well."

"Of course," she offered. "A perfect place for an angry young man with no identity to lose, anyway."

"A perfect place, indeed." A rising note of conviction underlied his continuing words. "And we *were* perfect, Rayne and I. In the springs and summers, he taught me battle techniques and the art of subterfuge. During winter, I smuggled him back to England, where we trained with the best instructors in trick riding and swordfighting. Between it all, we volunteered for only the most insane missions—and succeeded at all of them. We were the perfect pair of avenging demons, killing off the grief of our boyhood with the fury of our manhood. We *never* left each other's side."

His smile fell then, as his body vibrated from a consuming grip of ice. "Until we decided to join the forces at Wexford last year."

Her stare widened. "You fought at Wexford?" she queried. "On *our* side?"

For a long moment—or perhaps a century passed, for this pain in his heart always seemed to last an eternity—Kris stood with fists coiled and eyes squeezed. When a reply finally came, it had to form itself out of the thickness wedged in his throat.

"It was really the bloodbath they speak of," he began in a low grate. "And worse. Rayne and I were separated quickly . . . we should have never let it happen. *I* should have never let it happen. But everything was so confusing; everything happened so fast. And there were so many more of them than us . . ."

Despite his effort, he lost the words then, dragging hard breaths past searing lungs. As if he ran across that battlefield in his tormented sleep again, breathing in naught but smoke and screams and hysteria, and searching, always searching for Rayne. *Rayne, damn you, answer me! Rayne!*

"It took the bastards one bayonet thrust to kill him," he finally uttered. "One thrust—it came from behind—past his spine and through his heart."

"Oh, Kristian." Her voice dropped to a rough whisper, as well. Her footsteps crunched closer in the gravel, but he slashed out a hand at her, needing to let out the rest of the nightmare, no matter how much the images rearranged his guts with more relish than Rhianna's rat scrambling a tin of mending thread.

"I—looked for him," he went on in sharp spurts. "I looked for him forever—and I finally found him—but he was gone. He was gone. I know because I kneeled down and I held him, but he wouldn't come back. Not even to say good-bye."

Suddenly, viciously, he whirled at the trees. A shower of leaves and mist rained upon them with the force of his blow at a thick-barked trunk. Kris sensed the trickle of blood oozing into his palm, but the damage could have meant his hand was falling off, and he didn't care.

"Damn it." He snarled. "God *damn* it. The bastard didn't even stay long enough to say good-bye. Damn you, Rayne. *Damn* you!"

"I know," came her assurance through the red smoke in his mind, along with her hands on the shuddering knots of his shoulders. "I know how it feels."

For a second, Kris wondered how she'd gotten so close again, so fast. But then he admitted his gratitude for her presence, no matter how she'd managed it. "I . . . want him back." The words spilled from him as naturally as the light raindrops now brimming out of the sky on them.

A thick, wet silence ensued. He expected that. He even welcomed the stillness, hoping to inhale it into his senses, as well.

He did *not* anticipate Shivahn's utterly serene response to his confession. "But Kristian, you *have* brought him back."

He fought back the temptation to fire her a sarcastic laugh. He instead opted for skeptically raised brows as he glanced at her again.

"You have brought him back with your work," she whispered, "haven't you? With your work . . . as the Griffin."

Kris spun and marched deeper into the trees. "You're getting wet," he growled. "Go home, Shivahn."

"And *you* go to Hell." She followed on his heels without a missed step, even through the slippery leaves.

"Been there already," he retorted. "And I don't care to discuss the experience any further with you."

"Well, I have a charming bit of news for *that*." She finished the pronouncement with a flourish of satisfaction. The next moment, Kris discovered why. The slope of rocks continued on around the shore and ended in a massive mound amid the trees, effectively ending his retreat. His glare having no effect on the boulders themselves, Kris pivoted on the maddeningly defiant leprechaun now posed similarly opposite him.

"Shivahn—"

"You killed yourself along with him," she cut him off. "Did you not, Kristian?" She advanced with a gaze full of lavender lightning and dark violet thunder, a force of nature now sweeping furiously upon him. "You wanted to die yourself that day, and so you did. You left the Insurgents, severing your life with them, too, so you and Rayne could continue on by being resurrected as the Griffin."

Kristian didn't answer. He refused to. He turned away, looked at *anything* but the soul-exploding tempest in her eyes—

But as he directed his glare to the lake, across the water, lightning scissored out of the clouds. The beam struck the water and ignited it into a sheen of purple-white light.

And for a moment, the flash blinded him.

For a moment, he saw nothing clearly any more.

"Answer me, damn you," she cried through the sizzling din. Kris looked to find her face centered in the sea of his vision, wet curls stuck to her forehead, lips slightly parted as she pulled in hard, violent breaths.

"Answer me!" she demanded again, this time on a sob

she tried to stifle. The sound knifed him like another slash of lightning, for nothing this consuming had filled him before.

The fire streaked up his arms, dug his fingers into her upper arms, and hauled her brutally to him. At the same time, it blazed his mind with a wrath he no more understood than had the ability to control.

Truth? he snarled at her from the tangled chaos of that mind. *You want the truth? Then you shall have it, damn you. You shall have it.*

And Kris gave it to her. He gave her the truth as he knew it only in that moment, the unbound reality of the only thing that made sense in his raging soul and his burning body.

He pulled her tighter to him and sealed his lips hard and hungrily to hers.

Chapter 10

he had pushed him too far.

The conclusion rang through Shiv-ahn's being, seared the ends of her fingers and reaches of her toes while it blasted away any rational thought from her mind and breath from her lungs . . .

Just like his kiss.

Oh, aye, she had pushed him too far. And dear powers of the *Sídhe* help her, she had never known such joy because of it.

Or mayhap this was why she had pushed so far to begin with. For was this not the burning bliss she had dreamed of for the last week, in the hours of the night where only deepest secrets lived? Was this not the bonfire she had felt in those midnight moments, brilliant and enthralling, sweeping her higher into its flames with every thrust of his mouth against hers, with every stroke of his tongue along hers?

Those flames climbed higher now, Shivahn realized, because his did, too. She recognized Kristian's need to purge the rage in his body along with the demons in his soul. Tears seared her lashes with the awe of knowing she could heal him in this way, too, the way only a woman healed a man, instinctually and naturally, since time began.

That was why she smiled up into the rain as he dipped her head back to suckle at her throat. That was why she gasped in elation as he slid those lips to her breast, further soaking the material there with his warm lickings. That was why she gave over to him, just as mist surrendered to thunder, when he cradled his arms around her to carry her into the bed of leaves at their feet.

The clouds embraced each other over the trees as Kristian embraced her with the length of his body. He felt like a force of gentle thunder himself, Shivahn thought as her hands roamed his back. He was so powerful and dark; commanding yet coaxing.

He kissed her again, rolling with her in the damp earth, filling the air with a new fragrance she savored in every corner of her senses: the earthen scent of fallen leaves mixed with the thick musk of their rising desires. Then she breathed in the scent of *him*, a captivating combination of spicy sea and crisp forest, of masculine warmth . . . and masculine arousal.

She loved smelling him. She wanted to smell *all* of him. Shivahn trailed her face into the dewy creases of rain and sweat at the base of his neck, down into the mist-touched hair mingled with leather shirt laces across his chest . . . then, as she tugged aside those laces, breathing in the planes of skin around his tautening nipples.

"*Shivahn.*" He gasped as she did. A tremor radiated from

the skin beneath her lips. His hands gripped the sides of her head as if in protest but instead dug into her hair, tangling in the wet strands, kneading in time to his quickening breaths and the soft-spattering rain. "Shivahn, you don't know what you're doing to me . . ."

She smiled against his skin. Knowing *she* caused that rough catch in his voice caused her senses to spark in delicious awakening. She raised that smile to him as she met his gaze again, his eyes now thickened to the green-gray hue of the mists surrounding them.

As she traced the brow above the left of those eyes, she returned to him in a whisper, "This feeling I give to you . . . is it the same as what you do to me?"

Kristian curled his lips back in a shaking but sultry smile. "And what do I do to you?"

She took a deep breath and lowered her fingers to the entrancing planes of those lips. "You make my belly curl with a wondrous smoke . . ."

"Smoke?" His lips parted wider, but he did not move to kiss her. He hovered there, but a breath away from her fingers; a breath neither of them took as they slowly, silently discovered the essence of each other, bodies reveling in the mingled, moist awareness of each other.

"Aye . . . smoke," she finally affirmed. "But 'tis an odd smoke, Kristian. It burns strangely . . ."

But her breath halted, unable to aid her in the rest of the description, as he slipped one hand to her lower belly. "Like this?" Kristian murmured in her ear as he fingered small swirls on the flatness between her hip bones.

"Oh," she rasped. "Oh, aye . . . like *that*."

"Hmmmm," he replied with a tone she had never heard in his voice before . . . a silken confidence, to be sure, but threaded with a note of something primitive and unpredictable. She liked this new sound, she swiftly decided. She urged him to speak it more by nudging her ear closer to his mouth.

"Mmmmm, you are right," he responded to her hint, thickening the butter cider in her veins into butter syrup. "This is a strange smoke. It swirls down rather than up." He demonstrated that fact with the corresponding path of his fingers. "And it grows hotter as it moves, not colder."

"Aye," she acquiesced in a choked cry, writhing at his touch upon the place that ached for him most. "Hotter. Aye, Kristian, that is where it burns . . ."

"I know." The silk in his voice roughened, as well. The rain began to fall harder, as if the heavens knew what kind of storm he stroked to life inside her. A lightning-white force gathered on the place where he caressed her, his thumb moving wondrously against the feminine bud of her.

"You do know." She gasped. "Oh Kristian, you do know, because it burns in you, too, aye?"

She thought she heard him groan then, though he restrained the sound beneath a heavy swallow. Yet finally, he did answer, "Aye. I burn, too, Leprechaun."

"Show me," she pleaded, perhaps even begged, but she cared not. At this moment, in this haven of rain and mist and wilderness and wetness, they were no longer English and Irish, nor pirate and rebel, nor even man and woman. They were, just as that first precious, anonymous moment they'd shared in Prevot's depths, only one soul, one shared understanding of a lifetime's worth of loneliness, one heart's outreach of need.

One.

Her heart sang it as her lips possessed his with the need of it. One. She wanted to be one with him.

"Show me, Kristian," she implored him again, when they dragged apart to inhale lungfuls of air. "Show me how you burn . . ."

His lips parted on a hard hiss, as if she had stabbed him with a smoldering blade. His head fell back, and she watched the sky bathe the surrendering grimace on his face in silvered rivulets. 'Twas as if the storm and he had become the same force: an assemblage of tears too long clamped inside clouds, of fury gathered over too much space and time, of passion waiting to be unleashed . . . waiting . . . *waiting.*

He was beautiful. So beautiful.

"Kristian." She sobbed, spreading her fingers upon the soaked expanse of his chest. By the *Sídhe*, she'd never touched a man so boldly, with such wanton intent, but every inch of his body felt so perfect to the sensitive pads of her fingers. "Kristian," she summoned again, sliding her hand along his neck, and insistently pulling him from there. *"Kristian."*

"God," he gritted, wresting from her, exposing the harsh desperation of his profile to her. "Ah, God, I . . ."

Shivahn did not make him finish the words. She already heard them in her heart. She knew what tormenting forces he battled, for the same conflicted cries echoed inside her. In this world that swirled around them so fast, how could they reach for Heaven now? For tomorrow, the call of his other-life would bring, at last, their good-bye. And then, she would hold these mists more easily than him.

But nay, came her sudden and joyous comprehension . . . she would not hold merely clouds. She would have the memory of Kristian in her heart, the lingering heat of his kisses on her lips . . . and the remembered strength of his body, teaching hers how to laugh, to cry, to soar, to live.

Oh, aye! her heart cried in joyous agreement, effectively drowning those merciless doubts in her heart. "Oh, *aye!*" her lips joined in whispered chorus. She offered the beautiful syllables again into the trees and the rain, joining them with Kristian's name as he descended to her like a cliff crumbling into the sea, finally succumbing to a force more powerful than natural comprehension could fathom—or control.

His lips met hers in a wet, hot kiss. Their bodies melded in wet, hot need. And his hands . . . oh, they were wet and hot, too, exploring her with a mindless recklessness, as if branding his personal claim to every inch he touched.

Soon that claim extended to kneading each place in time to the pulsing hardness between his legs, which now slid up and down against the crux of her own. In the doing, his body began to awaken hers in a way even his fingers had not: a shivering, shuddering way bonding her not only with the heightening storm around them but with every storm this glade had known since time began. Most important, she began to understand the storm gathering inside the man she held.

"Shivahn," he murmured on a jagged breath. His lips slid along the wet dew dotting her cheeks as his hands raked up her thighs, raising her skirts, seeking the moist, needing center of her. "Shivahn . . . oh, Shivahn . . ."

"Shivahn!"

Duncan's bellow crashed into their misted fantasy as if the *Sídhe* had truly allowed the glade to become their crystal ball of existence—only now, that Heaven was shattered.

And still, somehow believing the shards of their world would remold around them if they did, they lay there with bodies motionless and breaths held.

Nay, Shivahn's soul pleaded, as the heavens inexplicably stilled and the rain dripped from the trees in lonely trickles. *They cannot smash us apart; not now!*

Yet another shout came, closer and fiercer: "Shivahn! Shivahn, lass, are ye down here?"

A bizarre temptation to giggle pierced Shivahn's despair

as Kristian fumbled to set her skirts aright. Not a moment too soon, he stood, then helped her do the same. Duncan appeared at the top of the rock slope just as her head recovered from the shock of being yanked from a warm sea of passion to a cold shore of reality.

"Shivahn," the man pronounced on an exhausted sigh, "thank God; at last I've found you. Ye be needed in the village; now!"

At that, the chill of her sodden clothes soaked to the core of her bones. Her heart, racing with passion not a minute ago, now hammered against her ribs at a speed born of dread.

A dread she had known all too many occasions before.

"What is it, Duncan?" she forced herself to ask. But she already knew what he would answer to that. Locking her teeth and swallowing deeply, she thrust the more accurate words upon her lips: "*Who* is it? Who is it this time, Duncan?"

"Eric and Norman," her friend responded after a taut hesitation, his lean shoulders stiffening.

If the man had resurrected two ghosts with his statement, he'd not elicit a more shocked gasp from Shivahn. For in truth, 'twas what he had done. "Eric? Norman?" She repeated the names of her two childhood friends for the first time since placing heather on their graves last month. "But Sandys told us they were dead."

"He told us to *consider* them dead," Duncan corrected. "The filthy bastard." He fired a mouthful of spit into a nearby puddle. "But he had 'em. He had 'em all along. We could have gotten 'em when we went in to Prevot for Kris, but the lying whoreson—"

"*Duncan.*" Shivahn battled, in vain, to dull the fear-sharpened edge of her voice. "Where are they *now*? Take me to them *now*."

"We took 'em direct to the dining hall," he told her while helping her up the last few stones of the slope.

"The dining hall." Shivahn's breath halted once more— this time, because a wave of anxiety flooded her stomach and burned her lungs. "Powers of Heaven help me. That means they need stitching . . . or cutting."

"Aye," Duncan returned as they started off across the meadow at an urgent pace.

"B-both of them?" Shivahn asked past a throat dry as Billy's whiskey still on a Saturday eve. She skidded several times in ankle-deep puddles, unsuccessfully attempting to accelerate their journey.

"Nay," came the fast answer. "Just the one."

"Which one? Is it Eric or Norman? And how bad is it?"

When Duncan did not fire back an answer, she risked looking up from the uneven ground to cast her friend a perplexed glance. Unbelievably, she discovered Duncan's gaze arrowed in the last direction she expected.

The man stared past her, at Kristian.

"That's just the thing, lass," Duncan finally said. " 'Tis not Eric *or* Norman."

"Duncan," she prompted impatiently while skirting a five-foot-wide puddle, "what are you about?"

"They brought a third man in from Prevot," he finally clarified. "Calls himself Sir John, though he be the sorriest-lookin' knight I ever saw."

Halfway through Duncan's explanation, her friend's wary regard of Kristian began to make sense. Kristian's own mien told her so. His dark brows jumped. His eyes gleamed with near-obsessive concern. He caught up to Duncan in a stalking advance that might be perceived as threatening by a man less familiar with him.

"Sir John?" he echoed with an intensity she had never heard him use before. "John is here? How? Why?"

"So you do know him," Duncan returned. "Good, for he certain as bloody hell knows you. And he won't let a body near him until he sees you." Duncan threw his gaze back to Shivahn before uttering his last chilling statement. "Problem is, he may bleed to blazin' death because of his damn fool stubbornness.

"Unless ye can help him, lass."

By the time Kris sprinted with Shivahn across the clearing in front of the dining hall, both the night and the storm had descended on Trabith with full force. Rain knifed into the puddles at their feet; lightning streaked its blinding scythe across the landscape every other minute. Then surely as if Odin himself charioteered a stallion through the clouds overhead, a crash of thunder rattled every window and shook soaking leaves from trembling tree branches.

Without thinking about what caused his instinctual need to do so, Kris clutched Shivahn close to him for their final steps to the hall door, trying to shield her from the downpour before he could finally get her inside.

Had he known they'd only just experienced the *first* tumult of the evening, he might not have pulled her through the portal so impatiently.

As a matter of point, he might have been more assured of her safety in the storm outside than caught in the cyclone his first mate was creating of the hall.

Through some of the most brutal battles Kris had waged in his life, whether across high seas, across Grandfather's Persian carpet or across Castle Clay's fencing ring, John had been there, with massive jaw set and even larger loyalty in place, at his side. Yet through all those crucibles of fate, he had never seen the man carved away to the wild-eyed creature flailing from beneath bloodied blankets on the center table now.

Currently poor Maeve stood as the target of John's rancor. She backed away from the table wearing an apronful of the stew she'd just offered him. With a grimace, Kris wagered perhaps his friend had refused the food because the stew so closely matched the reds, browns, and purples of the cuts, bruises, and wounds peppering his body.

"Ah, God, John," he uttered, the words half choked by the rise of rage in his throat. "What the hell did that bastard do to you?"

At his mate's ensuing snarl, he considered whether he really wanted to know the answer. "Get *out*!" John finished to the outburst, adding the words to the stew he'd already barraged upon Maeve. "Get out, I told you, woman, and take your poisoned witch's stew with you. I said I'd not speak or consort with anyone but Kristian Montague, and I meant it!"

"Well, he's here," Kris boomed then. "So give the rafters some mercy, you bull-headed bastard, and shut up."

As John and Maeve darted stunned stares around to discover who had issued the order, he remained motionless by the door. He and Shivahn dripped a puddle the size of the North Sea on the floor, and he was chilled to the marrow, but he still clamped teeth tighter to the inside of his cheek to hold back the warmth of his giddy grin at the sight of his good mate again.

"Kris!" John barely finished the hoarse outcry before collapsing back to the table as if he'd just finished carrying an elephant over the Alps. "Kris," he wheezed from that position. "Thank God. They were right; you're really here. Thank God."

Kris moved to the table in three strides, yanking out the bench next to John, then straddling it. "You look like hell," he told the man in a husky murmur. He gave John's shoulder a gruff clasp, knowing that at this moment, the man's spirit cried more for dignity than his lips grunted in pain at the contact.

Still, he found himself regretting the action as John's eyes squeezed on a spasm of pain. "Well, you look worse," John rasped. "What'd ya do, ya nodcock, sell yer own hair to get outta Prevot?"

Amazing, Kris thought then. Sir John Petry had to be the only bounder who could induce a laugh in him despite a chest constricting in dread with the sight of a friend who'd been abused like a Michaelmas ham. "I'm afraid the new coiffure comes courtesy of Sandys's chambermaids," he cracked with a wry smirk.

John bunched his lips up to emit something between a grimacing growl and a hangover heave. "Sandys." He snarled. "Smarmy little piece of rat shit with feet."

Almost hating John for making him do so, Kris emitted another chuckle. John grunted a weak version of the same, and for the second time today, the years peeled away from Kris's mind easily as a rind from an orange, exposing a sweet fruit of a memory. For that moment, he and John sat together again in some secluded Castle Clay alcove, the two of them passing the time on a rainy night by exchanging anecdotes and stories, creating goals and adventures they would someday share.

But the adventures never had all this blood. All this pain.

"Kristian." Yet the adventures did not have that voice, either, as commanding as it was musical, pulling at him as urgently as two strong but gentle hands tugged at his shoulders. "Kristian, you *must* let me get to work now."

His head jerked up as he returned fully to the present. "Aye," he conceded to Shivahn. "I know." He swallowed deeply at observing his mate's face lose yet another shade of color. "John!" he called. "Hang on, mate. Hang on. This is Shivahn. She's going to take care of you. She's amazing, John. She tended me in Prevot—"

"*You?*" The man attempted an incredulous laugh. "*You*—let somebody—tend to you?" he said between the coughs that assaulted him, instead.

Kris let the quip go ignored. Instead, looking to Shivahn, he responded, "She was worth the surrender." He let his hand slip briefly into hers as he rose. "You'll see soon enough, my friend. You'll *feel* her magic soon enough."

Even as he said the words, he felt that incredible warming of her hands in proportion to the beautiful warming of her gaze. Yet the next moment, she nudged him aside, the efficient healer overcoming the affected woman once more. "*Back,*" she ordered him, nudging him aside— though doing so with a subtly intimate motion. With a rapid flash of a smile, Kris obliged—

Only to halt at John's protesting growl. "Nay!"

The man paid the toll for his outburst by writhing in another wave of pain, but seemingly found the fee worth it. Kris, on the other hand, leveled a glare at his mate dipped in everything but contentment. "Blast you, John! This isn't the time to prove the size of your cods with the size of your obstinance!"

"Blast *you*, ya halfwit nodcock." The man arrowed a hand up and wrested a quivering but unignorable fistful of Kris's shirt. "I've paid Zeus's own ransom to half the guards in Prevot, bloody near promised my firstborn child in service to the Insurgents, then let them haul me through those hills as some kinda initiation rite. You think I did it to pass along the latest White's club gossip?" The tirade concluded with John shutting his eyes and concentrating on taking a deep breath. "Sit . . . down." He snarled and rasped at once. "Just sit down, and listen to me for once."

Kris looked at John's fingers, clammy and trembling, against his shirt. After a half moment of deliberation, he lowered himself back to the bench, waving Shivahn away even as she tugged at his other arm in objection. He'd become the bridge between patient and healer, and he was determined that link was erected properly. And swiftly.

"What is it, John?" he asked.

Amazingly, his friend smiled. Yet even the sheen of his fever sweat seemed to wane as he beamed that grin. "Spread yer wings, Kristian. 'Tis time for ya to fly again."

Kris didn't say a word as he responded with a hard swallow. "John—do you know what you're saying?"

"I know how to use the code, damn it."

"But you're saying the *Sea Wing* is—"

"Fully rigged and stocked, and ready for her captain to take her wheel again."

Kris dragged an agitated hand along the side of his head. "Praying your pardon, Sir Confidence, but she's also tethered in Dublin Bay under the nose of a round-the-clock patrol."

"Not anymore." John emitted short, puffing laughs as he savored Kris's reacting gape. "Aye, lad, we did it. We broke our girl right out from under those fop-arsed bastards. Navigated her outta the bay myself, exactly fourteen days ago."

To his surprise, Kris encountered little problem envisioning *that* occurrence. The net his brain kept floundering in was dropped earlier in the scenario—namely, when he tried to comprehend what had happened to that "small matter" of the battalion posted to shoot anyone aboard his ship, let alone hauling anchor and sailing the *Sea Wing* off the dock.

"But . . . how?" the net finally freed him enough to query.

" 'Twas Nathan," John supplied. "He forged the false

release papers, then snuck them into a stack of other documents Sandys had to sign."

"Is that all?" Kris slanted a sardonic brow. "And Nathan just sauntered into Sandys's headquarters with the daily bread delivery, did he?"

"Nay. 'Twas his own face and prisoner's rags he wore. He'd merely spent the whole week telling every guard and soldier he'd rather kiss their arses before dying in the bowels of Prevot."

"And they believed him?"

"He got his audience with Sandys, did he not? *And* the signed release papers for the ship."

Kris couldn't voice a word of argument to that. "The little sly-sling," he murmured, shaking his head. "He might have made a decent living in the theater, after all."

Still, one last confusion needled his mind. Kris raised sights back to his friend with a furrowed brow. "John, if you had the *Sea Wing* free and clear of Dublin, how the hell did you end up back in Prevot?"

John wanted to laugh in reply to that. Kris observed that much; he watched his mate fight for the breath in his lungs and another smile on his lips, but John's broken body obliged with neither. "You really—don't know—the answer to that, do ya?" the man finally muttered.

But at that moment, Kris did know the answer. Oh, yes, he knew, and that explanation flooded his mind with slow heat and filled his gut with hot bile. Still, he shook his head in denial at his old friend.

"Nathan and I—went back to—get you, lad."

Kris tried to jolt up from the bench. John wouldn't let him. The man poured every ounce of his remaining strength into his clamphold around Kris's wrist, strength he could have—should have—been using to stay alive.

"Kris," he rasped, stringing his odds yet thinner by wasting his breath on words. "Kris, damn ya, now listen—"

"Damn me?" He sat back down with violent force. "Damn *you*, you half-brained oaf, when *you're* the one who risked not only your own neck—"

"And now you're gonna render my effort for naught?" came the retort, which might as well have been a murder accusation.

"Your effort was stupid," he slung back.

"Hmmph. Look what ocean is calling the river green."

"I didn't sneak *in* to Prevot."

"But ya would have, for either Nathan or me." Then, in a hoarse mutter, "And been thrice as reckless about it, as well." When Kris only clenched his jaw harder in reply, John stated more solemnly, "Lad, we volunteered for the mission. We knew the risks. I . . . just got caught, 'tis all."

Kris hurled a rough snort of his own before snapping, "Oh, 'tis *all*."

Surprisingly, not a growl or grumble preceded John's rebuttal. "Nathan didn't get a scratch on him," the man offered on a sudden surge of diplomacy. "They never connected us. He even threw Sandys and his men off our trail." Amusement twinkled at the back of his gaze. "The worms are no doubt slogging their way through Lough Erne by now."

Kris found no grounds for returning the man's jocularity. "And that's supposed to make me feel better?"

"That's *supposed* to get your head out of your bum and thinking straight about this!" With vehemently snarling glory, the real John Petrey had returned. "Damn it, Cock 'n' Bull, ya've *got* to listen to me!"

Shivahn reappeared then, moving in to spread a bright red rose salve across John's chest. But gently, Kris motioned her away once more. He wished he could return her frustrated glare with a genuinely remorseful look of his own. But he wasn't about to start lying to her now.

Cock 'n' Bull. John hadn't called him that since he really was twelve, when he'd strut his way through fencing practices with an overconfidence that more than earned the nickname. But once John resorted to using the insult, Kris had always known to do nothing else except stop, listen, and obey.

Tonight, he stopped. And he agreed to listen. As for the obeying part—

Some rules, Kris decided, were meant to be changed.

"Nathan—and the *Sea Wing*—are in the secret cove south of Rosslare Harbor, waiting to set sail—as we speak," John stated between shallow breaths. "But beyond Saturday—at midnight—he's waiting no longer. He won't wait for me—*or* for you. We decided it as the best—"

"And it was a good decision," Kris assured his friend. "A good decision, John."

The man gave what he could of a satisfied sigh. " 'Tis about—bloody time—ya agreed with me."

"Right," Kris murmured past the painful constricting of his own chest. "Right, John."

"And now that—we're in agreement—you're gonna leave—right away."

Kris smiled at his mate with deceptive calm. "I'm going to do nothing," he answered with the same smooth defiance, "except wait to kick your arse when you wake up, old man."

John's reaction didn't come as a surprise. A slew of creatively filthy curses served as prologue to his growled, "Kristian Rayne Bastion, you're beginning to piss me off!"

"I know." *And thank God. Because if you stay alive just for the privilege of rearranging my balls, I'll gladly take you up on the challenge, my friend.*

At the moment, however, he only had to deal with the

verbal brunt of the man's ire. "Are you—listening to me?" John demanded. "Saturday is—*two* days away—"

"And Nathan knows the way back to England."

"Oh, sorry. *My* mistake," came the sardonic return. "And he—knows his way past the port authorities, too? I suppose—ya taught him *that*—one afternoon while I was napping?"

Kris suddenly found his impervious veneer not so easy to maintain. He inhaled deeply against the weight that closed around his skull like an iron helmet three sizes too small.

The port authorities. No, he had not factored them into his confidence in letting Nathan guide the *Sea Wing* home. Once Nathan had gotten the vessel to London, of course, the mighty Emery Montague name would protect ship and crew better than a brigantine-size suit of armor—but many miles of the Thames stretched between Margate and London. And in those many miles, there existed the strong likelihood of many a watchful eye or ear; eyes and ears no doubt alerted within days of the *Wing*'s disappearance, via Sandys's ocean-crossing talons of corruption.

It wasn't that Nate couldn't handle the bastards, if they really tried to board the ship. The man had more than proven himself an expert in the art of kissing British arse.

But the moment would inevitably come when he'd have to *kick* some British arse.

Nathan was an appalling fighter.

Tension squeezed tighter against Kris's thoughts. He should be on board that ship. *His* ship. And *his* crew, 150 men for whom he was responsible.

Impossible. One look back at John inscribed the word on his brain as his final decision. He couldn't—he wouldn't—return to the *Wing* without John. 'Twould be like going home without a father. And he'd lived *that* hell once already, thank you.

But Hell, he discovered the next moment, was more than happy to grant repeat visits. Helplessly he watched as John erupted into a fit of coughs, concluded by a consuming shudder, a long groan, then limp stillness. His mate had at last surrendered to unconsciousness.

"John." It emerged from his throat as more a choke than a syllable. But the next moment, he erupted into a bellow. "John!"

He lunged back at his friend, thinking if he shook the bastard hard enough, he'd awaken him from his stupor, as he had in so many dockside taverns, when they'd listen to the cock's first crow through their drunken headaches. "John, you bastard, you're not going to win the fight by pulling this!"

"Kristian."

He heard Shivahn's voice, demanding his attention in no tone to be defied. But he didn't want to heed it. He didn't want to let go the last few inches of line he still held on the mainmast of his friend. Who would hold that line if he didn't?

"Kristian, I must have room. Now!"

He turned and confronted his own desperate gaze, reflected in the urgent brightness of her own. "Help him." He heard the hoarse desperation of his plea but didn't abdicate an inch of his stance next to her. He would drop to his knees in that spot, if necessary. He affected the verbal form of doing so as he repeated, "Please . . . Leprechaun . . . help him."

She smiled at him swiftly but tenderly. "I shall try. I shall try, and you must believe that I will."

"The fencing teacher . . . Shivahn, he's the one I told you about, who helped me—"

"I know. I know who he is, and I shall try very hard." She finished with a fast squeeze of his hands. In amazement, Kris looked down to those beautiful fingers, entwined with his own for a moment that passed too swiftly. Her skin was warm despite the worsening downpour outside and the permeating chill inside, a warmth that so completely suffused his hands that everything from his wrists to his fingertips ignited as if he'd just entered the hall from a summer day in the meadow. His nerves danced as if he'd been picking heather for hours; even his blood picked up an extra pulse as her life force permeated him.

Then she was gone, as she spun and bent to the task of giving John her attention. Kris stared at her compressed profile, her gaze focused as she sliced away clothing and murmured directions to Maeve. Her hair, still wet, still smelling of the leaves and earth they'd lain in, now had a leather thong hastily twisted around it. Along her neck and arms, raindrops mingled with sweat, making her clothes cling to her damp frame. He could see the strain of her every muscle as she concentrated on her patient.

Her patient—but his mate.

He shuffled back, but he couldn't leave, not until she knew if the man needed *his* heart to keep living. He'd give it, Kris vowed; he'd give it gladly.

If Shivahn heard his pledge, she didn't indicate so. Her hands continued to fly across John's body. All too clearly, Kris remembered the magic those hands wrought inside *his* broken and battered body. Gorag's words echoed through his head next, as he'd murmured them during that sweet song of an afternoon last week. *Shivahn is a special lass . . .*

Could she be special for John, too?

In response to that, his spirit answered only with another question. *Do you believe she can be? Do you really believe?*

"You must believe that I will try, Kristian . . . you must believe."

Kris tipped his head back, looking to the shadows flickering across the dining hall's roof . . . while his soul peered into its unsure recesses.

He had to believe.

In what?

I know it sounds odd, but she worked magic on those men . . .

We did it, lad . . . worked magic, we did!

Magic. Ah, God. He might even have laughed at what Fate asked him to do this night, if only the life of his best friend didn't serve as the collateral plunked on that gambling table.

Chapter 11

Three hours and thirty mugs of cider later, the downpour ceased with a strange suddenness. But the ensuing stillness around the cottage throbbed even harder at Kris's ears, like the ringing echoes left behind by funeral bagpipes.

John wouldn't want bagpipes at his funeral.

The man would demand the bawdiest acts from the nearest pleasure fair, complete with bare-breasted fire dancers and lewd-lyricked minstrels.

"Bloody hell." Kris sliced his thoughts to shreds with the vehement growl. He attached a slew of the filthy oaths he'd learned at John's side in those long-ago London taverns. Those *wonderful* London taverns.

"We shall see them again, John," he murmured as he gripped the frame of the window he'd stood in a few days ago, watching Shivahn dance through daisies. "We shall drink a pint of ale to your health in every one of those taverns."

The sentence tightened as he uttered it, turning the final syllables into seething grunts more than spoken words. And he knew exactly where the fuel for that ire came from: the cauldron of acid and self-loathing rising to a boil in his gut.

Four days ago, he'd stood here listening to Shivahn sing Celtic fairy tales.

Four days ago, his first mate had shared moldy bread and stale water with the Prevot Prison rats.

The cauldron simmered hotter as he envisioned John in that cell now, waiting through the hours much like these, the minutes sliding torturously by as he waited for one of two voices to join his labored breaths in the darkness: either his captain, coming to break him out, or his guard, coming to guide him to the gallows.

In response to *that*, Kris's arms quivered, weathering the force of his mind's terrifyingly calm statement. *I'll wager John's guard wasn't busy listening to Celtic fairy tales.*

"Bloody *hell*."

What, in all the conceivable forces in the universe, had happened to him? There used to be a time when fury like this wasn't wasted on sulking through rainy nights. There used to be a time when fury like this wasn't allowed to *become* fury like this. No pain was allowed to haunt his days, no lust permitted to distract his nights. Most of all, no vulnerability was tolerated to any man, anymore.

No vulnerability to any man.

He'd never realized his mistake until he made it. He'd never realized a *woman* could so easily tear down his ramparts, mounting her assault with the wisteria-eyed, soft-touched force of her presence, until it had been too late. Until he'd cranked wide not only the portcullis of his body's desires but the gates of his mind and heart, too.

The same mind and heart that thudded to life as she entered the cottage now.

Angrily Kris battled the force of her—for about thirty seconds. Willing away a curse was one thing. But ignoring Shivahn was like disregarding his arms and legs. And at the moment, he needed those arms and legs to help him turn to her and ask the sole question screaming in his mind.

"Is he"—he forced out—"John?" He tried to start again. But he officially declared the words casualties when he looked fully upon the woman who'd labored over his friend through the night.

Blood spattered her bodice and skirts. She'd finally gathered her hair into a hurried bun, but tendril escapees fell loose down her cheeks and neck. Her skin was still waxy with perspiration, but appeared, even in the fire's glow, at least three shades paler than the moment Kris left her in the dining hall. Three shades *too* pale.

She looked drained. Literally. As if she'd actually mixed her warmth and magic into a concoction that flowed in her veins until she shared it with John through the spigots of her fingers. And now the spigots ran dry. Kris didn't have to touch her to understand that. The moment he met her gaze and beheld a diluted glaze instead of brilliant violet fire, he knew she'd been depleted of every life-giving drop she'd been able to give this night.

"John," Shivahn echoed him then, and startled Kris by punctuating with a weary laugh. "John is a stubborn man."

Kris didn't know how to interpret that. So he said the only logical words that rose to his brain. "That he is."

"I wager it has made him interesting to live with sometimes."

Kris still didn't know whether to add his laugh or his grief to hers. He'd not ever imagined this moment would happen, that the link between their thoughts would feel sewn of raw silk, not forged of solid bronze. As a result, he stood there as awkward and lost as an altar boy without his hymnal.

"Interesting," he finally compelled himself to stammer. "John does add *that* to a voyage."

"Well," came her heavy-sighed reply, "tonight, he was interesting enough to save his own life."

Now Kris laughed. Then he swayed, his body allowing his own exhaustion (and the whiskey Gorag had snuck into the last batch of cider) to crash through his dam of tension and dread. At last he reached for her, gathering her fervently into his arms. "Say it again," he requested into her hair, squeezing her tighter.

Shivahn laughed then, as well, and he knew their bond had been remolded—this time, of solid gold. " 'Tis true," she told him with a sexy touch of sarcasm. "Your mate shall live to torment you again, Kristian."

"Thank you," he whispered, kissing her neck, her ear. *"Thank you."*

He willed himself to remember the hours of strained exertion she'd just been through; he envisioned the battle she'd waged for the life of his mate. So he stilled his hands atop each other along her spine, and he tried to think of draining bilge water instead of her lips, nestled warm and close against the base of his neck. He tried not to think of how he hungered to kiss those lips once more, just as he had in their misty lakeshore haven, only this time, taking her mouth with the tenderness of his gratitude, not the violence of his frustration.

He tried not to think of kissing her in the same way she lifted her mouth and kissed him now.

Kris groaned: partly in overt shock, mostly in uncontainable arousal. He wanted her, immediately and intensely. And, if he rightly assessed the tiny cries emanating from her own throat, he knew Shivahn's desires didn't lag far behind. The ladder to the loft was just two steps behind him. Across the room, Gorag snored deeply in the storage nook that doubled as his bedroom.

Shivahn pushed her tongue between his lips.

He groaned again and slid his hands around her bottom.

Eagerly she slid into position against him. They fitted hip to hip, heartbeat to heartbeat, moist desire against hard desire. They shook with anguish, knowing daybreak hovered on the other side of the hour. They also knew what that dawn would now bring: the reality that had crashed back upon them sometime between a lightning flash and a thunderclap yesterday, with the arrival of four horses and a wagon on the road from Dublin.

One hour. Then the world would become England and Ireland again.

One hour. It was enough. It had to be.

Kris lifted his lips long enough to direct in a whisper, "Go upstairs. I'll bank the fire, then follow you."

Shivahn grabbed gentle handfuls of his shirt, using them to haul him to her for another thorough kiss. "Come quickly," she softly commanded.

Kris kissed her back through his growing smile, as his mind drawled the thought, *No, my beautiful leprechaun, that's not my intention at all.*

"Shivahn!" a shout ripped through the air, just outside the cottage. "Shivahn! Come quickly!"

'Twas Duncan who shattered their passionate haze once more, but now, the man's voice cracked on a note of strident panic. Kris bolted to the door ahead of Shivahn, ironically thankful for the blast of chilled air, which helped reduce the swell in his breeches.

"What is it, Duncan?" he demanded. But his heart already thundered its way to his throat as the man jabbed a frantic finger toward the dining hall.

"He needs ye, lassie," the man blurted. "He needs ye bad."

Kris's grip on the door tightened to painful severity—he chose that reaction over pounding it off its hinges in his renewed fear and frustration—as beside him, Shivahn hurried back into her cloak.

"But he was fine when I left him," she said in a shaking rush, her own dread all too potent in every syllable. " 'Twas but a half hour ago!"

Duncan scratched his head, guiding their attention to his perplexed scowl. "But *I* was with Eric a half hour ago."

"Eric?" Shivahn squinted as if a fog bank had fallen between her and the man. "What do you mean? Eric only had a black eye and a few broken ribs. He shall be up and about before tomorrow, and boasting his way through every step of the deed."

Her forecast did *not* hearten the man. Duncan's features screwed tighter in a combination of impatience and anguish, until he ripped off his faded tricorn and stabbed it at the sky. "I nay know what the hell is wrong with him, Shivahn. I only know my only nephew is sweatin' like Jesus in Hades and screamin' like Cuchulainn's bloody phantoms. Come *now*, lass, please!"

With each word of the explication, Kris watched the face of the woman next to him drain another shade of color, until nothing remained except a visage of pale dread. "You are right, Duncan," she answered in the same low but decisive tone with which she'd dismissed Kris in the dining hall earlier. "I must see him now."

Yet as she turned back to retrieve her herb sack, the confidence escaped her on a shaking sigh, leaving only trembling uncertainty to permeate the words that followed.

"God help me," Kris heard Shivahn whisper. "One more time."

Time was a bizarre companion to the mortal inhabitants of this world, Shivahn contemplated with some last shred of lucid thought left in her brain. She had never been less caring of its presence, yet she had never been more aware of its presence. She labored over Eric with single-minded desperation, uncaring whether the minutes turned into hours or the hours turned into days. Yet through it all, there sat Time on her shoulder like a bird of prey, talons digging mercilessly into her conscience . . . reminding her. Reminding her that all Fate had to do was dictate the moment he could swoop down, those great claws poised to snatch her friend . . .

The image scorched her mind more cruelly than the day's sun blinded her eyes as she stepped from the dimness of the dining hall on aching legs and cramped feet. She threw up a hand to shield her eyes from the light, cold and unfeeling in its after-storm brilliance, and wished, perhaps for the first time in her life, the sky still wept on the land. Nothing would make a better companion to the climate saturating her soul right now.

The worse realization was: She had yet to endure the darkest part of that storm.

Before she dragged her hand down, she heard the scufflings of the small crowd that had gathered there awaiting her. She suddenly wanted to run; she yearned to flee back to the wilderness from which Duncan had pulled her yesterday, where she didn't have to be anybody's "special angel," or "miracle healer" or "heaven's gift"; where she had only been all she really was: a woman, reveling in the touch of a man. She yearned to return where she was only known as—

"Leprechaun."

For half a moment, she dismissed his strong murmur to the realms of her mind's desperate creation. But then he took another step, and she smelled his essence along with the wind, all man and forest and hearth smoke.

She dropped her hand with clumsy urgency and ran to him. She threw herself into his open arms, banded her arms around his waist, pressed her face to his chest, and prayed to Heaven she never had to let go.

She also prayed for the words of confession to go away. The heat of them seared the breath from her lungs and throat and ignited tears behind her eyes. But Heaven denied her behest. She spilled the words into Kristian's chest, between her gulping sobs.

"I did . . . all I could," she rasped. "I did . . . all I could, but it was not . . . enough. Oh, Kristian . . . it was not . . . enough."

"Leprechaun," came his murmur, warm in her ear. "I'm sorry . . . I'm sorry."

"He was too . . . deeply hurt. I could not help . . . not enough." The words overpowered her heart's battlements. "Oh, God, what kind of a healer *am* I? He is gone, and there was nothing I could do . . . *nothing* . . . and now he is gone. Eric is dead."

Eric is dead.

She emitted the words in but a whisper, but like one of

the teardrops that accompanied the confession, when dropped upon the expanse of the crowd gathered around them, caused a fast-spreading ripple toward every outskirt of Trabith.

The problem was, that ripple did not remain a ripple.

It turned into a tidal wave. In every violent meaning of the phrase.

Shivahn hardly cleared the moisture from her eyes before beholding the crowd around her swell to a mob numbering at least seventy-five. When—and where—had these peaceful people she called "neighbor" suddenly obtained the new "accessories" to their attire? The men girthed themselves with sword belts, strapped daggers to their thighs, and carried everything from obviously stolen rifles to barbarically simple axes. The women donned no such gear but stood by with extra cloaks, dented helmets appearing to be salvaged from the Spanish armada ships themselves, and even a few battered shields.

Again, Shivahn gaped at the scene and silently queried: *Where? And why?*

Her answer, unfortunately, came more swiftly than the formation of the mob itself. A cart, headed by two wild-eyed horses and guided by a scowling Billy, sliced through the throng. The crowd re-formed itself around the cart's bed, which supported a sole figure.

Duncan. Or at least Shivahn *thought* 'twas he who stood there, based on the height, stature, and clothing of the man who towered even higher over his fellow villagers now. Other than those factors, she did not recognize the person she could nearly call "Uncle" as legitimately as Eric had, considering the countless times she had quarreled with her mate like a brother. Duncan had always broken in to their rows, coercing them into truces with a shared slice of spiced apple or an adventure trip to explore the monastery ruins at Glendalough.

She saw none of that gentle uncle in the figure on the cart now. Not a glimmer of peaceful intent showed in the deep-socketed glare he scanned across the crowd.

"What on earth is going on?" she asked Kristian. His answer only deepened the strange coldness that had effectively doused the fire of her tears and now coursed an icy path through her veins. He clasped both her hands, gave them quick kisses, then stepped away from her.

"Kristian," she queried with a frown, "*what* are you—"

"My friends!" Duncan shouted then. "It is time!"

Shivahn found herself pressed forward in the crowd's reacting surge, as Duncan raised his bayonet-topped rifle like some knight wielding a battle pennant. "Aye, I even say it is *past* time!" he went on, his voice peaking with a hard savagery. "It is far past time that we keep sendin' off our lads down this road, only to welcome them back by diggin' their graves!"

The crowd agreed with a roaring cheer. Shivahn's senses spun in confusion. Who *was* that person up on that cart, and what had he done with Duncan, the man who refused to carry naught but a cutting dagger when helping her free Kristian from Prevot? For that matter, where was *Kristian*? She executed a frantic twirl on tiptoes, but saw naught but the undersides of arms swung high in support of Duncan's continuing diatribe.

"Most of ye know me well," he declared then, a few syllables actually leveling enough to sound like the Duncan Thornberry she recognized. "And ye know Eric was treated like my own son, Nicholas. Well, now my Nick is out there smugglin' and spyin' on Satan's blue-blooded demons, with nobody to watch his bum for him. There's nobody to follow him anymore. Nobody to come home with him. Nobody to call his best mate . . . because tonight, we must *bury* his best mate!"

He pounded the rifle's butt to the cart bed in emphasis of that. But he continued in a decidedly softer rasp. "What rankles me deeper is that I cannot send a word of notice to Nick about it. I cannot send a messenger, even a letter, because I am afraid of what Nick would do when getting it."

"What would he do, Duncan?" The query came with equal roughness from Billy, who'd tethered the reins and now leaned on one of the cart's back wheels.

Duncan lifted his head, first meeting his friend's earnest gaze, then turning his sights to the crowd again.

"He would come home." Each word was clearly steeped in his raw yearning for such an occurrence . . . but every inch of his face was carved in his raw fear of such an occurrence. "Damn it," he grated then, "my son will *not* come home to his own grave!"

Not a bird twittered during the hushed moment that followed. Then a voice near Duncan's feet called out, "Mine, neither!"

"Nor mine!" another joined in.

"Nor mine!" one more yelled.

Duncan acknowledged each of them with feral-eyed nods. "Ye are with me, then," he said, then spread his arms to include the whole crowd. "Say ye are *all* with me now, to at last level the odds with the butchering British bastards!"

"Aye!" the trio at the front chorused.

"Say ye will stand with me, to show them why we are called Ireland, not New Britain!"

"Aye!"

Shouted by the entire crowd this time, *that* sent the birds bursting from the trees.

That, Shivahn thought as her heart collided with her

lungs, was how the bards would record the start of Trabith's first uprising against the British.

The realization flooded her stomach with bile and inundated her mind with shameful shock. There had been many an eve, when bent over rows of battle-battered Insurgents, when she had envisioned this occasion with searing want. Aye, she had even prayed for it, dropping to her knees before any heavenly or magical power upon which she knew to call, angrily begging for her sleepy little village to do something about the pool of blood their country was sinking into, rather than watching the spectacle from their safe hiding place of this forgotten valley.

Yet then, she came home. And then, she always took the requests back.

Did she not?

It did not matter. Not now. Clearly, enough others had delivered similar prayers to hers, and they received their answers now from a clamoring, outcrying mob.

To her bizarre horror, Shivahn could only watch the scene unfolding now. She could only stare in bewilderment at the transformation of the people around her. She gaped at faces that had crinkled in laughter and shone with smiles only yesterday, now repoured into molds of wrath and revenge. She watched Maeve's Monday eve knitting group sharpen swords and bayonets. The village's apprentices and sheepherders—boys of but eleven and twelve—now practiced with flintlock pistols and poison-dipped arrows instead of hammers, awls, and herding rods. The frenzy sucked in even the smallest of the children: Rhianna raced by with her father's dagger belt; Sarah and Rachel added twin-size quotation marks to everything their own papa said by proudly skipping around his huddled strategy session with Duncan and Billy.

The strategy session in which they plotted how to kill as many Englishmen as possible.

As many Englishmen as possible.

A sharp, hurting sound tore at her throat. The outcry nearly burst past her lips before she restrained it behind locked teeth. Shivahn did not summon the strength to her legs so well; her buckling knees sent her flailing for support against a pointy-barked pine tree.

But she barely noticed the bright red cuts the tree inflicted across her palm. Not when her soul fought the pierces of deeper wounds. "Kristian," she grated, already breathing hard in her battle. "Kristian."

As many Englishmen as possible.

How long would it take them to remember they already had an Englishman ridiculously close by? she thought. *Two* of them, as a matter of fact?

About two seconds, her mind answered with ruthless brevity. Mayhap less than that, she determined, if Duncan's fury churned deeper than she fathomed. Oh, aye, she had seen such things happen before—and she shook clumps of pine needles loose from above by merely thinking about such a scene now. They would forget everything about the man they had once called mate, except for the fact he was the first Englishman they could mutilate on their mission of frenzied revenge.

"Kristian!" She emitted it now as half a rasp, half a sob. She shoved away from the tree and frantically stumbled toward home, fighting her way through the chaos of humanity all pressing the opposite direction.

All, that was, except one person.

Twenty feet ahead of her, sending mud chunks flying in his terrifyingly determined wake, was Norman MacLewis. Nobody else in Trabith had such an unmistakable mane of black hair—and nobody else would be racing his way toward her cottage with one intent so discernible in his unfaltering gait:

Revenge.

"Oh, God!" Shivahn blurted, yanking her skirts past her knees to catch Norman. Yet as she did, another part of her seemed to glide effortlessly over the ground, not laboring at all to breathe, completely warmed from the inside out. She had never experienced this duality of person before; an occurrence similar to how she felt before the Giving, only stranger, hotter . . . stronger.

She had no time to question the bizarre sensation. Instead, she was forced to let the invader help her, a lightning bolt of force sizzling up her arm and into her hand as she caught Norman by the shoulder and spun him about.

Along with the sharpened hunting dagger he gripped in his fisted hand.

Aided again by the strange surge of inner power, Shivahn leapt back with half a second to spare before her belly knew a lethal slash of the dagger's blade. "By all the *Sídhe*, Norman!" she cried out. "You are going to bloody *kill* someone!"

That was also when she beheld the full, wild force of rage in her friend's gaze. " 'Tis the general intent a man has when his best mate has been murdered," Norman snarled without a trace of remorse. "Now get out of my way, Shivahn."

She expelled a quick breath. He still knew her name. Part of Norman—the part she and Eric had laughed with over many a poteen and soda bread—was still left inside this man. Swallowing deeply, Shivahn stared deep into her friend's eyes, looking for *that* Norman once again.

As she did, the heat grew stronger. This time, she shook her head against the force, not wanting to obey its consuming command.

Its command for her to lower her fingers to Norman's wrist . . . on the hand with which he clutched the dagger.

And yet, as she did just that, she heard herself murmur to her friend, "Kristian did not kill Eric."

"Don't," Norman seethed back, his muscles struggling as if she held him with steel bands, not the tips of her fingers. "Don't, Shivahn! You loved Eric, too!"

"I loved Eric, too." She trembled then, knowing she was as frightened as he. Nay, *more* frightened. *What was happening?* Her voice . . . 'twas hers, yet not hers, as if another person lived inside her and only now, in the midst of this suddenly insane day, had clamored free of the bonds in her brain. Had clamored free for the sole purpose of healing more than just her friend's body. This time, she had to heal his *heart* . . .

For only then would she save Kristian.

"Let me go, Shivahn!"

"Drop the dagger, Norman."

"Nay!"

"Drop—the—dagger."

At first, she did not recognize the strangely soft *thunk* at her feet. Then, looking down, she thought Norman's action an accident—until she realized her friend gaped at the fallen weapon with more unblinking disbelief than she. Still, her mind could not accept the import of what her eyes so clearly proved; her senses could not comprehend the force that had overtaken her as mysteriously as the wrath that had descended upon Trabith.

Norman suddenly wrenched free of her and, with naught but one last, crazed glare at her, ran back for the mob at the dining hall.

The mob raised another round of air-splitting shouts. Shivahn fought a sudden and sickening onslaught of dizziness and tried to discern what words they bellowed to the treetops and beyond. But it nay mattered; not really. Whatever they shouted, it would surely involve more of them coming to hunt down Kristian. She did not have the strength to thwart a mob.

"God help me," she whispered, wheeling around and forcing her legs to stagger on to the cottage. "God help me," she repeated when she stumbled through the door with heart thundering and lungs heaving. "Kristian . . . Kristian . . . oh, God, please—"

"Leprechaun!"

The urgent whisper came from the storage nook. Shivahn reached it before releasing her next breath, which burst from her on an elated outcry while she hurled herself against his beautiful, proud, *living* body.

"Damn you!" she rasped into his neck, as her head spun again, and she clung to him tighter. "Damn you, I thought they—that you—"

"I know," he murmured back, his lips pressing her neck as his arms surrounded her in unalterable strength. "I'm sorry."

"You are not forgiven."

"Then I'm really sorry."

He pulled away enough to show her the darkening ocean mists of his gaze, telling Shivahn he wanted to prove his penance by kissing her, and kissing her well. Despite the spinning snarl of her senses, Shivahn admitted she yearned for naught more fervently than for just that kiss.

And yet, naught terrified her more acutely. That terror infused new force into her limbs, thrusting him away as she exclaimed, "Kristian, you are *not* safe! Duncan has lost his head, and yours may be soon to follow!"

His eyes' sensual haze now solidified to the gray-green determination of a storm front. "I know."

"We must get you out of here."

"That's the plan." He made the statement while turning and completing the task of stuffing bread and cheese into a small shoulder satchel. "It should have been the plan a week ago," he added, yet finished the clenched growl by surrendering to a wince of pain. With that, he all too clearly told Shivahn he had indeed cast aside his splint too early.

Despite the increasing thunder of her heartbeat, thanks in no small part to the distant but growing tumult outside, she summoned every drop of self-control not to push him into a seat in front of the fire that instant. Once she had him there, she would lecture his witless brain while she fixed his arm again.

Instead, Shivahn grabbed the second bag from him and set about packing the thing herself. "I hope you have included my comfrey roots and dried yarrow in this pile," she groused as she did. "They are my best help with bones on the mend. And that arm of yours needs all the help you can beg, borrow, or steal for it."

She knew a moment's surprise when Kristian did not respond to that with a sarcasm-drenched quip. She knew a moment's more bafflement as, with his back still turned to her, he sucked in a tight breath and did not release it.

Finally, he muttered, "I'll get the arm taken care of as soon as I'm back on the ship."

"Back on the . . ."

The words did not sink in until she looked down and truly observed what she had loaded into the sack. One coil of lean but strong rope. Two wood-handled instruments that could have been gardening trowels, save their wickedly sharp end points. And three round balls that could have been the lettuce heads those trowels dug up—save their "leaves" of cast iron and their odor of loose gunpowder. She had never seen grenades before but had overheard more than enough infirmary tent conversations to know a trio of the devices when she saw them.

As well as what they were used for.

For one more moment, Shivahn stared unblinking at the collection of weapons bunched in the cloth between her hands. Over the years, when forced to, she had wielded the occasional pistol or dagger during her service to the Insurgents within Trabith's proximity—but she had never held *this* much potential for destruction by herself before.

If the bag became the head of Sandys himself, she could not have dropped it more swiftly. "The *ship*?" she repeated, stripping all camouflage from her demanding tone as she leapt back over the bag to follow Kristian in his sudden flight across the room.

"You heard me correctly." He did not break stride, even as he flashed a quick glance between the front shutters. "Gorag's gone to sneak John out of the dining hall, then see us to the mouth of the pass. John and I will continue to Rosslare from there—" His tone dipped as his eyes did. "And we'll pray we're not too late."

At that, at last, he halted. As if putting his words into action, his head remained bowed as he jerked a chair out from the table and straddled it backward. From where Shivahn stood she now only saw his profile, his eyes tightly closed, his jaw rigidly set, the waves of his hair tousled in a thousand hand-worried tangles . . . so like the emotions twisting in her own heart as she watched him and watched him and tried to think of not ever watching him again.

She could not. By the saints, she *would* not. She could not flick away this urgent pressing on her chest any more than she could on that black night in Prevot, when her Brave One had turned from her with that same cloak of clenched tension around his shoulders, before telling her he would be gone forever on the morrow . . .

Just like then, Shivahn began her battle against Fate with one clenched, resolute word. "Nay," she ground out, setting her shoulders and pressing her hands into the folds of her skirt. "You cannot go. For God's sake, Kristian, have you so swiftly forgotten that English maniac who wants to kill you?"

He did *not* help her resolve with his dismissing bark of a laugh. "Have you so swiftly forgotten the Irish maniac who wishes the same?"

Shivahn drew in deep air at that, certain the perfect words of a comeback stood ready to dance across her tongue. But no such defiance came, or would be coming. The maddening mule before her was truly right this time. They could not simply hide him and Sir John in some nearby cave or forest while the majority of Trabith traipsed the countryside with a few decades' worth of hoarded weapons at their ready.

The best place for Kristian was on his bloody ship.

She trembled as the realization swept her with the force of a January gale. But in another way, she welcomed the tempest, for its invasion also blew aside the excuse of rational thought and all its boundaries. Sheer survival instinct now took over her heart—and her next words.

"I wish you a swift and safe journey, Kristian," she murmured with calm compliance, surprising even herself.

"Thank you, Leprechaun."

"Especially because I shall be on it with you."

He did not waver his tone, but he did not have to. As he delivered his dagger to its boot sheath with one sharp jab, Shivahn instantly grasped the sentiment beneath his low words. "The bloody hell you will."

"I did not *ask*," she countered before he finished. She had expected, and prepared for, his response. "You have no choice about this."

"The bloody hell I don't."

Kristian moved to step around her. Shivahn stepped with him. When he persisted in continuing, she did, too. She stepped *on* him, her boot toes atop his, forcing him to haul her along with each step.

"Damn it"—he growled—"Shivahn—"

"You need me. It is an inescapable fact. Simply admit it, Kristian."

"Nice try," he shot back. "I hate to break up that little celebration in your head, but I can cross the Irish Sea blindfolded in a rowboat."

"And you can cross the Wicklow Mountains as easily?" She hoisted her chin in mayhap too much assurance, but by now, she followed instinct too desperately to care. "You know where and how your countrymen have carved their Military Road through the ravines in those mountains and where they've hidden their outposts along the way? And you know the alternate routes to take that will not kill you even more mercilessly?"

She could have halted there, her argument well made, judging from the tighter scowl across his lips. But like a warrior heady on the encroaching taste of triumph, she plunged more ardently into her siege. "Once you descend to the Vale of Clara, I assume you know the swiftest route to take across the bogs. 'Tis not a mere skipping distance to Rosslare, as I am certain you also know, and you do only have until Saturday midnight, if I heard correctly last eve, and—"

"You heard correctly," Kristian finally cut her off. With a pair of swift, jerking motions, he stepped back from her.

Shivahn decided prudence best overruled instinct through the next moment. She said nothing, and held back excited twitches from her lips as his own muttered a string of agitated curses.

At last, he spun and commanded from between his teeth, "Rosslare." He jabbed an equally dominating finger at her. "You'll come as far as Rosslare, then you'll return your devious little arse back here faster than Gorag can spit. *Those* are the terms, Shivahn. Don't *think* of crossing me on them."

Shivahn only laughed at that as she sailed into his chest and pressed her cheek against the wonderful, rigid, rain-dampened strength of him. "Why ever do you think I would do such a thing?" she quipped, wrapping her arms tight around him.

She ignored his incredulous grunt of a reply. Who was he, to presume she did not mean every word she said? After all, *this* time, the man's orders made sense. Sailing with the ship and Kristian and his whole crew back to England . . . 'twas not only an utterly improper idea, even for a maid from a village the history books would never remember, but an invitation to danger even in the thinking of it. An impossibility. Aye, most definitely an impossibility.

So said her head.

In her heart, Shivahn refused to give up the dreams from which magical happenings were often born. The happenings that became the rhymes of the minstrels' songs and the grand moments of the bard's tales. The happenings in which Brave Ones and Leprechauns were bound together, no matter what the forces scheming to tear them apart, to accomplish the feats destined for them by the powers who saw all and knew all.

The thought bloomed like a lover's promise in her soul, spreading warmth throughout her limbs despite Kristian's frosty new demeanor as he stomped around adding provisions for one more traveler. Shivahn merely smiled at his stiff spine and felt the warmth thicken to an aching, womanly sensation at knowing she would be near him for at least one more sunrise and sunset.

Be angry for now, Kristian, she told him from a suddenly peaceful realm inside. *For all too soon, we will behold your great and grand sea. And in the hours between now and then, I will pray for a way to show you I have a heart filled with enough dreams to bridge it.*

Chapter 12

ris didn't know how he'd let himself forget the most important characteristic about leprechauns.

They were devious as hell.

But forgotten that fact he had, and this particular imp had used the weakness against him at the most opportune moment she could.

He twisted the reins harder, slowing the cart over a rocky patch in the path and allowing at least an iota of his tension free. Still, the leather burned his fingers as memories of her *coup de grâce* assailed him in agonizing detail. Again he saw the crafty wench literally walking all over him, stepping on him rather than moving aside for him like any docile, *normal* woman.

He should have been filled with rage at her audacity. Instead, a wash of arousal, instant and hot, had diluted his wrath to uselessness. The mere press of her toes upon his had begun reverberations of sensual sensation he'd never experienced before. He recalled trying to ignore how strange—and sexy—it was to become aware of a woman from the opposite direction of normalcy . . . appreciating first her shins, *then* her thighs and their warm juncture, *then* her breasts and her mouth . . .

God in bloody Heaven, her mouth. He recalled trying to ignore the triumphant, adorable grin that had spread on that mouth, as she spouted her case with witful candor that should be outlawed at such a level of potency in one woman.

By all of her ancient saints, he'd tried to be furious with her again. He'd *been* trying for the last ten hours, as they'd traversed the heights of the Wicklows, escalating what seemed the ramparts of the gods' own citadel. All around them, cliffs had jutted into the heavens, dark purple and slate gray into cloud-studded blue, a display of might and majesty unmatched by mortal efforts. After the mountains, a man's breath rushed from him again when descending into the vales: first Clara, with its mists tucked like a maid's treasured laces among hidden meadows and medieval forests, then Avoca, where the Avonbeg and Avonmore became the hypnotizing elixir of the River Avoca.

It was all unashamedly wild, unabashedly bold, unmercifully beautiful. It was land that transformed a man's soul through his senses, making all the stories of the great Irish pagans no longer exciting fireside fare but easily conceivable truth. On the crests of these broad ridges, Kris saw the mighty Finn MacCool, leading his warriors with a bold swagger. Against this stormy sky, he beheld the noble Niall of the Nine Hostages, gazing toward the sea that would carry him on another grand foreign conquest.

Just one disconcerting element recurred with each of

those scenes. In each of the imaginings, his mind all too easily painted Shivahn into the wild, mystical picture, as well.

Paint her back out, *Montague. Paint her out of your mind and your life. You were insane to have thought this story would have any other ending than this.*

Insane, or enchanted.

He vented a snort as that thought became a full realization. How many times in Trabith had he gazed around him, wondering if the place was really the subject of some storybook spell, or if he finally was out of his mind, when neither conclusion was the truth? All the time, the enchantment had flowed from the woman in the cart behind him, rendering a man unable to discern his nays from his ayes, or the head above his waist from the head lower . . .

Making a man act much the way John did now.

Kris's teeth sawed against each other as another of his mate's chortles rocked the cart. Every muscle from his shoulders to his wrists coiled in expectation of Shivahn's answering laugh. She didn't render his effort for naught, but she hadn't since they'd skirted the mixture of old and new structures at Enniscorthy, and the two of them had struck up this little party of a conversation—and John had swiftly, obviously decided himself besotted with her.

Two hours had easily passed since then, and Shivahn had made *no* effort to diffuse the man's interest.

Not that he'd noticed, Kris qualified. Or cared. He *didn't* care. The wench had been a pleasant diversion during a badly needed holiday. Now, thanks to John, he wouldn't have to worry about what he'd say when leaving her at Rosslare, or about the expression on her face as he did . . . or about the pain he'd expected in her eyes. Now he actually looked forward to seeing his bunk on the *Sea Wing*, for he didn't have to worry about her haunting one minute of his dreams.

Ah, God, what she did in his dreams . . .

He wound the reins tighter around his fists, grateful for any pain on which to focus other than the fire suddenly razing his chest and sending red smoke across his vision. He narrowed his concentration on those fists through the next countless miles, shifting his grip only to guide the horse at the landmarks Shivahn had briefed him to observe.

So fell the night, and so continued the journey—until they topped the last high hill overlooking Rosslare.

Just as the horse judged the slope to be passable and began the downward hike, Kris glanced to their left, where Johnstown Castle rose majestically from its acres of surrounding estate.

The moment he did, he hauled the reins back with a slew of oaths. The horse skittered in protest. The cart jolted, then violently swayed.

"Jesus, Mary, and Joseph," John blurted from where he'd been knocked against the cart's right side, if Kris discerned the accompanying *thunk* correctly. "What the hell has jumped your skin, Cock 'n' Bull? Some screaming banshee?"

"Worse," Kris snapped, though not swerving his glare from the scene illuminated by every lighted window in the castle. "Sorry to break up your little *tête-à-tête*, friends, but we've got company. The red-coated type. And plenty of it."

John fired off a string of profanities that turned Kristian's oaths into lullaby lyrics by comparison. Yet despite the flush saturating her cheeks as she listened, Shivahn wished she could join the man.

Kristian's grim tone hardly did justice to the panorama she beheld with increasingly painful breaths and a heartbeat echoing in her ears louder than Billy's *bodhrán* drum. Johnstown Castle bled everywhere in unmistakable British red. The bastards in crimson poured from the main portal and oozed along the front drive, a festering wound she yearned to obliterate with a swipe of her hands.

That was, if they did not notice the cart, overcome it with but a third of their numbers, burn it to the ground, and add her head to the embers.

Before they did God-only-knew what to Kristian and John.

Her mouth suddenly became dry and hot enough to bake bread.

"Must be at least three battalions' worth," John growled. "Maybe four, depending on who's inside or on patrol."

Shivahn moistened her lips enough to rasp, "Do . . . do you think they are here waiting for you, Kristian?"

"They're not looking for fairy dust." She watched his posture stiffen against the thick, gray night sky. He did not turn even a glance at her. Then again, Shivahn noted with an uncomfortable quirk in the pit of her stomach, he had not since they had departed Enniscorthy.

"They know *something* is brewing around here," John muttered darkly. *"Damn."* He whacked a fist into the cart bed. "Nate had 'em swarming north faster than fleas on a nag. I woulda bet my balls they were swimming the North Channel by now."

"I can hear everyone rushing to the dice table now," she answered that before thinking to control her sardonic words or tone—to which John reacted with a short yet equally inappropriate chuckle.

"Christ on a bed of nails," he finally uttered. "Where *did* ya find this minx, Kris?"

Despite their perilous situation, Shivahn allowed half a smile to break free as warmth took the place of the twist in her belly. She nay knew why, but it had been important to gain the goodwill of Kristian's best mate before they left. With John's affectionate tone, she knew her endeavors neared success.

The missing spark of that victory had yet to be even a glimmer in the eye of the man she stared at now—the man who pivoted long enough to snarl at them. "Mayhap you two would like to offer these bastards some tea, as long as you're announcing our presence to all Rosslare."

"Trim your sails, Cock 'n' Bull," John countered. "I'm thinking. And while you're at it, why don't ya steer this contraption to the side o' the hill where they *can't* see us?"

Kristian grudgingly heeded John's suggestion. But his spine straightened once more when they saw what waited for them on the other flank of the rise.

Rosslare Harbor. And another half mile down the coast, so she had been told, the nearly invisible cove where the *Sea Wing* awaited its captain and first mate for another hour at best.

"So close," John murmured, the clench to his voice aptly matching the frustrated strain in her own muscles. "We're so damn close, but we might as well be . . ."

Chivalrous tact transformed his words into a trailing sigh, but Shivahn could have have finished the sentence for him, so clearly did she know what the words would have been.

We might as well be back in Trabith, he would have grumbled, *taking our chances with Duncan's mob instead of half the red-coated bastards in Ireland.*

She should have gone ahead and voiced the statement. Mayhap the truth cold have cleared enough air to breathe in the thickening cloud of vigilant tension surrounding them—

the haze gaining access even to *her* thoughts, strangling each hope she mustered. She envisioned the *Sea Wing* as best she could from the mentionings Kristian had given her about his vessel; she saw the proud bow carved with its gold-edged wings; her mind's eye watched the dedicated scramblings of its crew along the plain but polished decks . . .

Suddenly she gasped. Her spine nearly impaled the back of her skull, so sharply did a terrible thought yank up her gaze.

"Kristian," she blurted, rising up on her knees in the cart bed, "Kristian, what if they have found your ship already?"

"They haven't."

He issued the rebuttal swiftly and coldly, as if merely speaking to a parlormaid in his grandfather's castle. A there-but-not-there person. Certainly not a person he had lain with in the mists of a lakeshore twilight, consuming with his kisses, igniting with his touch, traveling deep inside of with the magic of his tender whispers.

Defiance surged through her, hot and strong. On its crest rose the inclination to hurl his icy indifference back at him just as her forefathers had flung broadswords through the necks of Diarmuid Macmurrough's traitorous knights.

But you swore more to him, came the rankling if damnably truthful reminder. *You swore you would show him the sea of your heart is bigger than his sea of pain. You even prayed Heaven would give you a chance to show him that.*

Your chance has all but crashed in to your dock, Shivahn. How the next leg of the voyage is navigated is up to you.

"If they'd found the *Wing*," Kristian continued then, still directing his glare out over the horizon, "there wouldn't be so many of them left here. And whoever *was* left wouldn't be just lolling about. They'd be gathered around the cove, waiting to ambush us at our weakest moment."

"You've hit the bull on the butt with that one, lad," John confirmed. The man spit over the side of the cart as if he'd just eaten rotten fruit. "Pansy pisspots wouldn't want to chip a fingernail by facing us the honest way."

"Well, then," Shivahn responded with forced brightness, "that should make it easier for us, aye, once we get around them at this point?"

Neither man's response remotely rewarded her for the effort. At least John tried, giving her shoulder a gentle pat.

Finally, Kristian cocked his head to emit on a sardonic drawl, "Would anyone like to present any suggestions on how to carry through Mistress Armagh's brilliant strategy?"

Let us begin by throwing our captain into the ocean. Shivahn's lips trembled against the temptation to spit out the words. Heaven's chances be burned; she should let the man sail off to his own bloody island and give him her ecstatic farewell in the doing.

"Well, we're asking for capture and killing as long as we're in *this* contraption," John ventured with an ironically breezy back-wave of his hand. "Which, in my humble opinion, only leaves one answer to your question, Cock 'n' Bull."

"Oh?" Kristian returned with equally feigned civility.

"We get out and hike to the cove."

He might as well have suggested they storm the castle. As Kristian spun back to the horse, he retorted with equal vehemence, "The bloody hell we do."

"The bloody hell we *don't*. We're as appetizing to them right now as fat, juicy ducks, and you know it."

"Need I remind you, Sir Petrey, that twenty-four hours ago, you were a half-dead slab of flesh with more open wounds than a harpooned whale?"

Kristian delivered the comeback with more confident relish than Billy threw darts. He even swung one leg back around as he did and leaned a cocky-angled elbow on his bent knee.

Astoundingly, John gave him naught but a serene smile in reaction. "And need I remind *you*," he drawled at last, "that twenty-four hours ago, this lassie began working her magic on me? I feel like a new man today, thanks to her."

Normally, Shivahn would have replied to those words with at least a small smile. Instead, her brow rumpled deeper as she moved her stare to Kristian, who swiftly averted his glass-hard glare. She watched his hand rake a stiff path to the back of his head, and she felt every taut notch of frustration in the motion—but the thoughts that had driven the action had been thoroughly, purposely sealed off from her.

By Saint Patrick himself, 'twas if, when healing the wounds in John's body, she had somehow inflicted them on Kristian's spirit.

"Kris," John broke the pause in a determined murmur, "do ya understand what we're facing here? We have no other choice! Listen to me—this plan *will* work. If you move ahead and scout the route, and Shivahn helps me along behind—"

At *that*, Kristian bolted to his feet. "No." He snarled. "No. If we leave the cart here, we leave Shivahn with it. I'll not have her driving back when they're finally on to us. They'll immediately search the streets for accomplices. 'Tis too risky."

Five seconds passed of a telling pause. "Bloody hell," John rumbled then. "You've hit another bull on the ass, haven't ya?"

"You are asking that question of the wrong friend, Sir Petrey," Shivahn immediately returned. Both men's gazes shot to her, but she focused her own attention on the glare emanating from the driver's bench, hard and dark as a lichen-covered gravestone, set above a mouth locked in determined impassivity. "Who are either of you to decide the risks *I* take?" she leveled with tantamount conviction and unwavering tone.

Yet in her veins, triumphant satisfaction bubbled—for in Kristian's eyes, shadows suddenly shifted. As for what those shadings meant, or where they had come from, she did not know, nor would she allow herself to care. She would revel in the knowledge that she still affected him somehow. *Somehow.*

But like the countless other contests waged between Irish and English bloods over the centuries, her victory was chopped ruthlessly short. "No," Kristian quietly decreed, into the air heavy with approaching fog. "No. Shivahn stays here, and that's the decision."

" 'And that's the decision!' " John echoed in a mocking baritone. "Thank you, ya blue-balled Napoleon. I'll remember ya the next time I meet someone soliciting for a controlling bastard to—"

A sudden slash of Kristian's hand cut short John's tirade. But the action was not resented. Shivahn watched as John rose cautiously to his knees, uniting himself with his captain once more as they peered hard into the surrounding shadows for the source of Kristian's alarm. Shivahn joined them from her own position in the cart bed but heard naught but the ocean waves in the distance and the closer scufflings of field mice and badgers. In the recesses beneath the birch trees, she detected only moon shadows and fallen leaves.

But she allowed her posture to relax only when Kristian did so first. 'Twas only some loud night creature, she assured herself, probably as perturbed by these boys' debates as she.

That was when her heart was jerked out of her chest by one night-rending bellow.

"Freeze in the name of His Majesty George the Third!"

A collective clunking of boots, bayonets, and muskets gathered into a dauntingly huge half circle behind them. *I am dreaming,* Shivahn's mind pleaded her in the ensuing half second of silence. *Every moment of this day has been but a strange unbelievable dream, and now it is becoming a nightmare. There are truly not a hundred British bastards standing there about to murder me, and I am truly not this horridly petrified.*

But then John shifted next to her, raising his hands in surrender, and the all-too-real wafting of his body odor told her just how real the nightmare had become. "Bloody hell," he muttered under his breath.

That was why Kristian's laugh, not only loud, but dramatically so, clapped her muscles into even more shocked paralysis. "Gentlemen!" he called through the final chuckles of that outburst, "I believe you have made some sort of a mistake here." The corner of her eye caught the easygoing outspread of his good arm. "My mate and I are merchants who sail beneath the same flag as you. We were on our way home from the market in Cork when an knotwit greenhand put a rip in our spanker sail. We dared not attempt the crossing without it, so we have put into Rosslare to have it repaired.

"In the meantime, my friend and I have sought out a little . . . diversion, you might say, during the delay."

A suggestive smoothness took over his tone then. If that did not make his meaning clear, Kristian lowered his hand atop Shivahn's head, stroking her possessively there. The action, so simple, restarted the maelstrom of confusion inside her. Did she kiss him or kill him? Oh, aye, his swift thinking might just save their lives—she only wished the plan did not entail stirring up the carnal side of these soldiers' imaginations.

One soldier moved forward from the rest. A lantern-bearing lad of about twelve years accompanied him. Then again, the two could have been brothers, so young did the features of the soldier himself appear. Except his eyes. In another ten years, Shivahn thought, this lad would have the eyes of a monster like Sandys. He had well begun the process already.

The soldier surveyed Kristian for a moment which felt like a century. "And your name, Captain?" he finally demanded.

"James Summerall." The syllables slipped out as if Kristian gave the name a thousand times a year—or at least a thousand times before tonight, Shivahn suspected. A glance John's way confirmed her theory. Though his arms remained skyward, he looked for all the world as if about to stifle a yawn.

"And the name of your ship, Captain Summerall?"

Kristian released an indulgent chuckle. "Really, gentlemen, I fail to see how that matters in this—"

"You were ordered to halt, sir!" The shout came as Kristian hooked his leg back over the driving seat and reached for the reins.

"And I told *you* there's been a mistake, soldier." The amiable merchant disappeared from his mien. Shivahn easily recognized the persona who stepped in: the defiant warrior whose presence had dominated a Prevot dungeon cell, even when facing Sandys himself.

And this field soldier was not Sandys—not yet. He did not surrender a step at Kristian's rejoinder, though he looked like he wanted to. He blinked rapidly, as if mentally tearing through the pages of some sacred procedures manual and not finding the answer for situations like *this*.

Finally, the soldier motioned forward a comrade, who looked even younger than him. "What think you, Philip?" he asked tightly of his friend.

Philip had obviously been awaiting his chance to speak. "They have a woman," he asserted eagerly. "And you remember what the orders were from Sandys. Montague might have a woman with him. A woman—"

"With those odd purple eyes," the first soldier finished, grinning triumphantly. The pair locked hands with swift excitement—probably the same handclasp they had shared when mastering their Latin lessons or drowning their first cat, Shivahn surmised. If they topped the act with falsetto giggles, she would gladly give in to the nausea clawing at her belly.

They did not giggle. Instead, the first soldier marched closer, becoming the monster-who-would-be-Sandys once more. "We would have a word with your wench, Captain," he demanded.

It seemed the nausea would gain the better on her after all, Shivahn concluded between the wash of dizziness in her head and the loss of all known strength in her legs. She flashed a wild stare up at Kristian, her eyes translating what her soul desperately begged him: *Nay! Do not let them take me—you* know *what they shall do to me!*

"Captain Summerall! We would have a word with your wench!"

This time, Kristian replied to the soldier. But he did not do so with a falsified chortle or an easygoing gesture or even the sharper side of a growl.

He muttered the comeback beneath his breath as he grabbed up the reins and snapped them hard.

The words were "The hell you will!"

The cart lurched to life, knocking John off balance in half a second. Shivahn gasped, envisioning every stitch she had put into him ripping asunder, until she realized her fears were for naught; *she* broke his fall. They rolled together into the left side of the cart as Kristian drove the horse to a hard right, down the back side of the hill, straight toward the curve where the harbor made its bid inland.

"Get down and hang on!" he directed over the crossbow-taut line of his shoulders.

"*Now* he tells me," John groused at that, which made his next action even more astounding. John's hearty laugh filled her head as he released it but an inch from her ear, followed by a sound giving vivid life to the war cries of her heathen ancestors. "Here we go, lassie!" he cried gleefully. "Bet ya've never seen your bonny country from *this* angle, eh? Hee-heeee!"

Through the next whirl of minutes—or it could have been seconds, or it could have been hours—Shivahn could surely answer the man with an adamant *aye*. Over the rumbling thunder of the cart wheels beneath them, outraged shouts and pummeling hoofbeats confirmed the Brits no longer believed in the existence of one Captain James Summerall and now have full chase to the escaped traitor Kristian Montague and his Irish wench accomplice.

Over several more hills they bounded, bumped, and raced; through countless night-damp meadows they streaked; through at least a dozen moments did Shivahn survive the complete cessation of her heartbeat, certain her body would not care about it the next moment, anyway, because she would be dead.

The worst of those instances came when she dared a glance up, peering through the window made of the cart's driving seat and floorboard on top and bottom, and Kristian's braced legs on either side. A joyous grin exploded on her lips when foam-topped waters met her gaze. The next moment, a shocked scream stole the smile. A hand was clamped around her arm. She wrenched around to find the most horrid of her nightmares come to life: a British horseman, leering greedily, preparing to haul her onto a ferocious-eyed steed.

The soldier had made only one lethal mistake. While freeing his second arm to secure his grip on her, he swung his bayonet flat against his back. 'Twas the moment John awaited. The next moment, the bayonet was in his grip. The moment after that, it was buried in the soldier's chest.

They sped on toward the water.

As the rumble of the cart now gained an echo of crashing waves, the smile curved its way back onto Shivahn's lips. The scent of her fear began to mingle with salty mists and a bracing wind. At last they cleared the crest of a broad hill, and the waters of Saint George's Channel spread before them, magnificent even though inky blackness shrouded the cresting waves.

"We are here!" she exclaimed to John, who only grunted in reply as he busied himself reloading his confiscated crossbow. The sight of the weapon, sleekly dangerous, sharpened the edges of her ecstasy with the fear she still should be clinging to, but it did not diminish the core of that hope-kindled flame. They were here, so close, *so close;* how much farther could the bloody cove be now?

Besides, she heartened herself, not a single horseman gave chase to them any more. They had run Sandys's gauntlet, and won! The only reason Kristian still drove on like a madman was the ever-rising arc of the moon overhead. 'Twas almost midnight. Shivahn felt it in the increasing impatience of her spirit—as well as Kristian's.

Kristian's spirit. A small cry escaped her, uncontrollable yet unnoticed by either man, as that comprehension flooded her heart with joyous understanding. Before tonight, she had grown so accustomed to the invisible connection of their souls that she began even to take the link for granted, like the gift of a precious ring, always there around her, but not always acknowledged. Until tonight, when Kristian had strangely and suddenly blocked her access to his half of the ring . . .

Their pursuit by half the forces in Rosslare must have effectively diverted his attention from that effort. Sometimes, Shivahn supposed, even murderous British bastards served their share of wondrous purposes.

But Fate had a way of eavesdropping on somebody's most incriminating thoughts, then expounding on them. And Shivahn never wished her thoughts more into meaningless oblivion than she did with Fate's intervention of the next moment—when what looked like an entire battalion of horsemen crashed through the trees at them.

"Saints in Heaven!" she gasped.

"Bloody hell!" John yelled.

"Hang on!" Kristian ordered.

He meant it. Very much. Shivahn found out how much as the cart went up on its left wheel, presenting her with a reeling, blurry view of the clouds, the channel, the shore. Then the ground swept periously near again, freshly churned by the horses that now plowed into the forest to their immediate right.

The jarring *thunk* of the next instant signaled they rode level again. Years of dried undergrowth crunched beneath them and flew up at them, joining an army of pine needles, flailing at them in the wake of their intrusion. In the midst of it all, it seemed the fairies themselves guided the horse over every fallen log in the wood, sending Shivahn three feet into the air every time they jolted over one of the moss-covered obstacles.

After the tenth of those bruising ordeals, she began to search her memory for some of John's more satisfyingly colorful curses. She picked one out and even, in a small and strange way, looked forward to using the forbidden words—

When the cart broke from the trees and skidded to a stop in a small bank of gravelly sand. Though *small* was the grandest of exaggerations in this instance, Shivahn decided during her next moment of scrutiny. She looked out to observe this mound comprised the only serviceable "shore" to a vast, tree-shrouded lagoon.

A lagoon currently occupied by one of the most magnificent brigantines she had ever seen.

"Oh," she breathed. "Oh." With sails fully flung to the silver shadows of the sky and decks shifting in the reflections of night waters, the reasoning behind this vessel's name no longer remained a mystery. Indeed, the *Sea.Wing* looked more than ready to take flight over the trees, riding the wind on its canvas expanses, its keel trailing a wake of star shards.

The envisionings did not strike Shivahn as one bit fantastical or unreal. After all, she surmised, with Kristian Montague at a vessel's helm, anything was thoroughly and incredibly possible.

The awestruck pulses of her heart doubled into the meter of renewed panic as an ominous creak suddenly reverberated around them. Along with John and Kristian, Shivahn watched as their exhausted horse strained his foam-flecked muzzle toward the cool waters and dragged the beaten cart right along behind.

With their first step, the left wheel shuddered.

With their second step, the right wheel followed suit.

With their third step, the whole thing careened into the water with the grace of a dying goose.

Shivahn nay knew if the horse took a fourth step. When she regained her footing on the lagoon's mushy floor, 'twas to find Kristian's hand on her forehead, plunging her under the frigid water again. Furiously she flailed at him—until her brain reverberated with sharp-accented shouts, slicing through the night:

"They're here!"

"We've found them; sound the trumpets; they're here!"

"Ready all guns and fire at the captain's mark! We'll carry 'em back to Sandys the way we should, mates, in their coffins!"

"In their coffins, aye!"

"Aye!"

Oh my God! The phrase echoed in Shivahn's mind, screaming the words her lips were too paralyzed to form. *Oh my God oh my God oh my God oh My God.*

Next to her, his nearly submerged face draped in ghoulish lagoon moss, Kristian invoked the opposite end of the spiritual kingdom in a scathing oath. "First Mate Petrey," he followed to it as the distinct *thwacks* of loading muskets resounded across the water, "open ears will receive your suggestions of what to do now."

" 'Tis a bit obvious, Cock 'n' Bull," came the physically labored but heartily spirited reply. "We do the backstroke."

"But . . . can you make it? John, are you sure?"

If she did not concentrate so hard on forcing air to her lungs and sanity to her brain, Shivahn would have shed mirthful tears at the image John presented, rolling his eyes below moss-drenched brows. "Shut up and swim, Kris," he retorted, and splashed toward the ship.

But for all of Kristian's promise of the contrary, he did not need John. Instead, he turned back to her. And for one moment, just that facet of a moment in the middle of this impossible night, Shivahn found the magic of the moon in the silvered planes of his gentle smile. She found the emerald strength of an Irish midnight in his penetrating gaze.

But more *thwacks* ripped the moment asunder. Shivahn blinked again, and once more her gaze was filled by the Kristian of focused command and impenetrable control. 'Twas that Kristian who shot one more glare back at the bastards who grew closer by terrifying degrees, then arrowed his stare back into her.

"You *do* know how to swim," he commanded—not asked—of her. Quickly, Shivahn nodded. "Good," he responded, "because you're going to swim for your life now, Leprechaun. Let's go!"

Chapter 13

e had not meant the words lightly. Shivahn swam for her very life, especially as shouts erupted from the shore: soldiers calling to each other as they stripped out of their weapons and boots for a chance at capturing bare-handed the prize of Kristian Montague . . . or, as second prize, his "healer harpy."

With that thought, she not only caught up to Kristian but churned through the water past him. Stimulating her strokes were the splashes of lead rifle balls, plunking lethally into the water all around her, as well as a frantic glance backward, to discover the arrival on shore of a truck cannon the size of a vicious dragon.

She nearly cried in relief when John's bellow reached her, and she looked to see him directing her to the port side of the ship. There, a rope ladder dangled and swayed in the midnight winds. As she doubled her strokes, aiming herself there, she spied a myriad of crewmen scrambling up and down the shrouds, positioning the sails to capture the full power of those winds. The other half raced along the *Wing*'s rails, returning the Brits' fire with lusty war cries.

As she neared the ladder, Shivahn felt smaller than a sand crab encountering a chunk of driftwood fitted with masts and sails. Her fingers shook as she reached for the first rung; her muscles quivered as she pulled herself out of the cold water, into an even icier wind, and began the wobbling climb up the towering height of the hull.

When she'd covered what seemed half the distance, she paused to allow herself a small smile of triumph—

Until the ship suddenly rocked from more than just the swell of the lagoon waves.

"Coming about!" she heard John exclaim above. "All hands to stations; we're coming about and breaking out! Hee-heeee!"

Shivahn shot an astounded glance upward. Coming about? They were coming about *now*, and John was laughing about it? He *laughed* as the now-pitching rail sent the ladder—and her—into a crazier career of motion, with no more security than a heather bud possessed against a high moor wind?

Even as the thought churned through her mind, her senses rejected it as impossible. John had just guided her to the ladder himself. Surely he had not forgotten her here, especially when his own captain had yet to board behind her!

Dear God and all the precious saints, her heart rattled off at that, *Kristian is still behind me . . . isn't he?*

If the heavenly hosts deemed to answer her, John's cackle, even louder now, drowned their response. "Aye, come after us now, ya milk-sopping, ball-sucking donkey's arses!"

Mayhap he *did* need a reminder that not all guests had arrived at the party yet.

With that conclusion, Shivahn tossed back her head and called to the upper deck ten times over. Then ten times more. But the wind now snapped the *Wing*'s sails to full attention. She heard the dull but rapid thuds of every crewman hurrying to his duties, effecting the turn of the ship toward the veil of trees which, until tonight, had guaranteed the cove's secrecy. That meant the *Sea Wing* had nearly "flown free" of its red-coated pursuers—

It also meant, for the next ten or fifteen minutes by her estimate, that this side of the ship would be vulnerable to fire from the shore. Including anyone hanging on rope ladders against the hull.

John or no John, 'twas time to get herself up the second half of this ladder. Now.

She cleared the next five rungs with the ease of an old jack-tar. Then a blast of wind whooshed over the *Wing* from behind. 'Twas a boon for the sails and a disaster for her. Shivahn shrieked as the ladder twisted on the gust. She screamed as her left hand slipped loose and her right quavered visibly. She begged the rest of her body for any scraps of remaining strength; her muscles responded with trembling futility.

"Oh, God," she rasped. "Oh, God and the forces in all Your heavens—" She finally rewound her left hand around the rung again, but she might as well be paralyzed for all the help it gave her there. "Help me!" she pleaded. "Oh, help me!"

"Shhh." The sound filled her ear in the same manner his body moved up and around her: like molten steel, with unmistakable strength. "Shhh now, and do as I say."

"Kristian!" She nearly wept the word as she dropped her head back into the crook of his neck. "Thank God!"

"You'll be saying those thanks to Him in person, if you don't listen to me," he snapped. She gave a fast nod of understanding.

"All right," he continued, "let go with this arm first, and then your left. Wrap them both around my neck, and follow with your legs around my waist. Got it?" The last two words came out as terse bites, as he shifted into position around her.

"Nay," she protested. "Nay, I do *not*. Kristian, you want me to—"

"*Trust me.*" His tone wasn't terse this time. The words were blatant commands of anger now. "Just as I asked you to trust me in the tunnel at Prevot, Shivahn. Just as I trusted you with the life of my best friend. Well, now 'tis time for *you* to trust *me* again." He had to yell his concluding charge over the cannon blast now erupting from shore. "Make your decision and follow it, woman—now!"

Whether she whirled around and against him as unthinking reaction or an actual act of trust, Kristian had no time to contemplate—or care.

No, he ordered once more to himself, he did *not* care. He did not care how his muscles surged with strength from the instant she pressed around him, her shivering smallness igniting a primal need to show her she was secure in his care. He did not care about the sea-spiced sexiness of her wet curls as the wind spattered them against his face, nearly blinding him. Nor did he care about the magical resurgence of stamina she gave him with a fervent kiss on his neck when, because of that blindness, he didn't gain enough footing on a rung and slipped, nearly sending them both back into the gunpowder-encrusted water.

"Kristian," she'd followed that kiss with the press of her soft lips to his ear, "I believe in you, Brave One."

But he didn't care.

Who the bloody hell was he fooling?

He cared with gut-tearing intensity, especially as he at last heaved them both over the top rail and saw he would not get away with simply slipping the *Sea Wing*'s new passenger down the back hatch and into the safety of the secret hold. He cared as he watched the head of every crewman on deck glance their way a first time then a second, as they realized the captain didn't bring the ladder up with him, but something with more captivating legs and more interesting . . . rungs.

"Gentlemen!" he bellowed, sweeping them all with one glare. "The last time I looked, this ship was under pursuit!"

They gave him no reason to elaborate. But as he watched them scatter to different stations like ants disappearing back into baseboards, Kris savored no satisfaction at being the captain who had bullied them there. He drafted a swift promissory note to order the Barbados rum and the French chocolates to be brought out as recompense, perhaps at tomorrow's supper, as soon as they'd gotten Shivahn safely back on land and were well on the way back home.

As soon as Shivahn was safe. As soon as they'd set course back home. He greeted both the thoughts with deepening degrees of a grimace. How simply his mind popped out the assumptions; how swiftly reality blasted him into remembering those dreams still lay on the other side of impossible—not to mention what seemed half the British militia stationed on Ireland.

The same militia that now detonated a white-gold cannon

blast fifty yards off the port hull and succeeded in aiming the shot through the *Wing*'s galley window.

The hit sent a column of debris-laden smoke into the already murky air. Kris took in the sight with a mixture of gratitude—they hadn't gotten an inch of the hull, after all—and fury. Mostly fury.

"John!" he roared across the main deck. He found his first mate precisely where he'd expected to: in the middle of the thickest gunfire and the deepest wreckage. "Send Adam and his crew down to the gun deck, and tell them to use the truck cannons. We're through playing manor host to these bastards!"

The eager readiness of John's nod confirmed he'd already anticipated that order. Kris followed his mate's gesturing hand in time to watch Adam and crew dash to, then drop down the aft deck hatch as if a bevy of long-legged doxies waited instead of the truck guns.

He grunted in grim satisfaction at the sight, but only during the moment it took him to whirl back upon the woman at his side. "As for you," he ordered, "come with me."

It took just one moment to discover his not-to-be-questioned tone was unnecessary. For the first time since he'd known the woman, Shivahn responded with a completely obedient nod.

Kris scowled—until she lifted her gaze to his. Her eyes were brilliant with focused attention. She began to slide her hands back and forth against each other, as if priming them for action. Before his eyes, she became an even bolder, more powerful version of herself—the legendary Insurgent healer, now ready to leap into action on behalf of his crew.

Not now. Ah, God, not now.

As if he really needed more endorsement of that, another cannon blast rent the air. The vibrations of the decks identified the unnaturally swift handiwork of Adam and mates, but that only meant they had now asked for the full brunt of return fire from shore.

Which only intensified the need now burning its way through every inch of Kris's system. The need to keep this woman alive during this chaos—no matter how much she was going to hate him for it.

"Come on," he growled, putting a halt to her eager hand-rubbing by grabbing her fingers and hauling her down the starboard deck, toward the same hatch Adam and crew had disappeared through. But halfway there, a frenzy of shouts on the shore preceded a new profusion of gunfire. The resulting pounds and pongs on the decks began to correspond with every terror-induced lurch of Kris's heart.

"Hell," he gritted. The next moment, the oath emerged as part of a stronger epithet. He shouted the words through another spattering of rifle fire, as he finally surrendered to the urge to scoop her off her feet and press her close to his torso. To his deepened surprise, Shivahn didn't utter a word of protest, even helping him by wrapping her arms around his neck.

He molded as much of himself around her as he could, holding the position until he at last let her down again, in front of the door to the only cabin at the rear of the ship. His quarters.

As he threw the latch and shoulder-butted the door open, he allowed a sardonic grimace to flash across his face. He'd never let a woman enter this, his private sanctum, though he'd sure as hell indulged visions of the day he'd find both a woman and a moment worthy of the risk.

Sizzling gunfire off his starboard bow and bellowing cannons off his port bow had *not* been part of those fantasies. But ah, God, how perfectly Shivahn fulfilled her role in the scene. Kris watched her enter the cabin while he ignited the lamp secured to the bulkhead. Even soaked to the skin, she was femininity incarnate against the dark woods and brass fixtures of the cabin. He took in the curlicues of her hair, stuck to the wind-flushed curves of her cheeks; he even noticed the granules of sea salt lingering on the ends of her eyelashes, forming glistening fans around the inquisitive depths of her eyes.

Oh, yes, he greedily drank in every wet, wild, womanly detail of her. That was when he realized she didn't just fulfill his fantasies . . . she surpassed them.

As his hand lowered from the lamp, she asked, "Where are we?"

"My cabin." He crossed to his bunk as she advanced toward the constellation chart tacked to the hull over his desk. *Good girl,* he silently encouraged her. Mayhap if Cassiopeia and Orion absorbed her concentration, she wouldn't notice his next action until it was too late.

But Cassiopeia and Orion weren't about to be so benevolent. "Your cabin is nice, Kristian," she declared, pivoting back around as Kris secured his knees on the feather and ticking mattress. "But now I would like to go back above."

She issued the declaration even as the hulls around them quivered violently again. The crisis was more than enough to dissolve any other woman into grateful monologues about what a valiant captain he was, to ensconce her in the safety of his own quarters while cannon balls and rifle fire dueled through the air above. Any woman, Kris amended, but Shivahn Armagh, who'd been ready to face Sandys again rather than the confines of a tunnel that could easily accommodate this cabin.

Which meant the next five minutes might become the bloodiest battle he'd ever fight.

With that conclusion, he commanded his mind to stay focused on one critical point: Battles were won with careful strategy, not overpowering brawn. He repeated it as an inner litany while he extended his hand to her, softly dictating "Come here, Leprechaun."

She looked at his upturned hand as if it had become a dragon's claw. "But I do not like it down here, Kristian."

"I know, Leprechaun."

"It is *crowded* down here, Kristian."

"I know." He kept his arm extended and his stare fixed upon her, while reaching his other hand back to push at the wall behind his bunk. The panel acquiesced after a short jerk then a soft-scraping sound. He revealed a compartment able to easily hold half a dozen shipping crates—or one sweetly-curved Irish rebel.

"Come here, Shivahn," he repeated, making no effort to mask the meaning in his tone. He owed her the honesty of knowing his intention, no matter how huge of a monster she deemed him for it.

Or no matter how tormentingly huge her eyes grew, as she peered to that blackness behind him and realized she beheld the depths of her own fate.

"Nay!" She slammed back against the hull, looking as if she yearned to become *part* of the hull. "Nay, I will not 'come here'!"

"Shivahn, *don't* make this harder than it has to be."

"Go to hell! What do you know about how *hard* this is?" She'd barely finished before attempting a desperate lunge for the door. But Kris had kept his arm extended with instinctual foresight. With a rough grunt, he caught her around the waist, swung her back against his chest, and began counting bruises as she flailed, kicked, pummeled, and elbowed him.

His fantasies had certainly not prepared him for *this*. But somehow, he ruminated, contemplations of pulling a woman into one's bunk should not have to include the variation of wrestling her there.

"Shivahn—" He managed with impressive composure, considering her elbow had just landed three inches shy of assuring he'd never sire children. "This is for your own good!"

"This is for *your* own good!" came the fiercely flung comeback. "You would lock me up in this hold like an animal rather than—"

"Let you get raped and abused and mutilated?"

Like the growl upon which he emitted them, the words lashed savagely through the air—and finally, it seemed, into Shivahn. First, she went utterly still in his hold. After a moment in which neither of them breathed, she squirmed again, but this time, she deliberately fought to be closer, not farther, from him.

Before Kris could recoup from that startlement, he found himself confronted by her upturned, scowling face. "What the bloody hell is that supposed to mean?" she demanded.

He raised both arms at the elbows. "No hidden meanings," he replied simply. "Because you know if those bastards get aboard, they won't have any hidden meanings, either. Think of your own experiences with them, Shivahn, and you know I speak the truth."

Ironically, 'twas the bastards themselves who provided the most convincing confirmation of his assertion. Corresponding to the final word of his statement, another cannon blast exploded from the shore and streaked across the water like a sharpened dagger through Chinese silk. The sound ended in a shattering crash above, echoing in violent shudders throughout every beam in the ship.

Shivahn's hands raced up to Kris's shoulders. "Dear God," she whispered, trembling more visibly than the hull.

"Kris!" came John's bellow from the top of the aft hatchway. "Galley's been hit again! Get your arse back up here!"

Kris slid a hand to her suddenly pale cheek. "You heard the man, Leprechaun."

Pure fear shimmering in her eyes as she did so, she gave a faltering nod and rasped, "Aye."

The sound pressed a primal, painful weight against Kris's chest. He battled the unseen enemy with a hard swallow. No use. The only assuagement of the pressure came in tunneling his hand through to the back of her hair and pulling her tight, then tighter still, against him.

"Shivahn," he grated into the wet mass of her curls, "I'm asking you to trust me again. Can you do that?"

His ears heard the desperate supplication of his voice. His mind reeled in questioning shock at where and how his pride had so easily fled.

His heart didn't give a damn. "Trust me," he breathed to her again and again, realizing the plea was now a litany as much for himself as her. He began to taste her between each word, kissing his way around the salty-sweet crescent of her ear, suckling his way along the dewy line of her jaw. He finally sealed himself atop the damp, expectant upturn of her lips. Shivahn moaned. He moaned. Mouths parted. Tongues mated. The world disappeared.

Almost.

"Kris!" John's roar again. Every oath the man had ever taught him screamed through his brain. Raw want for this woman flared hot and consuming through him, even stronger than the first time she'd incinerated him, on that filthy floor in Prevot.

Kris remembered what he'd wished for in that long-ago moment. He'd wished to have her here, in his bunk, on his blankets, writhing against him. And now all he could do was devour her in one last crush of his mouth to hers, sweeping his tongue into every moist corner of her delicious wetness, before dragging himself away, trying to rip his gaze away from the hypnotizing sheen of hers.

"Slide the panel shut after you're inside," he told her, though pausing midsentence to suck in breath between the pounding of his heart and the throbbing between his legs. "There's a handle on the inside. Don't let go of it until *I* come for you." He reached and slammed his hand over hers for one last second. "Do you hear me, Shivahn?" he demanded. "Don't open up for anyone but *me*."

She nodded sharply. Then she raised one last stare, filled with the courageous smile she strived to work to her lips, but their kiss-reddened surfaces tremored too fiercely to cooperate.

"I'll be back," Kris promised her, the weight on his chest compressing his voice to a taut growl. "I'll be back *soon*."

He whirled and dashed from the cabin before observing her reaction to that. If he did otherwise, he admitted, he'd capitulate to her damn fool notion of accompanying him above. And doing that would be as good as inviting these animals aboard for tea and scones—not to mention a tasty "piece" of his little Irish guest. For if *that* happened, he'd really have something to worry about.

Because if they touched Shivahn, they'd have to kill him first.

With that resolution, he hit the deck at a full run, sprinting straight for the thickest mass of the gray-white haze, which now blocked even the tops of the masts from view. As he'd expected, he found John there. *And* the heap of wood, glass, and lead pans that had been the galley. *And* the majority of the rest of the crew, charcoal-faced and weary-eyed—

And grinning at him like a band of pirates who'd just absconded with a hold full of booty.

At the perplexed scowl he raked at them in reaction,

those leers threatened to dissolve into outright laughter. All, that was, except for John, who knew his roar of a laugh would garner him naught more than a disgruntled glower from his captain. Which it did.

His thumbs hooked into the length of thick rope acting as his belt, the man sauntered forward to regard Kris with the mirthful stare that hadn't changed since their adventures in Castle Clay's forest, when he'd topple Kris from whatever tree limb had been drafted into service as the "main yard-arm" for the day.

"Well, Cock 'n' Bull," he announced, "yer timing, as usual, sucks as bad as those bastards' aim." That consumed the last inch of latent gunpowder on the touch holes of the crew's composure. The explosions of their laughter formed the background to John's explanation. "We've cleared the lagoon, Kris. Ya missed all the fun!"

Instantly, Kris navigated a reversal of his expression. From a crunched frown, he hoisted eyebrows into slants of astoundment. That fervor took his legs on a direct course to the port rail. Once there, he stared hard into the haze that some supernatural doxy had dropped over the Rosslare Coast like her gauzy underthings.

Sure enough, as his sights grew acclimated to the muck, solid shapes took form: the jagged tops of the trees that had been unflagging guardians of their hidden cove, then the slopes and cliffs of the ensuing shore.

Kris still stared into the fog as John joined him at the rail. Still puffed with more cheek than a cabin boy who'd docked his first whore, John flashed a smirk. "Figured ya'd have yer hands full with the minx, so I told Nathan to chart the course for Portsmouth. Those red-coated wankers are more'n likely expecting us at Cardiff or Plymouth, so I wagered we'd cruise down the Channel a bit and keep 'em guessing long as possible. Besides, Nate needs the practice."

Kris delayed for one moment before responding to that. When he did, low yet steadily, he didn't veer his sights from the depths of the fog. "Then he'll be getting some more practice now."

"What do ya mean?"

"Tell Nate to chart north, not west. We're putting in at Wexford first."

John's reaction came as no surprise. "By Jesus and all the—did we use yer brain for cannon shot by mistake back there?"

Kris allowed himself a trace of a smile. "My brain is where it's always been, thank you."

John did *not* see the humor, however minuscule, in the comment. He shoved from the bulwark to adopt a hands-on-hips stance he must have picked up from Maeve. His whole mien bore the stamp of Trabith's fiery matriarch. "Then what is this about?"

With his response, Kris at last looked to his mate. "You mean *who* is this about?"

John's gaze darted from deck to shrouds and back again, reflecting his scramble to interpret Kris's look. Kris hoped, in this rare instance, the man's wickedly astute instinct would fail him and, ergo, drop him into prideful silence.

But John's instincts were damn near invincible—as proved by the next moment, when he looked back to Kris with an enfuried gape. "Awww, *no!*" He drew the second syllable out on a disgusted groan. "Don't do this to me, lad. Don't tell me yer gonna risk this vessel *tonight* because of one wench—"

"That one wench is more danger to us than three of Sandys's battalions," Kris cut him off. He emphasized his explanation by scooping both hands into the air, a symphony conductor refitted in Irish country clothes. "Her hands have well nigh earned her a sainthood with the Insurgents. Do you know what that means?"

After a telling instant, John's face screwed into a capitulating glower. "Aye, damn you," he muttered. "Those Irish heathens will be racing the red coats for our arses. The stubborn shits will win, too."

At that, Kris did let a chuckle slip free—though inside, he conceded that getting the better of John comprised only half the cause for his celebration. He'd be able to go and free Shivahn from her dark prison now, and he hoped, regain control of his breathing patterns in the doing. From the moment she'd looked into the secret compartment in his cabin as if gazing into the mouth of Hell, some hidden chunk of his own heart had begun a dreading thrum of its own . . . as if, beyond his consent or control, her fear had entwined itself into his senses, as well . . .

It was irrational, he knew. Beyond understandable; defiant of all explanation. And yet, he barely gave the occurrence a passing shrug. Wonders like this, Kris conceded with a resigned grunt, were going to be thousand-times-a-day incidents as long as he and Shivahn remained within a bird's flight from each other. And *that* condition would be modified inside another two hours. Thank God.

Kris lingered at the rail a moment longer, allowing himself a self-pleased smile in anticipation of his soul's approaching peace. Thank *God*.

During that moment, that grin plummented. The same way his confidence plunged into horror's ice-encrusted grip.

The same way he watched a longboat splash down from the main deck of the British frigate that had suddenly materialized out of the fog next to them.

As soon as the ten-passenger boat hit the water, a row of muskets and rifles appeared along the frigate's rail: a line of black circles so meticulously spaced, one would think an oversized black pearl necklace were laid atop the bulwark, instead. Steel chinked coldly against steel; now the weapons were not only aimed but ready to fire—and despite John's earlier jibe, across the distance of only fifteen feet separating the *Wing* from the frigate, the soldiers *would* hit whatever, or whomever, they sighted down their barrels now. With deadly accuracy.

Still standing next to him, John wished the musketholders to a dozen corners of Hell in as many painful ways. Kris silently seconded each of the epithets. If some part of his mind had pondered how intense his dread could *really* get tonight, he doubted that question lay unanswered now. He didn't know if his heart had given up in shock or still thundered in rage; an explosion of a headache blocked that knowledge as completely as it overpowered every other awareness in his body.

Except for the awareness of the red-coated swine on the opposite deck now shouting an order for their halt and surrender. As if they could or would do much else. How *had* the damn frigate appeared nearly atop them, Kris raged, without a swish of bow waves or snap of rigging to betray its approach?

The possibility of the whole circumstance was irrational. Beyond understandable. Defiant of all explanation. And just happened to occur when he had a healer harpy stowed in his hold who sprinkled buds of impossible circumstances around her like Fate's little bridesmaid.

Shivahn!

The outcry hurricaned through every corner of his senses, eclipsing even the din of his headache. But not a sound emanated from his throat. Kris swallowed as he threw a quick glance to the rear hatchway and issued a silent roar of a command there:

Shivahn—ah, God, Shivahn, if there was ever a time for

you to obey me, 'tis now. 'Tis now, *Shivahn! Stay in that bloody compartment, Shivahn!*

As the contingent from the frigate hoisted themselves through the port gangway, a moment of dark humor gave his terror an instant of reprieve. Comparing the vessel's leader to swine had been a more accurate presumption than he'd dreamed. Captain's braid adorned the shoulders of o̅ne man in the group, who waddled forward with such ponderous steps and nostrils flared so wide, Kris wondered how Gorag's prize hog had gotten itself promoted so fast in the ranks of His Majesty's navy.

Kris strode forward to meet the man. They stopped opposite each other in the middle of the main deck. He continued to hold his tongue. The bastard may have appeared like tomorrow night's boiled ham, but at least twenty-five marksmen awaited but a breath of a firing order from him. Kris knew it; the swine knew it; the swine lifted a greasy smile because of it.

"Well, well." The bastard's voice still resonated with the nasal squeal that had issued their boarding order. "What a pleasant surprise this is. I have the pleasure of meeting you at last, Captain Montague."

Pleasure didn't describe Kris's perspective on the situation. He prepared perfectly sardonic yet seething words to tell this little pisspot just that, and shifted his jaw into an angle of defiant insolence with which to fire them—

When another voice erupted through the mists instead. A voice filled with musical strength yet steel-strong conviction, as it called out, "Begging your pardon, sir . . . but he is *not* Captain Montague."

Everyone on the deck snapped startled stares toward the aft deck—except Kris. He drove his own sights to the deck at his feet, beseeching whatever forces were listening that the voice had been an angel, a fairy, or even a kelp-haired sea witch; anything or anyone except the voice he now affiliated with pagan Gaelic songs, sweet-belled laughter, and passion-breathed sighs.

But the next moment, he recognized John's slightly limping step, sidling cautiously next to him. He also recognized John's surreptitious murmur, meant for his ears alone:

"Christ's toes, Kris. What the bloody hell does your minx think she's doing now?"

Chapter 14

That was certainly the question of the hour. The question Kris craved to shake out of "the minx" himself.

No, he corrected himself while forcing his gaze toward the aft deck, he wouldn't shake it out of her at all. He'd shove aside every layer of her sodden skirts, throw her across his lap, and spank every word out of her, one commanding whack at a time. Mayhap receiving the punishment befitting a recalcitrant wench would make her think twice about so easily casting herself to the role next time.

If she ever had the chance to contemplate a next time.

If the swine and his piglets didn't decide to make her the next main course in their trough.

And who the hell are you thinking to fool with those hopes, Montague? More important, who the hell is she thinking to fool?

The litany of both those questions throbbed in every agonizing pulse of his blood as he along with every other gaping dolt on the deck watched Shivahn approach the frigate's captain with serene gaze and steps taken so smoothly, a body would think she floated instead of walked . . . that was, if she wore flounced silk instead of wool still wet enough to form a clinging silhouette of her hips and legs.

Damn her. Damn her. *Damn her.* The sight of her, far too alluring for her own good in front of these animals, rushed his senses past possessive rage and into the envisionment of his helplessness as he and John lay in chains with the rats in the frigate's hold, listening to every pitch of her screams as the swine forced himself upon her. *This* was undoubtedly their fate, he told himself, as soon as Shivahn sashayed close enough to the swine, and the bastard indulged his first touch of her incredible skin.

Only with the help of John's grip and the effort of his shaking muscles did he restrain himself as she glided closer to the frigate's contingent. Leaping across the deck and strangling the life from a Royal Navy captain would only assure a bloodbath on this deck, and he refused to sacrifice his men in that way. This current tactic slaughtered only him, by slow and tormenting chunks, from the inside out.

Another of those chunks writhed in its death throes as she stopped before the swine. Shivahn's footing placed her a clear foot from the man, but his girth separated them by another foot. Good, Kris concluded. Very good.

But he still had to live through the moment when the bastard claimed *his* leprechaun.

God, came the plea from a deep, aching part of him, *dear God, help me through this.*

And dear God, help her.

But as he willed himself to observe the encounter across the deck, Kris found his gaze held by more than his own self-volition. As a matter of point, he saw it was the *swine* who looked in need of Heaven's intervention.

Just like the members of his crew around him, the officer couldn't rip his gaze away from Shivahn. And while that in itself wasn't so odd, as proved by the reaction of the *Wing*'s own crew to her a half-hour past, Kris registered a distinct difference in the way she held this group's attention now— as if she really *held* their attention . . .

In much the same way she reached out and held the swine's hand.

Kris blinked hard and shook his head. Surely, in watching the encounter from twelve feet away, his mind created incidents that weren't really occurring, as well as the officer's docile acceptance of them. Yet even after Kris dared three steps closer; even after he really beheld her slender, pale fingers entwined with the pudgy stubs of the swine's hand, he had yet to observe even a crack of a lascivious leer at the captain's mouth. He didn't see a twitch of temptation to slip a quick feel of breast or thigh, either.

Not usual operating procedure for the esteemed bastards of His Majesty's Royal Navy.

The next act of this spectacle commenced with a queenly nod of Shivahn's head. A smile traced its way around her lips as she prompted the swine, "You are . . . Captain . . . ?"

"R-R-Reisinger," the man supplied for her in a rolling stammer. "C-Captain Reisinger of His Majesty's Royal Navy, my lady."

At that, Kris snapped a stunned glance to John. Already awaiting him: the startlement stamped on John's own features. Together, they mouthed, *My lady?*

"Captain Reisinger," Shivahn repeated, the words flowing like Celtic folk harmony off her half-smiling lips, "I think you have all made a terrible mistake."

Reisinger's brows arched into his pasty-skinned

forehead, actually appearing to give that suggestion serious consideration. "Beseeching your pardon, lady, but that's not so likely. This ship is the *Sea Wing*, former property of one Kristian Montague, who is wanted by my comrade, Major Sandys of Prevot Prison, for heinous crimes to the crown of England."

Comrade my arse, Kristian allowed at least his thoughts to rage at the man.

"Montague escaped from his cell three weeks ago," Reisinger went on, "and this ship disappeared shortly after that. And now, it appears we have felled both birds with one stone, as it were. Both Montague and the *Sea Wing* . . . must be our lucky night!"

He included his men in the last of that, and they joined in his cocky chortle. Yet as one, their grins fell just as swiftly, when they glanced to Shivahn's expression of very *un*chortling sobriety. An almost eerie sadness had begun to fill the gaze she swept on them, like candlelight straining to gain clarity behind lavender-tinted glass.

A damp stillness befell the deck. That was the moment Kris *felt* the change beneath her gaze, as well. He felt the frantic beating of her heart against her ribs, even as he felt the contrast of the bizarre mist that had inundated her mind, like some unininvited yet ever-powerful spirit. Then suddenly, he felt that spirit solidify into a frisson of lightning heat, racing down her arm and into the fingers she squeezed tight, tighter still, around Reisinger's hand.

"This is *not* Captain Montague," she said to the man then, and Kris didn't think he'd ever heard a more eerie yet unignorable sound. Her hand trembled against Reisinger's, and she inhaled an equally faltering breath, yet he had never witnessed her features set in such desperate intent, even when she'd first clutched him in Prevot; even when she'd first bent to healing John in Trabith.

"Pre-preposterous," the swine stammered back, his eyes now battling to look away from her, but his hand still caught limp and helpless in hers. "Of *course* this is—"

"Captain James Summerall," she finished, as if having rehearsed the words to perfection. "He is a merchant, only seeking kind harbor for the night, and he was kind enough to show a local lass around his fine ship. Mayhap," she ventured, dipping her tone into gently chiding meaning, "you have chased the wrong vessel."

"Th—that is not possible!" Reisinger sputtered.

"That *is* possible."

"No!"

"Aye."

With that, Shivahn lifted her hand and pressed it against Reisinger's face. *"Aye,"* she repeated, grave and soft.

Every muscle in Kris's body coiled in a possessive craving to lurch forward and haul her free of defiling herself on the swine. But the next moment, Reisinger himself saved him from the risk. The man jerked away from her with a gawk so mortified, Kris found his own sights doubling back to confirm Shivahn hadn't suddenly grown boils for skin and snakes for hair.

No, a tumble of goddess's red-gold curls still rained down her back. Pale cream perfection still denoted her goddess's skin. A goddess's rigid determination still defined her spine.

Reisinger snapped his own stance at Kris. The expectant tension on the deck thickened as palpably as the fog. Especially as the man's hand rose to the pistol at his thick waist.

On the other hand, Kris should have deduced Reisinger had long ago relegated his pistol to the sole purpose of serving as prop to his pompous poses. The weapon did exactly that now, as the swine yanked himself to the extent of his porcine height, sucked in a grimacing breath, and snarled, "We're getting the blazing hell off this deranged tub."

Reisinger's ensemble didn't acquiesce so easily to *that* directive. Riding a swell of their mutterings and oaths, one sailor stomped forward and planted himself next to the officer's ear. "Captain, you don't mean—"

"The devil I don't," Reisinger cut him off. "*Move*, Jenkins; *now*."

"Captain! For the love of George, can't you see 'tis that harpy, casting some sort of spell on you? Captain, she's—"

"Are you defying my order, Jenkins?"

Led by the suddenly silent Jenkins, the boarding party snapped perfect, obedient turns before filing back out the gangway with equally unspeaking precision.

In the moment before he followed his men, Reisinger pivoted back toward Shivahn—and for the first time this eve, Kris actually conceded gratitude at his soaked discomfort, for at least the chill in his bones confirmed he looked upon the next moment with a conscious mind.

The moment in which an officer of George's navy bowed to an Irish country wench as if she were Elizabeth Tudor reincarnated.

Reisinger deepened the shocked breaths Kris shared with his crew by declaring against Shivahn's fingers, "Please accept my apologies for this disturbance of your outing, my lady."

Hell, Kris speculated then. Maybe she *was* Elizabeth Tudor reincarnated. For other than the slight quaver to the nicety she murmured back to Reisinger, the only other evidence of her true unsurety were the amethyst shards crashing each other inside the gaze she swiftly flicked back at him. Even the faces of his men said they'd believe the rationalization, if their slack stares could be interpreted correctly while they watched the frigate fade back into the fog.

Unless he'd built the comparison in nervy haste.

Unless he counted Shivahn's dizzy, backward stumble as another sign of her "queenly" composure. Unless he considered his crew's collective backsteps from helping her as "respect" for their reborn monarch.

Unless he attributed the answering rage in his heart as some weird rejuvenation of allegiance to the English crown.

Every pounding beat of that fury made itself known as he shoved forward himself, cleared the remaining distance to her in three strides, and scooped her in his arms. As he looked down to her now, her cheek pressed intimately to the heart of him, the hammering din in his chest threatened to pummel out the awareness of all else around him.

"They . . . they do not understand the way you do, Kristian," she whispered up at him then. "Do they?"

"Who?" he returned quietly, though in truth, the query was rhetorical.

"Your men . . . your friends. They truly think me a vexed harpy . . . do they not?"

Kris replied with naught but a deep swallow. He confronted the probing violet intensity in her gaze, and he could say nothing, though he felt like screaming everything.

He knew how she felt. Ah, God, he knew how she felt; here in the midst of a crowd, yet utterly alone, as if she were an oddity beneath glass, a soulless creature to be scrutinized and ogled. He'd experienced the same thing at every Castle Clay ball he couldn't excuse himself from. Years later, a shadow of the sensation had befallen him with his first steps into the Trabith dining hall.

But his ordeal at Trabith had concluded in triumph, thanks to her. And in recompense, he could offer her no such victory. One glance around the deck provided him with ample evidence to the harsh conclusion. This destruction was what he left behind in his life: scenes like this throughout the years, attesting to nothing but near-escapes and bitter battles—while the achingly beautiful woman in his arms had only to wave her magical hands and miracles occurred.

He owed her his life. And all he could do was flash her his grimace.

"You're wet," Kris muttered, realizing a frustrated tone wasn't so hard to summon, after all. "I'm taking you back down to the cabin," he added with increased terseness. "You'll catch your death of a chill if you stay up here."

"How convenient," came the unexpectedly quiet reply. "If I am dead, it shall be no problem for everyone to ignore me, will it?"

"Shivahn—" The mutter became a jaw-tight growl.

"And when I die, 'twould finally prove to everyone I am not the devil's doxy, either."

"Shivahn—"

" 'Twould be a good thing to die then, I am thinking."

Kris longed to growl a very long oath. "Gentlemen!" he bellowed over his shoulder, instead. "I believe there's a mess to be cleaned here and a ship to be sailed!"

The men broke into activity, though it took no court wizard to observe that each of these "seasoned" jack-tars managed to find a task placing him at least five feet from Shivahn—even as a scowling Kris made a path through them toward the rear hatch.

He made better time in reaching the cabin this time, though why that accomplishment startled him, he didn't know. A man's attentions generally *did* function faster when he didn't have cannon blasts and rifle fire distracting him.

But the moment he cleared the portal, those attentions also decided to remain deliberately outside the compartment. He grew aware of their mutiny just as he gently lowered Shivahn to his bunk—and his whole body tremored with the need to follow her there.

"I hate it down here, Kristian," she rasped to him, her husky undertone *not* helping him win his inner battle.

"Not as much as I do, Leprechaun," he forced himself to murmur back, when he really yearned to yell it aloud while hurling her back out to the deck, leaving him in the safe, sane darkness his world had known before she'd brought him brightness again with her damnably unforgettable touch. *Not as much as I want to hold you so close and tell you everything is all right; not as much as I want to chase the fear away for you, forever.*

But I can't. My touch will only destroy you, Shivahn. My touch will—

Kill you.

Oh, yes. He'd kill her. Maybe not next week, or next month, but someday, certain as January rain and August heather, she would die because of being with him. Hadn't the reaches of his soul screamed it at him since the moment he'd discovered her beneath those lad's clothes in Prevot?

But somehow, excuses had always arisen to drown those screams. Shivahn had needed him to stay in Trabith . . . he had needed her to get *out* of the village . . . and every time the *Sídhe* had justified those excuses, traveling with them through every episode of this insane adventure, and smiling favorably upon them.

So far.

Too many years of living on this sea told him their quota of smiles was running dangerously low. It was time to give a gift back to the *Sídhe*.

He beckoned every stone of remaining strength to help him push up and away from her. Up and away from melding his mouth with hers . . . pressing his body to hers . . .

That would be fine recompense to her, indeed,

Montague. Fine recompense for saving your ship, for saving your life. *You would repay her, then, by turning her magic into madness?*

All you have to do is avoid her eyes. Just don't look at her, Montague. Just don't *look at her.*

He could not even look at her. That much was evident the moment Kristian well nigh threw her down here, then pulled back as if *he* believed she had become some kind of haunted harpy, as well.

This was *not* the scene Shivahn envisioned when at last trusting him to haul her down this horrid hole again. It certainly was not the response she expected for forcing her "gift" to traverse the realms she'd experienced only once before, on the road in Trabith with Norman. Terrifying realms. Physically painful realms, if she arrived at correct conclusions from the dizzying thumps behind her eyes that felt like a tribe of wee folk practicing their rowdiest jigs.

She should sleep. Her body issued that order in undeniable echoes. But she never had been one for minding orders. The English had seen to that when she was still but a colleen.

Instead, she rose from the bunk and took one, then two soft steps toward the rigid spine Kristian had presented to her in looming force. Funny . . . even now, even with his back erected like some Cromwellian battlement at her, her thoughts of "the English," with as many faces and scenes as they possessed, did not include *him.*

Shivahn smiled then, emboldened by that wondrous thought. She approached Kristian with fervent steps now—

Just as he spun sharply back in her direction. They collided and momentarily tangled into each other; the only reason they now did not end up in a complete embrace was his restraining grip on her elbows.

Not that Shivahn would have minded embracing him again. Or letting his lips claim hers as they had an hour ago, making her forget he had ever arrowed her with black looks from the front of the cart, or all but commanded her to crawl into the black hole that still gaped at her from the far side of his bunk—

Or that he was capable of standing so close to her like this, feeling the same lightning-like pull of their bodies like this, and yet looking, yet not *really* looking at her like this . . .

"Kristian." She shook her head as a new wash of vertigo threatened to send her back to the bunk. His name, usually such a natural sibilance on her lips, now seemed the consistency of cold gruel. "Kristian . . . are you all right?"

He pulled his hands away, to drag them through his damp chaos of hair. "I'm fine."

"You do not sound fine." She managed a small smile, on her lips and in her tone. "And you certainly do not look it." Her senses focusing again, she reached up to finger a bunch of strands he'd missed. "As a matter of point, you look like hell."

He flinched as if she'd come at him with razors instead of her fingers. "I'm—fine," he stressed stiffly.

She gave up on the smile. "I believed you more the first time."

"Believe whatever you want."

He snarled the words at her like a condemning Protestant, though, in the ensuing moment, he appeared more the damned sinner himself. Yet then he vacillated between the two, as if not knowing whether to crucify her or drop kisses on her feet.

At that moment, Shivahn nay cared if he had her

canonized. She refused to accept this behavior from him. Not from the spirit her soul had recognized as her Brave One; not from the man who had brought her life a meaning of magic as she had never known before.

With the resolution lodged in her spirit, she firmly set her stance before breaking his thick silence with level calm. "Kristian . . . why can you not even look at me now?"

At first, he answered only by turning from her again. "Why did *you* leave your compartment?" he finally fired.

"This is not about the compartment."

"Mayhap it is." He gestured toward the bunk, his taut-ened muscles outlined by the wet fabric still pasted against them. "You sat there, Shivahn, and told me you would—"

"—trust you," she interjected. "I said naught about really getting into the compartment for you." She couldn't help the slight lowering of her eyelids and the soft smile that curved her lips as she added, "I also knew you would have never let them get near here."

At that, he lowered his arm. Then his head. The slow res-ignation with which he did both might as well have been a verbal agreement to her assertion.

But Shivahn did not want to gloat on her victory. Instead, she took advantage of the chance to reach and press a hand to the enticing stubble across that strong, beautiful jaw. She marveled at the distinctly male roughness filling her palm . . . she marveled as well that Kristian did not shrink away from her.

"Besides," she said then, emboldened by his acceptance, "I think that betwixt the two of us, the adventure saw a rather happy ending."

At that, he *did* look at her. Only the gold flecks in his eyes, rather than glowing soft as candlelight, glinted more like an army with battle torches raised at the ready. "An adventure," Kristian repeated, sounding out the words as if learning them in another language. "Is that how you describe it?"

By hesitant inches, Shivahn retracted her hand. "How would *you* describe it?"

"*Not* a bloody adventure."

He spun from her once more, now dragging both hands along the sides of his head. He strode to a weathered sea chest and slammed it open. In three concise grabs, he retrieved dry long hose, breeches, and a clean if wrinkled shirt. By the time he elbowed the chest shut and yanked open the door, she likened him to a member of Mogh Nuadat's army, fleeing for his life from Conn of the Hundred Battles at Moylena.

On the other hand, mayhap Conn and his pagan savages would be a more easy force to face than the figure filling the portal now. John stood with one hand propped against the door frame, the other "knocking" on what was now empty air. For the first time since she had known the man, rigid concentration defined every inch of his face. She began to see why Kristian called him first mate as well as best mate, for here, she saw the man who could easily step in as the *Sea Wing*'s captain if Kristian were busy doing things like being imprisoned . . . or dealing with a healer harpy from Hell in his cabin.

"Apologies for the interruption," John muttered, though the crinkles at the edges of his eyes spoke of a secret delight he gained from the situation.

The *Sea Wing*'s captain, on the other hand, certainly showed not an inkling to join that group. Without taking even a moment to acknowledge John's apology, Kristian snapped, "What is it?"

Like a child reminded he had not milked the goats yet, John reaffixed the stern mien to his face before replying "Nathan's about to navigate this tub in circles up there. Ya want to tell us what our course is now: Wexford or Portsmouth?"

Shivahn had not thought it possible, but at that, some winch inside Kristian notched harder, stiffening his spine tighter. Still, she doubted his heart echoed the throbbing chaos of hers. In the last hour, faced with wondering if she would live through the next *minute,* the course of tomorrow had seemed a meaningless concern, something that would never happen. Now she learned that Kristian had planned their good-bye for the dock at Wexford . . . but a little more than an hour away.

She also discovered that in spite of the vexing thunder-cloud that had settled over his attitude toward her—perhaps because of it—*she* was not ready to say good-bye in an hour.

But she dared not give voice to her fear. She hardly ventured breathe, lest her breath shift the unsteady winds on which Kristian's disposition seemed to now reside, and he decided they should toss her overboard rather than deal with her at all.

Thankfully, the man did not waste his time in coming to a decision. "There's no time for Wexford now," he stated grimly. "Even if we did make good time there, they've probably alerted every battalion from here to Belfast by now. God only knows who or what would be waiting for us."

John fanned out his arms with benevolent ease. "Ya don't have to force those clams down my throat. I thought Wexford was a barmy move from the start, remember?"

The crack did *not* slacken the tension in Kristian's muscles. "It seems Miss Armagh will be traveling with us, after all," he stated succinctly while stomping past his first officer and down the hall—actions that only increased the merriment dancing in his first mate's eyes.

"Get her into dry clothes as soon as possible," he ordered further. "I think Randolph left some shirts and breeches behind when he decided to be a banker instead of a cabin boy. I'll take care of the coordinates for Portsmouth with Nate, as well as sending Andre and Gerard back in the longboat to get word to Trabith."

"Understood, Captain." John stressed the final word with a sardonic enough slant that Shivahn bit back a sudden laugh. "Anything else I can do for ya, *Captain*?"

Surprisingly, Kristian halted in response to that. He turned in the hall with a contemplative stare, as if taking his first mate's words in their most serious context. "Aye, John," he finally replied, "there *is* one more thing you can do for me.

"Shut the bloody hell up and get to work."

At that, he whirled to the ladder and climbed it with lunging steps. In the silence he left behind, Shivahn witnessed yet another expression take over Sir John Petrey, which she had not seen before.

Confusion.

Kristian had tossed his own best mate into as deep a pit of bafflement as she.

Somehow, that observation did not make her feel any better. "Oh, I have made a fine muddle of things," she whispered as salty tears slipped down her cheeks.

"Cow's crap," came John's retort. "Ya saved our bums from swinging off that wanker's yardarm. In my book, *Miss* Armagh, there isn't a bloody thing wrong with that."

Shivahn tilted a look up at the man. As she expected, a smile tempted his lips and twinkled in his eyes. She could not help but smile back. When John offered both his hands in a gesture of friendship, she eagerly accepted them.

She was glad she did so. John's strength immediately began to seep into her—and yet, she wondered if her heart would ever know the full light of happiness again. Kristian had filled dreams she never thought would come true: dreams of a person who would believe in the magic of her hands yet believe in the humanity of her soul . . . dreams of a man who would regard her as a person and touch her as a woman.

Where was that Kristian now? Where was he in the stranger who had stood here five minutes ago, barely able to touch her, let alone look upon her?

The query weighted Shivahn's head down, as she watched more tears splat upon her whitened knuckles. "I have not see him like this before, John," she confessed from trembling lips.

"Neither have I, little minx," came the quiet reply. "Neither have I."

She sucked in a deep breath, as more words burned at her throat to be spoken. *What will happen to me now, John? What fate awaits me now, in the land full of people who would rather murder me than look at me? And how in the world shall I get through this, when it seems* you *shall be my only friend there?*

Yet somehow, she clamped the questions into unspoken silence.

She did not want to know the answers.

Chapter 15

"Shivahn Armagh, you owe us an answer!"

"And I second the motion!"

The hearty declarations filled the inside of the carriage with the warmth of their humor. Shivahn could not help but return a smile to their sources, who shared the seat opposite her and Kristian: a wide-grinning Nathan and wild young Patrick, the *Sea Wing's* wisely chosen boatswain.

These two had been the first of the crew to dare friendships with her after that first horrid night; therefore, she was doubly thankful to Providence for the decision made last night, as the ship dropped temporary anchor in Portsmouth Harbor, that they be included on the journey to London. She remembered the words John had muttered to sway Kristian's decision—something about Nathan and Patrick being there to "give ya help with the goods when it's time"—but she stopped trying to decipher the message's meaning when sheer gratitude had intervened. As far as she was concerned, Nathan and Patrick had been sent along to save her sanity.

After all, if the seamen were not here, she would be trapped in this coach with the quiet stranger whose murky stare should warrant him some kind of a citation, so flagrantly did it defy the glory of the land he beheld with nay so much as a blink. This part of England called West Sussex was dotted with hills carpeted in fresh spring grass, occasionally patterned with bold juttings of black-green forests, fairytale-old towers, and pasture walls draped in the rainbowed finery of wildflowers.

Since disembarking the *Sea Wing* yesterday, Shivahn had found herself in a state she could only describe as pleasant shock. She did not feel a bit frightened in this beautiful land. She did not feel threatened or awkward or dangerously out of place, either.

As a matter of point, "the land of the British bastards" felt a great deal like home.

Kristian, on the other hand, looked as if he were attempting to solve all the world's problems before they reached London. Unless he happened to throw an errant glance *her* way. On those rare occasions, his stare did turn from its dark contemplation, if only for an instant. Aye, for but an instant, her Brave One appeared again, like a shaft of sun piercing North Sea storm clouds, making her blink with the blindingly painful honesty of his soul's loneliness for her. And his body's desire for her . . .

But just as swiftly, the storm clouds rolled in over his gaze again. As they did now.

"Shivv-aaahhn." Nathan's singsong of a prompt saved her belly from balling into another knot of frustration. "You are shilly-shallying with us, Miss Armagh," the sailor accused with a teasing smirk.

"No shilly-shallying allowed," Patrick added. "Answer the question, Shivahn."

Shivahn gave them a mutinous sigh. "And just what do you two be wanting with the name of the first boy who ever kissed me?" She bolstered the finish of the retort by coiling arms across her chest, praying that if her defiance did not deter them, mayhap a passing angel or saint would interfere on her behalf.

Anything to escape having to tell them that boy's name was Kristian.

Alas, both Nathan and Patrick only cocked their brows higher her direction. Shivahn prayed harder, but not an angel or saint seemed within earshot of her plea.

Or mayhap she reached that conclusion too soon.

The coach lurched to a violent stop, and the horses let out equine cries of alarm. Yet from Cornelius up on the driver's box came nary a sound.

"What the bloody hell?" Patrick muttered.

"We've barely stopped in the last two days," Nathan stated. "Even Sandys's bloodhounds can't sniff out a trail that doesn't exist."

"Maybe they *can*," Patrick countered.

Kristian did not add his agreement or argument to the exchange. Instead, enveloping her shoulders with one arm and drawing his pistol with a yank of the other, he ordered with low calm, "I suggest we find out the answer to this little mystery, gentlemen. *Now*."

Only to her minimal surprise, the seamen reacted to that like boys set free on an adventure. Nathan sneaked out the door to her left with spylike stealth, while Patrick chose a pirate's approach, kicking the carriage's right side open and blasting himself out the opening, a human cannon ball.

To her not-so-minimal surprise, she discovered herself

trembling beneath Kristian's hold. She looked to him with unblinking eyes, awaiting her own instructions.

To her belief, they were, "Stay here. And stay the hell down."

After that, he pushed her to the carriage floor. He followed her there and, from that position, slid out the same door Patrick had just propelled from.

But in the instant before he disappeared, Kristian grabbed her hand once more and crushed it with the sudden intensity of his grip. "Shivahn, this time I *mean it*," he growled. "If I see so much as a hair of your head outside this carriage, I'll shoot it off your spine myself."

He shoved her arm back at her and slammed the door in her face—before she could swear that she had no intention of disobeying him this time. More than that, she wished she could have issued an order of her own at him. *Be careful, Kristian; by the saints, be careful!*

Because I love you, Kristian.

Dear God and all the angels help me, I love you.

She waited. And *waited*. The coach creaked and groaned through another violent jerk. Her heart raced to her ears, resounding so loudly through her head that the ensuing voices were not much more than a tide of tones upon tones, sounds crashing too heavily atop each other for her to translate into words, much less figure their meanings.

Were they arresting him even now? she wondered wildly . . . were they lashing his hands into manacles and forcing him to watch while they killed Nathan and Patrick in the road? Did they now command him to talk about the healer harpy, his accomplice, even as they eyed the closed coach and speculated what—or who—was inside?

The carriage's door opened again.

Shivahn swallowed her heart back down into her chest and forced herself to consider her options. Did she submit right now to these bastards and hope the *Sídhe* helped her mesmerize an entire battalion of them . . . or survive a multiple raping by them? Or fling herself at the ape who stood there now and hope to escape into lands that might have been Scotland for how well she knew them?

She estimated she had another three seconds in which to make up her mind.

They became the three seconds filled with a distinctly warm, strong voice, beckoning to her. "Leprechaun."

Shivahn wasted not a moment on some silly outcry of joy. She skipped straight to the act of hurling herself against him, then holding on with all her might despite his stunned *oof*. She didn't relent the hold even as Kristian clumsily tried to shut the door and maneuver them both back onto the seat.

He finally accomplished both, with a number of positions that would inspire a pained wince even from a pleasure fair tumbler. 'Twas the small penance he had due, Shivahn justified, for even the few moments her heart had started to crumble from the anguish of believing him dead.

A small chuckle escaped past his lips, preceding his soft utterance against her forehead. "Are you all right?"

She had prepared to show him just how "all right" she was, despite having just endured one of the most petrifying moments of her life then being chuckled at for it, when Kristian gave his concern an unexpected measure of proof. Tenderly he slid two fingers up to her cheek, capturing the errant strands of her hair that had fallen there from a chignon that now probably looked more a bird's nest. His touch only skimmed her skin for an instant, yet it sent delicious frissons of warmth into the depths of her belly. And beyond.

Oh, sweet fairy fire, how she had missed his touch!

"I—" Shivahn managed to stammer, before deciding a

change of subject might be the best conversation undertaken. "What has happened, Kristian?"

He took several moments to give over his reply. His delay maddened her; not because of his silence, but because of how he spent that pause: slowly twirling her lock of hair through his fingers, gazing at the tangled curl as if beholding spun gold.

" 'Tis a disabled wagon," he at last responded, reluctantly lowering his hand at the same time.

"A disabled wagon?" She tried to comprehend the meaning behind his words, which she apparently did not fathom. Just like the meaning behind his stare. "And *that* is why we have stopped as if Hell has surfaced in the road before us, and why you have all slinked out as if dreading your own shadow will shoot you?"

"Wagons and horses are as valuable as emeralds and rubies to the farmers of these hills," he explained. "To leave behind both together, despite a shattered axle, is a glaring enough situation to warrant caution. It might mean the owner is in trouble nearby, or Sandys's agents have come up with a clever diversion to slow us, then attack us."

Shivahn regarded him with a new measure of respect. "And you have decided to gamble on the former?"

Kristian jerked a rapid, almost uncomfortable, shrug. "They knew I would." He mumbled the admission as if confessing he was a highway robber in addition to a mystery-shrouded pirate, and they had truly stopped to steal some cowherder blind. "Fortunately," he said with a hopeful rise, "we've fairly well ruled out the latter. Nathan and Patrick are reconnoitering the immediate area to see if there's anyone about who needs our aid."

The last of that statement caused Shivahn to straighten. "Well, then, I should be with them," she declared nearly without thought, so instantly did her healer's instinct rush to life in her blood.

"The hell you should." Clearly, Kristian retorted on an equally inherent impulse. But Shivahn pushed aside the recognition. She had no time for his masculine paradings *now*.

"Kristian, damn it, somebody could be hurt!"

"Aye." This time, he spoke with maddening, commanding ease. "Somebody like you."

"You already said there was no danger."

"I said there was no sign of search troops. That does *not* rule out the thousand other bastards who would love to get their hands on a morsel like you."

She threw him a glare conveying her desire to slap him for that remark. Kristian only grinned, silently daring her to follow through.

"I want—to help," she asserted with enunciated resolve.

"You will—stay here," he returned, using her own cadence to prove its uselessness on him.

Oh, Kristian, how I would dearly love to punch you.

Oh, Leprechaun . . . please try. Go ahead and try.

And he grinned again. Wider this time. Reveling in his dominion over her—

Or so he thought.

If he wanted her to stay here with him, Shivahn decided with a small upturn to her own lips, then he would have to make the effort worth her while.

But she did not give voice to that conclusion. Nay, she elected to borrow the man's own insolent courage to act straight away upon her solution.

She braced her hands to the squab at either side of his head. Then she dipped lower next to him . . . lower.

At the first touch of their lips, he shook in surprise.

At the first slide of their tongues, he moaned in desire.

At the first press of their bodies, he glided his hands along the length of her arms, eliciting rapturous shivers throughout her body.

But then his fingers slid around hers. Just before he shoved them vehemently away.

When Shivahn finally blinked the shock back from her vision and commanded her lungs to breathe in more than painful spurts, she forced herself to look at him. In pushing her away, Kristian had propelled himself back, too. He now occupied the corner of the carriage opposite from her, looking much like a hunter cornered by a she-lion. The sight of him burned her stomach with nauseous humiliation.

"Nathan and Patrick . . . should be rejoining us in a moment," he murmured, before clearing his throat as if naught had just occurred between them but an indiscreet oath spoken. "Mayhap . . . you shall be warmer when they're back."

Shivahn surrendered her expression to the full force of outraged confusion. "Warmer?"

He cleared his throat again. "You're . . . shivering," he said with increased discomfort. "And you have my apologies for that, but a heated coach was nowhere to be had in Portsmouth at the late hour we arrived."

"I am not cold, Kristian." Though she *was* amazed he had noticed the tremors claiming the lengths of her arms and legs, which she only now grew aware of herself.

"I shouldn't have let you sleep up on the main deck," he went on as if *he* constituted both parties to this conversation. "No matter what you said about not being able to breathe in the cabin."

"I am *not* cold, Kristian."

"It did no good for the concentrations of the night crew, either," he amended with a surprising lilt of gentleness.

"Not that any of them minded. You made short work of dispelling everyone's shock after that first night."

"They would have lavished thanks on anyone who helped with the mess those pigs left of the galley," she returned crisply, suddenly yearning for his undecipherable mutterings of before. He could keep his gentle overtures to himself, she fumed, if they came punctuated with looks like what he now hurled at her—glances with spearheads molded of pure pain.

"Aye, and what about the primitive cooking conditions because of that?" came the fast—and *gentle*—rebuttal.

" 'Tis not difficult to boil willicks and prawns." She felt instantly contrite for her churlishness. She appended more evenly, "But they are a most decent group of men, possessing their manners as well as their wits."

She did *not* expect Kristian's reacting ring of laughter to that. Nor the strangely sardonic statement with which he finished the burst. "Wits. You say they had *wits*? Those men had not a wit among the whole of them, Shivahn, from the moment they fell in love with you."

At that, her blood pounded harder through her heart. She knew exactly what to do now. Leaning forward, she forced herself to meet his hard, dark gaze . . . then, on the softest of whispers, utter the words she could no longer hold secret and silent in that heart . . .

"And what of their captain, Kristian? Has . . . their captain fallen in love, too?"

He did not move. Neither did she. Their stares tangled through space, through time, mayhap even halting time. A breeze stirred through the carriage, smelling of churned grass and twilight mists. Shivahn's prayers echoed in her head, beseeching the fates that this time, her instinct would *not* prove correct—that Kristian would not render his answer in the form of an averted gaze and a saying-everything-but-nothing silence.

But his lips pressed tighter together, ever more silent, by the moment.

And yet . . . Shivahn still found herself composing a tiny litany of thanks to the spirits, for he did not look away. He did *not* look away; he continued to meet her gaze, almost looking as if he *needed* to, even though a vein beyond the corner of his left eye pulsed a clearly terrified beat.

But that was not the inspiration for her thanksgiving. Shivahn found that motivation when she looked *inside* his eyes . . . when she pushed her gaze beyond the surface chaos of his gaze and beheld the treasure for which all the angels received her fervent gratitude:

Two starpoints of light, gleaming at her with pure need, with pure want. They lived in the depths of his eyes like two last golden embers in a night where morning seemed very far away.

Aye, they were only embers. But embers could be fanned into flames.

She had always loved a good bonfire.

Twenty-four hours later, that confidence did not spark to life so simply anymore. As a matter of point, Shivahn wondered if it might have been doused for good . . . undoubtedly somewhere on the streets of a big, brash city called London.

In place of the temptation to smile, her mouth dropped into a wide circle, which she tried to maneuver into forming coherent words. Instead, she yielded only a soft-gasped, "Oh, my," every time they turned another corner.

"Oh, my," she said as they wheeled through a tangle of ornate coaches outside a grand park denoted as Vauxhall. She echoed the words eight more times before they cleared the throng of men swaggering by in peacock colors, escorting women in fancy-feathered masks and dark-rouged lips.

"Oh, my," she whispered as they traversed along the banks of a wide brown river to their left and came upon a grandly sprawling palace to their right.

"Lambeth," Nathan explained, putting an identity to the ornate stone gates and residential wings beyond. "Home of the Archbishop of Canterbury."

She nodded, dually fascinated and perplexed that one man needed more land than all of Trabith to live on.

But with the next turn of her head, she tossed aside her bewilderment for the more enjoyable sensation of awed delight.

"Oh, my!" she cried out this time as they crossed the river and came upon a green, lovely park, its width matched by a lake dotted with geese and ducks and the golden remnants of the afternoon.

"St. James Park," Patrick supplied for her this time. His lips curved into a devilish grin. "Ahhh, many fond memories in this head were formed 'neath the trees of St. James."

"Must stir up quite a crowd in your breeches," Nathan quipped. "Unless your head's as puny as I think it is."

Patrick jeered. "Wouldn't you like to find out, fairy boy?"

"Gentlemen!" Kristian stressed the charge with an upsweep of his hand—and irony edged to his tone. "We're not whittling away the hours on the *Wing*'s quarterdeck any more. You were brought along to be my extra eyes and ears—as well as halfway civilized examples of English decorum to our traveling companion."

"Begging your pardon, Captain," Patrick muttered.

"Begging your pardon, as well, Captain Montague," Nathan echoed. "But I don't think *we're* going to change

Shivahn's mind about the ins and outs of 'English decorum.' "

"As if you know your ins from your outs," came the sally from the seaman next to her. Patrick shot her a couldn't-help-myself look during the barrage of Nathan's peeved huff, Kristian's low growl, and *her* impulsive giggle.

" 'Tis all right," she declared to them all. "I *like* this decorum better." In a more serious murmur, she added, "It makes me feel at home."

"Which is why it's *not* all right."

Nathan and Patrick joined her in directing startled stares at the corner where the charge still vibrated the air with its irrefutable command—though in return, Kristian drove his intense gaze only at her.

"We shall be in London for at least the next seven days," he stated then, swiftly leveling his tone—and shuttering his eyes. "During that time, you are to venture in public only as necessary. If the situation does arise, and you are inquired of your purpose in Town, then someone *else* shall answer for you. *You* do not understand a word of English."

"But that is a lie," Shivahn contended. "I know English just fine."

"And every moment you prove it," came the sarcasm-dripped retort, "your lovely brogue is as clear as a shamrock tattooed on your forehead."

Shivahn dropped her brows. Blazes of Hell take the man. He was right. And, surmising from the arrogant fluidity with which he settled against the cushion again, he knew it.

Even so, when he continued detailing his plan, Kristian strained out all scorn in favor of a respectful tone to all in the carriage. "I think the simplest solution is to give you a new identity." Patrick and Nathan rendered nods of approval to the suggestion. "She shall be my distant cousin from . . ."

"China!" Patrick offered.

"Germany," Nathan suggested, slanting an incredulous brow the younger man's way.

"Germany," Kristian repeated. "Aye, Germany. That ought to stay the biddying tongues of this city long enough for us to get some business done and then be gone."

Through the following pause, Shivahn surmised she might as well have been the man's dunce of a German cousin, after all. The other men in the carriage acknowledged Kristian's assertion with far more grave a silence than the words warranted, and she could not interpret the meanings in the subtle nods they gave each other, either. Only one perception glared piercingly clear to her: These men treated a little "business" like some secret mission.

The kind of mission that could put a man in prison. In chains. Sentenced to be beheaded.

I am sorry to disappoint you, Mistress Armagh, but you get what you see. I was only going about my normal business in Dublin, when caught in a series of bizarre circumstances . . .

His "normal business." Shivahn would have laughed, however bitterly, at the recollection, if the memory was not dominated by the sight of Kristian as he had bantered that at her, his body covered with bruises, his eyes full of pain, and his tongue replete with lies.

The lies he had told her from the beginning.

You were speaking another language to me even then, Kristian, were you not? All your words—"your business"— it all meant something else, but what? What the bloody blazes are you hiding, Kristian? Why can you not reach out and share this with me?

Or mayhap I should ask . . . who *is stopping you from doing so?*

Mayhap I should ask right now.

Yet as Shivahn summoned as much height to her spine as she could, preparing to shatter the carriage's silence with her demand, a bellow routed her. A bellow she could not have matched if she multiplied herself tenfold.

"Montague Manor, Berkeley Square!" came the shout from the driver's perch. The compartment swayed in equal ardor as the portly driver swung to the ground. "Ye be home, Captain Montague!" he declared merrily. "Got ye here in three days, just as I promised!"

"I admire a man of his word," Kristian called back. "Excellent work, Cornelius. Find some oats for your horses in the stables round back and some food for yourself in the kitchen. Then I'll meet you in my study about that bonus *I* promised."

That gleaned Kristian a gap-toothed grin from the man who swept open the door with the zeal of a lad half his age. "I say aye-aye to *that*, Captain!"

"Imagine that," Patrick murmured to Shivahn from behind his cupped hand.

But she did not respond to her new friend. She could not. Once more, her mouthed formed into a dry O of wordless wonder, as she looked past Patrick, past Kristian, and even past Cornelius's rotund shoulders . . .

At another bloody palace.

"Oh . . . *my*," she finally managed to breathe, as a hand—she knew not whose, and she could not tear her gaze from the palace long enough to look—helped her down from the carriage and onto the red-bricked drive. Her head tilted back as her stare climbed walls formed of the same red bricks, their flawless assemblage interrupted only by two wide bay windows on the mansion's ground level, then flawless rows of rectangular windows indicating the mansion's upper two floors.

These elements, Shivahn recognized. She had walked by

many manors in Dublin constructed in this style. And she would be able to give this dwelling the same careless shrug she turned to those homes, if the buildings merely shared the same structure.

But they did not. Kristian's home affected her just as Kristian the man: It was more than the usual of its kind. The windows on the mansions in Dublin were mere windows. Montague Manor's windows were capped by small overhangs carved in intricate depictions of mythical ocean beings. Along their bottom ledges, wrought-iron sills brimmed over with pot after pot of multihued flowers. When Shivahn directed her gaze to the inside of the lower-level windows, she beheld draperies rich and dramatic enough to be waves for those carved sea creatures to loll upon.

Between soaring white pillars they progressed, through an outer courtyard where butterflies danced around ferns and roses and a masterpiece of a carved stone bench, then finally through the wide front doors, into an entry hall that had Shivahn pondering if they had taken a wrong turn and arrived at the halls of Parliament, instead.

A lake of a marble floor led to a stairway fit for a royal palace. The steps, made of a lighter-colored wood she did not recognize, flowed down and ended in balustrades of carved glory that again reminded her of waves to support the sea spirits themselves. To her right, double doors opened into a room easily the size of Trabith's dining hall, only this room had an oak table at which half the village could dine together, sitting in thronelike chairs as they did.

A small giggle tempted her throat, however, at imagining her kin doing jigs and folk frolics on the marble dance floor beyond that. And yet, just two months ago, would she have ever imagined standing in this portal herself?

" 'Tis all right to go in, Shivahn."

She jerked in startlement before thinking about the action, then wondered whether she had done so because of the hint of sensual smoothness to Kristian's voice, or the proximity at which he stood, his mouth just behind her left ear, as he said it.

She decided he had successfully seized her on both fronts. She confirmed his victory in the wobbling whisper of her reply. "Th-thank you."

Though now, she had not a care for the ballroom any more. She turned completely to him, rejoicing merely in the closeness of his presence again. She gazed up at him, and it wasn't long before she yearned to touch him. She lifted her hand and flattened her fingers over the strong, warm beat of his heart.

She should have kept her cursed hand to herself. Kristian moved away by a sharp step, as if he had been summoned out of an enchanted sleep by an evil sorceress.

"I would have you be comfortable during your stay at Montague Manor, Miss Armagh." He issued the decree while running a discreet hand across his chest, ridding himself from some invisible residue he obviously imagined from her contact. "Therefore, all the amenities we have are yours to enjoy, as well.

"I only ask that you refrain from using one area of the house." He pointed across the marble lake, to the only door that remained solidly closed. "My private study is unexplorable territory."

Shivahn looked at the carved oak door to which he gestured and wondered if she should actually salute her comprehension of his dictate. Instead, she dipped an awkward nod, dragged her courage from where it hid behind her anxiety, and compelled herself to state "You have a lovely home, Kristian."

" 'Tis not my home," came his courteous but curt return.

"But when I am in London, it suffices well enough as a roof over my head." Then, with a distinct tightening of his lips, "And it assuages what little my Grandfather has of a conscience."

Shivahn did not know what to render in way of a reaction to that. Yet the next instant, she was rescued from her quandary by another voice, resounding to the heights of the foyer like the first morning cry of an auk over the cliffs at Bray Head.

"Christ in the almighty heavens! Are ye broodin' a puddle o' despair on my new-polished floor before ye've been ten minutes home, Kristian Montague?"

Though Kristian's lips succumbed to the tiniest of twitches, his eyes gleamed with spring-green brightness. Eagerly Shivahn followed the pivot of his head, to discover who warranted this dawning in a man who, two moments ago, seemed so hell-bent on staying steeped in an inner midnight.

"Hallo, old wench," he said, curling his arms around the pleasantly well-fleshed form of a woman Shivahn gauged at a few years older than Maeve's age. But other than that detail, this stranger shared no similarities with her friend back in Trabith. Straight black strands, swept up into a neatly braided bun, replaced Maeve's auburn curls. Where Maeve easily looked many men in the eye at her proud five feet eight inches, this woman's bright blue eyes and plump bow of a mouth stared adoringly up at Kristian from a height of no more than five feet.

"Hallo, callow laddie," she fired back at him, clearly finishing out a long-established welcome-home ritual.

Shivahn found herself charmed by *that* factor. 'Twas another element to the scene that plummeted her jaw in astonishment once more. She managed to give voice to that shock with a stammered "You . . . you are Irish."

Unlike Kristian, the woman's amused smile twinkled over every inch of her expressive face. "Last time I checked, *Agra*."

Shivahn bounced an increasingly agitated stare between the two of them. "Then . . . this is a normal occurrence in London, that Irish and English embrace like old cousins?"

"Oh, dear," the woman murmured, arching a brow at Kristian. "I was afraid of this when Terrence arrived with your note. He said something of an 'unexpected guest.' He also wagered you would tell her nothing."

"Tell me nothing of what?" Shivahn left behind the scowl as she stepped forward with a look born of determined intent.

But she and Kristian's "old wench" might as well have been comparing recipes for potato soup with this last exchange. When Kristian cleared his throat and spoke again, 'twas to say "This is Fionna Shay, Shivahn. I greet her with an embrace because she is a valued part of my household."

"I *rule* your household, you wretch." Fionna jabbed him with a firm but playful elbow.

Kristian held up surrendering hands. "I am corrected, and properly so." He followed with an apologetic bow to the Irishwoman. "Needless to say, Fionna is more than able to see to your every need during your stay."

"Bloody right." Fionna bracketed the top corners of her apron with haughty fists. "Only I'd be having an easier time of it if I knew whose needs I was seeing to."

She lilted the end of that statement with a liberal dose of meaning, while pivoting that huge blue stare upon Shivahn again. Surprisingly, though, Fionna's regard did not give her a drop of nervousness. 'Twas only when Kristian looked upon her again that Shivahn fought the need to laugh and cry at once. Or to drop her head in shame yet lift it high in readiness for his kiss. To hate him for the tension etched to every inch of his lips . . . or to love him for the reverence hiding in the forest-deep shadows of his eyes.

"Fionna," he finally said, "this is Mistress Shivahn Armagh. And she is . . ."

"Yes?" Though impatience threaded Fionna's prod, delight twinkled in her eyes. As if the woman *savored* the sight of her master's disconcertment.

At last, she *did* press Kristian: "By Saints Peter and Patrick, laddie, spit it out!"

But Kristian did not "spit it out." Instead, he kicked a violent toe at the floor, jabbed his arms across his torso, and emitted a snort more harsh than the exhausted exhalations of the horses outside.

And then, he did what Shivahn suspected he would yet prayed he would not. He wheeled his sights wildly about the foyer, until he found sanctuary in the closed door of his study.

"Our coachman is wanting his bonus," he stated. "And I've no doubt a pile of papers on my desk."

"No doubt," Fionna echoed, like a mother indulging the "invisible mate" of her child.

"Then I shall wish you a good evening, ladies." He whirled like that same boy Fionna had just humored, just told he could skip his bath, and now escaping before anyone changed their minds about the situation. "Fionna," he called over his shoulder, "I'm famished. I'll take supper in my study this evening."

"Aye-aye, Captain Montague."

The slamming study door made a strangely contradictory finish to Fionna's easy-drawled comeback. As the sound evoked hollow knells from the two waist-high Oriental urns flanking the entrance of the ballroom, Shivahn listened to her heart echo with the same directionless emptiness.

That was why, she supposed, she felt entitled to another surprised gape as Fionna brushed her hands together in satisfied slaps, cracked a merry grin and declared, "Well. Isn't this going to be fun!"

Three nights later, Shivahn still wondered when or how the *fun* factored in to this bewildering episode of her life.

She weathered a wash of guilt as soon as the thought assaulted her mind, its ambush perfectly waged as she diverted her attention to the rooftops of a midnight-shrouded London.

Oh, aye, for as many mysteries and questions still lingering in the labyrinth below, she could match moments surely considered "fun." There was the clandestine visit to the market with Fionna and her first ecstatic taste of a swan-shaped chocolate tart. She had reveled in the more "approved" excursion to the Chelsea Physic Garden with Patrick, where, to Patrick's pique, she had crooned with more enthusiasm over the Lebanon cedar trees than his riding prowess. And earlier this eve, she had known heaven in a bath with water scented just like wisteria petals.

Shivahn sighed softly with that particular remembrance as she pulled the folds of her robe more snug against the night's damp air—though she admitted the chill constituted only half her desire to feel the garment more fully on her skin. The robe, a breathtaking creation of seashell-colored satin and lace like enchanted ocean foam, had appeared after the bath on the arm of a smugly smiling Fionna and had not left Shivahn's body since. She had refused Fionna's demands to don even a chemise first and did not regret the decision even in this late hour of banked fires and slumbering ovens.

She did not regret it because with the robe closer to her, at least she had *some* part of Kristian close to her.

Oh, aye, the garment had come on Fionna's arm, but Kristian might as well have sent a card with the beautiful gift, so clearly did it betray him in its lavish generosity . . . its inherent sensuality . . .

Its smooth silence.

"Come now, Shivahn," she murmured to her cynically smirking reflection in the window glass. "Surely you leap to unfounded accusations. After all, Kristian *has* granted you one hour and four words at the dinner table each eve. 'Tis a generous donation, do you not think, for a man so busy with—"

What? Her mind vented the shriek she so longed to unleash into the ear of the man she pictured now. *If* she could summon a memory of Kristian without his head stooped over a soup bowl, his backside hurrying into his precious study, or his legs swinging over the saddle of his horse to disappear on another "business" outing of mysterious destination.

Oh, Kristian, how high the mountain of gold I would pay right now for one of your lingering stares. The powers I would surrender for one day spent the way we used to, laughing and talking, kissing each other . . .

Loving each other.

Her choked sob echoed in the room. Hot tears trailed down her cheeks. She welcomed them. A dry rawness burned her throat, but she welcomed that pain, too, for the rawness induced one very helpful result. It grated not just at her throat but stripped away the layers of her patience, as well.

In short, it made her mad as bloody hell.

Mad enough to search out and find one maddening,

brooding English bastard—*tonight*—no matter what rules she had to break.

It's late, Kris's brain exhorted him for the dozenth time since the mantel clock across the study had *donged* that many times, that many minutes ago. *Go to bed, Montague. Take advantage of your feather mattress and satin sheets. Soon enough, you'll be back to a narrow tick bunk on the* Wing *again.*

"And I can't wait," he replied aloud in a weary combination of a sigh and a murmur.

His brows jumped together in surprise. It *was* late. What other reason justified the vehemence of this need to depart London again so fast? He was safe here, for all intents and purposes; his close connection to the mighty Emery Dominick Montague served at least one use in its protective powers against Sandys's minions on the home front, as long as he made no moves too swift or blatant.

Besides that, he still had more than a few ledgers to inspect now that the tea plantation on Barbados had turned a profit, not to mention the obscene success of the interisland sailing service he'd partnered with Mast Iverson last year.

That musing prompted him to a softly sardonic grunt. Who would have thought so many people would be so giddy about skipping from one Caribbean isle to the next?

An old heathen like Mast Iverson, he readily mused to that. *Or a young heathen like Shivahn.*

Shivahn.

Damn it, his mind growled. "Damn it," his lips muttered. He snatched up a tall-plumed writing pen from the Renaissance desk he'd done nothing but scowl behind for the last fifteen minutes. Grimly he anticipated ripping the thing apart quill by quill until either his frustration was spent or the onslaught of her image finished its conquest of his thoughts.

If the matter were tossed into the *Wing*'s wagering pool, he'd slam down a hundred pounds on the former scenario occurring first—though he had *no* fathoming, even now, of how the woman kept achieving the latter. Aside from the one hour at dinner each night Fionna refused him any excuses from, he could compile another wildly successful ledger of the time he had managed *not* to spend with a certain violet-eyed house guest of Montague Manor.

Yet there she appeared in every other minute of his days, her smile tormenting him from every sunrise . . . her touch caressing him with every sunset . . . and through the hours in between, her laughter and her musical voice echoing in his memories. As for the nights . . .

The nights, his mind saved for fantasies of their passion-fused mouths and their desire-slicked bodies. Through the hours of interminable midnight silences, his mind was filled with their enjoined sighs as they climbed to mutual heights of ecstasy . . .

During the nights, Kris concluded while untangling himself from sheet after sweat-covered sheet, she performed her deepest and most dangerous sorcery.

At that conclusion, he swallowed. Hard. And watched the as-yet-unplucked plume begin to shake in his sweating fist. Because that conclusion did not stand alone. It came followed by a realization, an epiphany so completely confirmed by the thunderclap of his heart that no corner of his senses remained quiet enough to give audience to a protest, anyway. Especially when the truth of that realization chanted its way across his mind, louder with each accusing refrain:

You're not afraid of giving in to her sorcery, Montague.
You're afraid of giving it up.

Of giving her *up.*

"The bloody *hell* I am." His snarl vibrated across his teeth as his mind clawed through a fury-red haze. *And I suppose 'tis why I'm pacing like a caged lion to get back to Ireland again. I suppose 'tis why I'll face the chance of swinging from Sandys's gallows in order to deliver her home, where she'll be safe again; at least safer than chasing around on the ocean with me.*

Where she'll be happy again . . . eventually. Where she'll forget me . . . eventually.

He hurled aside the pen and shoved up from the desk, toppling a glass of water in the doing. He ignored the puddle turning from dark crimson to dark brown as it spread from the Turkish area carpet to the polished teak floor. He scooped up only the crystal glass, crossing quickly to the spirits cart.

Tonight, he'd flood her out of his mind with imported brandy.

Tomorrow, he'd concentrate on washing her out of his soul, as well.

He jerked the stopper out of the brandy decanter, pouring himself a liberal dose. The brandy sloshed out upon his hand, as well, but he didn't care. It trickled down his arm as he brought the glass to his lips in eager anticipation of the numbness about to consume him.

"Put it down this instant, Kristian Montague. No spirits will cloud your brain from what I have to say."

Kris didn't know which collision sounded loudest in the room: his lungs smashing against his ribs, or the door *whack*ing against its stopper.

Hell, he surmised, it didn't much matter. He doubted neither impact would jar Shivahn into surrendering an inch of her stance. Her arms folded across her chest; she planted her bare feet evenly at the edge of the carpet. Every inch of her spine and legs were pulled so erect, he could only remember the last time he'd seen a woman so unflinchingly incensed: when his French tutor, Madame Genoix, had caught him "studying" a copy of the *Kama Sutra* instead of *Candide.*

Only Madame Genoix never had hair that tumbled and danced in firelight like a wild golden flame. She never had a gaze like the indigo core of that flame, so intense it didn't destroy a man, but transformed him. And Madame Genoix had never, never bounded barefoot into his domain in the middle of the night, wearing only a robe making her appear an avenging fairy exploded to human form, with a milky column of a throat disappearing into the lacy shadow formed by two beautiful breasts . . .

God, Kris decided then, was finally exacting His revenge for those *Kama Sutra* "lessons."

"I specifically told you not to trespass this room," he stated with calmness possible only from years of acting fearless even when his gut felt like imploding.

"My name," came the immediate reply, "is not 'you.' I have a *name*, Kristian, and you know what it is."

Against even his battle-honed will, his gaze flinched away from her. He pulled his shoulders back and wondered what the hell it mattered if he looked at her or not. He had not glanced away at seeing the tortured look in her eyes.

Yet as she whispered her next words, no other description existed for it but tortured. "You used to whisper my name like the wind itself. When you called me 'Leprechaun,' it made me wish I could truly become one."

Kris jerked the violent shrug again. "Yes, well," he muttered, "I used to do many things."

"And now?"

"And now I don't."

"Why?" But she didn't stop her siege with the verbal charge. Before Kris could blink in reaction, she snatched the glass from his hand, lobbed it with shatteringly perfect aim into the fireplace, then grabbed up his hand into both her own. "*Why*, Kristian?" she pleaded again, sentencing him to the torment of cupping her cheek as she did so.

"Shivahn—" With a clenched growl, he yanked from her. "Go to bed. You are speaking—"

"The truth between us," she interjected with fast, hard surety, "and you know it. Turn from me, Kristian; go ahead and leave the bloody room if you like. It will not change the fact that you are a butter-blooded, lack-of-a-spine coward who will no more admit the truth of your heart than the nose on your face."

She hadn't just challenged him to pistols at dawn. She'd gone ahead and fired the first shot. Which meant, despite the clamoring protest of his gut and the heartbeat now pounding its way to his head, he had to turn and return her fire with the most lethal weapons at his disposal—in this case, a narrowed, burning glare he had, until tonight, used only on his most vile enemies.

"And what," he leveled with the sneer properly accompanying that stare, "might that 'truth' be?"

The tremor he induced in her was clear to see, claiming her from head to toes, but she maintained every proud inch of her stance. She uttered her reply to him with the same unfaltering conviction.

"The truth that you love me as much as I love you."

The glare drained from his face. Kris managed to draw in a lungful of air, but beside that, he didn't move. His feet might as well have been chained to the floor with Sandys's leg irons. "I—" he finally gritted, "I have no idea what—"

"You have *every* idea what I speak about!" Her retort trembled with encroaching tears. "Damn you, Kristian. *Damn* you! Look at me, Kristian. Look at me as you did that first night we ever held each other . . . as if it were the last night of the world . . . as if we were the last people in the world.

"I am that same woman you gazed upon that night, Kristian. I am that same woman who needs your love. Look upon me again, Kristian . . . and *see* me!"

A growl, low and taut and desperate, resounded in the depths of his throat. *Run—you can run now and never have to do this!*

But he wouldn't run. He knew that as clearly as the uncertainty written so beautifully, bittersweetly on her face . . . the tiny tremors that showed him when she spoke of self-doubt and fear, she spoke of terror she knew all too well.

No, Kris realized, he would not run. And he *would* look at her.

And as he did, she lifted violently shaking fingers to her shoulders.

And when she lowered them, the robe came down, too . . . falling away from her completely nude body.

Chapter 16

The room threatened to close in around her. 'Twas a large room, Shivahn observed in some distant, odd part of her brain; large and comfortable and warm . . . and yet, she shivered.

Oh, God, she shivered. She could not stop, as she stood here enduring the claws of terror as she had never suffered them before. All the soldiers she had seen too late, who already stared at her with death in their eyes; the battlefields where blood had saturated her feet along with the mud; even confronting the heinous glare of Sandys himself . . . those were merely fretful moments compared to the terror of this. They were never a time where the fate of her soul lay in the words of one person's answer. Kristian. *Kristian.* The man she loved . . .

This man who now said naught. Moved naught. Did

naught but gaze at her with eyes she could no more fathom than the green depths of the sea they had crossed together.

The sea they had crossed *together*, she thought with new awareness and hope. The foundations of the bridge they had already begun to forge. A bridge their peoples refused to build from steel and rock, but a bond *they* could make with their passion, their bodies, their love.

Kristian, she supplicated him with her gaze, with every pulse of her heart, *help me bridge the sea. Please help me.*

Why could she not stop shivering?

Her body already knew the answer to that. Her skin eagerly recognized, and came alive with, the intensity of his stare; first the places on her body that had known his attentions before, then the shadows and recesses and secret places that had not. Her breasts tightened and puckered, yearning for the sucklings of his lips. And the moist place centered between her thighs ached in readiness, its want becoming need when Kristian's gaze at last traveled there.

He emitted a harsh breath and, in return, Shivahn held her own. Was his exhalation a sound of denial, or surrender?

She waited through another interminable moment. Yet at last, she decided she could easily claim the ribbon as largest self-made idiot in all of the city this night. Mayhap in the entire country. She blinked back tears, trying to clear her vision enough to find her robe and hide the mortified flush certainly claiming every inch of her now.

Yet it was in that blind moment that a hand curved around her waist. A wonderful, careful, large, and caressing hand.

A soft cry escaped her as he dipped his lips to the base of her neck, his own breath escaping him on a ragged sigh this time. He navigated a soft-suckling path to the sweetly sensitive area beneath her ear, at last rasping there, "Shivahn ... ah, *God,* Leprechaun, I cannot fight this any longer."

At that, her world truly did close in and tumble down. She found herself enveloped in the power of Kristian, the passion of Kristian, as he nearly fell into her, seemingly seized by a need to hold her, tighter, tighter.

"Aye," Shivahn answered to the question he spoke not in words but with his hands, as they covered her back in fervent-fingered strokes. "Aye," she begged him again, laughing and crying at once. She wrapped her arms around his lean, tapered torso, which was sheathed, thank the fates, only in the billowy cream lawn shirt earlier bound in by a gilded waist-coat and stiff linen neckband.

Her touch elicited a rough sound from deep in his throat, a sound both tormented and pleasured. It awakened sensations in her own body, which she could no more give title to than control; sensations strangely frightening to her in their newness yet exhilarating in their primal rightness. Oh, aye, these feelings were as right as the fate and magic that had brought them together in the first place.

They surrendered to a kiss fused of needs too long denied, of hunger too long starved. Shivahn moaned as Kristian swept his tongue through her mouth, taking her like a man indeed famished, kissing her in the same way he low-ered his hands around the spheres of her bottom: hotly, urgently, completely.

When their lips at last broke apart, another groan tore up his throat, the sound bordering on an outcry of a word—only no word would come to express the completion they now discovered. Shivahn knew that as she gazed upon his face, every angle of his features etched in exquisitely savage torment, and she found not a word to describe how beautiful she thought him.

Yet the next moment, even that perception fled her mind

as Kristian introduced wondrous new feelings to her body. He followed the direction of his hands with the trail of his mouth, gliding his lips slowly down between her breasts, over the expanse of her stomach. Then, smoothly kneeling before her, he placed a small yet lingering kiss on the golden curls where every drop of blood in her body seemed to race at once.

"Oh." She gasped, digging her hands into his sweat-dampened hair. "Oh, *Kris* . . ."

She knew not how she remained on her feet as his hands cupped more firmly around her buttocks, pulling her more intimately against his parted mouth and exploring tongue. She cried out as he licked and kissed, suckled and delved, unabashedly opening her. In return he only chuckled wickedly in his throat, then urged her closer to a pulsing tension for which there seemed no ease, only ever-spiraling heights of need.

Beyond her control or caring, her head fell back. Her hair tangled in his fingers as he rocked her pelvis in time to his sweet strokings. His mouth became her anchor and her wings, the core of her earth and the breadth of her sky.

He splayed his hands up to the base of her back, finally allowing her knees to crumble and her body to collapse against him. Together they descended to the crimson rug in front of the waning fire, where Shivahn looked down at his face, now cast in flickering shadows and depthless desire.

She hovered above him for a moment, then kissed him awkwardly but deeply, suddenly unsure about what to do and how to move.

He smiled softly then, as if he had heard her deliberations like spoken words. Shivahn was nay too positive he had *not*, for he coaxed her with rough breath—"Here . . . like this"—before gently prodding her thighs apart to straddle him, sliding her woman's cleft directly against the hard masculine ridge of him.

Now 'twas her turn to smile, as she watched him quake visibly with the contact. His neck arched, and his features smoldered with arousal. When Kristian at last looked back up at her, the depths of his hooded gaze swirled as she had never seen them do so before, caught in maelstroms of an unnameable but unstoppable force.

'Twas with that force that she found herself hauled down next to him the next instant, then swiftly rolled to her back, consumed in another sweeping ecstasy of a kiss. She welcomed Kristian's body upon her, around her, feeling so right against her.

She wanted to feel more of him.

She acted on *that* decision by shyly shifting one button of his shirt free. Then another. But her movements took on jerking brazenness as Kristian pumped his breaths into her ear with each liberated button, rasping to her *"yes"* as he shuddered with the brushings of her fingers.

When she at last freed him from the garment, he wrapped himself closer to her. His mouth consumed hers in a thrusting kiss. Tongues mated. Nipples hardened. Heartbeats joined. And all the world became only fire and need, skin and sensation, a promise pulsating more loudly to its fulfillment . . .

When his lips at last rose from hers, Shivahn let out a reluctant sigh. She opened her eyes in languid anticipation, already envisioning the mesmerizing emerald facets that awaited her from his own gaze.

But naught filled her stare except the shadow that suddenly befell Kristian's features. He kissed her again, yet the offering was as chaste as a peck on the cheek from Gorag. "Kristian," she whispered, writhing beneath him. She no longer wanted but needed surcease from the ache he had kindled inside her woman's core. Dear God, certainly he ached like this, too—if only, mayhap, just a little.

"Kristian," she begged again, *"please . . ."*

In answer, he only gathered up her hand and pressed it to the center of his chest. Shivahn's knuckles vibrated with the wild pummeling of his heartbeat, which added to her amazement that he compelled his voice to such careful steadiness.

"Leprechaun," he said softly to her, "do you know what you are begging me for? Do you know what you are pleading me to do?"

Shivahn knew she owed him an apology for her soft laugh of reaction to that, but her penitence would have to come later. *Much* later. Right now, the sound felt too good on her lips, and she felt too wonderful in his arms.

She followed the outburst by deciding not to tell him what she wanted but to show him. She released her hand from his and glided her own hold up to his nape. With undeniable command, she pulled his lips down to meet hers in the carnal kiss she now craved more ravenously than a chocolate swan tart.

She did not release him from that kiss until harsh breaths and shaking growls raced each other from his chest to his throat—until she felt him quiver violently and press the swell of his sex at her inner thigh. All the while, she let curiosity take over her hands, directing them down the valley of his back, where lengths of corded muscles flexed and tautened at her exploration. He was magnificent, unquestionably sculpted by an angel in the mood to create a sensual masterpiece, and she marveled over every hard, captivating angle of him.

'Twas but another minute before she could no longer repress her urge to travel her touch around his waist, to the top of his black silk breeches, where her fingers skimmed the buttons there. Shivahn swallowed in hesitation, recognizing another crossroads in this exciting but confusing journey they shared.

Yet somehow, Kristian magically read even that thought, for he smiled knowingly as he murmured to her "Go ahead, Leprechaun. *Please,* go ahead . . ."

Her heart now soaring to triple its cadence, she did. As she loosened the fabric between his thighs, Kristian moaned in encouragement. As she pulled his long hose back, the fullness of his desire filled her hand. And his husky groan filled her ears.

"Ah, *God,* Shivahn," he rasped. "Yes . . . *yes.*"

For long minutes, she did not respond, too captivated by the feel of him to bother with speaking. She ran her fingers along the contours and veins of him, the length and velvety knob of him. She even explored the two sacks nestled in the curly hairs at the base of his hardness.

"Kristian," she at last whispered on dry lips, "you are hard."

He had to remoisten his own lips before responding. "Yes."

"And you are hot."

"Oh, *yes.*"

"I . . . I am hot, too, Kristian . . ."

She rasped the last of that against his lips, which parted hers with impassioned urgency . . . at the same time his knees opened her legs with gentle but undeviating intent. As if she wished him to deviate at all! *Do not stop, Kristian,* rang out the bells of her soul, *do not* ever *stop making me feel this way . . .*

And yet, she knew there was more. Oh, aye, there was so much more to feel and to have; there was the completion they both hungered for as Kristian locked his hands into hers and pressed her against the carpet, fully beneath him now.

Awe-filled tears burned to her eyes and rolled down her temples with the sight of him. He had never appeared more her Brave One than he did now ... her damn-the-odds outlaw, her bold sea rebel, her heart's fire. As he rose yet higher over her, she lifted her face to meet him, to accept him into her mouth as she accepted him into her body.

Kristian kissed her hard and deep, his throat vibrating with the labor to breathe as his body shuddered with the exertion of entering her by careful increments. His tongue drove back and forth against hers in time to the small slides of his hips inside hers, until Shivahn thought *she* would explode from the tremoring tension now cleaving them together.

Together ...

Together, they soared to heights far beyond the clouds and the thunderstorms, the stars, and the *Sídhe*. Together, they raced to speeds faster than stallion stampedes and more breathtaking than waterfalls. Together, they became an entity more wild and uncontrollable than they had ever known they could be.

"Oh," she cried with that realization, as she suckled his chin, his jaw, his neck. "Oh, Kristian, it feels so good!"

He nodded to that and added a half-sighed sound of assent, but she somehow knew he did so only with intensely concentrated effort. Affirmation to her impression came the next moment, with his body-consuming quaver.

"Shivahn," he grated against her ear then. "Forgive me ... I don't know how much longer I can—"

Then intense heat burst inside her—a barrier burned away, a long moment of skin-torn pain—but the sound that reverberated through Kristian made her gladly swear she would bear the ordeal to its conclusion. 'Twas what she had dreamed of hearing from him since he sighed in her ear at Trabith's lakeshore . . . mayhap before that, too, in some part of her imagination that lived only in the nakedness of midnight fantasies. 'Twas a sound born in the center of his being, the part of him she now became truly one with, she fitted so hotly and perfectly with.

Let me have the pain, she cried from inside, *if I can also have this joy!*

Yet as the following minutes unfolded, so also did the realization that she might be wrong about her conclusion . . . wondrously, magnificently wrong. For at sometime in those following minutes, Kristian no longer hurt her but began to fill her. And enflame her. To new and amazing heights.

For during those minutes, even as he slid himself again and again into her, he began to touch her in tingling places. He began to stroke her with the slick length of his erection, angling himself to rub her in delicious ways before sliding back into the wetness of her womanhood. 'Twas not long before she found herself echoing Kristian's gasps and moans, as his body exhorted hers to seek some mysterious fulfillment to its burning pressure—

Until suddenly, the fire exploded inside her.

"Kristian!" She cried the beautiful word on a high, hard gasp, as the flames swept her from the inside out. The tip of her every nerve shimmered and shattered in the eruption, until her whole being consisted of naught but an ecstasy of endless fire.

Half an instant later, the conflagration took Kristian, too. 'Twas no confusion to feeling the flames sweep over his body, as he matched her call with a guttural outcry of his own. Shivahn basked in deep satisfaction as she listened to the sound, filled with utterly masculine fulfillment.

They lay there for a long while, heat of skin shared with beats of hearts, still joined as one body, one breath, one being. The way, Shivahn thought, they had meant to be since the moment she first held this man on a cold prison floor. This was the reason she had escaped down terrifying tunnels, sneaked past a mob of her own people, run from battalions of English soldiers, and, aye, even crossed an ocean to the land of her sworn enemy.

Nay, she corrected herself, she had crossed *two* oceans to be here: the wind-lashed waves between two warring islands and the mystery-bound expanse of a man's soul. She did not know which had been the more perilous ordeal. Nor, she conceded, did she care. Both journeys had been worth their ordeals, their setbacks, their seemingly hopeless horizons.

She had arrived now. She was home now. In Kristian's arms now.

Kris awoke with a distinct cramp in his back and a distinct soreness between his thighs.

Both brought a slow, satiated smile to his lips.

Nonetheless, he clamped back a moan as he finally forced himself to move, attempting an escape from the velvet throw pillow wedged between his head and arm and the lap blanket entangled around his legs. He'd recruited both off the couch after Shivahn had burrowed into his arms last night—then fallen promptly and peacefully to sleep. She'd felt so perfect there that he could find neither the heart nor the inclination to awaken her for the trip upstairs. So he'd rekindled the fire and created a bed for them right there.

Then enjoyed the deepest sleep he'd had for days.

He harbored no doubts about the source of his sudden nocturnal peace. The added presence in his "bed" was worth every bruise and cramp he endured now.

No, he modified that, he'd subject himself to a bloody broken leg in order to gain this moment of satiated serenity once more. Shivahn . . . ah, God, she'd freed more than his body last night. She'd let loose, at last, his spirit . . . she'd run with him in realms of completion he'd never imagined; showed him meadows of joy he never knew his soul possessed; dipped him in oceans of need he thought he'd already navigated. And in the end, he'd discovered a peace in his heart he'd assumed long dead inside of him.

Along with a terror not so unfamiliar.

And yet, though he had long ago made room for terror's presence in his life, he rubbed his hand over the depths of the gut it burned into with more searing force than ever before. But the new sensation still didn't come as a shock. Kris knew the vulnerability he opened inside himself the moment he first pressed to Shivahn last night . . . the moment he admitted he loved her.

That realization spurred him into a sitting position, as he gazed around the room for its golden-haired cause, who was now glaringly absent from the immediate area.

He had little trouble locating her. Still clothed only in her pale cream nudity and her cascade of hair, Shivahn wandered among the heavy furniture and ancient knickknacks on the far side of the study with the ease of a forest fairy taking a stroll through morning dew. Except, he noted, for the look of concentrated curiosity on her face as she arrived at one knickknack in particular.

The knickknack that had warranted her banishment from this room in the first place.

She sensed that fact somehow, Kris comprehended then, as well. He came to the conclusion while observing the way she lifted her fingertips to the glass dome enclosing his treasure. She touched the glass as if beholding some sacred

Celtic cross in her own land: with contemplative reverence and quiet honor.

As she halted in that position, Kris greedily drank in the sight of her. As he did, a heated sting filled his head. By all her bloody saints, she was beautiful.

She was his.

He made his way across to her and, having brought the blanket with him, wrapped it around her from behind as he moved into the same position, joining his hands in the valley below her breasts.

"Hallo, callow laddie," Shivahn murmured in emulation of Fionna's affectionate greeting.

"Hallo, gorgeous wench." Kris smiled, reveling in the way he had elicited a giggle strong enough to gently jostle her breasts atop the suddenly sensitive hairs on his arms.

She didn't giggle for long, though. Not after he nudged aside her hair to nuzzle wet kisses up her nape, then behind her ear, finally nipping at the enticing lobe itself. At that point, her breath dissolved into a contented sigh. Kris echoed the sound a moment later, as he rested his cheek atop her hair.

That was when he looked again to her fingers, still rested atop the glass dome in front of them.

She did not have to speak her questions about the object beneath the dome. Kris knew all the words, *felt* them beat out to him in the thumps of the heart beneath the skin he now stroked steadily with his thumbs. He also knew Shivahn demanded no reply, would be content not knowing all the business of his life, now that he'd let her into his soul.

But his soul and his business were inextricably bound, and now that he'd entrusted her with one, he longed to have her know the other. Perhaps even needed to tell her. God, oh, God, just to have one person—*this* person—to share in every aspect of his world and, yet, still love him atop it all . . .

Was such a miracle possible? Once, not so long ago, he hadn't believed it. He'd resigned himself to living out the rest of his life, what there would be of it, with a part of him missing, a part quietly sacrificed for the greater picture he'd painted himself into. Just like Rayne had done. Only Rayne had made the sacrifice look so easy . . .

Rayne had also never known Shivahn. And the miracles she didn't just ask a man to believe in, but *showed* him how to.

Miracles. Yes, Kris decided, they were well worth the risk—even the risk of the truth.

With that resolution lending strength to his will, he broke their silence in a low murmur against her temple. "You were right last night, you know."

Her smile reflected in the dome she still fingered. "Which time?"

Kris did not answer her yet. He wrapped himself tighter around her, waiting for the wordless melding of their souls to form into a tangible warmth around their bodies, as well.

When that happened, he whispered to her once more. "I love you. I . . . have loved you for a long while, perhaps since the night I first gazed upon you."

Shivahn said nothing to that, yet as complete as her silence came the surety that she held her tongue on purpose. For which Kris thanked her with equally mute fervency. He had more to say. Much more.

"I did not tell you last night," he continued, emboldened, "in the middle of—" The word fizzled on his lips, suddenly not so emboldened. "While we were—well, so you'd think I only—"

"Used the words to bed me?" came the laughter-edged return.

His lips twitched with the temptation to join her—for one second. "Leprechaun, I'm serious."

"So am I." Yet as she turned in his embrace and looked up at him, bright glints of mirth still sparkled in both hues of her beautiful eyes. "Kristian, who dropped her clothes for whom last night?"

He could return nothing to that but a capitulating quirk of brows. She had a point. He knew it, and *she* certainly knew it, as she gloated over her victory with a grin more she-devil than fairy. As a flag of surrender, she demanded a lingering kiss from him. When she'd collected her concession to satisfaction, she settled her cheek to his chest . . . both of them looking again to the glass dome and its contents.

And again, her unspoken questions hovered in the air. Echoing in the trills and tweets of the rising morning birds. Clacking in the wheels of a morning merchant's cart on the cobblestones. Reverberating in the encroaching thunder of his heartbeat.

Kris swallowed hard on that painful thunder before softly stating "It belonged to an ancestor of mine."

Her head stirred against his left nipple in a small fidget of confusion. "What did?"

"The battle helmet," he explained, "beneath the dome. 'Tis why it's there . . . it's over four hundred years old. It was made in 1308 for a man named Symon de Montagu, my grandfather many times over." He paused for a moment, marveling at how the act of releasing information instead pushed open the gates inward, letting in a flood of deep pride across his soul. With renewed veneration to his voice, he added, "He was a great man."

During his accounting, Shivahn didn't move. Nevertheless, he felt her encouraging succor around his soul as if she'd physically wrapped herself closer to him. "Tell me more," she prodded, her breath warming the skin directly over his heart.

At that, Kris smiled wryly. "Well, he didn't carry out his knighthood under the most pleasant pair of kings to rule England. Edward the Second was nearly a madman when he was forced to abdicate his throne, and Edward the Third, while more stable, ascended to the throne at fifteen. I wager many of his monarchial decisions were made using both heads on his body."

Though Shivahn raised a soft slap to his face at that, she did so while chuckling.

Dear God, it felt wonderful to speak this freely, to stand this freely, naked in the middle of his study with a woman. The woman he fell more madly in love with by the minute.

He grabbed her hand long enough to imprint a kiss upon her palm before continuing. "Still, even in the midst of the chaos around him, Symon bridged a better path for his life and for the welfare of England. And those bridges were *not* easy to erect. George's atrocities on Ireland now are toddlers' games compared to what the Plantagenets did to cripple Wales . . . and I suppose you can wager on who was called upon to clean up the mess when they were done."

Shivahn's curls tickled the underside of his chin as she nodded. "The new knights of the realm."

Kris nodded, as well. "Knights like Symon de Montagu, whose lives depended on their ability to create peace out of destruction, bounty out of hunger . . . something whole out of something some murdering bastards destroyed."

He couldn't rein back the savage growl underlining the last of his words. Nor, Kris concluded, did he have to. This was Shivahn in his arms; Shivahn, who understood his snarls and his rage, his vulnerability and his fears—understood them because she had lived them all, too.

Because of that comprehension, he didn't shirk her hand

when she again lifted her hand to his face. This time, she used the contact to guide his gaze into hers. He did not find another place to avert his stare, but let her see every contortion of the unbridled anguish still yet to be avenged in his soul.

After gazing at him as if physically drinking in his features, she looked back to the helmet once more. She said nothing through the next breath-held moment, but Kristian waited for her whispered words to come. The words that would save him . . . and condemn her.

"The beast . . . sculpted on the top of the helmet . . . 'tis a griffin, Kristian, isn't it?"

Chapter 17

lowly Kris nodded.

Softly Shivahn pressed herself to him and rose up on tiptoes to brush every surface of his lips with hers.

"Thank you," she told him. "Thank you, my brave Griffin." Her eyes were a tear-glimmered magic spell, her smile a tremulous offering of love.

She was the most breathtaking thing he'd ever seen.

And he had probably just signed her death warrant with his confession.

The realization speared a ragged inhalation up his throat. *"Thank* me?" he returned on the equally harsh release of that breath. He framed the side of her face with the whole of his right hand. "Ah, God, Leprechaun, don't. *Don't* thank me." He slid his hand into her hair, her thick curls winding around his fingers as desperate fear entwined around his senses. "You don't know what you've just asked for. What kind of life you're—"

Shivahn twisted herself free of him with such sudden ire, she yanked the rest of the words from his tongue, too. "I think I *know* about the 'kind of life' you speak of, Mr. Montague. Mayhap more than *you*."

"Mayhap," Kris conceded quietly.

His assent prompted her to a calming inhalation. "As for what I have 'asked for' now, do you think this new knowledge will glean me any more trouble than what I shall get from Sandys eventually, being implied as your accomplice across the whole of Ireland?"

At the brows he furrowed in unexpected comprehension, she beamed a gloating smile. "Ahhh. The Englishman finally sees the light."

At that, Kris's lips curved upward, too. He guided her hands up and around his neck, before he raked his hands around her waist. "Right now, I see only you," he told her thickly, uncaring about the blanket now falling away from them. She was truly here, he reaffirmed to himself; he wouldn't wake up to an empty bed and his unfulfilled fantasies, for the heated shimmers of her touch spread all-too-real magic into the place where they traced circles into his nape.

"My little accomplice," he murmured, brushing kisses across the sprays of freckles on her nose. "That has a nice ring to it, I think."

"Mmmm." She sidled closer to him, tilting her chin back so her lips received his oral caress, instead. "I think so, too."

Her following sigh opened a surge of desire through Kris. He didn't try to fight the flood, deepening his kiss as the wave crashed through him. Shivahn reacted with a wanton sound in her throat as she welcomed the bold stroke of his tongue, suckling him back with equal passion, perhaps even more, than the impassioned fervor she'd given him last night.

Kristian matched her mewl with a rough groan, as his blood simmered and his body hardened. The press of her stomach against the length of his arousal did *not* aid matters, only reminding him of the tight velvet walls inside her, as well. He couldn't stop kissing her, craving more of her, too long denied the warm, intoxicating taste of her.

"Kristian," she rasped when they pulled away to draw breaths of heavy need, "I am wondering . . ."

"Please do," he urged, shifting his hands around her bottom . . . imagining himself holding her like this as he drove deeper inside her.

"I . . . I have never been an accomplice before."

He smiled against her neck. "Mmmm-hmmm?"

"And I imagine the duties of the position must be many."

"Oh," he agreed, "many."

"And I suppose you will have to tutor me how to do everything correctly."

Her voice's harmony of sensual intimation yet guileless unsurety nearly proved his undoing. Kris clenched his jaw and took a pair of hard breaths before he could answer her. "Oh, Leprechaun . . . I'm a good tutor."

"I hope so." Again, her words vibrated with an irresistible combination of mock solemnity and true determination. "I so want to serve you well, Kristian."

A handful of wit-filled comebacks swirled readily to his mind in reply to that. Just as swiftly, they vanished. More accurately, they were burned away, as the skin of his shoulders, then his chest, then his stomach came alive beneath a tremoring pair of hands . . . ah, *God*, such a magical pair of hands, igniting pure-flamed ecstasy to every inch they roamed.

For the first time in his life, Kris looked to the study's

gaudy clutter of furniture in gratitude, for 'twas the back of the velvet settee next to them that offered him salvation from completely crumbling to the floor, his muscles on their way to becoming blocks of scorched ashes. But sweet Christ, he thought, what a fire in which to be torched alive . . . this conflagration of her touch, like no other heat he'd felt off her fingers before, as if her newfound depths of passion now poured like molten sparks through her skin.

And through *his* skin . . .

His harsh rasps echoed through his head as she rained those sparks around his navel, then spread to both his hip bones. At last Shivahn converged her hands inwardly again, igniting him into hotter need as her fingers trailed closer and closer—

"Dear *God*," he cried hoarsely. His head arched back as her hands surrounded the length of him. Now he did crumble, folding to his knees, almost laughing from the intensity of his sexual anticipation, especially as Shivahn descended with him, still holding him in her hands as she showered small kisses along his shoulders.

"Leprechaun . . . Leprechaun," he heard himself babble, trying to remember if he really *had* tossed back that brandy last night. He felt half drunk and wholly delirious. "What are you doing to me . . . what are you doing to me?"

But all he heard in answer was a slow, low throb, gathering force through the white-hot buzzing in his ears. The sensation drowned out all else except for the recognition that suddenly her mouth replaced her hands.

He felt himself fall completely back against the carpet, helpless against the sweet, wet assault of her tongue and her lips, on him and around him, shyly yet exquisitely nursing the very life from him . . .

In a torrent of rushing heat, Kris at last gave her what she wanted, surrendering to a soundless scream and a celestial-force climax. An appropriate analogy, he thought then. Surely no man would be given a gift of such shattering magnitude, then allowed to live beyond the experience. He only hoped his Creator would be as generous on the other side of mortality.

When he summoned the strength to open his eyes again, an angel indeed peered down on him. In turn, Kris drank in the sight of multifaceted amethyst eyes, a wild array of gold curls, and a grin favoring an all-knowing creature from the clouds.

Or a she-wolf who'd just bested her hunter.

'Twas that last observation that convinced him God had decided to give him another go at mortality's adventures. Kris even released an appropriately earthy chuckle before quipping "You're very proud of yourself, aren't you?"

"Aye," Shivahn returned without hesitation. Only then did her stare flicker with doubt. "Unless," she ventured, nervously nibbling the inside of her cheek, "I did not please you."

"No . . . *no.*" Kris tried—in vain—to repress his deep laugh. "My love," he went on gently, "you pleased me. You *pleased* me. But"—he allowed a scowl to crunch his features then—"there *is* one problem I still have left . . ."

Now she really reminded him of a she-wolf, every inch of her pricking to silent tension with the first hint of trouble on the air. "What?"

"If I could only find a way to wipe that self-pleased smirk off your face."

The very expression of which he spoke spread wider across her lips. "Of whatever do you speak?" she countered with innocent coyness, only increasing Kris's craving to kiss her senseless.

"Oh," he replied with a wolfish note or two of his own, "I think you know of what I speak."

He gave her no chance to even ponder a comeback. He took her lips as first hostages in his own siege of passion, while he entrapped her breasts against his chest with commanding hands upon her spine. Into her mouth he swept his relentless tongue, until he felt her limbs grow weak and her heartbeat pound against his own ribs.

Eagerly he launched the next stage of his campaign: Still engaging her mouth in teasing nips and licks, Kris pressed her back, slowly back, until she lay below him, both the carpet and their discarded blanket forming a luxurious pallet beneath them.

Still, neither layer of their bedding held a fraction of the incredible softness his fingers met at the apex of her thighs. Shivahn gasped as he slid a finger between her golden curls; she seized his shoulders as he continued his foray deeper into the tight core of her. When a consuming tremor claimed her, Kris recognized the unsteady cadence of his own breaths . . . the erratic ecstasy washing over his own nerve endings.

He never knew that bringing joy to another would fill *him* with such exhilaration, as well! Oh, countless were the moments of quiet satisfaction at witnessing children hugging the gifts the Griffin had left the night prior, or hearing the new note of hope in tavern songs because of prized information the Griffin had smuggled to Insurgent troops. But like an uninvited wedding guest, he'd never allowed himself to become a part of the celebration. He'd lifted mugs of ale and smiled wordless smiles—to do any less in Ireland would single him out more glaringly than sporting a green feather in his hat—but danger's necessity had always kept the mask of his performance firmly tied in place, never really gleaning the elation he gifted to others . . .

Until now. Oh, yes, until now, as the gates of the wedding feast at last flung open for him. The sweet bells of

Shivahn's sighs rang in his head . . . the lush wine of her passion filled his mouth . . .

"Kristian," she whispered with a bemused half smile, "now *you're* smirking."

"And you're wet," he replied with grinning flippancy. Yet the next moment, his voice dropped to a rough rasp as his lips dipped to her breast. "So wet and tight and hot . . ."

He shifted over her then, locking his hands atop hers against the carpet as he positioned his sex, hard and erect once more, at her moist folds. He brushed his lips to hers as he savored the half moment of anticipation before sheathing himself inside her. He couldn't wait to be deep and hot inside her . . .

"Kris!"

No, came his mind's first roaring answer. *No, you didn't hear that. Or maybe you did . . . maybe that's really Shivahn gasping your name, and your imagination has turned the sound into John's bellow, instead.*

"Kris, where the bloody hell are you?"

Kris inhaled the necessary air for a filth-drenched oath, only to find himself bested in the feat by Shivahn. To his vexation, the profanity only made him harder for her.

Still, he somehow found the fortitude to chuckle as she moaned into his chest with a girlish pout, "Is he *not* supposed to be somewhere repairing the ship, Kristian?"

"He must be finished," he informed her with an assuaging kiss.

"Kris, where *have* ya gone off to?" John's voice rang closer. "We've nearly finished with the *Wing*'s repairs!"

"Imagine that," Shivahn grumbled as they struggled to their feet. Yet halfway during their trip back to their array of shed clothes, Kris pulled her against him once more, capturing her in a kiss intended to accomplish one purpose: to underline the authority of his next words.

"We shall continue this later," he dictated with a meaningful growl, "in a proper bed."

Shivahn did not, however, make the order so effortless to abide by. "Aye-aye, Captain," she acquiesced past her dreamily closed eyes, as the effects of the kiss clearly lingered on through her slightly swaying body. There, in her unguarded, unabashed nudity, she tempted him to take her again more than all her other seductions combined.

Dear God, 'twas going to be hard to keep his hands off her now.

No, he determined within the next ten minutes, 'twas going to be bloody near impossible to keep his hands off her.

In the space of those ten minutes, he dressed quickly and opened the study door just as Shivahn disappeared out the servants' door on the other side of the room. She reappeared at the top of the main stairs with timing that might as well have been staged, so perfectly did she materialize at the same moment he finally dragged John in from flirting with the kitchen maids.

His first mate clearly forgot about the wenches, however, upon beholding his "little minx," who'd literally thrown herself into a blouse, country jacket, and several skirt layers, and still looked regal as Queen Josephine while descending to greet them. With good-natured laughs, she endured John's bearish embrace and three twirling circles—while Kris battled shockingly potent stings of the same possessive urge that had plagued him during their flight from Trabith. He clenched his fists against the longing to march over, sweep her into his own arms, and haul her upstairs.

Instead, he had to settle for sauntering back toward the library with painstakingly deceptive ease. He set the limit at modulating his voice, however. Heaven could only demand so much decorum from him on four hours' sleep. "All right, damn it," he fired irritably over his shoulder. "You're here to report, not cast your anchor for purchase in my front hall."

"Nice to see ya, too, Cock 'n' Bull," came the sneering reply.

When Kris declined to relax even at the invocation of the nickname—mainly because John still kept an arm snaked around Shivahn's waist as they entered the room—his first mate finally stiffened to a more pragmatic mien. "I'll be happy to start the reporting whenever you like, *Captain*. I was just of the thinking we were waiting to . . . dismiss the delicate ears from the room."

At that, Shivahn stepped forward with her own stiffened spine. Kris only wished she didn't have to be so damned adorable about her outrage. "I do *not* have delicate ears," she snapped.

John swept his arms into a surrendering U. "Guess I didn't tackle *that* headwind right."

"What I believe she means," Kris interjected, "is that reports don't have to be secrets around here anymore, John."

It took but half a second for the light of comprehension to spread across John's face. The man filled the other half of that second with a triumphant whistle. "I guess I really owe thanks to yer *Sídhe* folk now, little minx." He chuckled. "I don't know how ya got him to spill the swill, but I'm sure glad ya did."

Shivahn accepted the congratulations with a grin to match John's, though she added a knowing slant to that look as she wrapped her arms around Kris with proud boldness. "I . . . got him to spill many things."

Now they all joined in a laugh, though when John lowered his head, his features tightened into a glower. "Hell's bloody hounds," he growled, "it took you two long enough." He wheeled to the spirits cart. "I think my patience deserves some o' yer fancy brandy, Cock 'n' Bull."

"*Your* patience?" Shivahn fired to that, squirming in Kris's embrace, her unfulfilled passion clearly turning her into a spitfire leprechaun looking for the tiniest excuse for a fight.

Kris, however, held her fast and firm. "John," he prompted, "the report? Remember—the reason you're here at this ungodly hour to begin with?"

"Aye," his first mate agreed with a satisfied smack of lips and an admiring look at his half-empty tumbler.

"Well?"

"In a few words, things have gone more seamless than satin," John finally said. "The necessary mendings have been put to the sails, and we've got the shell of a new galley up." Then, with a mischievous glint in the wink he flashed back at Kristian: "I've checked every inch of the hold, too. The false bottom is worth every shilling ya paid for it, lad."

"Damn straight," Kristian returned. "I had the work done in Ireland."

"Right under those red coats' high-faluting noses, too." John directed the aside to Shivahn, who in turn lifted her gaze to Kris. And though he kept his own eyes fixed on his first mate, he felt her regard, filled with a quietly intense awe, seeping into him like rays of a summer sunrise—too bright to look at, too addicting to ignore.

"All right, John," he forced himself to press on, before those images of dragging her upstairs took over his mind again, "give me the straight shot from the barrel. How soon do you think we can make the crossing to Ireland again?"

John lowered his gaze into a probing question, and Kris sensed Shivahn seconded the look. "You're that anxious to leave, then? You've barely rested, Kris."

He compressed his lips and dragged a hand through his hair. "Rest wasn't the purpose of this trip, John."

"I'm aware of that. But once we've hoisted full sail, your dear granddaddy's protection blows out with the wind, too." John leveled an even more somber stare. "Are ya ready to go the next round with Sandys? Are ya really ready?"

Kris deliberated how to respond to that. In the moment he took to choose his words—of which his mind possessed a vexating dearth—a cavalry arrived to help his quest, in the form of Fionna's recognizable rap on the door. When Kris bade her enter, the Irishwoman presented a sealed envelope with his name alone on the outside, penned by a distinctly educated hand.

That was when Kris lifted his gaze back to John before sliding his finger beneath the seal on the missive. "Do I *want* to leave?" he replied as he did. "My friend, the choice may not be mine any longer."

With her heart beating inexplicably faster, Shivahn watched Kristian's fingers flip open the fine parchment of the letter. Her gaze rose to his face as he silently read the contents; she took in the multiple stages of reaction across the captivating angles she found there. First, his brows and eyes narrowed in concentration. Next, he flashed a fierce smile. Then he looked up to them again, a renewed decisiveness outlining his jaw.

He looked to John, and after a moment, they exchanged even wider smiles. Shivahn knew not what message they shared, but John's next question did not come as a surprise to her, either.

"I take it the Griffin is flying again?"

"The Griffin is flying again." Kristian issued the confirmation with an attempt at calmness, yet Shivahn felt the excitement beneath his words. "And this time, with quite a treasure."

The excitement, she witnessed the next moment, was infectious. Kristian's statement jerked John off the couch faster than a passing doxy with half her chest spilling from her corset. "The guns?" he exclaimed. "The bastard came through with the guns?"

Kristian's lips parted on a dazzling grin of his own. "All two hundred of them. With ample balls and patches, too."

John exploded with a heathen outcry and swept Shivahn into a reckless half jig of a dance. After he swung her back to the couch, he bounded to Kristian. "Ya got 'em," he muttered as they embraced roughly. "Ya really got 'em, Cock 'n' Bull, and I'm proud as hell of ya."

Kristian disengaged himself to pace her way with an alluring emerald sparkle to his gaze, an irresistible dimple forming itself in his right cheek and an inviting swagger to his hips she could *not* tear her stare from.

"Forgive our furor, Leprechaun," he said softly as he sank to the cushion next to her, slipping his arm around her with an intimate surety she did not mind at all. "We *do* have a good reason for this celebration. I have been carefully persuing a . . . friend, if you will, who plays a strong part in choosing and ordering supplies for His Majesty's troops in Ireland."

"Supplies," Shivahn echoed. "Supplies . . . such as rifles?"

"Supplies such as rifles," he verified. "And now, my friend has sent me word that he'd like to help me level out the battlefields a bit." He displayed the letter again between two raised fingers.

John added a hearty chortle to that. "Two hundred shiny new flintlocks are likely to do a *lot* of leveling."

Shivahn, on the other hand, felt like doing much more

than chortling. She felt capable of jumping to the bloody moon. Instead, she threw herself somewhere much better: into the arms of this man she loved for new reasons every passing hour. In *this* hour, most certainly, 'twas for the unspeakable courage that had led him to contact someone with possible access to King George himself.

"Oh, Kristian," she exclaimed into the curve of his nape, "this is wonderful!"

Kristian accepted her gratitude with a deep masculine sound of pleasure, which quickly translated itself into more obvious form . . . between his thighs. "I can think of a few ways we can celebrate further," he murmured into her ear.

Shivahn found his own ear for her whispered response. "You are the captain of this mission, Mr. Montague . . . therefore, your wish must be my command."

Just as his lips found hers, but before his tongue plumbed her anticipating warmth, a sharp groan annihilated their reverie. "Good Christ," John followed to the eruption. "Would you two throw a bucket of ice on it long enough to discuss when and how we're moving the goods to the *Wing*?"

Reluctantly Shivahn joined Kristian in recognizing the use of John's suggestion. She rose from the couch as Kristian gave his first mate an impressively composed reply.

"That information isn't given here," he stated. "Just in case the messenger—"

"—was followed," John concluded in unison with him. He followed with an approving nod. " 'Twas a shrewd precaution to take. So yer to meet him in person for the rendzevous information, instead?"

Kristian answered with his own nod. "Tomorrow night. In the gardens at the Shropton estate."

Shivahn started as John pounced across the room with thrice his intensity as before. "The *Shropton* estate?" he charged. "Correct me if I'm spouting wrong, lad, but is that not the big, new place up off Manchester Square, where they're tossing that fancy ball tomorrow night?"

Kristian reacted to his mate's theatrics as if John had merely confirmed directions to the market. "Precisely."

"Precisely? What do ya mean, precisely? Unless yer man's as barmy as the stunt he's let ya talk him into."

"No. I'd say he's more a genius."

Kristian reached to his desk and began to dally with an instrument comprised of mirrors, knobs, and an open metal triangle—a sextant, Shivahn remembered Nathan calling one of them on the *Wing*'s quarterdeck. "If *you* were one of Sandys's minions," he posed to John then, "would you suspect the Griffin of the audacity to carry out his business at one of the premier London social events of the year, beneath the noses of nearly everyone in George's court?"

John exhaled slowly. "Ya . . . got a point," he conceded. "I think."

"Point or no point," Kristian responded, "there is still one thing I am very much lacking."

"What's that?" queried John.

Kristian set down the sextant as he raised his head with a sole target for his sights. As his gaze locked to her, Shivahn noticed a glint to his green eyes she had never beheld there before. She almost laughed at the observation . . . if dread didn't clutch so oddly in her throat. 'Twas *he* who had the look of a mischief-minded leprechaun this time.

"I need a lady fair to accompany me to the ball."

She was *not* his lady fair. At least not when the duties extended to things like gala ball attendance in the center of London, England. Shivahn had proclaimed as much when the absurd suggestion had erupted from Kristian's lips—

only to encounter the full force of the determination that had well earned the man a place on Sir Symon de Montagu's bloodline.

"Look at me, you halfwit!" she had shouted at him. "By the saints, I am a country healer from a village half the size of St. James Park!"

Kristian's comment to that had entailed marching across the study, hoisting her off her feet, and carrying her up the stairs meant for a queen. But she was no queen!

"Look at my feet," she had cried in desperation, kicking as they dangled from his hold. "They are as big as a duck's. I cannot *dance* on them!"

"You'll follow my lead," he said—nay, commanded—to that.

"But—my hair—"

"Is beautiful. And will be even more so with fresh wisteria woven into it."

"And I am to wear naught else but wisteria buds?"

"You'll wear only the finest satin." With that, his voice had descended to a protective growl. "Something in indigo, I think. Aye, I'll make sure Fionna tells Madame LeTroux to bring over several bolts of indigo."

By that time, they had arrived at a large, carved oak door at the end of the north wing. As Kristian maneuvered the door open without losing an ounce of his hold on her, she had still been concentrating too hard on her list of protests to fully appreciate the mahogany beauty of his bedroom, or its view of a garden that looked plucked straight from the Beara Peninsula itself.

"Kristian, you are not listening to me," she pressed as he kicked the door shut and set her down. "For that matter, *listen* to me. My brogue—'twas *you* who pointed out the problem of it the day we—"

"Which is why you became my cousin from Germany,"

he parried, still maddeningly sure in voice despite the increasing urgency of his caresses on her body. "Remember?" he had murmured into her neck, before taking wet nips of the skin there.

"Stop it," she had attempted to order him. "*Stop it.* We have not even discussed my eyes—even that lad back in Rosslare knew to look for my eyes—and my hands—sometimes I cannot control what they—"

He first cut her short with a swift but deep kiss. After releasing her from that, he directed in a murmur *not* to be defied, "Your eyes and your hands, you shall keep to yourself. Both those treasures belong to me, and I shall never share them. So, Mistress Armagh, I suggest you put them to very good use *now*."

For the next hour, Shivahn had joyously done that. And she would have been ecstatic doing naught else with the rest of their day, but Kristian, in his infuriating Montague tenacity, was avowed to seeing her in indigo satin before the sun dipped behind the trees of Hyde Park that day.

And so, just as she had surrendered to the first moments of a warm nap atop his chest, he slapped both cheeks of her bottom and leapt from the bed with breathtaking grace. Shivahn's ire had brewed hotter when realizing she could not even level him a proper glare of reaction. The sight of his thoroughly naked muscles had dominated her sights beyond all other purposes.

Now, however, she exacted her revenge for that moment. Standing three feet from the floor atop a stool surely made for a two-year-old, Shivahn recruited every feature of her face to the sole mission of giving Kristian Montague a glower to plague his dreams. The task, she admitted, did not demand much effort. She had spent the better part of the day staring longingly out at the garden, its paths awash in summer's warmth, while *she* was awash in yards of stiff

satin, then more yards of itchy lace. The torture session did
not end there. She had also been forced to scrunch her feet
into all manner of torture devices that were cleverly dis-
guised as, in Madame LeTroux's own words, "zee most
booteeful new shoes you weel ever wear, *ma petite!*"

The little Frenchwoman approached her with those
high-heeled beasts again now, beaming like a little girl
showing off her new doll. Shivahn felt stupid as that play-
thing, too, and she told Kristian as much with another
clenching glare.

"Turn around!" came Madame LeTroux's excited coo.
"Turn around now, *ma petite*, and behold zee butterfly and
her new weengs!"

Shivahn did not want to turn around. She longed to jump
off this awful stool and into Kristian's strong, savoring
embrace. By the increasing play of intensity across his lips,
she knew he wished for the same thing, too.

Then why did he play into Madame LeTroux's silly
game, striding forward like a French cavalier to the
woman's giggling courtesan? Why did he bow before the
stool and extend his hand to *her*, as if requesting a dance of
Queen Titania herself? Why did he stupidly kiss her hand
and murmur, "*Madmoiselle* Armagh, may I escort you to
the mirror?"

"Oh . . . *my.*" Shivahn gasped the next moment. Why had
they both acted so giddy, indeed. A sensation akin to giddi-
ness showered like rainbow crystals through her own senses
now, as she stared at the incredible woman in the three-part
looking glass.

The gown was far from finished. Earlier, Madame
LeTroux had promised Kristian her seamstresses would
work shifts through the night to complete the dress in time
for the ball. Madame had rebuffed Shivahn's protests to
that, with assurances she would be well compensated for the

effort, including the reward of seeing Shivahn dressed in the finished creation.

For the first time, Shivahn believed what the woman said. The satin fabric, dyed the deep purple of a king's robe, fell in equally royal swags from her waist to the floor, then again in glorious flounces behind her. Along the curve of each swag were bunches of silk stitched to look like miniature wisteria buds; those lavender flowers also lined the sides of the squared neck, which topped a stomacher comprised of tiny purple satin bows. Hanging from the centers of a few of the bows were seed pearls shaded of the lightest pink. Tomorrow night, Madame informed her, all the bows would be finished and adorned as such.

Tomorrow night.

Shivahn's heartbeat lurched to her throat as her mind repeated the words. Tomorrow night was truly to be a reality, then. She would truly enter a den of people who would slaughter her rather than look at her. Who would rape her rather than dance with her.

Yet tomorrow night, the battle lines would not be even that clear. And the spoils of the contest so much more critical. Which made Lady Shropton's ballroom the most dangerous battlefield she would ever cross.

And cross it, Shivahn admitted with a resigned sigh, she would.

Aye, she would enter the lions' den tomorrow night, and she would do so in this grand contraption of a dress, with this frightened but brave smile on her face. Because she would do so on the arm of the man who still lit up this room with his approving smile, the man she loved . . . the man who had crossed many lions' dens for people who would never know him or thank him.

She would do this, she pledged, for Kristian . . . the man *and* the Griffin, both inextricably bound in this incredible being and, therefore, she now realized, bound inside *her*, as well.

In short, she also realized, her decision had really been made hours ago.

God help them both if that choice had been rendered in error.

erhaps, Kris thought, he really had made the wrong decision in bringing her here.

They had been in the Shroptons' main ballroom for mere moments before a dozen male stares greedily appraised the woman on his arm. Not that he blamed them. Donned in Madame LeTroux's finished gown, adorned with the amethyst necklace he'd sneaked out and purchased for her on Jermyn Street, her curls cascading around a spray of fresh wisteria, the sight of her had stolen his breath and left him with a thoroughly wonderful tightness in his chest.

He had no idiot but himself to blame for this quandary. He had reasoned, even argued with himself that a partner at his side would dilute the flood of attention he usually endured at these affairs. But only at this instant did he recognize the "logic" for the excuse it really was: to spoil

Shivahn with all the capacities at his disposal for at least one night; to give her a few hours of magic and beauty as recompense for the multitudes *she* had given *him*.

It seemed he had succeeded at his task. In blazing glory. In doing so, he had sealed himself into the most uncomfortable pair of breeches in the room: those of the man forced to stand by as every man in the room preened and fawned for his "cousin." He, on the other hand, could not so much as curl a hand around the waist that had laid bare against his through the hours of the previous night . . . and damn it, he swore, which would lay with him *again* after this bloody ordeal was through.

Uncontrollably, his mind slipped ahead four hours, into a heated vision of just how he'd savor the ecstasy of stripping her inch by tantalizing inch, kissing each exposed portion of her milky skin as he went—

He never saw Julia Shropton approach them until escape clearly ceased to be an option. "Damn," he muttered from locked teeth, stiffening instinctively.

At the same moment Kris rigidified the veneer of his defenses, Shivahn's gloved hand seized tighter around his arm, as well. He didn't blame her. The Viscountess Shropton cut a path through a room intimidating as a black cat's—an appropriate comparison, he ruminated, as it aptly represented the level of her morals.

"Kristian, you naughty boy," she greeted in a husky purr. "You have been away much too long." The last of that, she emphasized with the slide of a thin finger down the length of the arm Shivahn didn't occupy.

"Lady Shropton," he replied, dutifully bowing over the bony hand attached to the wandering finger. As he forced himself to brush Julia's knuckles with a gentleman's kiss, Kris wondered if the woman had taken a whole bloody bath in her cloying, fake-flowered perfume. Nevertheless, with a smile that couldn't be more false if he'd hammered it on, he ventured, "You are looking every inch"—*the desperate trollop, with that bodice plunged halfway to your navel*—"the quintessential hostess this evening."

"Oh, my word," Julia drawled back. "So I am 'quintessential' now. Well, you are forgiven from calling me that this evening, Kristian, only if you do not address me as 'Lady' *anything* anymore."

She graduated her emphasis from a finger to an eyebrow this time, the brow's etched black perfection arching at him as a suggestion to let her body follow suit. Yet the next moment, Julia transmuted into a flawless party hostess again, turning a gracious smile upon Shivahn. "Your penance also consists of introducing me to this adorable creature on your arm. She has swept away half the gentlemen in my ballroom, and I insist on being the first to know her secret."

Despite the lilt of droll bemusement to Julia's voice, Kristian didn't miss the woman's trace of genuine amazement, as well. Julia truly found it a mystery why Shivahn had distracted half the men off the dance floor, even away from the lavish buffet spread along the far wall of the room.

Fighting the urge to laugh at them all became as excruciating as tamping the urge to show them she was no "cousin" to him. And after drowning her in a kiss nothing short of ravishing, he could slide them all an arrogant grin, while declaring they'd all temporarily forgotten their wives and lovers for a magical beauty from the heart of Ireland. By God, just to witness the moment of raw shock on all their pompous, presuming faces might be worth the risk alone.

Yet there lay the reins tying back his tongue. Tonight, he was *not* taking risks alone. He had a partner—a recognition as strange in its newness as it was wondrous—and he looked to find that partner steadily adhering to her role in their mission now. *God, Shivahn,* he told her with his soul as their eyes fleetingly met, *I do love you.* With his heart, he prayed she heard him, before he addressed Julia with his reply.

"Julia Shropton, I am pleased to present my cousin, Margaret Von Kludow, who is here visiting from her home in Germany."

As they had rehearsed this morning, Shivahn watched him intently throughout the statement and reacted to her "name" with enough of a shy curtsy to produce an enchanted smile on Julia's deep-rouged mouth.

"Germany!" the woman exclaimed, now beholding Shivahn like a rare trinket in a Piccadilly window. "My *word.* Now you *do* owe me some explanations, Kristian Montague. You've never once mentioned relatives in Germany. For that matter, neither has your grandfather."

"Margaret is second removed," Kris filled in; again as they'd practiced. "On my mother's side." Then, with a contemptuous grimace he didn't have to feign at all: "I doubt Grandfather knows about her. Or cares."

"Now, *Kristian,*" Julia chided, though Kris didn't doubt his comment would be the talk of the Ladies' Salon in under two hours. "These boys and their quarrels," the woman uttered conspiratorily to Shivahn. "You are a patient little dear, enduring his thunder with such sunny patience."

If he had to select an instant as the evening's "moment of truth," the stretching silence after that would surely make Kris's final round of judging. He looked on as the two women regarded each other for a full half minute, one stare full of catlike expectancy, the other an astonishingly well-performed blank.

"Julia," he interceded after an appropriately "awkward" pause, "Margaret doesn't speak much English." He borrowed again from morning rehearsals to affect a bashful shrug. "And I'm afraid, as languages went, Grandfather managed to force only French and Latin down my throat."

"Oh," the woman responded—though the word possessed meaning far beyond its monosyllabled simplicity. "How . . . interesting." The black eyebrow snaked upward again. "So she cannot understand a word we're saying?"

"Mayhap a word," Kris answered. "Not much more." He had to force the last of the statement past his lips, which tensed along with the rest of his stance. He could predict Julia's next move as if she were the character at the mercy of his playwright's pen. *If* he wrote erotic farces.

"Well," she murmured, once more raising the wandering finger, this time to the folds of his neck stock. "How unfortunate for little Margaret. Yet how fortunate for little Julia."

Kris disengaged her caress by pretending to readjust the stock himself. "Julia . . ." he hedged in an equally discreet undertone. The last hitch he needed in tonight's plan was an attention-getting outburst from the lady of the manor. "Julia, I don't think this is the time or the—"

"Oh, I think this is well past the time, Kristian," came the determined rejoinder. "You've been away so long, toiling on that wretched boat of yours. I even heard something about you being in Ireland, of all places." She closed her eyes and shuddered as if envisioning him in a waist-deep pool of cockroaches. "Dear God, it must have been dreadful for you there. Between the potato pickers and the cutthroats, I can well imagine—"

"It was *not* dreadful," he cut her off, perhaps more gently than she deserved, but he directed the tone more to Shivahn, whose shaking fists belied the "bashful" dip of her head.

Julia, utterly ignoring his undertone, pressed her lips to his ear and one of her nearly exposed breasts to his chest. "Whatever you endured at the hands of those heathens, darling, I'll make you forget it."

"Julia—"

"You want to, Kristian. I know you do. Hand over Margaret's sweet little reins to someone else and come with *me*."

The suggestive breath upon which she finished went drowned by the opening measures of a lively waltz. But if the orchestra had struck into a high mass overture, Kris didn't doubt Shivahn would hesitate any more about the course she suddenly plotted for the dance floor, taking him along as hostage by way of one nearly dislocated elbow. He had enough time to feign an apologetic glimpse back at Julia before finding himself hauled against a leprechaun with a grip of iron and a slew of curses brimming at her lips.

"Dance with me *now*, Kristian," she seethed, "else watch me repaint this ballroom with that witch's blood."

Quickly Kris cupped her right hand in his left, slipped his other hand to her back, and swept her into the flowing twirl of the dance. "Smile, Sweetling," he said low as they rounded the far side of the dance floor, "or look down while you fume. Julia may be a witch, but she's damn smart about where she flies her broom. If she sees your lips moving, she *won't* think you're teaching me *Das Lied de Deutschen*."

Through a smile stiff and sugared enough to joust against one of Fionna's sweet sticks, she returned, "I hope she flies the broom into a tree and breaks both her bloody legs."

Perhaps 'twas the vehemence with which she ground out the words. Or the way her incensed gaze perfectly matched the brilliant shade of her gown. Nevertheless, Kris found himself borrowing one of her own mannerisms to curb his bellow of laughter down to an indulgant chuckle. As he bit hard on the inside of his cheek, he told her with loving softness, "Margaret Von Kludow, you are breathtaking when you're jealous."

"I am not jealous!" Reluctantly she heeded his caution,

spitting the rejoinder toward the floor. "I am . . . well, *I* am not the subject of this! Your darling Julia, on the other hand—"

"Has cold, hard fingers and a heart to match," he interjected. "*Your* fingers, however . . ."

He let that note of intimate promise swirl between them. Shivahn glanced up at him long enough that he witnessed her lips warm from their artificial mirth to an expression of equally sensual understanding. "Go on," she pressed softly.

He chuckled again. "Greedy girl."

"Mmm-hmm," she concurred smoothly. "Now go on . . . about my fingers . . ."

At that, Kris subtly pulled her closer to him—much closer than the dancing distance between the other couples on the floor—hiding the actual proximity of their bodies with the volumnous folds of her skirt. He fit his lips into the curve of her ear to give her his answer in a low, rough whisper:

"I wish your fingers were wrapped around my body right now. I wish they were making my skin hot as I made hotter love to you. I wish you were clutching my thighs as I made you shiver with—"

"Kristian *darling*."

Kris broke away from Shivahn like a peasant caught with his hand up the mayor's daughter's skirt. Yet instead of the village sheriff, he and Shivahn turned their flushed faces to a more frightening force: Julia's serenely smiling countenance. The Viscountess Shropton slid that smile up by a disconcerting inch as she curled a hand out to Kris with balletlike fluidity, an unmarked, white vellum envelope sandwiched between her two longest talons—er, fingers, Kris corrected himself.

"Darling," she repeated, "this just arrived for you. The

messenger stated it was urgent." She pitched a brief but meaning-filled glance at Shivahn. "And private."

"Thank you, Julia," he responded, managing at least the smile she clearly expected for seeing the message through its final ten steps of delivery. Then he centered his concentration on preventing himself from giving in to the rush of anticipation in his veins and tearing open the note there in the middle of the ballroom. Instead, he flashed Shivahn a knowing glance before nodding toward a long, sparsely populated hallway off to their left.

"Julia, I must ask you to excuse us," he murmured. "There is . . . a family matter that has suddenly come up."

"Ah," their hostess returned to him, though Julia secured her stare to Shivahn as she did so. Both her look and her voice carried the edge of a jewel-collared Siamese who'd just been ousted by the new kitten in the manor. "Please," she concluded tightly, "do not let me detain you."

Kris didn't waste time on a further farewell. Roping Shivahn's arm back under his, he made off for the hallway like a man intent on teaching his little cousin some new "steps" at the gala ball. And for the first time tonight, he relished every moment of the smug half smile and urgent pace that went along with their pretense.

He began testing doors when they'd traversed halfway down the hall. As he expected, most were locked, yet none completely muffled the moans and passionate cries rising from the social rooms and libraries beyond the portals. Suppressing his amused smile at Shivahn's widened eyes of reaction, he tugged her toward the room that finally proved vacant: the morning room behind the corridor's final door. Yet as they entered the room now, moonlight bathed the room instead of morning sun. A hazy gray glow illuminated collections of dark green velvet settees and easy chairs, all accented with arrangements of fine-embroidered pillows.

After locking the door, Kris crossed the room to the fire, a decently burning blaze no doubt seen to by a head butler with keen foresight. Shivahn's skirts rasped as she followed him.

"What does he say?" she asked before he'd even pulled the note out of the envelope.

When he'd done so, Kris read the message exactly as it was written. "Your flowers will be ready at midnight." He grinned. "Clever bastard. He made the note look like a flower order, in case Julia got her claws into it. I wouldn't put it past her, either, though the envelope shows no signs of tampering."

"But . . . what does it mean?" Shivahn put a visual version to her confused tone while watching him toss both envelope and note into the fire, then poke the cinders to assure the missive's thorough destruction.

"No doubt that we're to meet him at midnight," Kris supplied, setting the poker back against one of the miniature Greek pillars serving as chimney sidepieces. "And at that, I would wager, in the Viscount Shropton's prize rose garden."

Shivahn tilted another puzzled look his way, though twinkles of amusement now joined the shards of anxiety in her eyes. "The *Viscount* Shropton's garden?" she echoed with a mirthful lilt. "You mean our beloved Julia is not fond of *roses*, of all things?"

"Only when they arrive by the dozens, in cut crystal containers," Kris answered. "Never when they're still growing in the *dirt*, of all places."

"My *word*." She deliberately used their hostess's phrasing, pronunciation, *and* wandering finger up his arm. "What *was* I thinking to ask something like that?"

She had no awareness of the opportunity she presented so openly to Kris until he'd taken full advantage of it, grasping her finger in order to gain access to her hand, then pulling that hand around his neck. The rest of her body moved easily against him at the coaxing press of his other hand.

"I have no idea what *you're* thinking," he answered her then, his lips sliding against her temple, "but I'll give you a hint of what's on *my* mind . . ."

"Kristian!" she protested, albeit while arching yet closer to him. "We are here for a purpose!"

"Which we are fulfilling," he rebutted, his breath fanning into the curls Fionna had so carefully styled around her ears. "You must think ahead of the game, Sweetling. If we go back now, more eyebrows will rise across that ballroom than not. Everyone does, after all, believe I am in here ravishing every last *nein* from your lips."

To demonstrate his point, he captured her mouth in a slow, savoring kiss. "Oh," she whispered when he at last dragged away, "I think I am beginning to understand now . . ."

"Mmmmm." Kris finished the rough purr with a deep inhalation as they sank together to the nearest settee. He filled his senses with her perfume of fresh wisteria, soft-scented soap, and increasingly aroused woman . . . and swore no bouquet of flowers or wine smelled any sweeter. Nor did he imagine any man on earth any luckier, as Shivahn's hands roamed down his body, eager in their quest to cup around the hardening swell beneath the satin brocade of his breeches.

"Dear God, Leprechaun," he rasped through the magnificent tremors she induced when finding her prize, "you are becoming an incredible little accomplice . . ."

She had a dilemma. Shivahn admitted that fact at approximately three minutes until midnight, as she stole glances at

Kristian from beneath the lashes she'd kept vigilantly lowered all evening.

The dilemma was excruciatingly simple . . . yet excruciatingly serious. *What would she fantasize about in her sleepless hours, now that Kristian had made all her dreams come true?*

Lit only by the silver moonlight and the golden firelight flickering across the abandoned morning room, he had made love to her with a silent, slow intensity, even using the necessity of their fully clothed bodies to his sensual advantage. Instead of feeling her with his hands, he caressed her with his gaze, letting her behold the primal forces building throughout his body.

He had looked at her like that until the very last moment, when the surge of his climax struck him like a physical blow and his eyes squeezed shut as his head fell back. Shivahn followed him to heaven a moment later, her body convulsing around him in waves of sensation she'd never before experienced.

After that, they discovered the clock hands barely inched past eleven. Shivahn had enthusiastically suggested filling their remaining hour with a fireside snack of fresh fruit brimming from a miniature Roman urn on the nearby table, but Kristian had tugged her to her feet, an alternate plan clearly on his mind.

She had complied with dragging steps—though she soon found he would not accept such a pace from her for long. With the same masculine grace demonstrated on the settee, he twirled her into a series of intricate dance steps, perfectly timed to the orchestra's notes that floated down the hall . . . and from his softly humming lips. Every once in a while, he had interrupted his tune to quietly instruct her in a certain movement, or to praise her in a tone that flowed over her like a vocalization of the silken moon glow streaming in through the windows.

That dance had swirled into another, then another, until, for a few precious minutes, she had believed midnight would never come. She had believed they could truly exist like this, bodies and souls dancing forever as one. She believed time had finally halted inside one of her fantasies.

But alas, a spattering of distant applause knifed into her beautiful bubble. Following the incursion 'twas the smaller but no less distressing blade of Kristian's voice, now raised to a gentle but pragmatic tone: " 'Tis the musicians' resting period, Leprechaun. We've fifteen minutes to prepare for our rendezvous in the rose garden."

With twelve of those fifteen minutes now drained through the hourglass, she *definitely* knew she had a dilemma. How *did* one concentrate on things like rifles and ammunition, when just the sight of a man carrying wine punch across the room made her chest ache with skipped heartbeats and her mind dance with remembered waltzes?

As Kristian strode closer with the two glasses in hand, Shivahn's mind threw back only one inevitable answer to that. *You shall force yourself to concentrate on those things, because Kristian is depending on you to navigate* this *sea by his side.*

And is this not also another dream come true for you?

She let her instant smile serve as ample answer to that.

An answering smile grew across Kristian's lips as he arrived. "Your libation, my lady," he said with overtly gallant inflection, then added beneath his breath, "and my love."

"*Danka,*" she murmured, using one of the German words he had taught her. She sipped the crimson drink in hope 'twould cool the flush swirling again through her blood.

"And now," he suggested, sweeping his hand toward the Greek-columned terrace, "how about a stroll through the garden as we finish these?"

Shivahn nodded and took his arm, still in a surprised daze that people smiled, even wished them a good evening as they passed. Kristian's peers accepted her none-too-feigned uneasiness as the agitation of a foreigner in a daunting new world, and as for Kristian—well, her time would be better spent worrying about a magician relinquishing his secrets than this man surrendering an iota of his relaxed facade. She glanced at his charming profile in waves of alternating awe and curiosity, praying she could soak in his strength as naturally as she had come to absorb so much else about him in these last few amazing weeks.

Yet as they traversed down a wide set of polished stone stairs, then along meticulously groomed walkways, her heart accelerated to double the cadence of their pace on the empty path. Nevertheless, she found the presence of mind to notice Kristian's "friend" had wisely selected their meeting time and location. The midnight mists now swirling off an immense reflecting pond, coupled with Julia's "midnight surprise" of a flaming five-tiered dessert, had conveniently routed all their fellow party attendees from the garden. All the attendees, that was, except—

"Lord Shropton." Kristian issued his salutation in low respect, moving forward to clasp the gloved hand of an older but elegantly dressed man. Shivahn imagined the gentleman might even be handsome, when he smiled. He did *not* smile right now.

"Good evening, Mr. Montague," Shropton replied in a voice conveying the same firm but fair character as his features. Shivahn decided Julia an imbecile for not valuing the treasure beneath her own nose—or, for that matter, in her bed.

Yet with the second half of that thought, she also questioned why Kristian tarried here with Shropton, when their contact could now officially deem them late to their assignation. Her frustration grew as Kristian stroked a finger to the petals of a nearby rose and said conversationally, "The garden is flourishing, I see."

"Aye," Shropton answered. "Only the primroses aren't coming around as I'd like. I'm attempting a new hybrid from China, and the evening air seems too cold for them. I suppose that means I shall have to get around to building a greenhouse, after all."

"I suppose," Kristian concurred.

A small but sudden noise behind Shropton snapped both men's heads up, their mouths taut as their gazes anxiously scanned the area. When the interruption proved to be a small bird taking wing over the pond, they released their breaths in tandem and even traded relieved half smiles.

During that moment, Shropton's hazel gaze fell to her. His smile widened, and Shivahn discovered herself smiling back. She had guessed correctly; he was indeed an attractive man when he smiled.

Shropton flicked a glance back to Kristian as he inquired, "This is your special stowaway, I presume?"

"You presume correctly, my lord." Kristian slipped an arm around her waist. "This is Mistress Shivahn Armagh, of the village Trabith."

"Enchanted." The other man bowed over her hand. As he did, Shivahn angled a baffled look at Kristian. Did she actually stand here with a British viscount kissing her hand, even when Kristian had blatantly blurted where she came from?

The explanation to her confusion hit like a cannon ball to

a spritsail—and sent her reeling backward with identical force. She held up the hand Shropton had just honored, only to press those numb fingers to her mouth. "Y-you—" she stammered, then locked wide eyes on Kristian. "*He* is our—"

"You didn't tell her, I take it?" Shropton looked to Kristian, as well, his brows lifting bemusedly.

"You know how I do things, Leland," came the quiet reply. "People know things only if they have to. 'Tis—"

"I know, I know," Shropton cut in on a good-natured sigh. " 'Tis safer that way."

Shivahn recovered her wits enough to stomp back to Kristian's side. "Safer or not," she muttered at him from clenched teeth, "you might have told me *this* part before I doddered before the man like an imbecile."

"I might have," Kristian murmured back, infuriatingly gentle about the apology in his tone and the kiss upon her forehead. "I am sorry, Sweetling."

The viscount responded to their exchange with a laugh she imagined he hadn't used since a youth filled with his share of misty-midnighted rendezvous. "Well, well, well, Montague," the man drawled, "it seems you've finally found yourself an accomplice with spark to match your kindling."

Shivahn readily recovered her grin at that. "I am an incredible accomplice. Kristian told me so!"

"Good," Shropton returned with a swift wink, though his features returned to their initial set of focused solemnity. "We'll need *everyone* with their aces up tomorrow night."

Next to her, Kristian stiffened tangibly at that. "Tomorrow night?" he echoed. "Leland, that's bloody damn fast."

"That's also the only way we'll get the guns, my friend," came the stern answer. "After your episode in Dublin with the hens, Pitt and Sandys ordered supply transfers to Ireland to take place expediently as possible."

"The hens," Kristian grumbled, shaking his head. "I've smuggled out cows, cannon balls, battle plans, and even people. Now they won't forget a hold full of bloody chickens."

"They're also not likely to forget that warehouse piled with rifles. The shipment will be stored there overnight only—from six o'clock to six o'clock—before they load it onto the brig for Dublin."

Shivahn watched Kristian acknowledge his friend's information with a succinct nod. She had never seen his profile more stern, or more strong—or more breathtaking. "We'll be ready," he vowed to Shropton. "We'll have to be," he murmured as he looked down at her.

Shivahn responded with a smile as powerful as the exhilaration and hope she felt in this moment, standing at the side of the Brave One she so completely loved.

"Of course we shall be ready," she declared then. "We are, after all, flying on a Griffin's wings."

Her prediction came true. Twenty-three sleepless hours later, she, Nathan, and Kristian waited motionless in the shadows of Thames Street, ready at the side of a spirited mare hooked to a small, empty wagon. Fifteen miles away, Sir John and the *Sea Wing*'s crew had dared to sail as close as Rochester, then dropped anchor to await their arrival with a fully repaired and stocked ship. Somewhere in between, Patrick drove another cart packed with their personal belongings, including her gown and a book of love sonnets Kristian had donated for properly pressing her wisteria hairpieces.

Shivahn attempted to conjure the sweet fragrance of

those beautiful blossoms now. She closed her eyes tight and remembered the waltz Kristian had hummed to her in Shropton Manor's morning room. She envisioned the fruit in the urn, the fire in the hearth, the misty moonlight through the windows—

Then she inhaled. And came to the choking conclusion that not even her imagination could cut through the combined stench of gutted fish, damp bricks, tobacco smoke, stale beer, standing sewage, and the entire Two Fighting Cocks Inn, which lived up to its name in bawdy, brawling sounds as well as unbearable odors.

"Kristian," she at last regained the air to whisper, "how much longer?"

"Any minute now," he answered in a voice just as hushed, but a level above a whisper. Shivahn listened in rapt fascination, wondering how he managed the smooth combination of tones—just as she marveled at the man's infernal composure, when *she* felt like joining the crowd in the inn for the pleasure of letting out a simple scream or two.

"There!" Kristian's murmur kicked with a punctuation of excitement. "There he is." He motioned to a figure emerging from the shadows of the warehouse opposite the inn. A tricorn cast the man's face in darkness and a greatcoat swathed him from neck to boots, but he moved with the same careful strength she had observed in Lord Shropton's pace last night.

"Eleven fifteen." Kristian broke a smile of feral confidence. "Right on time." He turned that smile to her and dropped a quick kiss on her forehead. "It's Christmas Eve at last, Leprechaun. Bring the wagon forward when I motion."

Tears emerged from her eyes again, but this time, she did not choke them back. It had been a long while since she had cried in joy, and she savored the sensation as she returned both Kristian's kiss, then watched him stride out on the quay to meet Shropton.

As Kristian neared the man, he emitted some sort of quip, chuckling and nodding back toward her as he did so. Shropton nodded back and waved her forward. As she led the mare forward at a peaceful *clop-clop*, she struggled to breathe evenly against the contrasting gallop of her heartbeat.

Until the next moment, when both her breath and her heart seized to a stop.

They did so because Kristian let out a sudden, frantic shout. "Shivahn, *no!*"

He yelled out more orders at her, but the raw fear in those first two words sliced into her like sheets of paralyzing ice.

The fear. In Kristian's voice.

He was not supposed to be afraid! *He* was the charming cavalier, the composed gallant—he was the Griffin!

He was being clasped into wrist shackles by Lord Shropton.

Only the man was *not* Lord Shropton, Shivahn finally saw. The greatcoat fell away to reveal a British captain's uniform, and the face beneath the tricorn turned into the light, leering with savage triumph.

More soldiers emulated his look as they materialized from the shadows, rifles raised at the ready around Kristian and her. Shivahn gazed unblinking at them all, her muscles numb, her mind reeling with confused questions. Where *was* Lord Shropton? And if he had not betrayed them, who had?

As intense her need for the answer to that, she almost wished her mind had gone to the numbness of her limbs, as well. For as soon as the words streaked across her thoughts, one shadow mutated into another living thing . . . only it did not become another soldier. The person paced forward on a swish of black skirts, as sleek and serene as a beautiful, calculating cat.

'Twas a cat indeed, Shivahn observed with belly-deep horror.

A cat named Julia Shropton

Chapter 19

"**Y**ou *bitch*!" Kris snarled, charging at the beauty who approached as if she engaged in a Sunday stroll in St. James, not a midnight mission of betrayal. He almost got to her, too. His hands, though shackled, almost reached Julia's creamy white neck, where he would have joyously squeezed until she turned as putridly purple as the greasy fog around them.

But when he'd gotten two steps from her, a rifle butt jammed him between the ribs. He crumpled to the dock at Julia's feet, nausea and pain filling his gut, Shivahn's terrified shriek filling his ears. Bloodred fury coated his vision and thundered in his heart.

Through the ominous pause to follow came Julia's slow-taunting tongue clucks. "Temper, temper, darling Kristian," she crooned, as if she stood in her ballroom foyer holding him back from calling someone out for impugning her honor. Only there was one problem with that analogy, he thought caustically. The harlot had no honor.

"You knew about this—last night—didn't you?" he ground out, the words stiff and halted as he tried to regain his breath.

"Of course," came the breezy reply. "And I knew your little 'friendship' with Leland was not due to your 'interest' in his pathetic little roses. I knew all I had to do was watch, wait, and listen, until the spoils of the game were big enough to seize." A throaty laugh occupied her meaningful pause. "Prime Minister Pitt and this fine Captain Hewes have indeed made *these* spoils worth my time."

Kristian seethed as two soldiers hoisted him back to his feet. As soon as they did, Julia sidled closer, her only reaction to his silence showing in tiny lines at the corners of her perfectly rouged lips.

"Remember," she murmured huskily, her eyes dropping with seductive deliberation, "I gave you many chances last night to up the ante. After we'd both had a little fun, Captain Hewes would have peacefully taken you into custody. This horrid little scene wouldn't have been necessary . . . and right now, your Irish slut would be free to offer her charms on the Southwark street corner of her choice."

Before thought, reason, or control could inconveniently interfere with his fury, Kris lunged at the bitch with his entire body. "I'm looking at the only slut around here!" he raged, grappling against the three soldiers now restraining him.

"You shall halt and desist this instant, *traitor*!" boomed the bastard Julia had identified as Captain Hewes, and not Leland.

Leland. the strength again drained from Kris as the anchor of that thought suddenly dragged at his mind. Ah,

God, what had become of his friend who loved beauty enough that he forgave his harlot wife her liaisons and risked his life for an ideal called freedom? Dare he ask the question of Julia? Dare he want to know the answer?

Julia, it turned out, settled that quandary for him with her next sickeningly coy statement. " 'Tis such a shame about you, Kristian. You're a pea in the same pod as Leland . . . and now you shall end up as dead as him, too."

"Only he'll be going twice as painfully as his traitor friend." Hewes sneered knowingly. "I've special orders to keep him alive until Major Sandys in Dublin personally takes care of him."

"Whatever," Julia replied with a flippant toss of her head. But a provocative smile slithered back up her lips as her gaze roamed to Kris again. "Well, my darling," she murmured, "I suppose this is truly good-bye."

With that, she came forward so that she molded against him from groin to shoulders. Her nails dug into his scalp as she forced his mouth to meet hers in a union she used more to devour him than kiss him. When she plunged her tongue along his, Kris finally ripped away with disgust he didn't bother to disguise. He ridded himself of her false, fruity taste in a wad of thick spit he directed at her polished leather shoes.

"Rot in Hell, Julia."

"No, darling," she merrily retorted, "I believe you're going to beat me to it."

After that, a blinding blow joined the sting from her nails along the back of his head. A second later, Kris's senses tumbled into a vast, terrifying darkness.

Consciousness didn't offer a much better alternative. As his mind swam out of painful oblivion into excruciating reality, he first heard the deafening growl of his stomach.

The last thing he remembered eating, in all of two hurried chomps, was one of Fionna's mushroom and chicken pies. He might just kill for one of those pies now.

Hunger sat low on the priority list, however, when he moved his head. A thousand miniature savages raced through his brain, hurling their battle spears as they went, kicking up a dust storm of dizziness in their wake. More of the little demons assaulted the rest of his body, driving their heels into every inch of muscle he possessed.

But not even the din of his belly or the chaos of his bruises tormented his senses like the clenched sobs piercing the air, somewhere off to his right. *Shivahn.* He felt her sorrow in the core of his soul surely as he recognized the musical beauty inherent even in her weeping. *Don't cry, my love. Don't cry, Shivahn . . . please.*

"Please," he finally managed in a pasty rasp. Kris forced his head up, despite the additional volley of spears he sent flying across his skull. "Shivahn . . ." he called again, swallowing what little saliva he had, working his tongue against his teeth. "Shivahn . . . please, Sweetling; don't—"

"K-Kristian?" came the answering gasp, from the darkness of what he now recognized as the cargo hold of a small ship. 'Twas probably a lightweight schooner or frigate, built for speed rather than volume shipping.

"Leprechaun," he answered, the moisture and the volume slowly returning to his throat. "Please don't cry."

"Oh, God!" Her tearful exclamation was accompanied by a clanking of wrist cuffs and chains, as she scurried through musty tarps, rotted ropes, and hissing rats. "God," she repeated, her fingers fervently finding his face, "I didn't think you would ever wake up!"

"Shhh." He reached to her in the darkness and kissed her tear-salted lips. He knew that even as he was comforting her, it was *he* who drank of *her* touch, parting her lips with the selfish sweep of his tongue.

When at last he drew away, Kris ran his hand down her arm, to confirm he'd actually heard shackles clinking at her wrists. His back teeth ground together until the pain in his head shot down the length of his spine, but he could no longer claim control for his rage, much less shove it back into the corner in his soul from which it had burst. The corner reserved for pure and unforgiving hatred.

"God *damn* them for doing this to you." He snarled. Tenderly lifting her arms, he felt the chafed welts already beginning to form on her beautiful ivory skin. "And God damn *me* for bringing you into this."

"I beg your pardon, Mr. Montague, but I remember bringing *myself* into this on my own two feet, thank you."

He almost laughed. Almost. Preventing the chuckle was a long, weary sigh, expelled as he brushed reverent kisses on the insides of her wrists. "I'm sorry, Leprechaun," he whispered. "So sorry."

"I am not," she retorted lovingly. "Not for a moment Heaven has given me with you."

"Did they bash *you* over the head, too?" he cracked at that, yet yielded his sardonic bravado to a swallow of fresh fear. "Shivahn," he forced himself to ask her then, "Leprechaun . . . they didn't—the soldiers, while I was unconsciousness, they didn't try to—"

"Of course they tried to rape me," she answered with the somber calm that came only from confronting such a possibility for probably the last ten years of her life. "But Hewes ordered them off. There wasn't enough time."

Kris's breath escaped him in a relieved rush—as Shivahn inhaled with markedly different intent. "Kr-Kristian," she stammered, tears threatening to destroy that wobbling gasp, "I am so frightened."

He stroked her cheeks with his fingertips. "I know."

" 'Tis so *dark* in here."

"I know." Now looping his hands around her head so he could cradle her against his chest, he continued with his lips against her forehead, "But do you remember how we got out of the cavern beneath Prevot? And how we escaped those bastards in Rosslare? How we've gotten this far at all, when we should be long dead?"

In reply, Shivahn first only tilted her face up at him. Kris barely discerned the outline of her head in the darkness of their shipboard dungeon, so he didn't even attempt to make out her features. But he did not have to see her with his eyes; not when his heart had memorized every nuance of her two-toned eyes and her freckle-sprinkled nose, her incredibly full lips and her dimple-dotted cheeks . . . and her full leprechaun's smiles, too, just like the one that grew across her mouth now.

"We did all those things together," she finally answered him, her voice warm from the memories he had evoked of the last four weeks.

Four weeks, Kris pondered, squeezing his eyes shut in amazement. Twenty-eight days and almost as many nights, which all felt like twenty-eight *seconds.* And yet, how in the fleeting light of those days and nights had they come so far?

"Together," he filled in to that and affirmed to Shivahn at the same time. Yes, he sustained, they had done it all together . . . and as long as they still *were* together, he had to cherish each moment like a perfectly chiseled diamond . . . like the magic in the fingers now stroking his face . . .

Like the magic in the woman they belonged to.

"You are right, Kristian," that woman whispered to him now, and so much hope permeated her voice that for a moment, he kept his eyes closed and imagined they merely tarried late in bed together on a Sunday morning, in a cottage on the shore of Lake Trabith . . .

"And what am I right about *this* time?" he bantered back on a soft smile, even anticipating her answer. She'd most likely relate something one of their six children had done yesterday . . . or maybe his prediction of an early spring had come to pass, and she would tell him the heather was blooming in the meadow, and they should go pick some today . . .

"About being together," came Shivahn's response. "Aye, as long as we stay together, I promise you I will not be afraid . . . not even when they kill us."

His eyes slammed back open. The shackles cut into his wrists again. The pain pounded through his head again. The cottage on the shore of a mist-covered lake vanished into the blackness of a rat-infested cargo hold, which suddenly shook from the repercussions of two thunderclouds deciding to wage battle over their course on the Irish Sea.

That skyward skirmish had turned into a full war of the heavens by the time the ship dropped anchor in Dublin Bay. When two of Hewes's men hoisted open the hatchway, raindrops knived down the opening, accompanied by a cold broadsword of a wind.

"Bring the wench up first," Hewes shouted over the increasing fray of the storm. "And blindfold her well. Reisinger told me all about some hexing-vexing trick she does with her eyes."

As she overheard this, a panicked whimper vibrated in Shivahn's throat. She furrowed tighter against Kris, curling her hands into his shirt, shaking her head. Beneath her trembling knuckles, his lungs dragged in the suddenly icy air, fighting the craving to vent his own protest, to tell Hewes's lackeys to keep their lecherous paws off her.

Instead, he summoned every force of composure in his

body to aid him in gently thumbing back the hair from her cheeks, then gazing into her eyes with a strength he easily termed the most brilliant deceit the Griffin had ever accomplished. " 'Tis all right, Leprechaun. Go ahead. I'll be right behind you."

"B-but Kristian," she rasped, "they want to—"

"I promise," he stressed. "I shall be right behind you, or they'll slay me where I stand on the deck."

That earned him a brave attempt at a smile, which faded when the first soldier jerked her toward the ladder. Yet true to his promise, Kris trailed that guard step for step, looking on while the soldier bound her in a wide strip of dark fabric, even growling instructions at the halfwit when it seemed he would either slice off her ears, her breathing, or both with his inept version of a blindfold.

He inserted himself behind her as they crossed the deck and made sure he occupied the same position when they boarded the longboat. Through it all, he fed her directions on where and how to step, knowing she didn't need to be told, the guard by her side sufficiently showed her limbs how to move—but only his voice could reassure her heart, telling her they remained together even in the terrifying darkness she endured.

Half an army of red coats and two sizable open-bed wagons, all drenched in the downpour, awaited them on the dock. Yet as the rowers churned through the whitecaps, bringing the longboat closer, Kristian saw their arrival had been expected by another contigent, as well. A huddle of two dozen peasants, every man, woman, and child in the group clad in rags that clung to their shivering bodies, watched him with veneration in their eyes perceptible even from the distance they maintained from Sandys's corps.

Kristian looked to the group as he disembarked, acknowledging a respectful nod from the tallest of the men in the huddle, valuing their silent demonstration of thanks to new depths of his being. Depths that knew how seriously they all risked catching pneumonia by being here in this rain; that knew they did not have dry shirts or dresses waiting when they returned home . . . depths that now truly believed them his family, because a beautiful leprechaun from their midst had never stopped believing in him.

He would never see them again. They knew that, too—for as gruff hands shoved him toward the first wagon, that same towering man took a large step from the rest of the group and saluted him.

In the hand the man raised to his temple, he held one sodden green feather.

Somewhere in his soul, Kris actually thanked the *Sídhe* for stirring up this storm. Because of the tempest, the moisture in his eyes would not be seen as anything more than spattered raindrops on his face.

He finally dipped his head away from the sight and turned back to Shivahn. Now he actually looked forward to the journey on to Prevot. He knew he'd bring at least another small smile to her face, as he used the time to tell her of the courage shown by their compatriots on the dock.

Only Shivahn was no longer at his side.

"What the—" he began, only to emit a violent choke in place of his final word. He located her—being lifted onto the bed of the wagon behind him.

"No!" Despite his rage, he forced himself not to pitch the protest any stronger than this enraged growl. 'Twas already too late to hide her importance to him, and he well knew these animals would use that knowledge to their advantage if crossed.

Instead, he poured his strength into wrestling against the additional chains they clamped to his wrists, which attached him tightly to the wagon. As he witnessed them secure

Shivahn in the same way, savage frustration pulsed in every beat of his blood. Her head snapped right then left, anxiously seeking him, but he could only send out the words of his spirit to soothe her now. *I'm still right next to you, Leprechaun. Just look inside your soul, and you'll find me holding you, loving you.*

He sent the words out in a continuous litany as the wagons jerked into motion, splashing through the streets of Dún Laoghaire under a sky sagged with pillows of thickening rain clouds and a blanket of night's black velvet. Within thirty minutes of the journey, Kris's clothes hung sodden and heavy on his body, and his arms screamed with the unrelenting jerks and pulls of the manacles at his wrists. Yet his physical agony comprised half a drop of torment measured against the flood of his soul's ordeal: having to keep his heart open, calling out to her, and, in turn, laying bare his most vulnerable core to every sensation in Shivahn's spirit.

Aye, he shivered each time she shivered. His chest tightened each time she swallowed a terrified sob. His stomach roiled each time a soldier's hand strayed too close against a thigh or a breast in pretense of "checking" her shackles.

But he never let his soul stop talking to her. He never faltered his spirit from reaching to her. Even after two, then three hours, he swore to her, *I'm here and I'm not leaving, Leprechaun . . . never.*

That was why, when lightning suddenly flared around them, Kris paid the burst no attention other than a faint recognition that the storm had intensified with their approach to Dublin.

He jerked his sights up when the ensuing thunder blasted on them with a savage violence. 'Twas accompanied by a strangely comprehensible chorus of curses followed by a human deluge of shrieks, bellows, and war cries.

"Death to the red coats!" erupted a shout to his left.

"Life to Ireland!" boomed a voice to his right.

"Life to the *Griffin*!" somebody bettered that while running by.

"Holy, bloody God," croaked the youngest of Kris's dozen guards. " 'Tis an ambush!"

Another lightning flash, along with approximately fifty bobbing hand lanterns, confirmed the lad's declaration in a chaos of detail. Like Moses's locusts, the rebels swarmed from the forest lining both sides of the road. They wielded everything from axes and broadswords to common pitchforks and butcher knives—but held not a rifle among them, he noticed with grim irony.

Which, despite their numbers, made them a pathetically useless force against the small arsenal these red coats carried.

Nevertheless, the commanding officer for the front wagon, a lieutenant of twenty who glared like a man of forty, wheeled to their driver and shouted, "What the hell are you waiting for, Woolworth? Crack that whip *now*, or we'll be corpses inside a minute!"

Kris almost added his seconding motion to that. While he'd gladly pick up the tavern tariff for every iron-balled rebel in this raiding party, dread stuck in his gut at the primitive disorganization of the attack—and the terrifying danger that tactic posed to a village healer chained to the wagon behind them.

"Woolworth!" the lieutenant bellowed again. "Now!"

Woolworth finally heeded with a loud crack of his whip. The wagon pitched forward again, listed as it ran over a rebel in its path, then leveled out with a hard *thunk* and picked up speed. After sending a swift petition heavenward for the Irishman's soul, Kris set about determining the best way to take advantage of his captors' distraction.

But whatever form his plan took, he decreed to himself, Shivahn's safety had to be its pivotal cornerstone. That vow burned through him as he looked to the second wagon, hoping at least her blindfold had come loose in the chaos.

He turned—and did not see the second wagon following them.

As a matter of fact, he barely saw the second wagon at all. Too many rebels had overrun the conveyance, swiftly hacking the driver and soldiers aboard like so many slabs of prize beef cows. They leapt bareback to the shrilling horses and dunked the British flag in a bucket of grease. Within seconds, they hoisted the flag as a fiery banner of their conquest.

Those acts only manifested the beginning of the warriors' bloodlust. Now they took to destroying the wagon itself, slat by slat, screaming in exhilaration as the boards came free in violents rips and snaps.

The same way they tore apart Shivahn, too?

"Ah—*God*," Kris boomed. "Ah, God; stop the wagon! Stop the bloody wagon!"

He didn't know where his lungs had at last gleaned their commanding volume, but Woolworth found the order intimidating enough to saw frantically on the reins. "Woolworth!" the lieutenant roared at him, lurching forward with bulging eyes. "Are you listening to the *traitor*?"

"Stop—the—wagon," Kris commanded, all but daring the officer to kill him now, in defiance of Sandys's directive.

The lieutenant didn't touch him. "Drive *on*," he snarled at Woolworth, as he used the butt of his rifle to convey the order to Kris with a more personal touch. Kris doubled over in silent agony with the blow to his abdomen.

Just as he heard her cry cut through the night.

"Kristian?" came her yearning, sobbing shout. Yet the

next moment, her voice rose with the strange strength possible only through panicked fear. "Kristian? *Kristian!*"

"Shivvv ..." he croaked, trying to draw breath, welcoming only a thousand arrows of torment into his lungs. "Shivahnnn ..."

"Shut up, *traitor*," somebody shouted over his head. A knee bashed him in the face, while the lieutenant gave an approving grunt.

Shivahn, his heart roared while his senses reeled, fighting to reach her. *Oh, Leprechaun—oh, Leprechaun—*

"Kris—" Her screams now came in spurts of strident terror. "Kristian—I am lost here!"

Lost ... Leprechaun ... his whirling mind echoed. *No!*

"Kristian! Find me! Please!"

Please—please—can't leave her—please!

"Kristian—lost here—find me—pl—"

Then he heard her no more.

Shivahn? his heart whispered.

"Shivahn?" his throat rasped.

Silence.

Until he lunged against his chains; until he hurled himself toward the horizon. He threw himself into the black abyss that was marred only by silver, slashing raindrops—just like the daggers of anguish gashing into his soul.

Just like the name that sliced in a grieving howl from his lips.

"SHIVAHN!"

And still, only the rain answered.

Don't take her away from me, God ... not now, God. Not like this, God.

Through the night, his mind bellowed the words as his mouth whispered the prayer to the Prevot rats and vermin.

Over and over he rambled the entreaty, hoping if he spilled the sounds enough, they'd fill the caverns inside him now echoing with empty winds . . . and the memories of Shivahn's desperate screams.

She had gladly accepted Heaven's gift of their fleeting moments together, and so had he. She had also accepted the inevitability of their deaths, and so had he—on the condition he would be there for her, his loving gaze her last sight, his heart her safe fortress against the violence her body was about to know. His spirit would numb her terror as she climbed the gallows steps, surrounded by men with only one design in their minds: to kill her.

He had failed her.

She had been alone as the violence exploded around her. She had been alone in the midst of a chaos Kris knew with tormentingly vivid detail: the sweating clash of enemy upon enemy, the snarling frenzy for blood, the brushfire of primitive fury that seared away logical discretion of where a man's sword and dagger slashed and plunged, until his own kinsman lay at his feet, slain by his hand.

She'd been trapped in the vortex of at least a hundred of those blades. She'd been chained there, powerless to move. She'd been unable to do anything but scream for a man who'd promised he wouldn't leave her.

And he'd only been able to watch.

Just like he'd watched as Mum died. Just like he'd watched as they'd destroyed Gregory and Faye.

No, God. Why, God? Not her, too, God . . . not her!

But his mutterings, no matter how fervent, failed to shield his sanity from the sickeningly casual banter of the guards tossing dice outside the cell next to him.

"Bloody bogtrotters came out o' nowhere, so they're sayin'."

"Aye, heard the same thing myself. When Woolworth

brought in the traitor, he told me at least a hundred of the buggers poured from the forest like ants."

"Ants. Ha! And we squashed the little bastards just like ants, too!"

"Yeah, well, don't forget those 'little bastards' took out Thompson and Freeland and a whole lot of others before we tossed their own balls to Hell."

"Wait! Freeland, too? Awww, Jesus. I didn't hear that. Damn it. Freeland. He was a good man."

"He was."

"Damn. *Damn.* Well, I'm sure as blazin' glad we gutted just as many o' them in return."

"*I'm* sure as blazin' glad we're shortening their numbers by a dozen more in the morning."

"I only wish we could do it in the same way our lads got the privilege. My dagger sure could use a rebel's throat for sharpening."

"And my jigger sure could use a little rebel whore to warm it up whilst I was doin' it."

"Ahhhh, that's right . . . the healer harpy. I could use a little of her 'magic touch' myself. Where'd they put her?"

"They didn't. They only found one of her shoes and part of her dress. They think she's part of the rebels' dead pile, which *we* sure as hell aren't goin' to clean up."

"Yeah, well, good riddance, I guess. Who knows what kind of spell she hexes on a lad whilst he's doin' her . . ."

Kris didn't hear the rest of the words. His agonized roar resounded through his senses as he slammed himself against the slimy stone wall, his mind lost in a sea of pain without a shore.

Hours later, as he finally slid to the cell floor, Fate did bring merciful silence. The black void of his soul at last wrapped paralyzing numbness around his mind, deadening the shrieks in his head . . . and the prayers on his lips.

The peace didn't last long. Not an hour had passed before a door pounded open somewhere, and Sandys entered. Directly behind him, a line of soldiers marched in with enough torches to turn the cell block into an impressive simulation of Hell.

"Everyone on your feet," the soldier at the front of the line boomed after Sandys's approving nod. Another lackey quickly unlocked the cells. "Come forward as you're called."

"No." It was the first sound Kris had emitted in two hours, and the syllable grated with dry roughness. No matter. The determined step he took into the light, staring unflinchingly at Sandys as he did so, clearly communicated his demand would be heeded, in whatever manner he had to assure it.

Nevertheless, he narrowed his regard of Prevot's commander by the slightest fraction, silently daring Sandys to give him any excuse for murder as he voiced his edict in a low, level murmur.

"I'm going first."

Sandys said nothing.

They proceeded out to the execution yard.

he sky was watercolor gray; the mud looked like mushed offal. A damp wind blew in off the Liffey; it would likely rain again in an hour and through most of the day.

Kristian thought it one of the most beautiful days he'd ever seen.

As they emerged into the yard, he breathed in the moist air, identifying each precious scent swirling through his senses. Fresh-baked morning bread. Rain-dripped trees. The warmth of chimney smoke, the chill of wet cobblestones. He even savored the fetor of the over-worked horses and their scowling masters.

He roamed his eyes across the courtyard, into the sky, across the horizon to the distant silhouettes of the Wick-lows, shrouded in what Shivahn would probably call "fairy mist." *Shivahn,* his soul echoed on an aching whisper. *Ah,*

Shivahn . . . I shall meet you there, m'love. In the mist . . . I shall meet you there soon.

With that, he circled his sights back to the raised platform at the center of the courtyard. Then he lifted his gaze higher—and watched the noose above the stage sway with deceiving nonchalance in the cool wind.

Kris barely altered his expression, but Sandys had become an expert in reading his expressions. A master of torture, after all, had to properly exploit every nuance of his victim's demeanor. Therefore, the man replied to Kris's unspoken question: "Our guillotine has fallen into disrepair. It seems you shall receive the noose, after all."

Kris didn't look at the man, but as a victim who'd learned to read his persecutor in equal detail, he knew Sandys's lips now curled into his gloating rat's smile.

Sure enough, the bastard sneered a moment later, "Nonetheless, it shall be a pleasure to watch you die like this, traitor. The swift mercy of the blade has always been so unsatisfying to me."

"Right," Kris returned, though maintaining his level gaze on the waiting gallows. "I know I can die in peace now, Major, knowing precisely how you get your *satisfaction*."

With that, he turned his back on the fuming Sandys and strode forward to his execution.

A square-jawed soldier and a priest awaited him atop the platform. Kris accepted the priest's blessing only because he knew Shivahn would give him a blistering tantrum otherwise—only to remember there would be no more such scoldings. No more watching her eyes ignite like two opposing flames of violet fire, dark and bright fury contained in one captivating face. No more softening those eyes into passionate pools as he coaxed her into making peace with him once more . . .

No more light to his world. No more life to his life.

God, he couldn't wait to die.

"Let's get on with it," he growled, leaving the priest agape in the middle of a long Latin sentence. He turned as rough fingers bound his hands. Those same fingers lowered the noose around his neck then slammed the knot against his nape, burning the skin beneath his ears with the fast *thwick* of action. He swallowed and closed his eyes yet otherwise reveled in the peace that enveloped him then . . . the sudden, serene anticipation of finally stepping into the mist where Shivahn awaited him once more.

His heart beat once. His heart beat twice.

Somebody screamed.

Kris's senses lurched from their reverie. He scanned the yard in shock. That scream. *That scream.* Surely, as some insane predeath hallucination, he alone heard the sound. Surely nobody else witnessed the woman accompanying that outcry, now streaking into the courtyard on a horse black as night yet with hair brilliant as daybreak, fronting a band of equally appointed Irish rebels.

Then surely nobody cared if he blurted the essence of that hallucination, embodied in one grated word.

"Shivahn?"

"Kristian!"

She had cost herself precious extra seconds with her scream, which snapped every head in the courtyard her direction, but she nay cared. She nay cared about the rifles pivoted and aimed at her; she nay cared about Sandys, flashing his beady eyes in fury, waving droves of soldiers at her.

She cared only about the man on the platform with the noose tight around his neck, now staring at her as if he beheld a ghost materializing before him. He did not heed, of course, the fact he was about to become a specter in his own stead.

"Kristian," she cried again. "Oh, Kristian, if you give up on me now, I shall—*Kristian!*"

Her voice exploded into a shriek as she watched Sandys wrench that choice from either of their hands. Obeying a commanding hand signal from the bastard, the burly soldier next to Kristian threw the release for the platform's trap-door. The rope snapped taut. And Kristian dangled help-lessly from the end of it.

Shivahn barely needed to prod the black. The horse, pricked to attention by the exigency in her voice, sprinted into a gallop that, under other circumstances, would have exhilarated her in its powerful speed. But right now, the only intent making her heart race faster than the black's hooves centered solely on getting to that gallows.

True to the plan they had created last night, four rebels appeared to flank her advance. Two of them, Gig and Kier, were the same pair who had smashed her chains during the raid on the wagon and carried her to the safety of the forest. She had waited out the skirmish with the other two, Daniel and Jason, spending the time in whispered thanks that she had emerged from the fray missing only a shoe and the hem of her skirt.

The rebels, two on each side of her, fought the advancing guards with rash fearlessness Shivahn had never under-stood, even in all her years of hearing warriors' tales of bold battle feats, until now. Until, in this crazed, careening, dust-swirled moment, she experienced every lightning-charged sensation of those wild stories. Her body remained a part of her yet strangely removed from her; it knew naught else mattered but their target, still so far away—*Kristian, don't you dare die!*—it did not even feel the two rifle balls that found their way into her left arm—*Kristian, I am coming!*—

not even the bayonet thrusts that maneuvered past her defenders and nicked deeply into her legs.

Nay, none of it mattered—not when her Brave One swung closer to death with each passing second.

Ironically, the gallows provided a modicum of cover in the moment they needed protection most: the half minute required for Shivahn to position the black beneath Kris while Kier and Gig dismounted and set about cutting him down.

As she waited, her whole being pulsing in time to the frenetic rush of her heart, she looked to see the second wave of Insurgents storm the prison yard. This mob came in on foot, exploding with sword-waving bellows. They immediately increased their number by ten by making short work of the chains on the prisoners who had been waiting for execution after Kristian. The men scooped up weapons from dead or wounded guards and joined the mob with yelping enthusiasm.

"Shivahn!" came Gig's shout. "Here he comes!"

Her heart beat once. Her heart beat twice.

Then his wonderful weight toppled down behind her.

Yet the sudden jolt caused the black to whinny nervously and sidestep rapidly. Shivahn worked to control the horse with one hand and hold Kristian on with the other. She succeeded at the first and failed at the second.

Or so she thought. Just as she cried out in frantic frustration, especially as three new English battalions appeared, she looked to see Kristian had not slipped completely from the horse. The length of noose still secured around his neck had tangled in the left stirrup, preventing him from tumbling over the right flank. Only his left leg remained on the horse, curled at an assuredly painful angle behind her, with his knee dug into the small of her back.

She would have gasped in amazement, if Kristian did not

eclipse that shock the next instant. From his unconventionally half-saddled position, he hooked a hand around the pommel and shoved his way up so his mouth slammed against her ear. He wasted no time in commanding her "Let's go!"

Still, Shivahn hesitated. She would trample the man, not save him!

But she carried that worry only until his command turned into a fervent kiss against her neck. *Then* she knew Kristian Montague, in all his reckless, carnal glory, planned to stay with her through this wild journey. She pressed the black forward with a burst of resolute energy, and they wheeled around toward the gate.

"We have done it!" she exclaimed. "Kristian, we have—"

A horrified cry shattered the remainder of her celebration. Pure panic rendered the same destruction to her senses. Shivahn hauled back on the reins so forcefully, the black reared, front hooves churning the air, eyes glaring back to her in frightened confusion.

She did not blame the poor animal. The same rampant fear pounded its consuming fists through her own body as she assessed their path to the gate—

Now blocked by a twelve-foot-high wall of fire.

A torch came arcing through the air behind them, landed on the gallows platform, and in under a minute, added the whole tower to the conflagration—which also completed the circle of flames around them.

They had been, Shivahn concluded with terrifying finality, truly trapped.

As they looked on, Sandys continued to order more "kindling" added to the inferno: tinder such as whole wagons, barrels, and felled trees. Through the flames, she watched the man pace with leering excitement, a rat version of Lucifer, now creating a Hell in which he had captured his most prized mortal prey. He had forgotten the rest of the raid, now raging in different stages around the yard, and Shivahn struggled to comfort herself with the sight of the escaping Insurgents, many newly set free from their cells today, running to freedom behind the bastard's back.

But as her gaze followed those fleeing figures, she did not see them dashing across a Dublin prison yard. With every stinging blink of her eyes, those people began to sprint down a hard dirt road, instead. A dirt road surrounded by towering pine trees, majestic mountains, and houses with rose-draped thatched roofs . . .

All, that was, except *her* house. Orange and red flames now leapt the roof of the only home she had ever known, where at night, Ma and Da had played funny tunes for her on the *bodhrán* and pipe whistle; where during the day, the robins and blackbirds danced in Da's stone birdbath.

But she could not see the birdbath now. She saw only fire and smoke and people running down the lane. She saw Maeve's face contorted in anguish, screaming *They're dead; dear God, they're all dead!* She saw her own hand reaching out in protest, her small hand, only grown for five summers, as she tried to shout out in answer *but I am not dead, Maeve . . . I am not dead!*

And yet . . . mayhap . . . I am.

As the flames climbed higher around her, the same suffocating darkness billowed around her. She opened her mouth and breathed in naught but thick, black smoke. The smoke enveloped her aching lungs. She felt so weak, so tired, no matter how hard she tried to fight, to get up, to escape. She trembled all over, alone and afraid. She could not move. *I cannot move! Somebody help me move; please!*

"Shivahn!" came a voice, sounding so close, and yet . . . so distant. "Shivahn, we have to move—now!"

The voice sounded so familiar. 'Twas a friend, she knew

that much . . . yet why did the voice seem upset with her, like Da sounded when she neglected her chores?

"Shivahn . . . Sweetling . . . I can't do this by myself. I haven't eaten in two days and they just tried to hang me."

She knew that voice! She *loved* that voice! Sweet saints, who was it? Who called to her?

"Leprechaun, you've got to remember for me . . ."

I am trying . . . I am trying!

"Do you remember, m'love . . . when we were in the ship, in the dark? Leprechaun . . . do you remember what I told you then?"

Leprechaun, her mind echoed. Who in the world was calling her that? Only Kristian called her—

"Kristian!"

She blinked, gazing through the flames, and she saw Dublin again. She saw Sandys again, parading through his maniacal death dance, cackling joyously at them.

Most of all, she felt Kristian again, somehow properly saddled behind her at last yet slumped heavily against her back. His breathing was labored; his arm hung weakly around her waist.

And she remembered. She was *not* in Trabith anymore. And she was not dead! She was here, very much alive, with the man she loved! The man who was also very right, as she affirmed to him the next moment, with the wondrous, magic-making words he had beseeched her to recall:

"As long as we are together, I do not have any reason to be afraid." She pulled his arms tighter around her, while excitedly rewrapping the reins around her hands. "I do remember, Kristian . . . and I promise I shall never forget again!"

She finished her vow in a shout over the heightening roar of the fire and the heated pound of her blood. She repeated it as she guided the black in a preparatory circle, feeling even the horse's anticipating enthusiasm as they gained a little speed, then some more, then some more—

Before she gave the black full rein in a ground-eating gallop toward the flames.

"I love you, Kristian Montague!" she whispered one last time, before dropping her head as they leapt directly into the fire.

"Kristian, please! I am cold!"

His answering chuckle did not amuse her, Kris could tell, but he couldn't help teasing Shivahn for just one moment longer, holding the blanket out of her reach with one hand while keeping her pinned to the bed with his corresponding leg. He didn't think any man alive would blame him, either, if they saw her right now. Lying here at his side, clothed only in the waning firelight and the predawn glow filtering through the lakeside cottage's windows, she lacked only wings to convince him he had caught a fairy goddess to fill his arms, his heart, and, very soon, his life.

"My," he murmured, before dipping his lips to one obviously chilled nipple, "this *is* a change from just three weeks ago, my little fire-jumping leprechaun."

As he'd expected, she reacted to that with a musical laugh. As he'd hoped, she pulled his head up from her breast, to her mouth. He brought the covers down then, wrapping them in a cocoon of homespun wool almost as warm and soft as the skin his hands roamed with increasing aspiration.

"Hmmmm," Shivahn drawled languorously against the curve of his chin, "I really must stop letting you pull my strings with all that pretty fire-jumping talk, Mr. Montague."

"Ahhh," Kris quipped back, "but what strings."

She laughed again, but her gaze was earnest as she pulled back to say softly, "I would not be alive today if not for you. Thank you, my love, for believing in me when I did not."

Kris tried—in vain—to suppress a second chuckle as reaction to that. When Shivahn crunched her brows at him in a questioning scowl, he explained, "It's funny, 'tis all. Look who's thanking *me* for teaching *her* how to believe."

As he spoke, he gently checked the two bandages still wrapped around her arm. Upon confirming the well-healing flesh beneath, he bestowed a reverent kiss on both. "Leprechaun, don't you see?" he continued. "You had that strength inside you all along." He kicked up a corner of his mouth. "It just took a brilliant bloke like me to point it out."

With a grin of her own, she swatted his jaw. "Aye, and such a humble bloke, too."

He added a cocky brow to the tilt of his smirk. "You're not marrying me for my humility."

"A point well made," she replied—while taking advantage of his relaxed moment to escape from the bed. "Come, Mr. Montague, *up*. We must hie ourselves out of here before Maeve and the ladies make their way down here to find we have already given this place its wedding blessing."

Kris let out a protesting groan. "But the lake looks incredible this morn. Why don't you open the shutters a little wider and come back to bed?"

Shivahn peeked back over her shoulder at him, though clearly torn about doing so—for the moment their eyes met, they both knew he'd begun to win her. Kris beckoned her with an outstretched arm and a meaningful gaze. "Come on."

"Kristian." She drew out the first syllable in a sweet little hiss that introduced an adorable pout to her lips. That, coupled with the mussed fall of her hair down her naked back, transformed his erection from a mildly uncomfortable

ache to an irrefusable demand. "Kristian," she repeated, as if knowing how much she tormented him now, "they might be here any minute!"

"Let's live dangerously," he responded at the ready to that. "After the Griffin's had himself a honeymoon and a bit of a rest, 'tis to be the story of our life, anyway."

He'd said the right words. Her features ignited with a smile surely created from a sprinkle of fairy dust—and Kris didn't think he'd find her any more heart-haltingly lovely today, in or out of her wedding raiments.

"*Our* life," she whispered, as she slipped back into his arms. "I think I like the sound of that."

"Me, too," Kris answered, as she not only told him of her love but showed him, touching him . . . touching his body with her magical hands, touching his soul with her honest spirit, touching his heart with her incredible love.

"Oh, my love," he repeated, smiling as he considered a lifetime of those wondrous touches. "Me, too."

If you're looking for romance, adventure, excitement and suspense be sure to read these outstanding romances from Dell.

※

Antoinette Stockenberg
- ☐ **EMILY'S GHOST**   21002-X $5.50
- ☐ **BELOVED**   21330-4 $5.50
- ☐ **EMBERS**   21673-7 $4.99

Rebecca Paisley
- ☐ **HEARTSTRINGS**   21650-8 $4.99

Jill Gregory
- ☐ **CHERISHED**   20620-0 $5.99
- ☐ **DAISIES IN THE WIND**   21618-4 $5.99
- ☐ **FOREVER AFTER**   21512-9 $5.99
- ☐ **WHEN THE HEART BECKONS**   21857-8 $5.99
- ☐ **ALWAYS YOU**   22183-8 $5.99

Christina Skye
- ☐ **THE BLACK ROSE**   20929-3 $5.99
- ☐ **COME THE NIGHT**   21644-3 $4.99
- ☐ **COME THE DAWN**   21647-8 $5.50
- ☐ **DEFIANT CAPTIVE**   20626-X $5.50
- ☐ **EAST OF FOREVER**   20865-3 $4.99
- ☐ **THE RUBY**   20864-5 $5.99